MARY BALOGH

Someone Perfect

PIATKUS

PIATKUS

First published in the US in 2021 by Jove, Berkley,
an imprint of Penguin Random House LLC
First published in Great Britain in 2021 by Piatkus

3 5 7 9 10 8 6 4

A CIP catalogue record for this book
is available from the British Library.

ISBN 978-0-349-43154-3

Printed and bound in Great Britain by Clays Ltd, Elcograf S.p.A.

Papers used by Piatkus are from well-managed forests
and other responsible sources.

MIX
Paper from
responsible sources
FSC® C104740

Piatkus
An imprint of
Little, Brown Book Group
Carmelite House
50 Victoria Embankment
London EC4Y 0DZ

An Hachette UK Company
www.hachette.co.uk

www.littlebrown.co.uk

Someone Perfect

The Westcott Family

Stephen Westcott m. Eleanor Coke
Earl of Riverdale
(1698–1761)   (1704–1759)

Andrew Westcott m. Bertha Ames
(1726–1796)   (1736–1807)

David Westcott m. Althea Radley
(1756–1806)   (b. 1762)

George Westcott m. Eugenia Madson
Earl of Riverdale
(1724–1790)   (b. 1742)

Mildred m. Thomas Wayne
Westcott   Baron Molenor
(b. 1773)   (b. 1769)

Boris   Peter   Ivan
Wayne   Wayne   Wayne
(b. 1796)   (b. 1798)   (b. 1799)

Louise m. John Archer
Westcott   Duke of Netherby
(b. 1770)   (1755–1809)

m. Ava Cobham
(1760–1790)

Jessica m. Gabriel
Archer   Thorne
(b. 1795) Earl of Lyndale
            (b. 1787)

Evan
Thorne
(b. 1820)

Humphrey Westcott m. Alice Snow
Earl of Riverdale
(1762–1811)   (1768–1789)

Matilda m. Charles
Westcott   Sawyer
(b. 1761) Viscount
            Dirkson
            (b. 1761)

m. Viola Kingsley
(b. 1772)

m. Marcel Lamarr
Marquess of Dorchester
(b. 1773)

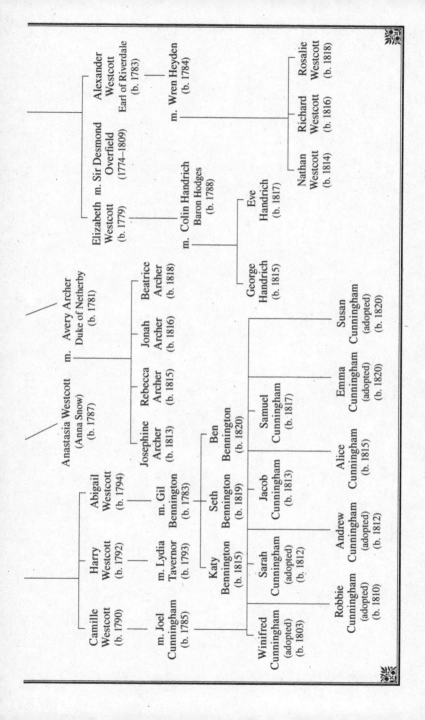

One

England was not renowned for long runs of perfect summer days. This year so far even brief runs had been in lamentably short supply. It seemed something of a miracle, then, when the morning had dawned with the promise of being yet another lovely day. The second in a row.

By the middle of the afternoon, the sky was a deep indigo blue and cloudless. The air was hot without being oppressive—the merest hint of a breeze saw to that. It also caused the leaves to flutter on the trees and the water to ripple on the river. The grass on both sides of the river was green and lush after all the rain, and liberally strewn with daisies, buttercups, and clover. Birds trilled from among the thick foliage of the trees, though it was not always easy to see them. Unseen insects whirred and chirped in the grass.

So much life. So much beauty.

Lady Estelle Lamarr had been walking along the riverbank, but she stopped in order to fill all her senses with

the perfection of the moment, wild nature at its most profuse and benign. Even the old single-arched stone bridge
farther along seemed to be an integral part of the scene
rather than a man-made intrusion upon it, just as a bird's
nest or an anthill or a beaver dam would be. There surely
could not possibly be anything to surpass the loveliness of
the English countryside on a summer day. How very privileged she was to live here.

Yesterday she had fretted a little at being kept at home
on a similar day by the impending departure of her uncle
and aunt and cousin, who had all been staying at Elm Court
for the past three weeks. Although Aunt Jane had talked of
leaving early, by eight o'clock at the latest, it was actually
after three in the afternoon by the time their carriage rolled
out of sight down the drive and the chance to enjoy the
outdoors had been virtually at an end.

First Uncle Charles had lingered over breakfast as though
he had all day, deep in conversation with Bertrand, Estelle's
twin brother. Then Ellen, their cousin, had decided she
really ought to send a quick note to her betrothed to explain
that their return home would be delayed because her mama
had decided they must call upon friends who lived not far
off their intended route, and those friends were bound to
invite them to stay for a few days. The conversation finally
at an end and Ellen's letter written, Aunt Jane had been
hopeful of a midmorning start. But that hope was dashed
when the vicar arrived from the village and was positively
delighted to find that he had come in time to send the travelers on their way with a blessing.

The Reverend John Mott, a deeply pious man, was a
longtime acquaintance of Aunt Jane's and a great favorite
of hers. At her urging, the blessing had developed into extended prayers and scripture readings in the sitting room

and had been succeeded by a lengthy discussion, initiated by Aunt Jane, about the deteriorating moral fiber of the nation, especially its heedless youth. And since by then noon was fast approaching, Estelle had invited the vicar to join them all for a light luncheon that she had guessed—correctly—their cook was already preparing with feverish haste for six people instead of the two she had been planning for.

After the dishes had been cleared from the table and their second cup of coffee had been poured, the conversation had turned to a discussion of the uncertain future of the monarchy, since King George IV was in perennial ill health and the only heir closely related to him was a young girl, Victoria, daughter of the Duke of Kent. The other royal dukes had been prolific in the production of children, it was true, but not, unfortunately, of the legitimate variety. It was all quite scandalous, in Aunt Jane's opinion.

The carriage had been outside the door at three o'clock, had been fully loaded with its three passengers by quarter past, and had finally rolled on its way at half past, all the last-minute thanks and well-wishes and reminders to do *this* and be sure to avoid doing *that* having been called out the window. By Aunt Jane, of course.

"So much for a perfect summer day," Estelle had said, turning to her brother—but with a twinkle in her eye. For of course she was exceedingly fond of her relatives and had actually enjoyed the day as it unfolded.

"All in a good cause," Bertrand had said. "We will miss them. There will be other lovely days to spend outdoors."

And sure enough, along had come the unexpected gift of today.

When she had left the house earlier, Estelle had intended to walk all the way to Prospect Hall to call upon Maria

Wiley. The heat was giving her second thoughts by now, however. The hall was a mile or so beyond the bridge, on the other side of the river, and she had already walked more than a mile. She looked down at the wildflowers at her feet and stooped to rub a hand over the grass. It was dry. And blessedly cool to the touch. She changed her mind about going farther and sat down close to the river's edge. She arranged her skirts neatly about her legs and clasped her arms around her raised knees.

Aunt Jane would have been horrified at such unladylike behavior, especially in a public place where anyone might come along at any moment and see her. Estelle smiled fondly at the thought. Aunt Jane and Uncle Charles had raised Bertrand and her. Their mother had died in a horrible accident before they were even a year old, and their father, overcome with grief and guilt over his conviction that he had caused their mother's death, had effectively disappeared from their lives except for brief, unsatisfactory visits twice a year or so. He had acquired an unsavory reputation as a rake, though they had not known that, of course, until much later.

He was back in their lives now and had been for the past eight years. Estelle loved him dearly, but that did not change the fact that their formative years, from one to seventeen, had been spent in the care of Aunt Jane, their mother's elder sister, and Uncle Charles. And in the company of Oliver and Ellen, their cousins, both older than they.

It had been a strict upbringing, with much emphasis upon duty and moral rectitude and self-discipline and piety. Estelle and Bertrand had also been loved, though. But there had always been a gaping hole in their lives, partly because their mother was dead, though mainly because their father was not. They had longed and yearned for him, watched for him from the attic room of Elm Court, where they had lived through most of those years and lived again now. Yet whenever he had come, they had held themselves aloof from him, waiting and waiting for him to . . . to open his arms and his heart to them. Or give some other sign. Make the first move. *Stay.*

After he left, usually sooner than he had intended, they hated him and wept for him—yes, Bertrand had wept too—and resolved to forget all about him, to cut him from their lives. Until, that was, they found themselves in the attic again, watching for his return. Yearning for him.

Ah. Estelle shook her head. She had not intended to sink into *those* memories today of all days. Today was for simple enjoyment. Tomorrow there might be clouds and blustery winds and chill temperatures and rain again. *Three* days in a row was too much to hope for with any confidence this year. Today she was free to do whatever she wished. Much as she had loved having her aunt and uncle and Ellen to stay, she had, as always, felt constrained by their presence. As though she needed to be on her very best behavior every single moment. And to listen meekly to almost daily harangues—though no, that was unfair. *Harangues* was a negative word. Aunt Jane loved her and wanted the best for her—and *of* her. She gave *suggestions* now, and they were often sound advice.

Her aunt did not approve of Estelle's living at Elm Court virtually alone, though Bertrand lived there too and they had always been extraordinarily close despite the fact that they were not, of course, identical twins. Estelle, in Aunt Jane's opinion, really ought to have a female companion living with her—just as Lady Maria Wiley of Prospect Hall did, and very proper too, though one could wish that her companion was a decade or so older than she was. It was bordering upon scandalous that Estelle did not have one at all. Aunt Jane could not understand why the marchioness did not insist upon it. *The marchioness* was Estelle's stepmother of eight years, her father's second wife. He was the Marquess of Dorchester.

Estelle did not want a companion. Not a female one, anyway. She had Bertrand, and he was enough for her. For a few years, just before their father's marriage to Viola Kingsley and then afterward, they had lived at Redcliffe Court in Northamptonshire, where they had been taken after their father inherited the title and property. Two years ago, however, they had come back to Elm Court, just the two of them, having found themselves overwhelmed by the life of the *ton* into which they had been thrust—with great success, incidentally, and even some enjoyment, until suddenly it had been enjoyable no longer.

They had already been in their twenties when it happened, an age at which Estelle at least ought to have been married, according to conventional wisdom. She had never really been tempted, however, though she liked a number of the eligible men she had met. Instead, she had wanted to . . . to *find* herself, for want of a clearer way to describe how she had felt. And of course it was how Bertrand had felt too. They so often thought alike about the important things.

So they had come back to Elm Court to live. Oh, not to become hermits. Far from it. Just this year, for example, they had gone to London for a few weeks of the Season and had proceeded from there to Hinsford Manor in Hampshire to celebrate the thirtieth birthday of Harry Westcott, their stepmother's son and therefore their stepbrother. It was a large family party that had turned unexpectedly into a celebration of Harry's wedding to Lydia Tavernor.

All of it had been thoroughly enjoyable—for both Estelle and her twin. But they had come back here well before the end of the Season. Sometimes Estelle wondered if they would grow old together here, to be known as *those weird and eccentric twins*. But life was ever changing. It was impossible to predict the future. She did not even want to try.

She sat in the sunshine. The heat felt very good. But . . . Well, it was really *quite* hot, and temptation beckoned in the form of the river. Poor Aunt Jane would have had heart palpitations. But Aunt Jane was not here, was she? And there was no one else in sight to be scandalized. It was why Estelle always loved walking beside the river north of their property, in fact. No one else ever came here. The bridge, sturdy and picturesque though it was, was rarely used these days, now that the main road nearby had been widened and resurfaced and was far more convenient to travelers than the narrow, rutted track that crossed the bridge. Most people would naturally choose convenience and comfort over a scenic route.

Temptation was not to be resisted, Estelle decided at last, perhaps because she did not put up any great fight against it. She pulled off her shoes and set them neatly beside her, peeled off her stockings and pressed them into the shoes so they would not go wafting away in the breeze, folded the lower half of her skirt neatly over her knees so that some remnant of modesty would be preserved, and lowered her feet gingerly into the river. She gasped at the coldness of the water, but she lowered her legs farther, wiggling her toes as she did so, and found that they quickly adapted. And oh goodness, it felt delicious.

She swished her feet and laughed when a few splashes spread into dark circles on her dress and doubtless penetrated each fold of it. One droplet landed on the side of her nose. She brushed it away and dried her hand on her skirt. She felt herself relax as she brought the whole of her attention back to the scene around her—and in her. For of course she was part of the scene, right to the very core of her being. It was not a case of *her* and *it*. She actually *was* it, just as the birds were and the insects and the grass and the daisies, and that butterfly fluttering over a cluster of clover. This, she thought, was contentment. Even happiness. Just this. She wished Bertrand had come with her.

Her bonnet was protecting her head from the full force of the sun. The brim was shading her eyes and preventing her from acquiring a red and shiny nose, which her maid would cluck over with disapproval and Bertrand would laugh at. But just for a couple of minutes she wanted to feel it all—the brightness and the warmth. She pulled loose the ribbons beneath her chin and took off her bonnet. One of her hairpins caught in the bottom edge of it, and while she wrestled to free it a whole hank of hair came tumbling down over her shoulder. Bother! But it served her right. She set the bonnet on the grass, pulled out the rest of her hairpins, and dropped them carefully into the hat. She shook her head and combed her fingers through her hair in the hope of achieving something like smoothness. It was impossible, of course, since she did not have a brush with her, but so what? She had already decided that she would not go visiting.

A sense of delicious freedom welled up in her and spilled over in exuberance. She kicked her feet, careful not to splash herself again. She propped herself up with her hands spread on the grass behind her, tipped back her head so she could feel the sun on her face and cool air on the back of her neck, and closed her eyes.

This was pure bliss.

Until, that was, she became aware of someone panting—someone who was not her. And then she heard low, menacing growls. And then angry barking. Her eyes flew open and she whipped her head about to see a huge monster of a dog dashing toward her across the grass, all bared teeth and ferocity and flying spittle and giant paws. If Estelle had not been half paralyzed with terror, she might well have jumped screaming right into the river. Instead she sat up sharply, spread her hands before her face, palms out, fingers spread, and cried out. Something idiotic like, "Good doggie," she thought afterward. By then she hoped fervently she had not actually said *doggie*.

"Heel, Captain!" The voice that snapped out the command came from somewhere behind Estelle. It was a harsh masculine voice—and instantly effective. The dog stopped in its tracks, a mere six feet from Estelle and towering over her. It growled menacingly once, tipped its head to one side, one brown ear flopping against its head, the other swinging free, black jowls quivering, black nose twitching, black eyes glaring death and destruction—and turned to trot to where the voice had come from.

Estelle sucked in a deep breath of air, perhaps the first since she had heard the panting. She turned more fully, drawing her feet from the water at the same time, curling her legs under her, and pulling her skirt down over them. All a bit too late for modesty.

People never came this way. Well. *Almost* never.

He was astride a massive horse, an equally massive man, or so he appeared to Estelle from her vantage point close to the ground. Oh dear God, her hair was all about her in a half-tangled, untidy mass. Her dress was soggy and clinging to her bare legs. He, on the other hand, was immaculately clad for riding, a man with wide shoulders and a broad chest and powerful-looking thighs. He was dark and dour of countenance, though the fact that his tall hat was pulled low over his brow and cast his face in shadow might account for at least part of that impression. His black-faced brown bloodhound panted up at him as though awaiting the order to attack and kill.

He was some distance away from Estelle, holding his horse quite still while he regarded her in silence. He made no apology. He asked for no assurance that she was unharmed. He uttered no greeting of any sort. Except that even as she noted this he touched his whip to the brim of his hat and inclined his head perhaps an inch and a half in her direction. Then he rode down the track, across the bridge, in among the trees that lay beyond the bank on the other side, and disappeared.

After that one slight acknowledgment of her existence he had not once looked her way.

Well.

Estelle gaped after him. She was trembling, she realized. Her heart was still beating at what felt like double time. It pounded in her chest and sounded like a drumbeat in her ears. Her hands were tingling with pins and needles. Her teeth were chattering, though certainly not with cold despite the fact that her skirt was definitely wet and uncomfortable about her legs. Her hair felt like a jungle and probably looked like one. She felt foolish and humiliated despite the fact that he was a stranger and it was unlikely she would ever see him again. She also felt indignant and ruffled. Downright angry, in fact. How dared he have a vicious dog like that on the loose where it might attack any unwary person walking alone—or sitting with her feet dangling in the water—and tear her to shreds?

Her heart speeded up further if it was possible and made

her feel quite faint for a moment. And how dared he not dismount from that monster of a horse and hurry to her assistance, all gentlemanly concern for her well-being? For all he knew, she might have swooned as soon as his back was turned and toppled into the water and drowned and floated away like Ophelia and eventually sunk, never to be seen or heard of again. At the very least he ought to have been abject in his apologies for frightening her. Instead, his silent stare had somehow put *her* at fault, as though she had upset his poor dog—had she *really* called him a doggie? *Captain!* Whoever had heard of calling a dog Captain?

So much for a perfect summer day.

It was ruined.

She wondered if she would tell Bertrand. She could narrate the encounter amusingly. He would laugh—*after* ascertaining that she had taken no real harm. But she would have nightmares for a *week*. Perhaps longer. Perhaps for the rest of her life. She was *still* breathless. She was almost whimpering. A butterfly fluttering past her face made her jump.

She pulled on her stockings, tried unsuccessfully again to comb her fingers all the way through her hair, gave up the struggle, and got to her feet. She pushed them into her shoes and made her way home, her bonnet dangling from the fingers of one hand, her hairpins tinkling around inside it.

Aunt Jane would have needed to be revived if she could have seen her now. Not, now that Estelle came to think of it, that she had ever seen her aunt swoon.

Justin Wiley, Earl of Brandon, was *not* in a good mood, and that was putting it mildly. He had no wish to go where he was going, was not looking forward to getting there, and was wondering even now if he should simply turn around and go back even though he had come a long way and was almost at his destination. He did *not*, then, appreciate a distraction on top of everything else, especially when it came in the form of a woman whom he had mistaken at first for a farm wench playing truant from her chores before realizing that she was far too finely clad to be anything other than a lady. But a lady out *alone* in the middle of nowhere? With her hair in a dark, unruly cloud down her back and skirts up over her knees while her bare legs and feet dangled in the river?

The very sight of her had irritated him because of course he had reacted as any vigorous male would have in the circumstances—with a surge of sheer startled lust. *After* he had called off Captain, that was, and watched the woman try to contain her terror and at the same time make herself look respectable. Her efforts had done the opposite by drawing attention to a heaving bosom and bare, shapely legs. And that wanton hair.

It had been a brief distraction, over in a matter of minutes as he rode across the stone bridge that spanned the river and in among the trees on the other side. But his already dark mood had been further darkened, and he did not appreciate it one little bit. He had frightened a helpless woman—or at least Captain had, which was really the same thing since the dog was his. And he had reacted to her in an undisciplined, quite despicable way, even if he had not acted upon his baser instincts.

Prospect Hall must be close, within a mile or so anyway. That meant that the lady who was behaving with such scandalous disregard for propriety back there probably lived somewhere close. It was a fact that accused him, and he did not need more guilt heaped upon him.

For longer than a year now he had had the sole charge of his sister. He was her guardian, but had procrastinated in fulfilling his duty to her simply because she wanted nothing to do with him. He had respected her wishes while she was in mourning for her mother and had stayed away. And so he had perhaps exposed her to the bad influence of neighbors who did not know how to behave. Yet even now, when he had come at last to take charge, he was reluctant to complete his journey and was even tempted not to do so.

Good God, they might be acquaintances, that woman and his sister. *Half* sister, to be precise. Perhaps they were even friends. It was true that Maria had Miss Vane as a companion for respectability and some protection. But he had never met Miss Vane and knew little about her except that she had once been Maria's governess. He really had been unpardonably derelict in his duty. Even while Maria's mother was still alive he had been his sister's official guardian after his father's death six years ago.

He had just this moment been deficient also in his duty as a gentleman, he realized with a sudden grimace. He had not apologized to that woman for frightening her or explained to her that Captain was far too well trained to attack anyone, or any creature, in fact, without his master's say-so—which had never yet been given. Or that Cap was far too good-natured a dog to *want* to attack anyone. Doubtless he had been galloping up on the woman in the hope that she would allow him to slobber and pant all over her in exchange for a belly rub. It was distinctly to the dog's disadvantage that he was so large and fierce-looking with his giant paws and black face and wobbling jowls. And that his bark was deep and loud enough to wake the dead.

Justin had not even stopped long enough to assure himself that the woman had recovered from her fright. His dog had not gone within eight feet of her, but she might well be a vaporish sort. She might even now be stretched senseless upon the riverbank, getting fried by the sun.

It was extremely unlikely.

But he resented the distraction and the way the incident had somehow put him in the wrong. He needed to concentrate his mind upon the coming encounter with his sister. Soon. A mile or so beyond the bridge, he had been told at the village he had passed through twenty minutes or so ago. A couple of miles all told. About three miles if he continued along the road, as he would have done if he had been traveling with his carriage. He had sent that by the road with his valet and his baggage and had taken the shorter route himself. Something he now regretted. So. Less than a mile to go.

Maria was the daughter of his father and his father's second wife, now deceased. She was fourteen years younger than Justin. He had not seen her for twelve years. She had been a child then, eight years old, thin and pale, with fine blond hair and big blue eyes, and he had adored her. And she him. But he had left home abruptly and been gone for six years before he inherited the title and properties and fortune upon the death of his father. One of his first acts as Earl of Brandon, before he went home to Everleigh Park, was to have the countess, his stepmother, and therefore her daughter too, sent here to Prospect Hall to live. It was one of his smaller properties, though the house was said to be a comfortable, attractive manor set in pretty grounds and run by a small but competent staff, most of whom had been here forever. Justin had never come in person.

His stepmother's health had broken down a year or two after the move and had deteriorated steadily over the following years. Her illness had become more and more debilitating, until by the end she could neither rise from her bed nor move her limbs nor speak. Even swallowing apparently had become well nigh impossible, according to the brief, very factual reports Miss Vane had sent him twice a month. He had sent a physician from London and a few nurses who had come highly recommended. Each of the nurses had been dismissed within a week. Maria had nursed her mother herself right up to the end. The countess had died a little more than a year ago, and Maria had been left alone with her companion. She would remain under Justin's guardianship until her twenty-fifth birthday or until she married—with his permission. Whichever came first.

His sister had been here, then, since she was fourteen, with a sick mother for three or four of those years. She had been in mourning during the year since her mother's death. One could only imagine the sort of hell she had lived through. Yet she had refused his summons, couched very carefully as an invitation, to return to Everleigh Park after the funeral and again a year later. On the latter occasion, just a couple of months ago, she had dictated her answer to Miss Vane, who had written it in her small, distinct handwriting.

Lady Maria Wiley must confess to a certain degree of puzzlement over the Earl of Brandon's invitation to return home. She is already at home. Unless, that is, his lordship should choose to assert his sole ownership of Prospect Hall and require her removal, in which case she will purchase a home of her own with the inheritance left her by her mother and thus free him of an inconvenience and herself of any future harassment.

He had read and reread the extraordinary letter with amazed incredulity. *Harassment?* Could she hate him so much? It was obvious she could and did.

Did she realize, though, that the money her mother had left her was in trust with him for another five years? Did she understand that he was her legal guardian?

He had thought himself hardened against everything life could possibly hurl his way. He had had long practice, after all. But Maria had found a small chink in his armor. She was all that was left of what he had once valued, of what he had once loved.

A long, long time ago.

A lifetime or two ago.

There was a cluster of cottages up ahead on one side of the track. A picturesque stone manor stood alone on the other side, set back some distance from the road within a large garden of lawns and trellises and roses and myriad other flowers. This must be Prospect Hall.

Even now he considered turning back or simply riding on by. Being hated wore upon one. He was, however, long inured to such pain. He turned onto the wide graveled pathway that led through an open gate and along beside the manor to a stable block behind and to one side of it.

He wondered if in her wildest nightmares Maria expected him to come here in person to fetch her home. But she had given him no choice.

Two

It rained heavily and relentlessly the following day, from the middle of the morning on. But, disappointing as it was, a rainy day had its own beauty. Estelle was sitting on the window seat in the study, her favorite room in the house, with her back against a cushion, her feet flat on the padded sill, her knees drawn up before her. She had an open book propped against her legs but was no longer reading it. She was watching the rain slanting against the backdrop of the tall trees in the distance, beyond the lawn and the parterres. The wind was bowing the branches. The grass was emerald green and a bit overlong, though it was not yet unruly. It was the way she liked it best, actually, just before it was scythed. Though she did love the smell of newly cut grass too.

She turned her head to look at her brother. He was inelegantly slouched in the ancient leather chair before the fireplace, though the fire had not been lit. Aunt Jane would have frowned at his posture, yet there was a certain grace to it, as there was to his every movement. He was long and lean, just as she was on a smaller scale and with a few feminine curves thrown in. He was darkly handsome. Charming too, with a smile that could warm a room. She had seen the effect it had upon London drawing rooms and ballrooms. Men instinctively liked him, and women of all ages melted before him in droves. Young women almost visibly fell in love with him on sight. It really was not much of an exaggeration. The fact that he was Viscount Watley, heir to a marquess's title and fortune, was no doubt part of his appeal, but it was only a small part. It was his person that attracted. Yet he never flirted or sent out deliberate lures—not in Estelle's experience anyway. There was no vanity in him.

His long legs were stretched out before him now, one of his booted feet braced against the hearth. One elbow rested on the arm of his chair while his fingers played absently with his hair, which was slightly ruffled on that side. The other hand turned the pages of his book, in which he had been deeply engrossed for more than an hour. It was, she knew, some ancient Greek play—in Greek. It lost something in translation, he had explained when she had pointed out that there was a highly rated English version of the same play on one of the bookshelves.

He sensed her eyes upon him and looked up to smile at her. "Still raining?" he asked.

"Is the world still turning?" she replied.

He laughed. "It *was* a foolish question," he admitted. "It feels good to be quiet again, does it not? Just the two of us?"

"It does," she said.

"Though that sounds disloyal to our aunt and uncle," he added, setting his book facedown across his lap. "It was good having them here."

"It was," she said. "And Aunt Annemarie and Uncle William last month." Annemarie Cornish was their father's sister. "And seeing Papa and Mother and all the Westcotts at Hinsford and in London during the spring. It was all lovely. But yes, Bert, it feels *very* good to be quiet and alone here again with all the autumn and winter to look forward to. I think we must be hopeless cases."

"Not hermits, but close." He smiled again and hesitated before continuing. "Do you ever feel damaged, Stell?"

Oh! Where had *that* come from? The question had hovered between them for years but had never actually been put into words by either of them. Until now. Right out of the blue. Or, rather, right out of the gray and the rain. *Damaged.*

"By our upbringing?" But it was the only thing he could mean. There was a longish pause while she gave her answer some thought and they stared across the room at each other. "No. Not *damaged*. It is the wrong word. *Influenced*, yes. Of course. All adults are influenced by their childhood and youth. It would be impossible not to be. For some people those growing years are difficult. Oh, I suppose they are for all people to greater or lesser degrees. There is surely no such thing as a perfectly idyllic childhood. And if there were, it would perhaps be a poor preparation for adulthood. But . . . Even difficult childhoods are not always *damaging*. They can be just the opposite, in fact. They can build character and understanding and even wisdom. And fortitude."

"Mama stumbled over the hem of her dressing gown and tried to steady herself with a hand against the wall behind her," he said. "Except that she set her hand where the window would have been if Papa had not opened it earlier."

And fell to her death. It had happened upstairs in this very house, in what had then been the nursery, hers and

Bertrand's, early one morning while their father was rocking them to sleep. They had been cutting teeth.

"It ought not to have happened," Bertrand added.

"But it did," she said. "I wish I remembered her. She had us for almost a whole year, held us, fed us, laughed with us, played with us. Why is it we do not start remembering things right from the moment of our birth?"

"Have you forgiven our father?" he asked. "I mean *really* forgiven him?"

"Papa?" she said. Quite frequently now Bertrand called him that. Sometimes, though, he still referred to him as *Father*. "Yes, Bert. I have. For opening that window, of course. He could not have predicted . . . It was pure accident. But yes, for the rest of it too. He cannot go back to change the sixteen years following Mama's death, though I believe he would if he could. That is always the trouble with life, is it not? We cannot go back, even by as much as a day or an hour, to change something we said or did, or something we did *not* say or do. Or everything that resulted from those words and deeds. I have asked myself what might have happened if Aunt Jane and Uncle Charles had not come here and stayed and taken over our upbringing and really done a pretty commendable job of it. Every time Papa came home, he must have seen that we were well cared for, with a substitute mother and father and even older cousins as a substitute brother and sister. And we never complained to him. We never even *spoke* to him unless he spoke to us. He must have felt like an intruder. Like a failure. He must have convinced himself—he has told us he did—that we were far better off without him."

"He was wrong," Bertrand said.

"He was," she agreed. "And of course he ought to have known better. But he cannot go back. Neither can we. I sometimes wonder what might have happened if during one of his visits we had thrown ourselves upon him and begged him to stay or to take us with him. But we never did. We had been taught to behave with quiet decorum, to be seen and not heard. And we doubted his love. So we can never know what might have happened. *We cannot go back*."

"No," he agreed.

"But though our upbringing was— Oh, it was really rather *cheerless*, was it not, Bert?" she said. "Even so, we were enormously fortunate to have an uncle and aunt willing to give up years of their own lives and even their own home to come here for our sakes. And they did love us, even though it was never in a really warm or demonstrative way. I think Mama must have hugged us a lot. Probably Papa too during that first year. He was the one trying to rock us to sleep, after all. He had been up most of the night with us because our nurse was exhausted and he had sent her to bed. Oh, *if only* we could remember. I have indeed forgiven him, Bert. And I do *not* feel damaged. Only different, perhaps, from what I might have been. Which is a foolish way to think. We are all different from what we might have been if *this* or *that* had been different. Life is nothing if not precarious. It is how we live it from day to day that matters, though."

"You are not damaged, then," he said. "Yet you are still unmarried, Stell, at the age of twenty-five, soon to be twenty-six. Even though you are titled, rich, and beautiful. Even though you sparkle with vitality and charm in company and have had so many offers I have lost count."

That was a bit of an exaggeration. Actually a lot of an exaggeration. She was usually able to deflect ardor before it organized itself into a formal offer.

"You are twenty-five, almost twenty-six too," she said.

"Though you will always and ever be twenty minutes younger than I am. You are titled, rich, and handsome. You radiate warmth and charm in company. Yet you are still unmarried too. You have not even made any offers unless you have been very secretive about it."

He closed his book and set it down on the small table beside his chair. "It is different for me," he said. "I am a man. There *is* a difference, Stell, though I can see you are about to bristle and give me a lecture on the unfairness of it all."

"And you believe I remain single because I am *damaged*?" she said. She closed her own book too after taking note of the page number, and slid it down between herself and the window.

"It has occurred to me," he said. "Do you *want* to marry, Stell?"

She folded her arms beneath her bosom and gazed outward for a few moments. The rain was still sheeting down. The flowers in the beds were getting buffeted.

"Are you afraid I will still be here, an aging spinster sister, after you bring a bride to Elm Court?" she asked, turning her head back to smile at him. "Causing endless trouble?"

He grinned back. "I will ship you off to Redcliffe," he said. "You can be a prop and stay to our father and stepmother in their old age."

"Poor things." She laughed. "And poor me. Of course I want to marry. But before you ask, I have no idea when and even less idea *whom*. I have not met him yet."

"Would you know if you had?" he asked.

She thought about it. "Maybe not," she admitted. "Though when I think of all the men I know—the single ones—I really cannot picture myself married to any one of them. Not that that is any indictment of them. There are some very pleasant and worthy men among them. But—"

For some reason she thought of the dark, dour stranger who had ridden into her life and out of it yesterday, passing her by without a word even though that vicious dog of his might have torn her limb from limb if he had been one moment later arriving upon the scene. She almost laughed. But Bertrand would want to know why, and she had not told him about the incident. He was quite capable of forbidding her to leave their property without male protection and they would end up squabbling and she would accuse him of sounding just like Aunt Jane and he would accuse her of not heeding good advice when she heard it simply because she found Aunt Jane tedious. Which would be grossly unfair. She *loved* their aunt.

"But?" he said, prompting her. "What sort of man *are* you looking for, Stell?"

"Oh, let me see. My dream man." She pursed her lips and gazed out at the clouds. "*Not* tall, dark, and handsome, or he would be you. I love having you as a brother, Bert, but I would want something quite different in a husband."

"Short, fair, and ugly, then?" he suggested.

"The thing is," she said, "that I cannot really suggest a physical type that attracts me more than any other. But he would have to be . . . *attractive*. The trouble is, though, that it is a difficult word to define. *Something that attracts*. Or *someone* in this case. What are attractive qualities in a man, apart from just looks? Let me see. An open, pleasing countenance, I think. Smiling eyes, preferably blue. Yes, definitely blue. Good teeth, preferably white. A kindly manner. But with firm principles and the courage to stand by them. Charm. Kindness to all. Fellow feeling for all.

Intelligence and some learning. A sense of humor. A regard for women as persons."

"Passion?" he suggested when she paused to think some more.

She considered it—and her mind yet again touched upon that man, who had seemed to be coldness to the core. She shivered and hugged her arms more tightly.

"And passion," she said. "And commitment and fidelity. No *chères amies* for my dream man."

"Position? Wealth? Property?" he suggested.

"Well, I am tempted to say that they are of no importance whatsoever," she said. "But that would be impractical. The idea of living on love alone goes too far into the realm of fantasy to be feasible. My husband would not have to be titled, but he would have to be of good birth and education, I believe. Otherwise we would have so little in common that there would not be enough to sustain a relationship when the first blush of romance had worn off. He would not have to be enormously wealthy or live in a mansion, but he would have to be comfortably situated. I do not believe I would be happy living in a hovel, waiting for him to snare a rabbit for me to skin and drop into a pot of stew with some thin gruel and vegetables I had pulled up from my scrubby little patch of garden."

"And you would forever live in fear that he would be taken up for poaching and transported for seven years or so." He laughed and sat up a little straighter in his chair.

"I would not," she said. "I would not have married him in the first place."

"But there would have to be a blush of romance?" he said.

"I did use those words, did I not?" she admitted. "Oh, I believe so. There must be something more than just a dispassionate decision that *this* man rather than any other will suit me as a husband. I just do not really know what that something is, though, Bert. Perhaps I will know it when I find it. *If* I find it. But he must be a man of impeccable character and reputation. I could not contemplate marrying a rake, even a reformed rake."

"Like our father," he said quietly.

"Well," she said, shrugging her shoulders and turning her face to the window again. "There you have me, Bert. For he was undoubtedly a rake, was he not? Yet I love him dearly. And I do believe he is the best of husbands now. He and Mother are terribly happy."

"Yes," he agreed.

"But I am not our stepmother," she said. "I could not do what she did. I would not take the risk. I could not marry a man with an unsavory past and be happy with him, no matter how much he had reformed. I want someone . . ."

"Perfect?" he suggested when she paused.

"Well." She laughed softly and turned to swing her legs to the floor. "It is not too much to ask, surely, when I have waited so long. Someone perfect?"

"Maybe not," he said. "But it may explain why you are twenty-five and unwed."

"And what about you?" she asked. "What are you looking for in a wife?"

"I am not," he said.

"But when you do?" she asked. "You are not intending to remain single all your life, are you?"

"I could not do it even if I wanted to," he said. "I have the succession to take care of. I am Papa's only son. And he has only the one brother. I cannot imagine that Uncle André will ever marry. Can you?"

"No," she said. She was dearly fond of her uncle, but he reminded her of an overgrown boy, ever cheerful but sadly addicted to all forms of gaming and convinced that the very next bet he made would bring him the fortune that would set him up for life. Meantime his pockets were almost always to let, and Estelle suspected he was never free of debt.

"I do not know what type of woman I will look for when I start searching," Bertrand said. "But definitely not someone perfect, Stell. Such a one sounds to me like more than a bit of a snore."

"Someone imperfect, then," she said.

"She sounds infinitely more interesting," he said. "Quite irresistible, in fact. Introduce me if you should meet her before I do. Are you going to ring for some tea? Or shall I?"

"I am on my feet," she said, standing up to prove it. "I will ring."

It *did* sound a bit dull when put into words—*someone perfect*. But then perfection would preclude dullness, would it not? A dull man could not possibly be perfect, for he would lack that certain something that would make him perfect. And if she thought any more upon these lines, her head would surely make a complete turn on her neck and make her dizzy at the very least.

She pulled the bell rope.

She had not asked Bertrand, she realized, if *he* felt damaged. She suspected he did, that he always had. Something she had worked her way past had stuck with her twin. She now loved their father without reservation. Bertrand loved him, *but* . . .

Well, there did seem to be a *but*.

Justin was outside walking. He had come around to the back of the house, because when he had been at the front he had felt as though he were being watched from the sitting room—with resentment and hostility. As though he had been preventing Maria from being out there herself, tending the roses. He had invited her to stroll with him, but she had refused.

She was like a block of marble, even worse than he had expected. She had been easily recognizable, though he had not seen her for twelve years. Of medium height, she was slender to the point of thinness, with blond hair that was thicker and shinier than it had been when she was a child. She had a pale, delicate complexion in a narrow oval face, with a pointed chin and large blue eyes. She was beautiful, but in the way of a marble statue more than of a living woman, and a woman of twenty at that. She ought to be vibrant with youthful energy and chafing at the bit, eager to start living again, to go out into the world to mingle with her peers and fall in love. She was free of what must have been a heavy burden of nursing her mother through a long, increasingly debilitating illness until her eventual death. She was at the end of her year of mourning.

He had not seen one spark of vitality in her since his arrival. He did not know if it was *just* because he was here. If she had been surprised to see him two days ago, she had not shown it beyond a certain stillness when the housekeeper had announced him and he had stridden into the sitting room perhaps with more of a masterly stride than he ought. But he had been nervous, damn it. Within moments, however, she had got to her feet, made him a deep curtsy, and greeted him with a single word.

"Brandon," she had said.

Her companion had curtsied to him too.

"Maria?" he had said. "And Miss Vane, I assume?"

His sister had said no more. Her companion had inclined her head to indicate that yes, he had correctly identified her.

He could not even remember what he had gone on to say. Nothing much. Nothing that had warmed the atmosphere even one degree.

Silence did not seem to disconcert Maria. She seemed to feel no social obligation to initiate conversation during a lull or to pick up and enlarge upon any topic he introduced. She was the mistress of the monosyllabic answer. She displayed no curiosity about the brother she had once adored and had not seen in twelve years. She asked no questions about his journey or his reason for coming here. She had said nothing during that first meeting about instructing the servants to prepare a room for him or set a place for him at the dinner table. She had not asked how long he intended to stay.

He wondered exactly what her mother had told her about him. And what their father had told her.

He had left Captain out in the stables, in the care of the lone groom who worked there. His dog had not been happy about it, but he knew how to take orders—and how to express his displeasure over ones of which he disapproved. Drooping ears and jowls, and eyes he could make look as though they too drooped at the outer corners. An ambling gait as he walked slowly on his large paws, head down, looking like an octogenarian. None of it had caused Justin to relent.

For what had remained of the day of his arrival he had contented himself with behaving more or less like a guest, though he had asked to be directed to a bedchamber. It was Miss Vane who had taken charge after a glance at a silent Maria. She had shown him to the room the housekeeper informed her had been prepared for him. It was Miss Vane who told him when dinner would be served.

Yesterday, since courtesy was getting him nowhere with

Maria, he had asserted himself as the owner of Prospect Hall. He had spent time with the housekeeper and inspected the kitchen and pantries with her. He had sat down at the desk in her office and examined the account books. He kept no steward here, just as his father had not, since the size of the house and grounds and the farmland beyond them did not justify the extra expense. He had a man of business who managed all the smaller properties of the earldom from his office in London and sent regular and detailed reports. The man had proved both honest and efficient, as Justin had expected. He had worked for the late earl for twenty years before his death.

Since it had been raining too heavily for him to go out, he had asked the housekeeper if he might have the use of her room for a short while longer and had summoned Miss Vane. He had asked her if she was satisfied with her position as companion to his sister when she had been originally hired as a governess. Yes, she had told him. It was Maria herself who had begged her to stay when the countess had decided that her formal education was over after she turned seventeen.

"Only seventeen?" Justin had said.

"The countess, her mother, needed her, my lord," Miss Vane had told him. "She was ill and required almost constant company and assistance."

"None of the nurses I sent were as good as they were reputed to be?" he had asked her.

"They did not suit the countess," Miss Vane had said. "She preferred her daughter."

"Not you?" Justin had asked her. "Did you help nurse her, Miss Vane?"

"She preferred her daughter, my lord," she had said.

She was a serious, dignified young woman. She had

looked him in the eye as she spoke to him, but she would not open up to him, he suspected, and give anything more than a brief factual answer to any question he asked. Which was fair enough. She was an employee. She had her livelihood to protect. He suspected she might be fond of his sister.

"It was Maria rather than the countess who persuaded you to remain in the capacity of companion after your duties as governess were terminated, then?" he had asked.

"Yes, my lord," she had said. "She persuaded the countess that she needed me. And she wrote to your man of business in London for permission, since it is you, I believe, who pays my salary."

"Nursing her mother single-handed must have been hard on my sister," he had said.

"Yes, my lord," she had said. "But it is what daughters do."

And hard on Miss Vane too, he did not doubt. She was clearly a gentlewoman. She was almost certainly impoverished, or at least her father was. This could not be much of a life for her. But one could not always choose one's own way of life or even one's occupation, as he knew well from personal experience. At least she was employed. And he knew she was well paid.

"You are prepared to continue as my sister's companion?" he had asked her. "Though it will entail a removal to Everleigh Park?"

She had hesitated. "I would be uncomfortable going so far from my own home, my lord," she had said. "From my father's home, that is. My mother gave birth again a year ago. She is not a young woman. Four of my brothers and sisters are under the age of ten. I believe she is finding it hard to cope. I . . . I would rather not go so far away."

He would guess her age to be somewhere between

twenty-five and thirty, Justin thought. How many children were there, for God's sake? And how old was her mother? Fortunately, it was not his concern.

"I understand," he had said. "I will see to it that you are paid the equivalent of six months' salary when you leave here, Miss Vane. And I thank you for your service to my sister."

"That is very generous of you, my lord," she had said.

He had got to his feet and indicated the door behind her. It was a disappointment. Compelling Maria to leave here to return to Everleigh Park with him was going to be even more difficult than he had thought.

This morning the rain had stopped and Justin had found the foreman of the farm and inspected the barns and granaries and fields and the cattle sheds and sheep pens. He had spoken with some of the laborers and even looked in upon the cottages of a couple of them and spoken with their wives. As he had expected, though, all seemed to be running smoothly. No one expressed any outstanding grievances.

This afternoon he was having a good look around the park—or garden, rather. It did not quite qualify in size as a *park*. It was very pretty, nevertheless, and well cared for. The showpiece was the front garden and its profusion of flowers, most notably roses. All the beds and trellises and surrounding banks of shrubs made of it the quintessential English country garden against the backdrop of the gray stone manor.

But Justin preferred the back with the stables and carriage house and paddock off to one side and herb and vegetable gardens half hidden behind borders of flowers destined for the urns and vases inside the house—it was filled with them. Behind the gardens were tall trees with rhododendron and azalea bushes blooming beneath them. Captain was back there, sniffing and marking out his new territory. He was more reconciled to the stables as a temporary home than he had been at the start. The groom, who had very little else to do, was lavishing a great deal of time and attention upon him, it seemed.

Justin stood on the cobbled pathway between the two halves of the garden, gazing back toward the trees. Yesterday, after talking with Miss Vane, he had repeated his invitation to Maria to come to Everleigh with him when he returned there next week, keeping alive the myth that he was asking her rather than telling her. It was her home, after all, he had reminded her. It was where she had lived until after her father—*their* father—died when she was fourteen. It was unfortunate that circumstances had prevented her from taking her proper place in society when she turned eighteen. But it was not by any means too late. She was only twenty now, and she was both the daughter and the sister of an earl. He would take her to London next spring for the Season and see to it that she had a suitable female to sponsor and chaperon her. In the meanwhile he would provide some company and entertainment for her during what remained of the summer and through the winter. There would be old acquaintances to renew, new ones to be made.

He had fumbled his way onward, without any help from his sister.

"No, thank you, Brandon," she had said when he had finished making his case. "I will stay here with Melanie. She and our neighbors are all the company I need or want."

It had been a lengthy speech for her. He suspected she was refusing the life he offered just because she had a grudge against him. She was *twenty*, for the love of God. It did not seem to him that there could be any robust social life to be found here.

He would have to force the issue, of course, and he suspected she knew it. He was going to have to insist, though he did wonder why. If she was content to stay here, shut away from society, gradually seeing her youth dwindle, nursing whatever grievance she had against him specifically and perhaps the world in general, then why not allow her to do so? She was a rational being and no longer a child, after all. And Miss Vane, who would probably remain in her employment if Maria stayed here, did offer her some respectability.

He could not do it. He could not allow Maria to remain here. He felt responsible for her. He *was* responsible for her.

He wondered again what her mother had told her about him. And their father before he died. Though he very much doubted their father had told her anything. Certainly not the truth—or the truth as he had perceived it. And his father had never told lies. He might have closed up like a clam, but he would rather have done that than utter an untruth. It had been one thing upon which he had always been firm and inflexible. Had the countess told her daughter the truth? Justin very much doubted that too. So what *had* she said to make Maria hate him so much?

There was no doubt that she *did* hate him. Without passion. The worst kind of hatred.

Could his stepmother not simply have told her that he had gone away, as young men will, to explore the world and sow some wild oats before it became necessary to settle down? Maria might still have ended up hating him, but surely with passion. She would be raging against him for neglecting and abandoning her. For not even saying goodbye.

Of course that explanation, if her mother had given it,

would no longer have sufficed when, six years ago, he had not returned home after their father's death. He had not returned, in fact, until well after he had given the command that the countess remove here to Prospect Hall.

Captain was dashing down the path toward him, woofing, and Justin became aware of the sound of horses' hooves and carriage wheels.

"Sit, Cap," he said, and his dog obeyed, but not without looking reproachfully at him, all panting intelligence and eagerness to be gone to investigate this new excitement.

The carriage did not come along the side of the house to the stables. It must have stopped at the front of the house, then. The groom was striding out of the stables and going in that direction. Maria had a visitor—her first since his arrival.

He stayed where he was for a few minutes. The last thing he felt like doing was being sociable to a stranger. However, he was the owner of Prospect Hall. He was Maria's brother and guardian. It would not do for her visitor to discover that he had remained skulking back here throughout the visit. He turned and strode off toward the stables, where he left Captain in his stall—it was spread with fresh straw and the water bowl had been filled, he saw—and nodded to the groom, who was leading a horse and gig toward the stables.

Justin let himself into the house by the front door. There were two hats on the side table, a tall-crowned man's hat and a fashionable bonnet with matching kid gloves. A couple, then. There was no sign of any servant. He proceeded to the sitting room and let himself in without knocking. Conversation, which had sounded cheerful and lively, stopped abruptly as the four occupants of the room, all still on their feet, turned to look at him.

The visitors were a man and a woman, both young, probably in their middle twenties, both smartly dressed in what he recognized as the first stare of fashion. The man was tall, dark, slim, and elegant. The woman was his feminine counterpart. And extremely, vividly lovely. There was a moment, a fraction of a moment, when he did not recognize her. Then he did. Perhaps it was the startled look upon her face, quickly suppressed.

"The Earl of Brandon," Maria said by way of introduction, without adding any explanation of his relationship to her. But perhaps they knew? Surely they did, in fact. "Viscount Watley, Brandon. And Lady Estelle Lamarr."

Not husband and wife, then. But he would have known it anyway. They were clearly brother and sister. No. More than that. There was something about them . . . They were somehow like two halves of a whole, masculine and feminine in perfect balance with each other. He would bet his fortune on it that they were twins.

"Brandon?" Watley inclined his head with easy courtesy and smiled. "Lady Maria's brother, I believe?"

"*Half* brother," Maria said.

Lady Estelle Lamarr acknowledged him with a nod of the head. No curtsy. Face like a mask.

And Justin, who might have said or done any number of things to set them all at their ease—like stepping forward with a smile of his own and an outstretched hand, for example, and some remark that would require a response—said and did nothing beyond making the pair a slight stiff bow.

Three

"Well, that was awkward," Bertrand said cheerfully as he guided the horse and gig through the gates and onto the road home, leaving Prospect Hall behind them. "Are you *sure* we stayed for only half an hour, Stell? It felt more like three and a half."

"Poor Maria," Estelle said. "She does not seem at all happy to see her brother, does she? *Half* brother, to be more accurate. I cannot say I blame her. I have rarely if ever met a more morose man."

The only thing she might say in his favor was that he had made no mention of that ghastly encounter by the river the day before yesterday. Not by the merest twitching of an eyebrow had he betrayed any sign of recognition. Perhaps he really had *not* recognized her.

"What with Lady Maria sulking and Miss Vane playing the part of demure, near-mute companion and Brandon seemingly never having grasped the concept of making polite conversation, it was dashed hard going," Bertrand said. "It is a good thing Miss Vane did at least open her mouth long enough to ask about Aunt Jane, Uncle Charles, and Ellen, and we were able to give an exhaustive account of their long-drawn-out departure. Lady Maria actually smiled when you described the prayer meeting."

"It may be a little unfair to say she was *sulking*, Bert," Estelle said. "I would say she was displaying a dignified sort of displeasure with her half brother without being openly ill-mannered about it. They must have quarreled. Not just now, I mean. Years ago. We have always suspected it. How could we not when everyone hereabouts was eager enough to inform us two years ago when we came back to live at Elm Court that Lady Brandon and Maria had not *chosen* to move here after the late earl's passing but had been *commanded* to come by the new earl? Neither of us puts a great deal of trust in unsubstantiated rumor, but it did seem troubling that the earl did not once come here in person while the countess lay dying. Yet she was his stepmother. Nor did he come afterward to comfort his sister or attend her mother's funeral. Maria herself has never spoken a word about her life before she came here, or about *why* she and the countess came. She has never made mention of her brother—not in my hearing, anyway. None of it has been *normal*."

"It is a bit strange that we had not set eyes upon him before today, either here or anywhere else," Bertrand said. "He has had the title for a number of years now, and someone mentioned—it might have been Papa or Avery—that he has taken his place in the House of Lords. That means he must have been in London."

"But never at any of the social events we attended," she

said. "I would not have forgotten that face if I had seen it before. It is really quite unpleasant. Almost menacing. I wonder how he broke his nose."

Bertrand laughed. "That detail has escaped the notice of the gossips hereabouts," he said as he slowed the horse and steered the gig skillfully over the stone bridge, having chosen the scenic route home, bumpy though the track was in parts. "It is amazing the breaking of the aristocratic nose does not have a story of its own. There are enough other stories to lift the hairs along the back of one's neck and remind one to keep the doors locked at night."

The stories about the wicked earl were still resurrected by the gossips whenever there was little other news to enliven conversation. He was said to have left home at the command of his father, the late earl, several years before he succeeded to the title. He was said to have indulged in every vice and debauchery known to mankind both before and after his banishment. It was even said that he had spent a few years at hard labor in some particularly notorious jail in the north of England. It was all wild conjecture, of course. No one had any hard facts or credible witnesses to substantiate the rumors. For the past six years he had been the Earl of Brandon and had apparently settled down to a life of sober respectability. Though no one was sure even of that, since he had never come here and no one had ever run into him in London or elsewhere.

"I suppose," Bertrand added, "no one knew about the nose in order to invent a story to account for it. That will soon be rectified, I am sure. I am betting on a jail yard brawl."

"Surely not *all* the stories we have been told can be untrue," Estelle said. "Or can they? Having seen the man today and spent half an hour in his company, I must confess I am half inclined to believe everything. Including the prison story. He looks like a thoroughly bad lot. Yet poor Maria cannot even ask him to leave. He *owns* Prospect Hall. I wonder if he is her guardian. I suppose he must be, though she has never said. She is only twenty, after all."

There was indeed a hardness to the look of him, and it was not just his broken nose. It was his dark hair and dark, unfathomable eyes, several shades darker than her own and Bertrand's—chocolate without the cream—and his weather-bronzed, harsh-featured face. It was his massive size, which seemed to owe nothing at all to fat but everything to muscle. *Not* the sort of muscle acquired by participation in gentlemanly sports, however, but the sort that came from manual labor. He looked like an impostor in his elegant gentleman's attire. He did not behave entirely like a gentleman either. He had no easy, sociable smiles, no conversation. Estelle was sure he had not strung more than five words together during their entire visit. He had not uttered a word of apology to her during their first encounter, though it must have been clear to him that his dog had scared her out of her wits.

"How disappointing for you, Stell," Bertrand said, turning his head to grin at her. "You were presented today with the unexpected opportunity of meeting someone new, a single gentleman, an earl no less, a man both eligible and below the age of sixty. But he does not fit your image of the perfect husband. He is missing a few attributes."

"Make that *all* attributes," she said.

"You cannot adjust your expectations?" he asked, still grinning.

"Alas, I cannot," she said with a sigh. "I might forgive

him for being tall and dark, but . . . No, Bert, it seems that I have become stuck in my ways in my old age. I must have blue eyes and a straight nose and a kindly manner."

"Mere trivialities," he said. "You are headed for eternal spinsterhood, Stell. Though I must confess I would not enjoy having a brother-in-law with such nonexistent conversation."

"Oh, Bert," she said. "Did you see his *hands*? They are huge. And *callused*."

"It is what results from unraveling all those hemp ropes in jail," he said. "But picture this, Stell. You could sit beside him on a love seat in your boudoir, rubbing a soothing salve into his hands while he entertains you with stories from his shady past. No? It does not sound like marital bliss to you? You do not think you could get more than two words at a time out of him?"

She punched him on the arm, and the gig swayed a bit drunkenly before he regained control of the ribbons. Estelle shrieked and her brother laughed.

But really, *poor* Maria! Exactly *why* had he come now, when he had never come before?

Estelle and Bertrand had called upon Maria two years ago, as they had upon all their neighbors, to make her acquaintance. She had been an eighteen-year-old then, thinner and paler even than she was now, but self-possessed and mature beyond her years and devoted to her severely ailing mother, whose declining health had already confined her to her own suite of rooms though she had not yet been totally bedridden. They had never met the countess, as she had stopped receiving visitors. The neighbors described her as a beautiful woman who always hated to be seen before she had spent hours with her maid making herself look perfect.

Maria had insisted upon caring for her mother herself, though it must have been an increasingly difficult task. She had dismissed a number of nurses who had come from an agency because they were not tender enough with their patient and caused her more distress than comfort. Or so Maria had claimed. Estelle had often wondered if it was in fact the countess herself who had sent them away. If it was, it had been extremely selfish of her. Though it was perhaps wrong to judge someone who had been very ill, when she, Estelle, had always enjoyed good health.

Estelle had returned to Prospect Hall at least once a week after that initial visit, at first out of pity for a young neighbor who must have been getting very little pleasure out of life, but then out of genuine friendship. If Maria was upstairs, tending the invalid, as she often was, Estelle would spend half an hour talking with Melanie Vane, the governess turned companion, a sensible woman who obviously felt a deep attachment to her charge. Though no, Miss Vane had said in answer to a question Bertrand had asked one day when he had been with Estelle, she did not help at all in the sickroom. Maria preferred to do all that needed doing herself.

By which Estelle had suspected that the countess preferred it. Or demanded it. Maria had never given the slightest hint of anything but total affection for and devotion to her mother, however.

Now, at the age of twenty, released from her duties in the sickroom and the year of her mourning at an end, Maria still looked fragile and probably appeared shy to anyone who did not know her. Actually she was neither, and Estelle was very fond of her. But she *was* still a minor, and there was something not quite proper about her living without the chaperonage of someone older than Melanie, who was close to Estelle in age. If the Earl of Brandon really was her guardian, then possibly he had plans for her. Marriage, perhaps. Did he have someone specific picked out for her? She would hate it if he did.

But there was nothing Estelle could do about it.

The Reverend Mott and some of the more socially prominent local families called at Prospect Hall over the next week to pay their respects to the Earl of Brandon, having heard he was in residence and never having met him before. More than one of them slipped that last fact quite deliberately into conversation, it seemed to Justin, as though to reproach him for neglecting his duty—to the countess, perhaps. To his sister, probably. To them, maybe. His father had made a point of coming here once a year and staying a couple of weeks in order to inspect the property and call upon his neighbors and even entertain some of them. He had been an affable sort, Justin's father, well liked and well respected wherever he went.

Justin accepted a couple of invitations to dine and took Maria with him. It was somewhat reassuring to discover that she had not been obliged to live here as a near hermit. There were a few genteel families with whom she could and did socialize, it seemed, though he did learn that during the final years of her mother's illness and the year since her death she had not left the hall for anything except Sunday service at church, and not always even then.

There were very few young people of an age approximate to hers in the neighborhood. Most of the young ladies were either married or still in the schoolroom. Most of the young men were absent—at school or university or kicking their heels elsewhere—though their parents spoke fondly of them and their promising prospects. Justin had the feeling one or two of them might have been summoned home if the parents had been given advance notice of his coming. Maria was very eligible, after all.

But it was really quite improper for her to be here all alone except for Miss Vane, who was not herself much older than her charge. He could not in all conscience allow his sister to remain here. He had known that before he came, of course, but now it was glaringly obvious. She did not even look twenty. She could pass for a girl of sixteen. She was going to have to return to Everleigh with him, whether she liked it or not.

She did *not* like it, of course.

She did not argue, however. She merely said no, though Justin suspected she knew her answer counted for nothing. She had turned from marble to . . . What was harder and colder than marble? Granite? Whatever it was, she had turned to it since he had told her what was about to happen. Like the tyrant his sister no doubt saw him as.

No doubt too she knew that when she left, Miss Vane would not go with her. He did consider asking the woman if she would extend her employment for one month in order to accompany Maria to Everleigh and offer her companionship through her first few weeks there. But it would be unfair to ask, he decided.

The neighborhood family most eligible to offer his sister companionship was the brother-and-sister duo. The twins. Watley's title, Justin had learned, was a courtesy one. He had suspected as much, actually, from the fact that the man's sister was *Lady* Estelle Lamarr rather than simply *Miss* Lamarr. Their father was the Marquess of Dorchester of Redcliffe Court in Northamptonshire. Justin had a nodding acquaintance with him from the House of Lords. Their stepmother was related in some way to the Westcott family, which boasted among its members more titles than almost any other noble family in England. Those twins were socially *connected*, even if one of them did choose to behave on occasion with a quite shocking lack of ladylike decorum. And they were of a suitable age to be his sister's friends. He would guess they were twenty-five or so. Both were single. Watley was elegant and good-looking and had the polished manners of a gentleman of superior rank. It had been impossible to discern in that one awkward meeting Justin had had with the man if he fancied Maria or if she fancied him. But it would not have been surprising. It would certainly be worth encouraging if there was some spark there. Lady Estelle was equally elegant and refined— despite the riverbank incident—with a certain liveliness of manner that must offer some of the light in darkness that Maria seemed desperately to need.

Justin would be happy to encourage acquaintances with brother and sister, but not under present circumstances. Maria should not be here alone and really ought not to have been during the past year while she mourned her mother. He ought to have insisted upon sending *someone* old enough to lend her countenance, though he could not for the life of him think whom. Lady Maple, perhaps? She was Maria's great-aunt on her mother's side, though he did not know if the two had ever met. The countess had quarreled with everyone in her family soon after she married Justin's father. Anyway, it was too late now.

It seemed that Watley and his sister lived alone at Elm Court two or three miles away as the crow flies, farther by road.

There was no question of his leaving Maria here even though he hated the thought of taking her to Everleigh against her will and without her longtime companion. He had had an idea, however, something that might ease her return to Everleigh and help her settle there during the crucial first couple of weeks or so. He did not particularly fancy meeting either one of the Lamarrs again, as he was fully aware that he had not acquitted himself well when they called at Prospect Hall. He had been a bit thrown at recognizing the woman from the riverbank, if the truth were known, and by the time he had recovered from that it had been too late to greet the two of them as he ought, with a warm smile and a handshake. That failure had set the tone for the whole of the excruciatingly painful half hour or so that had followed. If someone had tied his tongue in a knot he could hardly have done worse.

He *would* meet them again, though—by choice. Provided they were at home, that was. He learned the direction of Elm Court from the groom in the stables and saddled up his horse one afternoon and led it outside. He decided, perhaps against his better judgment, to take Captain too, since his dog had been leveling a more than usually hangdog expression at him lately, having not had a good run since their arrival here.

He set out to call upon Viscount Watley and Lady Estelle Lamarr.

The grass had been newly scythed and looked neat and smelled heavenly. Then, however, the four large flower beds, which, long before Estelle was born, had been cut into the lawn with geometric precision to form four diamond shapes in a larger diamond formation, had ended up looking sadly ragged in contrast. She could have waited for the gardeners to get to them, as of course they would, but she liked doing a bit of gardening and was out here now pulling weeds and cutting deadheads from among the flowers and dropping them all into the basket she carried over her arm. And what a difference the pulling and cutting had made! The flowers in the three beds she had already done were looking considerably brighter and more fully alive again, and now this one did too. She stood back on the grass to admire her handiwork. But something caught the edge of her vision as she did so, and she looked across two large diamonds to the drive beyond.

A horse and rider were just coming into view, and for a moment she brightened with the expectation that Bertrand was returning from his visit to the vicarage in time for tea. The Reverend Mott had once been his beloved and much-revered teacher and mentor. That was in the days before their great-uncle died and their father succeeded to the marquess's title and they all moved to Redcliffe Court— she and Bertrand, Aunt Jane and Uncle Charles, and cousins Oliver and Ellen. But not, alas, their father. It had taken another couple of years to bring him home to stay. Bertrand had gone today to discuss the Greek plays he had been reading. It all sounded as dry as dust to Estelle, but her twin had been full of eagerness in anticipation of an afternoon of interesting entertainment.

No, they were *not* identical twins.

The rider was not Bertrand, of course. He had *walked* into the village. It was the Earl of Brandon, and now Estelle could not even pretend to be away from home. He had seen her. So had his dog, which took a few menacing steps toward her across the lawn before stopping abruptly at something the man had said. She heard the low rumble of his voice but could not discern the actual words.

How very mortifying and unpleasant. Estelle was terribly aware of her ancient cotton dress, faded from innumerable washes and much despised by her maid, who always told her it was too old even for the ragbag. But it was cool and comfortable and was kept strictly for chores such as this one. Her straw hat must be almost as antique. Its brim was limp and shapeless and wonderfully effective in shading her face and neck from the sun. Her gloves were large and elbow length and bright green and ugly. But they kept her fingers and forearms from being pricked, and they kept the dirt from getting beneath her fingernails and the sap from staining her hands. Her shoes . . . Well, the less said about her shoes, the better.

She set down her basket, pulled off her gloves, and dropped them on top of the dead blooms and weeds. She could not do anything about the rest of her appearance. Let him think what he would. She did not much care about his good opinion anyway. She made her way toward him, skirting about the flower beds and eyeing the dog warily. It was panting, its tongue lolling out of its mouth. It was looking at her as though it would be happy to make her its afternoon tea if only its master would be obliging enough to ride out of sight for a few moments.

The man looked as morose as ever. Oh, it was wicked, perhaps, to have taken him in such thorough dislike. No, it was not. He had done nothing to make himself likable. Quite the opposite.

"Captain will not hurt you," he told her.

"Not when you are here to call him off," she agreed.

"Cap," he said. "Shake."

And the dog, still panting, still gazing intently and hungrily at her, sat on its haunches, lifted one of its giant paws, and dangled it toward her.

Oh dear God.

But he had done it deliberately to disconcert her—the man, that was. To make a cringing female out of her, as he had done by the river. How she wished now that she had left her legs dangling in the water and merely tossed her head—and her hair—in his direction. And raised one haughty eyebrow.

She took a few resolute steps forward, grasped the dog's paw in a firm clasp, and shook it. It was *gigantic*. It could flatten her with one swat. And it had lethal-looking claws. Was that what one called them on a dog? Or were they nails?

"How do you do, Captain?" she said before looking up at the earl. Man and dog suited each other. He was gigantic too. And he had those huge hands, neatly gloved at the moment and holding the reins. "How do you do, Lord Brandon?"

He removed his hat. "I wondered, Lady Estelle," he said, "if I might have a few words with you and Viscount Watley."

A few words. He had already had them—more than he had ever spoken in a row before now—and she wished he would go away. All the way away. Back home where he had come from. Maria did not like him even though he was her brother, and that fact merely confirmed Estelle in her own negative reaction to him. Perhaps those rumors about him were all true. Perhaps he was as dangerous and evil as he looked. Perhaps he really was an ex-convict. And perhaps she was overreacting, merely because she had embarrassed herself out by the river and called his dog a doggie and was embarrassing herself today. This dress, she remembered now, had been new when she was still living here with her aunt and uncle, before the move to Redcliffe. They had moved when she was *fifteen*. She was twenty-five now, going on twenty-six. How excruciatingly embarrassing. Never mind the ragbag. The dress was too old for a museum.

"Bertrand is not here," she said. "He ought to be back

soon for tea, but when he gets to discussing classical litera-
ture with the vicar, time loses all meaning for both of them.
It is altogether possible that eventually they will notice
darkness has fallen beyond the windows of the study,
though I daresay the vicar's housekeeper might insist upon
feeding him his dinner before then."

And what on earth was she prattling about now?

"But you may have a word with me if you wish," she said.

He glanced toward the house. "Perhaps it would not be
quite the thing," he said.

It was what Bertrand would think too. And, of course,
Aunt Jane if she were here. Though if she were here, then
there would be no problem, would there? And how mortifying that this man had had to point out to her what was
proper behavior.

"I will summon my maid," she said. "Perhaps you would
like to take your horse to the stables, Lord Brandon, while
I wash my hands." *And change my dress. And my shoes.
And comb my hair.* "The butler will show you up to the
drawing room."

Please come home, Bert.

She ought simply to have agreed with him that it was not
the thing to entertain a gentleman alone. He would have
gone away and returned some other time if the word he
wished to have with them was important enough. But she
could not bear the thought of waiting every day in anticipation of his coming back. Better to hear him out now and be
rid of him.

He returned his hat to his head and proceeded on his
way to the stables, his dog loping along at his side.

Four

Fifteen minutes later, Estelle entered the drawing room, wearing a sprigged muslin dress she had acquired in London during the spring. Her hair was freshly brushed and twisted into a knot at the back of her head—her maid's specialty when time was of the essence. He was standing with his back to the fireplace, his legs slightly apart, his hands behind him, his expression stern. Lord of his domain—in *her* drawing room. Well, strictly speaking, Bertrand's drawing room. But certainly not the Earl of Brandon's. Of Bertrand, of course, there was no sign. Olga, Estelle's maid, who had come into the room behind her, went to sit in the corner farthest from the window and busied herself with some darning.

"Please have a seat," Estelle said.

She thought he was going to ignore her invitation, but he was merely waiting, it seemed, for her to seat herself first. The man had *some* manners, then. He filled the chair he sat on, but there was no reason in the world why she should feel intimidated. She clasped her hands in her lap.

"You did not bring Maria with you?" she asked.

"No," he said.

Well, that was obvious. Her question had been meant as a conversation starter. *Why* had he not brought Maria? He either had not recognized it as a cue or did not like round-aboutation. Very well. She would be direct.

"What is it you wished to say to my brother and me?" she asked him. Were his eyes really black? Or would she see varying shades of brown if she were closer to him? She had no wish whatsoever to be closer to him, however. She could live very happily without knowing the true color of his eyes.

"My sister is twenty years old," he said. "It was un-exceptionable for her to live at Prospect Hall with her mother, even while her mother was gravely ill. I acquiesced to her wish to remain there to do her mourning after her mother died. They were extremely close, I believe, and Maria had given up several years of her own life to her care. She also had a companion with her, Miss Vane, a lady with whom she was long familiar, originally as her governess. I believed my sister would be so devastated by her loss that she would be content to live a retired existence with few social distractions or none. I judged that her situation would be respectable enough, at least temporarily."

Her mother. Her mother. Never *Lady Brandon* or *my stepmother.*

"You judged correctly," Estelle said. "Maria was physi-cally exhausted and emotionally drained through much of the past year. She received callers but never returned the calls, as far as I am aware. She certainly never came here, though we invited her."

But why had he not come sooner to check on her for himself? Why had he not come when Lady Brandon was desperately ill and dying? *Why had he not gone to her funeral?* She was buried in the churchyard here, not back at Everleigh Park beside her late husband.

"She does get some outdoor exercise," he said. "She spends time in the garden. I understand the roses owe a great deal to her hard work."

"Yes," she said. Tending the lavish beauty of the roses had given some consolation to a girl whose own life had been unendingly bleak, at least in the two years Estelle had known her.

"Lady Estelle," he said. "She cannot remain here, especially when her companion is herself unmarried and under the age of thirty, a woman who was hired as my sister's governess. There is no female relative of suitable age and circumstances on my father's side of the family and only one, probably too elderly, on Maria's upon whom I could call to live with her here. But even if there were someone, this is no place for the young daughter of an earl. She ought to have an opportunity to mingle with the *ton* and enjoy the company of her peers. She must return to Everleigh, which is her rightful home. She must take her place in society as soon as it can be arranged."

Why was he telling *her* this? Why had he wanted Bertrand to hear what he had to say? Did he merely wish to justify his high-handed desire to take Maria away? It was his decision to make, not theirs. Did he perhaps hope she and her brother would join their voices with his in persuading Maria that it was in her best interest to return home with him? Perhaps it was. But there was the fact that Maria appeared to dislike him, and that was probably understating her feelings. How would *she* feel if Bertrand had forced her to live with him here but she hated him? No, that was no good. She could not imagine ever hating her twin. And heaven help him if he ever tried to force her to do anything she did not want to do.

"Perhaps it is to Maria herself you ought to be making these arguments, Lord Brandon," she said.

"Do you believe I have not done so?" he asked harshly. "She will not even discuss the matter. Beyond the one word *no*, she remains mute. And though she knows she cannot fight me if I insist—and I *do* insist—she treats me with a silent sort of contempt that is intolerable. To me. And to her, I daresay."

Contempt?

"You wish me to persuade her, then, that it will be best for her to go with you?" she asked him, anger gathering like a ball in her stomach. "How can I know that, Lord Brandon? Perhaps happiness found in solitude is preferable to misery found in company, especially when one does not *like* the company."

Now he had goaded her into being downright rude.

He gazed at her in silence. He was very good at that. Silence did not seem to cause him discomfort. She ought to wait him out but she could not.

"And you wish *Bertrand* to add his persuasions to mine?" she asked. "He will not do it. He would consider it the height of impertinence to interfere between a brother and sister."

The drawing room door opened even as she spoke and Bertrand came in, all haste and smiles—and a glance toward the corner to assure himself that some female servant was there and his twin had not committed the unpardonable indiscretion of entertaining a gentleman alone.

"Brandon. Good to see you," he said, striding across the

room to shake the earl by the hand while Estelle nodded a dismissal to Olga. "I am sorry I was from home when you came. And I apologize to you too, Stell. I promised to be back in time for tea, but the vicar and I got carried away with our discussion and lost track of time. A poor excuse, I know, but the truth, I am afraid."

The earl had stood to shake hands with him. They were of almost the same height, Estelle noticed in some surprise—it had seemed to her on their first encounter with him that the earl towered over her brother. They were very different in build, however, her twin lithe and graceful, the earl broader of girth and solid with muscle. He was not the sort of man one would wish to come across at night in a dark lane.

"Lord Brandon wishes us to persuade Maria to return to Everleigh Park with him, Bert," Estelle said as her brother took a seat directly across from their visitor.

"It would seem to be the best thing for her to do," Bertrand said as the earl opened his mouth to speak. "I have felt some concern over the fact that she no longer has an older relative living with her. Not that Lady Brandon was able to offer any real chaperonage for a few years before her demise, poor lady. She was very ill. Nevertheless, her very presence in the house made everything perfectly respectable. I take it Lady Maria does not wish to leave? I daresay she has grown comfortable here, and Prospect Hall is a pretty place. In what way do you believe we can convince her to change her mind, Brandon?"

Estelle clamped her teeth together. Trust her brother to take his part. Men and their protective instincts!

"That is not quite what I came to ask of you," the earl said. "Lady Estelle has perhaps misunderstood what I *have* said."

"Indeed?" She raised her eyebrows.

"My sister must and will return to Everleigh Park with me," Lord Brandon said. "There is no question of her remaining here. She has been told, in fact, that we will be leaving within a week. Unfortunately, however, Miss Vane will be unable to accompany us. Family concerns make it difficult for her to move farther away from her own home than she already is. So I am going to have not only an unwilling sister at Everleigh with me, but also a very lonely one. I have taken some steps to make my house a more welcoming place for her while she settles there after six years away and accepts it as her home again. But I do not know how those plans will work out. Being there will not be easy for her. She has never lived there without her mother. Or for very long without her father. She has not lived there with me since she was eight years old. I would be a great deal happier if I could arrange matters so that she could have someone familiar there in whom to confide and upon whom to lean, even if only for a short while. It is my hope that you—both of you—will be guests at Everleigh for a couple of weeks or so."

Oh, heaven forbid! Estelle drew breath to speak.

"And how does Lady Maria feel about this?" Bertrand asked before she could.

"I have not asked her," the earl admitted. "I decided to speak with you first. It is a great deal to ask."

Indeed it was. Maria had been *eight*? He had been gone from home for six years, then, before his father died and he inherited the title.

Bertrand looked at Estelle, his eyebrows raised.

"We will need to talk this over," she said. "Between ourselves."

It would be intolerable. And Maria would surely not appreciate such interference in her affairs—*Oh, by the way, Maria, when you go to Everleigh Park, against your will, with the brother you hate? Bert and I will be going too to spend a few weeks there as his guests. Will not that be fun? I can scarcely wait!* But . . . Melanie Vane would not be going with her. She would be all alone—with her brother. That would be a blow indeed to poor Maria.

"We would also need to speak with Lady Maria," Bertrand said. "She is Estelle's friend and a close acquaintance of mine. Even if we should decide between ourselves that we are willing to accept your invitation for her sake, we would not be comfortable having her presented with a *fait accompli*. She may be your sister and ward, Brandon, and therefore subject to your commands, but she owes nothing to us."

"Maria is indeed my friend," Estelle said. "I would not do anything that concerns her behind her back, Lord Brandon. She may be a minor and a woman, but she . . . *matters*. As a person."

The Earl of Brandon got to his feet. "I will say nothing of my visit here, then," he said. "Until you have given me your answer, that is. May I expect it fairly soon?"

"You say you plan to leave here with your sister within the week," Bertrand said. "We will give you our answer before then. In the meanwhile, it is altogether possible that we will call upon Lady Maria. If we do, we would appreciate a word alone with her."

"You will have it." The earl inclined his head and made his way toward the door. "Good day, Lady Estelle."

Bertrand had got to his feet to follow him.

She murmured something as they left the room. She resented this, she thought as she stood up and stared at the door after it closed behind them. She deeply resented it.

There was *something* between the Earl of Brandon and Maria. Something old and ugly. Her father had died just before she and her mother came here—sent from Everleigh Park, it seemed, by the command of the present earl. Just as he had been banished by his father six years before that—if the story she had heard was true, that was. Was there a connection? But even if there was, it could not have involved Maria. She had been *eight years old*.

Estelle tried to imagine what would happen if her own father were to die—horrid thought. She tried to imagine Bertrand sending their stepmother far away from Redcliffe. Banishing her. She could not picture it. Their stepmother was not their *mother*. No one could take her place even though she had died before their first birthday and they had no conscious memories of her. But both she and Bertrand *adored* their stepmother—they called her Mother—and she loved them. She was a very real part of their family unit. She would always have a home at Redcliffe, even if Bertrand moved there with a wife and family. Even if she chose to go and live with one of her three children instead of remaining at Redcliffe.

Maria had never offered any explanation of what had brought her and her mother here. Estelle felt for her now in her obvious distress over the arrival of her brother and could only imagine how she must be feeling about having to return with him—alone—to the home she had not seen in six years. Nevertheless, that was *Maria's* business. She would adjust and cope somehow. She was a much stronger person than her physical appearance and her quiet demeanor suggested. Estelle very much resented being drawn into whatever secret passions lurked within that family story.

It was not *her* story. Or Bertrand's. They had dealt with their own demons when they had reared their nasty heads.

And they had emerged from the struggle stronger and happier. They had their father back in their lives, with the wonderful bonus of a stepmother. And now they really were contented together here at Elm Court, alone again after a busy spring and a round of family visits. Alone for the autumn and winter, they had been hoping, with the possible exception of Christmas.

Bertrand came back into the room.

"You do not want to go to Everleigh?" he asked.

"I really, *really* do not," she told him.

"But . . . ?" He tipped his head to one side and regarded her closely. "You will have sleepless nights if we leave it at that without giving it another thought? Is that what your frown is telling me?"

"I *despise* the fact that you know me so well, Bert," she said. "How dare he present us with this dilemma?"

"You really have taken him in dislike," he said, grinning at her. "Your heart is not in danger, is it, Stell?" He waggled his eyebrows.

"Oh! That is not even *funny*." She grabbed a cushion from the love seat and hurled it at him.

He caught it in one hand.

"We will talk about it," he said. "We do need to consider Lady Maria and what, if anything, we can do to help her. I know you have grown very fond of her, Stell, and I care what happens to her. But may we have a tea tray brought up first? I am starved. *And* parched."

"And whose fault is that?" she asked.

Lady Estelle Lamarr had been hostile. Watley had been wary and careful in his response. He probably ought not to have called upon them, Justin thought as he rode back to Prospect Hall, Captain loping along beside his horse except when he paused to sniff at something that caught his interest and needed further attention or went dashing off to explore the unknown. He never went far. He had been trained not to do so. A raised voice or a whistle would bring him back in a moment. The dog never needed a leash.

Inviting them to Everleigh had probably not been a brilliant idea from the start. But he was feeling a bit desperate. Maria had been a burden upon his conscience for the past six years, the innocent victim of a situation that did not involve her. He had driven her from her home not long after she lost her father and when she was at an age at which girls were starting to look forward to being young ladies and stepping out into the world of fashion and parties and courtship. But at least she had been with her mother. That had no longer been so for more than a year now. She had lost both her parents by the time she was nineteen. Clearly she could not remain where she was.

The only real solution was for her to live at Everleigh, where she had been born and spent her childhood. Where her brother and guardian lived. Where she belonged. Yet he had known from her clipped responses to all his letters, including the one in which he had asked if he might come for her mother's funeral, that she would resist coming home. If she were younger, he could simply have had her fetched home after her mother's death whether she liked it or not. If she were older, past the age of twenty-five, he would have had no further responsibility for her and would have been happy to allow her to remain at Prospect Hall as long as she wished and take full charge of her own life. But she was twenty, betwixt and between, and she was a burden to him.

Not a burden in the most obvious sense. Good God, he

had loved her when she was a child, and love never did quite die. Especially when there was no good reason for it to do so. The fact that she obviously hated him now was not a reason. She had been a *child*—and she had probably been fed misleading, even purely false information about him throughout her girlhood. She would surely not resent him so bitterly just for leaving home, leaving *her*, without an explanation or a goodbye. He had *tried* to say goodbye. He had run up to the nursery, leaving his hastily gathered bundle in the hallway, but he had been waylaid outside the door and escorted ignominiously to the stables and then all the way to the gates of the park by two burly, wooden-faced footmen—who were no longer in his employ, he had been relieved to discover when he returned home five and a half years ago.

When he had learned that Miss Vane would not go with them to Everleigh, he had wondered how soon he could hire a replacement for her. He must still do so, of course, but it would take time, and then her newly employed companion would be a stranger to Maria for some time. In the meanwhile, how could he find someone who *was* familiar to her, someone to be with her for the crucial first weeks following her return home? His mind had alit upon the Lamarr twins. They were a handsome, well-bred pair and sufficiently older than his sister to provide some steadying influence—he had chosen to ignore that scene on the riverbank—but close enough to her in age to offer genuine companionship.

If they would agree to be guests in his home for a couple of weeks, that was.

Damnation but he was so inexperienced at this sort of thing, Justin thought in some frustration, slowing his horse as he approached the stone bridge over the river and glancing along the bank to his left as though he expected to see

Lady Estelle Lamarr sitting there again, her loose hair touching the grass behind her as she tipped back her head. She had looked very fetching again this morning in her old, faded dress, which would have been shapeless had it not been for the curves of the woman beneath it, and her floppy straw hat, which had seen better days but was now at perhaps its most attractive. He had been almost disappointed when she stepped into the drawing room later, bareheaded, her hair twisted into an immaculate knot high on the back of her head, and wearing a dress that was in the latest mode.

Inexperienced and alone.

His *aloneness* would not weigh so heavily upon him, perhaps, if he had only himself to consider. His neighbors at Everleigh had not exactly welcomed him home with open arms when he had returned six months or so after his father's death. He did not know what his father had told them, but it would hardly have been what he had perceived as the truth. He had always been an amiable but private man, keeping his business, especially as it related to his family, strictly to himself. His father's second wife, on the other hand, would probably have had no such qualms, and goodness alone knew what stories she had told in the neighborhood and beyond. The neighbors had not openly shunned Justin, however, and he had had civil, if not warm, dealings with them in the years since.

It had been beyond his father's power to cut him out of the inheritance, of course, as he had explained to his son in bitter tones during that final, terrible interview—the last time Justin saw him. But his father could and would—*and did*—forbid him to set foot upon Everleigh land or that of any of his other properties during the rest of his own natural life. He had cut Justin's allowance as of that moment. If his son did not have a penny in his purse with which to remove himself elsewhere, then he would have to walk and beg for crusts of bread as he went.

Justin had had his horse—his own personal possession—and enough money in his purse to get him to his aunt and uncle's house sixty miles away with as many of his other possessions as he could carry with him. Aunt Betty Sharpe, always one of his favorite people in this world, was his mother's younger sister. Uncle Rowan, her husband, was a favorite too. Justin had poured out his woes to them and the full truth—the *only* people to whom he had ever told it.

His uncle had wanted to intervene, but it had been out of the question. His aunt had wanted to open their home and their bounty to him and shelter him for the rest of his life. That was equally out of the question. He had stayed for a week, borrowed twenty pounds from his uncle—who had tried to insist that it be far more and that it be considered a gift—and left early one morning. He had paid back the loan within a year but had not gone back there or to London, where he might have found a few friends and some genteel employment, or to his aunts, his father's sisters, who both lived in Cornwall. Instead he had ridden off into the unknown, a stranger in what he had soon come to see as a strange land. He had not returned home for six and a half years.

He had felt essentially alone ever since coming home, though perhaps that was his fault. He had felt—oddly—like a stranger in a strange land again.

He had friends—very close ones—but they were of a different world, and he chose to keep his two worlds separate and distinct. None of those friends ever came to Everleigh. He went to them, quite frequently and often for lengthy spells, but he had resisted the urge to stay, simply to disappear from his responsibilities as earl. During the past three years he had taken his place in the House of Lords as a peer of the realm and had been conscientious about attending when the House was in session. It had meant spending time in residence at his London home, though he had studiously avoided mingling with the *ton* or attending any of the various parties with which its members entertained themselves during the months of the Season. He had refused any invitations that had ever come his way.

His friends from long ago had fallen away. Or perhaps over the intervening years they had merely got on with their lives, as he had with his, and their paths had diverged so drastically that there was no longer any point of connection. He had some friendly acquaintances with whom he occasionally dined at one of the gentlemen's clubs. And there were a few actual friends, though he saw them only when he was in London. One of them, come to think of it, had a connection with the Westcott family and therefore, no doubt through several twists and turns of family ties and half ties, with Watley and his sister. He had learned of that connection during the past week from a few visitors to Prospect Hall. Avery Archer, Duke of Netherby, had married a Westcott, had he not? And was not Netherby's stepmother a Westcott too?

He was a bit of an intimidating man, Netherby. He was not the sort one slapped on the back and greeted with a dubious jest and a hearty guffaw. He was a man who exuded power and commanded universal respect despite the fact that he appeared to do nothing that would explain people's awe of him. He was slight of build, languid of manner, and soft of voice, with eyelids that drooped almost habitually over his eyes, though the eyes beneath them were keen and observant. He had made the strange comment during his first private conversation with Justin that if he ever had a vital secret that he absolutely must confide to someone— *"though I cannot imagine I ever would find myself in such a drastic or ridiculous situation"*—he would surely feel confident in entrusting it to the Earl of Brandon.

Which was indeed a strange thing to say. What he had seen in Justin to provoke it, Justin did not know. But they had been friends ever since and occasionally dined together at White's Club and even a couple of times at Archer House, the ducal town residence, in company with the duchess and the dowager duchess. He would not feel comfortable inviting Netherby to Everleigh to meet Maria, however. For one thing, he might scare her to death. The duke's mere presence scared a lot of people. For another thing, his duchess was increasing with their fifth child.

Before leaving home to come here Justin had considered organizing some sort of house party, but he had modified the idea in favor of a family gathering. That sounded cozy and safe, though in reality, of course, it was anything but. There were three families to consider and no guarantee that any of them would come or that they would mingle comfortably together if they did. Or that *Maria* would mingle with any of them.

He had sent off letters inviting them all. Aunt Betty had replied immediately. She and Uncle Rowan would come. His cousins, their children, would come too—Doris with her husband, Martin Haig, and their two young children; Sidney and Ernest, aged thirty-two and twenty-eight respectively; and Rosie, aged nineteen and known fondly to the family as *the afterthought*. They were all strangers to Maria, and in no way related to her. They had not come to Everleigh at all after the wedding of Maria's mother to

Justin's father. But they were good people, all of them, and would surely be kind to Maria. She ought to know them.

He had not heard from the others before leaving Everleigh to come here. There were his father's two sisters, his aunts—and Maria's. Aunt Augusta had married Peter Ormsbury, now Baron Crowther, and Aunt Felicity had married Harold, Peter's brother. And there were Maria's relatives—the brother and sisters of the late countess, her mother. Leonard Dickson had married Margaret—Justin did not know her maiden name. Patricia was married to Irwin Chandler. Sarah was married to Thomas Wickford. Justin knew no more about any of them except that all three men were apparently successful businessmen from Yorkshire. And there was Lady Maple, Maria's great-aunt. Justin had invited them all to Everleigh even though Maria had never met any of them. Her mother had quarreled with them all soon after her marriage to his father. He had no idea how likely any of them were to accept his invitation, or how Maria would react if they *did* come.

Now he was feeling queasy about the whole thing. What if they *did* all come, with children and possibly grandchildren? He had no idea whatsoever how it would turn out if they did.

For the past few days, however, he had focused his mind and his efforts upon making sure that Maria would have someone familiar with her for a while. He had not made sure of any such thing, of course. Lady Estelle had insisted that she would need to discuss the matter with her brother before deciding, and she had looked as though she was ready to dismiss the invitation without much discussion at all. Watley had insisted that *if* they were willing to come to Everleigh, Maria must be consulted first.

Nothing was sure, except that next week he would be returning to Everleigh with his sister.

If the Lamarrs *did* come, of course, and even perhaps if they did not, their friendship could be very good for Maria in the future. Their connections with the *ton* could be a considerable asset to her next spring, when he would move heaven and earth to see to it that she was in London and taking her place in society at last. If they were there too, that was.

She was vividly beautiful, Justin thought, still gazing at the riverbank where Lady Estelle Lamarr had been sitting the first time he saw her. That mane of dark hair. Those slim, shapely legs. But he shook his head firmly to clear it, whistled for Captain, who came dashing obligingly toward him through the long grass and clover and buttercups, and rode onward across the bridge. Yes, she was a strikingly lovely woman, but he must remember that it was not for himself that he was inviting her to Everleigh. It was for his sister. It would be as well to remember that, not least because he had seen the thinly veiled revulsion with which she had looked at him on all three occasions when they had met. And if *revulsion* was too strong a word—though he was not sure it was—then she certainly regarded him with disfavor. Maria had probably told her a few things. Though not necessarily, for there was also the fact that he looked like a barbarian, an image he had cultivated deliberately once upon a time out of the sheer instinct for self-defense.

With some success, it would seem.

Five

Estelle went alone to call upon Maria. It would be easier that way, she had suggested, and Bertrand had agreed—quite eagerly, it had seemed to his twin—that Maria was more likely to relax and talk from the heart if he was not there too. He went off instead to do some fishing with a friend from the village after urging Estelle to *please* take the gig and one of the grooms with her. It was a good suggestion, she had agreed without actually promising to do it.

She walked to Prospect Hall, it being a perfect day for some exercise, warm but not hot, breezy but not windy. And with no sign of imminent rain, a miracle in itself. And she went unaccompanied. It was less than three miles from Elm Court, after all, and it would be tedious to have Olga or a groom trailing after her and making her feel self-conscious and guilty about making them walk too.

The summer was already well advanced, but the roses were still blooming as though it were the middle of June.

Estelle could see them as she approached the house, covering trellises and trailing over bushes and filling beds, including the circular plot around the ornamental pond and in an arc behind the wrought iron seat overlooking it. Even if she had not been able to see the roses, however, their heady perfume would have given notice of their presence long before she turned through the gates and the gravel of the drive crunched beneath her feet. Maria, bent over one bush, clippers in hand, heard her and straightened up to smile a greeting.

"This is perfect timing," she called. "I was about to stop for a rest. Come and sit with me. Melanie is inside writing to her family. She has always been very faithful to them. Her weekly letter is always at least three pages long, though I do not know what she finds to fill it. She is going to bring some lemonade when she is finished."

She did not say where her brother was. There was no sign of him.

Maria had some color in her cheeks from her exertions. But there were dark smudges under her eyes, as Estelle remembered there had been during the final weeks of her mother's illness and for the first month or so after her death. They suggested she was not sleeping well.

Estelle sat while her friend brushed off the clippers and put them away in a cloth bag with her gloves.

"The rose garden is like a piece of heaven, as always," Estelle said. "You have a gift with plants that goes through to the marrow of your bones, Maria."

Her friend pulled a face. "But when one is in heaven, one is supposed to remain there forever," she said. "One is not supposed to be forced to leave it."

It had been the wrong thing to say. "You are going home to Everleigh soon?" Estelle said.

"*This* is home," Maria said, pulling the drawstrings to close the bag. "But yes. I will be leaving here within the next few days. I am glad to have the chance to say goodbye to you in person, Estelle. I will miss you. Dreadfully. And Lord Watley too. *And* Melanie." She looked for a moment as if she might cry, but she blinked her eyes determinedly and smiled.

"Bertrand and I have been invited to go to Everleigh too," Estelle said. "To spend a few weeks with you."

Maria gazed at her in openmouthed surprise.

"We have not said yes," Estelle told her. "Nor have we said no. We have discussed the invitation with each other but are agreed that the decision is not ours alone to make. We would be happy to give you our company at Everleigh Park for a while, but only if our going there would make *you* happy too."

Maria was frowning now. "He called upon you with such an invitation without saying a word to me?" she asked.

"The Earl of Brandon is your guardian, Maria, and obviously takes his responsibility seriously," Estelle said gently, though she still resented having been drawn into the apparent quarrel between brother and sister, about which she knew nothing and which was none of her business anyway. And where had he been for the past six years if indeed he took his duties seriously? "He must believe it is essential that you return to live at Everleigh Park rather than remain alone here when you are still a minor. However, he is fully aware that you do not want to go. And he knows you do not . . . *like* him. He fears you will be lonely and unhappy there without even Melanie for company. So he invited Bertrand and me to make the transition easier for you." Oh, why should she feel obliged to explain the earl's motives? That was for him to do.

"Easier!" Maria said with soft incredulity. "And what else did he say?"

Estelle sighed as her friend came to sit beside her on the wrought iron seat.

"About whatever is between you and him, do you mean?" she asked. "Nothing at all. We did not ask. And we do not wish to know or *need* to know. We have no desire to be caught in the middle of some old quarrel that does not concern us. But *you* concern us, Maria. I have grown very fond of you. You must go back to Everleigh Park, it seems. The Earl of Brandon has told Bertrand and me that, and *you* have told me. I will be sorry to lose you. You *and* Melanie. I will worry about you too because I know you are unhappy about having to go. But if Bertrand and I go, it will be solely for the purpose of giving you our company for a week or two until you feel settled and comfortable there again. Perhaps by then you will have employed a new companion. We will go *only* if it is what you wish, however."

"His *relatives* are going to be there too," Maria said.

"Oh?" Estelle said. "Well. Then you will have company even without us. That will surely be pleasant for you."

"His aunt and uncle and cousins," Maria explained. "His *mother's* relatives."

"Do you know them?" Estelle asked.

"No," Maria said. "They never came to Everleigh after Papa married Mama. I believe he might have gone a time or two to visit them. I do not remember. But if he did, he never took Mama or me. Brandon—the *present* Brandon— used to go there for a month each summer. He never took me." For a brief, unguarded moment there was something in her eyes that looked like wistfulness.

"They will surely love meeting you," Estelle said.

"They hated Mama." Maria's fingers were pleating the

muslin of her skirt and then smoothing out the slight creases they had made.

"How do you know that?" Estelle asked.

"Because she told me so," Maria said. "They resented her and were jealous of her. I suppose they thought Papa should spend the rest of his life mourning his first wife."

It could have happened that way, Estelle supposed. But it was all long ago. And Maria was not her mother. Surely they would not resent her too—especially if they had already agreed to go to Everleigh Park to meet her.

"Have you thought to suggest that Lord Brandon also invite some of *your* relatives?" Estelle asked. But oh dear, *were* there any? If there were, they had never come here. At least, they had not done so during the two years she and Bertrand had been back at Elm Court.

Maria made a few more pleats in her skirt. "They all hated Mama," she said. "They would have nothing to do with her after she married Papa."

Ah.

All sorts of questions crowded into Estelle's mind, most of them about the late Countess of Brandon. But it was not her business to ask any of them. She was almost sorry now that she and Bertrand had not simply decided to decline the earl's invitation without even consulting Maria. The atmosphere at Everleigh was not likely to be a happy one. They had had enough of family awkwardness and resentments in their own lives, she and Bertrand, before they had battled their way to the harmonious family relationships and tranquility they enjoyed now. She wanted the time and leisure to appreciate those things without taking on another family's problems. However, they were committed now—depending upon Maria's decision, anyway.

"Estelle." Maria turned on the seat and took one of her

hands in both her own. "I do beg your pardon. I try not to allow myself to be dragged down into gloom and depression. Sometimes it is difficult, but I had years of practice during the decline of Mama's health. I learned that there is always something to smile about and make life worth living. Just having her alive and still with me and sometimes without pain was enough to buoy my spirits whenever I felt them drooping. And to come out here and tend the roses and cut some to set in a vase in her room, where she could see them and sometimes smile at them. To have friends. To find joy in little things. I am so glad you have come to see me and are my friend."

Estelle smiled and squeezed her hand.

"But I am lonely here," Maria told her. "I love it; it is home. I have Melanie and some friends. But I am lonely. I had no chance really to feel it while Mama was still alive, and I was too sad during much of the past year to find it irksome. But . . . Estelle, I want to *live*. I want to . . . dance. And . . . *flirt*. I am not sure that is the right word, for it sounds rather wicked. But I want to be young. I want to be courted. I want and want and want. Is that horridly selfish and trivial-minded of me? Melanie talks often of fortitude, and she shows it herself all the time, poor thing, because she has never had a chance herself to . . . to *live*. Her father is not very wealthy but he has a large family, mostly boys who need to be educated so they can find gainful employment. And now her mother is tired but still has a number of very young children. Oh dear, I am talking too much. But, Estelle, I would not mind so terribly much having to go back to Everleigh if I did not have to go with *him* and live there with him."

She bit her lower lip and looked at Estelle in some dismay. She had indeed spoken more freely than she had ever done before. Estelle had thought she was happy here, as she and Bertrand were at Elm Court. But they had already lived the sort of life Maria craved, and still did whenever they chose to venture from home to participate in a family celebration or enjoy a few weeks of a London Season. They had chosen their present way of life because, at least for now, it was what suited them best.

"It will all happen for you," she assured her friend. "And perhaps you can take comfort from the fact that your brother is determined that it will. You may not like him, Maria, but he does seem to have your best interests at heart."

"I can never do anything less than hate him," Maria said. "He broke Papa's heart and therefore he broke Mama's too. And mine. I can never forgive him."

"Then you must find your own happiness," Estelle said. "But not just to be free of him, Maria. Choose with care." She laughed suddenly. "Listen to Aunt Estelle."

Maria laughed too. "Come to Everleigh," she said, patting Estelle's hand before releasing it. "Viscount Watley too. I shall show you the house and park and the countryside around. They are all lovely, though really there ought to be a far stronger word. *Magnificent*, perhaps? I will introduce you to people I remember there, though I was very young when I last saw them—just fourteen. I daresay Brandon's relatives will be polite to me even if not wildly affectionate. They could hardly *not* be polite, could they, when presumably he has invited them to come specifically to make my acquaintance? And I will not bear them a grudge. Old quarrels are foolish things when they are not one's own. Besides, they will be extra company for you, and you for them. You and Lord Watley have such polished manners that you bring warmth to any company of which you are a part. I have watched you do it and try to emulate you. Please, please come. It is a wonderful idea, even if it *was* Brandon who suggested it. I suppose it would be foolish to believe that he must be evil to the very core, would it not?"

And now there could be no going back, Estelle thought. She would have to make the best of spending two weeks at Everleigh Park when she and her twin had looked forward *so* much to a quiet spell at home together. But at least she would have him with her for moral support. And at least they had committed themselves for only two weeks. It was not a great chunk out of their lives, was it, in the grand scheme of things? Not when a friend's happiness was at stake.

"I shall have Bertrand write a formal acceptance to the Earl of Brandon's invitation, then," she said, and Maria leaned toward her and hugged her.

"Thank you," she said. "You will not be sorry. I promise. I shall see to it that you have a wonderful time."

Melanie Vane was coming from the direction of the house, a tray bearing three glasses of lemonade in her hands and a cushion tucked under her arm.

"I saw you through the sitting room window," she called to Estelle when she was within earshot, "and hoped you would still be here after I had finished my letters. You must be thirsty. You walked?"

"I did," Estelle said, taking the tray from her hands and setting it on the grass between her and Maria while Melanie dropped the cushion onto the lawn and sat on it, curling her legs beside her and tucking her skirt about them. "Did you say *letters*? Plural?"

"I address my weekly letter to the whole family," Melanie explained. "But I always include a brief note to one of the little ones—a different one each time. It makes them feel special."

Melanie was the eldest of eight children. At the age of eighteen she had made the decision to seek employment as a governess rather than marry the farmer who had offered for her. Maria had been her second pupil.

"Estelle and Viscount Watley are going to come to Everleigh Park to spend a few weeks with me," Maria said as she handed around the glasses.

"That is very good to hear," Melanie said. "Now I will feel far more at ease about going home instead of accompanying you. Did you know I was leaving, Lady Estelle? I have just been telling my family so. They will be very happy."

"So you see," Maria said, "I will have the company of friends and you will not have to worry about me."

Although Justin was not in the habit of standing at windows to spy upon what was going on outside, he did happen to be at the library window when Lady Estelle Lamarr walked across the front lawn toward Maria and then sat on the seat by the pond. She was looking very fetching in rose pink with a straw bonnet far crisper and more fashionable than the pretty, floppy thing she had been wearing when he called at Elm Court.

He had been hoping she and her brother would call, but it seemed she had come alone. He would wait for half an hour, the average time for a social visit. He sat down and opened the book in his hand, something by Miss Austen. He had been intending for some time to read one of her books. The library did not offer much else to attract his interest.

He looked out again twenty minutes later. Miss Vane had joined the other two, and Maria was handing around glasses of lemonade. He waited a few more minutes and then went out to the stables to fetch Captain, who had had a good run this morning but was always ready for more exercise. There was no sign of a strange horse or of a gig. She had walked here, then. Alone? He had not seen a maid when she arrived earlier. But she had been alone by the river more than a week ago. Perhaps she considered that she was beyond the age of needing a chaperon whenever she left the privacy of her own home and its grounds. But he was surprised Watley allowed it. It was not his business, however. *She* was not his business.

"Come, Cap," he said. And he set off on foot, taking a circuitous route around the paddock, beside a copse of trees, across a lane that hardly qualified for the name, through a meadow, and over a stile to come out on the road out of the village a mere few hundred yards from Prospect Hall.

He had a fifteen-minute wait. Not an unpleasant one. He had learned during the years of his exile to enjoy the sights and sounds and smells of the English countryside and to be content with his own company when there was no other to be had. He had even learned that stilling his natural restlessness was beneficial to his overall well-being. There was much chatter both without and within to drown out the only sound that had anything important to say. Silence, that was. The ultimate irony.

He saw her coming before she saw him. But then, of course, she was not looking for him.

"Sit, Cap," he said quietly, and leaned his back against the broad trunk of a tree. He crossed his arms over his chest and his boots at the ankles.

She saw his dog first and stopped abruptly.

"Oh," she said, now spotting him. "Lord Brandon. You startled me."

Captain, without any prompting, lifted one paw toward her. She came closer and shook it. Her gloves and the ribbons on her bonnet were a paler pink than her dress and spencer.

"Good day, Captain," she said before looking up at him. "Did you command him not to attack me? Or is he not as fierce as he looks? Is he not a bloodhound, though? A hunter?"

"Even hunters do not dash about the countryside tearing to shreds children and maidens and grandmothers and other assorted persons who appear in their path," he said. "It is possible to be amiable and gentle by nature and also deadly by training and upon command."

"And Captain is amiable?" she said. "And gentle? His looks contradict that notion. I would guess you are not here communing with nature by accident, Lord Brandon."

"I saw you in the rose garden," he said. "Though I do not know *why* you came or *what* you spoke of with Maria. I did not eavesdrop on your conversation. She has been feeling depressed."

"I daresay you would be too if you were about to be torn against your will from your home," she said, and he felt his abdominal muscles tighten as he remembered just exactly how it did feel.

"Everleigh Park is Maria's home, Lady Estelle," he said. "Being here was always a temporary arrangement for her, though it has lasted for six years. May I walk with you?"

He could see her hesitate. "I cannot stop you, can I?" she said.

"Ah, but indeed you can," he assured her. "A simple

no would do it." He was not going to have her tell herself and maybe her brother that he had forced his company upon her.

"I suppose it would." She half smiled. "Yes, Lord Brandon, you may walk with me."

He adjusted his stride to hers, though she was taller than he had realized and had long legs. He did not want his mind to dwell upon those legs at present, however. She was very slender, though not without enticingly feminine curves. Another detail he must ignore. He was good at self-discipline where women were concerned.

"Maria is displeased with you," she said, "because you came to Elm Court to invite Bertrand and me to Everleigh Park without first consulting her."

"It was a choice between the devil and the deep blue sea," he said. "If I had asked her first and *then* called upon you, she would have been displeased because she would surely have told me not to do it. If I called upon you—as I did—before asking her, then she would be annoyed that I had gone behind her back. As she is. I chose the option of the deep blue sea and invited the devil to do his worst. Maria is displeased with me full stop, Lady Estelle."

She did not say anything else for a while as they came up to the bridge. She stopped in the middle of it and set a hand on the stone wall before looking at him briefly and then gazing downstream.

"You *love* her," she surprised him by saying. She looked a bit surprised too, as though she had believed he must hate Maria just because Maria hated him.

He studied her face in profile. Perfect eyebrow and eyelashes, perfect nose and mouth and chin and neck. She was a true beauty, a fact that came close to irritating him. This was about *Maria*, not about him.

"I was fourteen when she was born," he told her, turning his head to watch Captain, who was sniffing about in the grass on the other side and then loping in halfhearted pursuit of a butterfly he had disturbed. "An age at which one might expect a boy to be least interested in a baby in the house. She was born early and was unusually small and frail. Nobody said anything to me about her chances of survival, but I understood that she was not expected to live. She cried a great deal. I used to go up to the nursery when no one else was there with her except the nurse, and I would persuade the nurse to let me hold her and walk about with her and find a position in my arms for her that would stop the crying and lull her to sleep. I used to spread her fingers over one of mine and marvel at the perfection of them, even her nails. I willed her to live, but very shortly I came to understand that she did not need my strength or my will. She had enough of her own. She lived despite expectations to the contrary. She grew to be a thin and pale child and—in my estimation—tough. I spent a great deal of time with her until she was eight. And yes, Lady Estelle, I loved her. Make that present tense. Love does not die simply because of a long absence and changed circumstances."

Lady Estelle stood very still, watching the water flow under the bridge.

"She says she will be happy to have us come to Everleigh Park as your guests," she told him at last, turning to face him. "We will come, then."

"Thank you," he said, and found himself gazing into her eyes. They were brown, like his own, but not nearly as dark. "If you wish to accompany us when we go, there will be room in the carriage for you, and Watley too, unless he prefers to ride, as I will be doing. The carriage would be at your service whenever you wished to return home."

"I believe it would be better," she said, "for us to give both you and Maria a chance to settle for a few days before we arrive. It will also be more convenient if we travel in our own carriage."

"As you wish." He inclined his head.

This was perhaps the natural time and place to take his leave of her. There was nothing more to say, and he knew she did not like him.

"I will escort you within sight of your house," he told her.

She gave him that half smile, which curved her lips but did not quite light her face. She led the way from the bridge, and Captain came dashing toward them to nudge *her* hand, not his. She smoothed a gloved hand over his large head, and he closed his eyes in momentary bliss before dashing off again.

"You have made a conquest," he said.

Again that half smile.

"You will not be the only guests at Everleigh," he told her. "My aunt, my mother's sister, will be there too, with my uncle and cousins."

"Yes," she said. "Maria told me. She has not met them before?" She doubtless knew the answer though she phrased it as a question.

"No," he said. "After my father's remarriage they felt it more tactful, I suppose, to stay away from Everleigh, though my father remained fond of them and they of him. I always adored them, and visited them every year. I believe you will like them. My uncle is all amiability and my aunt is . . . *comfortable*. It is the best word I can think of to describe her. Three of my cousins are closer to me in age than to Maria, though Rosie is younger than she by a year. I hope they can be friends."

They did not proceed along the track to the road as he expected. Instead, she turned to walk along the riverbank. There was no well-defined path, but he supposed she knew where she was going and that it was safe. He walked between her and the river.

"I have also written to invite Maria's aunts and uncle and their families from Yorkshire and a great-aunt," he said. "Her mother's siblings and aunt, that is. And our father's sisters and their families, all of whom live in Cornwall. I had not yet heard from any of them before I left home. So there may be just a small gathering, or there could be quite a large one."

"Lady Brandon was estranged from her family?" she asked. "And from her husband's?" Again her words suggested that she knew the answer. Even if Maria had not spoken of them, though, she must have noticed that none of them had ever come to see her mother while she was sick or attended her funeral. At least, he assumed none of them had. He had never heard of any such visits.

"Family quarrels," he said. "Unfortunately they afflict all too many families."

He did not even know the exact cause of his stepmother's estrangement from her own family, though he did know it had been from all of her siblings, not just one of them. They had been at their sister's wedding to his father, the only time Justin had met any of them. Soon after, however, they were all unwelcome at Everleigh, though Justin had never heard his father speak of having any disagreement with them. The same held true of his stepmother's aunt, who had married a baronet when she was very young. She had introduced her niece to society—and to his father.

"And such quarrels often endure for too long a time," Lady Estelle said. "I hope they will all come, Lord Brandon. It has occurred to me a number of times during the past two years, since Bertrand and I came back to live at Elm Court, that Maria is terribly alone."

Was there accusation in those words?

"She is not quite alone any longer," he said. "She has me."

She slanted a glance his way as though to say that that might be no great asset to her friend. But she did not say it aloud, or anything else.

They walked side by side and in silence until Elm Court came into view as they rounded a bend in the river. He stopped to take his leave of her.

"We will be setting out four days from now," he told her. "May I expect you and Viscount Watley to follow a couple of days after that?"

"We will leave a week from today," she said.

"I will look forward to welcoming you to Everleigh Park, then," he said, and held out a hand for hers.

He did not think she was going to take it. But after a moment's hesitation she set her own in it and he clasped the warm, gloved slimness of her hand. She did *not* shiver, but it seemed to him that she came close. She raised her eyes to his.

"Thank you for the escort home," she said. "One never knows what dangers and terrors might be lying in wait for an unwary woman walking alone." And this time that half smile lurked in her eyes as well as at the corners of her lips and suggested mockery—or just amusement.

He watched her as she walked away, and Captain sat on his haunches beside him, everything drooping—ears, jowls, eyes in their folds of flesh. As though his best friend were deserting him, the ungrateful cur.

"It is sometimes hard to be disliked," Justin said, realizing only after he had done so that he had spoken aloud. He was not much given to self-pity—not since leaving his aunt and uncle's house early one morning more than twelve years ago, anyway. "Come on, Cap. Time to go home."

Six

Justin rode all the way from East Sussex to Hertfordshire and Everleigh Park, leaving his carriage to his sister and her maid. It was no hardship. For years he had not set foot inside a carriage, and for a while even a ride in a cart or gig had been a luxury. The hardest aspect of this journey was the necessity of staying close to the carriage, of stopping more frequently than he would otherwise have done, for rest stops and refreshment at approximately regular intervals. He took his own meals separately whenever he could, in taprooms rather than dining rooms or private parlors.

There had been no hysterics when they left Prospect Hall. No arguments or dragging of heels. No tears, unless Maria had shed them privately or when she took her leave of Miss Vane, who would be leaving an hour or so after them by private chaise. Or when she walked for the last time in the rose garden. Or when she went with Miss Vane the day before their departure to the churchyard where her mother was buried. She was behaving, in fact, with a mature dignity, cool in her manner to him but not openly rebellious. She initiated no conversation, but she spoke in more than just monosyllables whenever he directed a question or a remark specifically to her.

"I have had the Chinese bedchamber in the east wing prepared for you at Everleigh," he told her when he joined her for breakfast on the final morning before their arrival. "I am sure you would not wish to return to your old room on the nursery floor. I recall that you always loved being taken to the Chinese room to see the screens and the paper on the wall."

Specifically, she had liked *him* to take her there because he had had the patience to wait, often by lying on the bed, his hands clasped behind his head, while she gazed at all the intricately stylized figures on the walls and screen and sometimes outlined them with a finger, though it was a rule that they were never to touch walls. She had also loved the Chinese fan, which she would wave with both hands before her face and then, leaning over him, before *his* face, giggling gleefully whenever she could raise the hair from his forehead and make him shut his eyes and wrinkle his nose.

"Thank you." He did not expect her to say anything else, but she did. "And I liked the colored lamps there. I loved to go in the dusk and dark if someone was willing to light them for me."

Almost always he had been that someone.

"Lady Estelle Lamarr will have the gold room next to yours," he said.

"Thank you," she said again.

They arrived home in the middle of the afternoon. It was a rather gray day, though they had at least avoided rain. And so, Justin thought, he was back to the cold magnificence of a stately house he had once loved as though it were an integral part of his very being. Now he hated it. But no, that was not quite true. *Hated* was too passionate a word. He felt nothing for Everleigh. Not even pride. Only a dull ache about the heart he had no wish to analyze.

He dismounted at the foot of the marble steps that led up beneath a broad portico to the great double doors of the house. He strode over to open the door of the carriage while Captain dashed off with happy woofs to greet a familiar groom who was approaching. Justin set down the steps before offering his hand to help Maria alight.

"Welcome home," he said.

Both Phelps, the butler, and his wife, who was the housekeeper, had come out onto the portico, Phelps stiffly formal, his wife smiling and curtsying.

"Oh," Maria cried, her face breaking into smiles. "Mrs. Phelps." And she grasped the sides of her traveling dress and dashed up the marble steps to be enfolded in the embrace of a servant who had been with them forever. "You are still here. And Mr. Phelps too."

Within minutes she and her maid had been borne off to the east wing and the Chinese bedchamber. It was the first time since she was a child, Justin thought as he went to the library even before going up to his own room, that he had seen Maria animated and smiling. She had scarcely spared a glance for him.

He checked his mail. There was a formidable pile of it on the large oak desk, or rather there were *two* piles. The larger pile consisted of letters concerning business his secretary had already been able to deal with. But even the smaller pile seemed alarmingly high.

Maria knew, of course, that the Lamarrs were coming. She had had to approve the invitation before they would accept. She knew too that his aunt and uncle Sharpe and his cousins—all four of them—were coming. She had made no open protest beyond a certain tightening of the lips when he told her. Her mother had wept when Justin's father had wanted to invite them to Everleigh for Maria's christening. They would hate Maria, she had protested between sobs, just as they resented *her* for marrying him and making him happy and helping him forget his first wife. At the time— Justin had been only fourteen—it had not struck him how inappropriate it was that she would make her complaint to his father in his hearing. He had felt only shock at the very notion that his father might *forget* his mother, who had been so very far superior to his stepmother in every imaginable way. Fortunately, perhaps, he had held his tongue and his father had said something soothing to his second wife. But he had *not* invited Aunt Betty and Uncle Rowan and the cousins to the christening, to Justin's great disappointment. Or to any event ever again, in fact.

He had not told Maria of the other guests he had invited, for he had had no idea if any of them would come or, in the case of her mother's relatives, even acknowledge his invitation. But they had responded to the letters he had written before leaving for Prospect Hall. And all except one had agreed to come. It felt more than a little overwhelming. It was also gratifying.

Sarah and Thomas Wickford, the late countess's younger sister and her husband, expressed regret. They were about to set off for a tour of Scotland, including the Highlands, with a group of friends. But Leonard Dickson and Patricia Chandler, the late countess's older brother and sister, would be delighted to come with their spouses and children, to meet their niece at last. Aunt Augusta and Aunt Felicity, sisters of Justin and Maria's father, would come from Cornwall with the uncles and cousins. Lady Maple, Maria's great-aunt, would be pleased to spend a couple of weeks at Everleigh Park to acquaint herself with her great-niece.

Justin shared the news with his sister when she joined him in the dining room for dinner. She did not react with the hysteria he had feared. She swallowed a mouthful of soup and set her spoon down beside the bowl.

"If I ever met my aunts and uncles and cousins on Papa's side," she said, "I do not remember. I do remember Papa telling me about them, though, and recounting stories of his childhood with his sisters. He used to make me laugh. But they lived far away in Cornwall and could not come here easily, he always used to say. Mama did not want to go there when Papa suggested it once. The sea air did not agree with her, and they lived close to the sea. I thought I would have liked to go, but it did not happen."

Justin remembered that. Maria would have been five or six and was excited at the possibility of a holiday at the seaside. He would have liked to go too. He had been there a couple of times when his mother was still alive and had had great fun with his cousins, running barefoot on the beach, building sand forts, climbing rocks, bathing in the sea and being bowled over by incoming waves. Swallowing salt water and pulling gargoyle faces. He remembered his aunts and uncles and cousins coming to Everleigh too, but only once after his father's remarriage, before Maria was born. His stepmother had complained afterward that her sisters-in-law had treated her condescendingly, as though she were a child of no account, and had not liked her.

"I have not met any of Mama's family," Maria continued, running a finger along the handle of her spoon but not picking it up again. "They were estranged from Mama. They were unkind to her."

"That was unfortunate," Justin said. "For them and for

her. Most of all for you, perhaps. As a child you missed the pleasure of being part of a larger family."

"Family is not of primary importance," she said, frowning. "That is what Mama always said. I have friends, and they are preferable to family. One can *choose* one's friends."

"I think Miss Vane might express a different opinion if she were here," he said. "She was really very happy to be returning home to her family, was she not?"

"Perhaps," she said, picking up her spoon and finishing her soup, though it must have been almost cold.

Justin wondered how many happy family memories she had of her childhood. Some of them might include him, though no doubt they had been clouded by her later hatred of him.

He had been ten when his mother died. Perhaps childhood recollections were not always strong on detail or accuracy, but they *were* on atmosphere and emotion. He remembered their little family—his father and mother and him—as an idyllically happy unit. He remembered sometimes when he was very young running down from the nursery floor in his bare feet while his nurse snored in her own room next to his, and letting himself into his mother's bedchamber and climbing onto the big, soft bed to burrow safely between her and his father—his father was always there even though he had a room that was nominally his own. If the door was locked, as it occasionally was, Justin would call out and rattle the knob until he heard the murmur of their voices within and sometimes laughter before his father, all flushed and disheveled, would open the door and call him a mighty pest and sweep him up in his arms and cover his face with kisses before tossing him onto the bed and following him there to cuddle both him and Justin's mother in his arms.

Ah, the innocence of childhood and his puzzlement over that locked door. It was a memory that could bring him to the brink of tears.

Why *the devil* had his father married Maria's mother?

"Lady Maple, your great-aunt, will be coming to spend a couple of weeks here too," he told Maria. "She will be arriving three days from now if there are no unexpected delays."

Lady Maple had married above her station years ago, having caught the eye of the notoriously lecherous Sir Cuthbert Maple. She had insisted upon marriage rather than the carte blanche he had offered. Or so the story went. It might be wildly inaccurate. She had been a wealthy widow ever since the demise of her husband a mere year or so later. She had sponsored her niece's fabulously successful debut into society when that niece was a mere seventeen years old and extraordinarily lovely. She had married the widowed Earl of Brandon, Justin's father.

Maria looked consideringly at him before nodding to a footman to remove her soup bowl. "She hated my mother and quarreled with her," she said. "I do not want to meet her, Brandon. I *loved* my mother."

"I know," he said. "She will be coming nevertheless, to meet you. It is why they are all coming. I thought it might be good for you to meet them. I thought it might give you the sense that your family consists of more people than just me. Any quarrels that have kept you apart from them were your mother's. You have never had a chance to decide for yourself if you want any of them to be a part of your life."

Maria did not argue with him. She waited for the next course to be served before she spoke again.

"You have given me no choice but to be polite to your guests, Brandon," she said then. "Unlike Estelle and Viscount Watley, these . . . *persons* did not insist that I approve of their invitations before they accepted them. I daresay they cannot be blamed for that, however. It is possible they have assumed that I am as eager to make their acquaintance as they would appear to be to make mine. I will be civil. You need not worry that I will behave like a child having the sulks or throwing a tantrum. I will not, however, stand for any disrespect to the memory of Mama."

"Then we are in agreement upon something," he said. "Neither will I, Maria."

"Well," Bertrand said, breaking a lengthy silence during which both he and Estelle had dozed on and off in their opposite corners of the carriage seat. "It looks spectacular, at least."

It did indeed. They had just turned off the main road and driven through high wrought iron gates between massive stone gateposts. Two young children, presumably the gate-keeper's, had been standing side by side outside a solidly square stone lodge, watching them pass. Bertrand had raised a hand and waved to them. Now the carriage was beginning the gradual descent of a long slope and would soon be swallowed up by a band of trees. But before that happened they had a panoramic view of the magnificence of Everleigh Park—of which this hill and the trees and the valley below were a part.

A river flowed through the wide valley floor, spanned by a grand Palladian bridge, a three-arched stone bridge with a roofed structure held aloft by stone pillars, like a Greek temple, built over it. On the near side a footpath followed the course of the river, bordered by rock gardens and low shrubs and flowers, all of them clearly intended to give the impression of profuse wildness. Beyond the bridge, elms and oak trees shaded cultivated lawns to either side of formal gardens, the parterres filled with flowers and herbs and edged with low box hedges. Graveled walking paths separated them and radiated outward from a central fountain. Over to the west there was a lake and what looked like a long waterfall cascading down the steep hill on the far side of the valley. To the east there was a large square maze near long rows of greenhouses. A two-story structure that appeared to be a summerhouse was half hidden among the trees on the slope above them.

And straight across, in line with the road they were on and just where the valley was giving way to the rise of wooded hills, stood a square gray-stone mansion of massive proportions. There were four wings of equal size. But where one might expect a hollow center and a courtyard, there was instead a great dome rising above the crenellated balustrade that edged the flat roof. Before the main entrance at the front, marble steps led up to a pillared stone portico, which somehow echoed the bridge. On either side of it long windows of diminishing size caught the sunlight on all three stories of the house.

To the right of the house the road they were now on continued up into the hills until it disappeared from sight.

"Oh goodness," Estelle said. "*Magnificent* does not seem quite superlative enough, does it? It almost robs one of breath. If we must feel duty bound to spend two weeks away from home, Bert, I daresay we could do worse than spend them here."

She was wishing even so that they *were* at home, though that was undoubtedly selfish of her. Maria needed them at least for a while until she had settled back into the home she had not seen since she was little more than a child. And until someone could be employed to replace Melanie Vane as her companion. It would not be easy for her with a brother she disliked and an imminent visit from relatives who were Lord Brandon's rather than hers and who she feared would judge her harshly because they had hated her mother. Though he had invited other relatives too. Would they come?

She and Bertrand could help, Estelle thought. They were adept at socializing with all sorts of people. The key was to be civil, to listen, to be interested, to smile, to look happy. She did wish, however, that she did not have to direct those skills at the Earl of Brandon himself. She found him . . . disturbing, not least because he had shown a human side of himself when he had walked home with her from Prospect Hall and told her how he had loved Maria after she was born and during her early childhood. Estelle had not wanted to know that about him. It had contradicted everything she had felt about him until then. And everything she had heard of him from local gossip—*which she claimed to despise.* It had contradicted Maria's intense dislike of him. But . . . he still loved his sister. It was hard to deny that. He had gone in person to bring her home from Prospect Hall, *not*, Estelle had been forced to admit to herself, because he coveted the role of stern guardian, but because he cared about her well-being and her prospects for the future. Sometimes one's prejudices and preconceptions were more enjoyable to cling to than inconvenient facts that pointed in a different direction.

What a horrible admission to have to make to herself. It made her dislike him even more and feel even more reluctant to be a guest at Everleigh Park. Oh, she *wished* they had not felt compelled to come.

"We will stay *only* two weeks," Bertrand said. "We will be quite firm about that, Stell, won't we? Oh, I say. This is quite a contrast. How clever."

The branches of huge ancient trees had closed in a canopy overhead, and the rays of sunlight that found their way through made a magical collage of light and shade over the drive and tree trunks on either side. But . . . *clever*? As though the trees had been grown for this specific purpose.

"It is like driving into a cathedral," she said. "How splendid it is, Bert. Imagine *living* in a place like this."

"Well, Redcliffe is no hovel," he said.

"It is not." She laughed. "Neither is Elm Court. But—imagine living *here*."

"If you can entice Brandon into making you an offer," he said, "you will not have to just *imagine*."

She let out a mock shriek and punched him on the arm. "I think I prefer my imagination," she said.

The carriage drew clear of the trees, passed by the colorful rock garden, rumbled through the bridge, and crossed the valley floor between trees and lawns before turning onto the cobbled terrace of the house and rocking to a halt. To one side of them wide flagged steps led down to the parterre gardens, which were spread before them in all their geometric precision. On the other side was the long flight of marble steps leading up beneath the great portico. The main doors had opened and Maria hurried out before stopping at the top of the steps to gaze down upon them, smiling warmly and then hurrying down.

The Earl of Brandon came out after her but stayed at the top of the steps while their coachman descended from his perch and opened the carriage door and set down the steps. The earl was not smiling, Estelle saw. His hands were clasped behind him, his feet set apart. Lord of his domain—but this time it really *was* his domain. She returned her attention to Maria.

Bertrand descended first and handed Estelle down. Maria came hurrying into her arms.

"I was so afraid you would change your minds," she said, turning to offer her hand to Bertrand. "Did you have a pleasant journey?"

"Long journeys are to be endured," he said as he shook her hand. "They are pleasant after one has arrived safely at one's destination."

"Then it must have been pleasant," she said, beaming at him. "For here you are, safely arrived."

The Earl of Brandon watched from the top of the marble steps. Estelle looked up at him, and he inclined his head. She wondered if he stood there for effect, if he knew how intimidating he looked from down here. But it was, admittedly, a spiteful thought. He might just as easily be standing back to give his sister more freedom to welcome her friends. She caught up the skirt of her carriage dress in one hand and climbed toward him.

"Good day, Lord Brandon," she said.

"Welcome to Everleigh, Lady Estelle," he said, offering her his hand.

She remembered from the last time, after he had walked her home to Elm Court, how large his hand was, how completely it enclosed her own. She remembered how she had thought then that he could squash every bone in her hand if he chose. Now, as then, he clasped her hand firmly but with some gentleness too, as though he was fully aware of his own strength and chose deliberately not to demonstrate it. Now, as he had *not* done then, he bowed over her hand and raised it briefly to his lips. She stopped herself from snatching it away, but only perhaps from long practice. Her hand must have been kissed a hundred times or more before now

by a hundred different men. It had not always been a plea-
surable experience, but never before had she felt such a
strong urge to pull her hand away.

"Thank you," she said. "Whoever decided to build the
house in this particular spot certainly had an eye for effect."

"My great-grandfather," he said. "He also chose to have
the drive constructed just where it is for the southern approach. He wished to awe the masses, I believe."

"I would guess he succeeded," she said. "I cannot speak
for the masses, but Bertrand and I were certainly awed."

Her brother and Maria had come up to them by then and
the two men shook hands, the earl with formal correctness,
Bertrand with easy grace. Oh, there was such a contrast
between the two men.

"Come inside," the earl said. "I will have Mrs. Phelps
show you to your rooms. Your baggage coach arrived a
short while ago, so all should be in readiness for you. She
will bring you to the drawing room for tea after you have
had time to refresh yourselves."

"Thank you," Bertrand said.

"I will take them up myself," Maria said, linking an arm
through Estelle's. "And I will remain with Estelle until she
is ready to come down."

Her brother nodded without comment. "In half an hour?"
he said.

The hall was vast and was clearly intended to awe the
visitor just as surely as the approach to the house was. The
floor was laid with black and white marble tiles. Huge landscape paintings in gilded frames hung upon the walls.
Marble urns set in curved alcoves about the perimeter over-
flowed with ferns and flowers. The high coved ceiling was
painted with scenes from mythology and edged with gold
leaf. Wide staircases rose on either side of the hall. The

grand double doors directly opposite the entryway must lead to the domed room, whatever it was. Maria had promised to give them a tour of the house, Estelle remembered. She looked forward to it.

They ascended the staircase to their right.

"You will both be in the east wing," Maria told them. "You will have the morning sunlight in your rooms. Some people might find that annoying, but I always love it as well as the sound of birdsong through an open window. I never mind being woken early to such bliss in the summertime. But if you do mind being disturbed, you will find that there are heavy curtains in each room to block the light."

"Provided a cockerel is not paraded beneath my window to herald the dawn each morning," Bertrand said, "I doubt my sleep will be disturbed."

Maria laughed as she indicated the door of his room and then led Estelle to the room next to it. Ah, it was like a spring garden, Estelle saw, all fresh greens and pale yellows and gold.

"It is known as the gold room," Maria told her. "It is next to my room, though there is a sitting room between them. You must feel free to share it with me."

"The room is quite lovely," Estelle said, turning to her friend as she closed the door. "But how *are* you, Maria?"

"It all seems surprisingly familiar," Maria told her. "Except that Mama is not here. Or Papa. I miss them both more now that I am here. Far more than I did when I was at Prospect Hall. I am determined to make this home again, though. There is no point in moping. I have not yet discussed with Brandon what my role here is to be. Am I just the younger sister whom he is hoping to marry off as soon as possible—at the great marriage mart of a London Season next spring, perhaps? Or am I the lady of the house until I marry, or until *he* does, the one who is to make certain decisions, like who will escort arriving guests to their rooms and what is to be served for meals? And . . . oh, and a hundred and one other things."

"It is indeed something you need to discuss with your brother," Estelle said, smiling at her. "I understand. I too live with my brother. I daresay you can come to an agreement that will suit you both once he knows your wishes and you know his thoughts."

"I am sure you are right," Maria said with a sigh. "There has been no chance for any such discussion so far, and there will not be for a while now. Instead of giving me time to settle here, he has decided to fill the house with guests and make my life far more difficult."

Estelle raised her eyebrows.

"Oh," Maria said, looking stricken. "I do not mean *you*. Or Lord Watley. You are my *friends*. His own relatives came yesterday—Mr. and Mrs. Sharpe, his aunt and uncle, and their two sons and two daughters, one of whom is married with two young children. They are all strangers to me and have no reason to be fond of me, though they have been polite so far. But today *Mama's* family has arrived. *And Papa's.* Oh, and Mama's aunt, Lady Maple. They are all strangers too, and there are so many of them, Estelle, that I feel I will *never* remember who is who, except that Mama's family all speak with broad Yorkshire accents while Papa's family have refined accents. Brandon did not consult me before he invited them. He thought I ought to meet all the branches of my family—though *his* relatives are not mine at all. I am feeling quite overwhelmed. Though there is no such thing when one is a lady, is there? Nothing is impossible. Even the worst ordeals can be endured. I will endure, then." She sighed and then, surprisingly, laughed. "At least

I will have you and Lord Watley with me now as moral support. What a huge relief it was when I saw that *this* time the approaching carriage brought familiar people. Friends."

"You have your brother to thank for our presence here," Estelle said. "I daresay he asked us here, and everyone else, because he cares about you, Maria."

"I wish he would not," Maria said, crossing the room to open the window. "Care, that is." But when she turned from the window she was smiling again. "Oh, I am determined not to grumble. And I have already admitted to myself that he must have meant well when he sent off all his invitations, just as he did when he went to call upon you and Viscount Watley at Elm Court. I will be civil to everyone. I will emulate you. I will even inject some warmth into my smiles. And I will make an effort to sort out who is who and who belongs to whom before the day is over. Now, you must be tired and hungry and thirsty. And you are probably longing to wash your hands and face and brush your hair and change your dress. There will be warm water in the dressing room by now, and that is surely your maid I can hear moving about in there. Come."

She led the way to a door at one side of the room and opened it to allow Estelle through.

"I will wait here for you," she said as she closed the door.

Estelle changed into an afternoon dress her maid had pulled from the top of her trunk and had a quick wash. She sat while Olga took down her hair, brushed it smooth, and coiled it neatly high on her head.

A short while later she left her room with Maria and knocked on her brother's door. He offered an arm to each of them as they went down to the floor below and along a wide corridor to the drawing room, a magnificent apartment directly above the great hall.

Seven

Justin stood by the fireplace in the drawing room later that evening, feeling cautiously optimistic. He had not really planned for everyone to arrive within a day of one another, but that was the way it had turned out. It had all been a bit hectic and dizzying, but here they were, and so far there had been no open disasters.

All his guests had arrived by the middle of the afternoon today, with the result that everyone had been able to meet one another at tea. Hearty Yorkshire accents had mingled with refined aristocratic voices, but it had all been perfectly amiable. He had half feared that the late countess's relatives might huddle at one end of the room while his father's took possession of the other end and Maria sulked between the two groups, the Lamarrs hovering on either side of her, and his aunt Betty and family tried to make themselves invisible wherever they could. It had not happened.

At dinner a short while ago he had deliberately not assigned places at the long table. He was not sure if anyone had been surprised by that or offended by it—he ought, perhaps, to have directed Aunt Augusta, Lady Crowther, to the place to the right of his at the head of the table, and Lady Maple to his left. But no one had made any comment, and none of the individual families had huddled together and shied away from everyone else. When he had come here to the drawing room with the men half an hour after Maria led the ladies from the dining room, everyone had mingled yet again.

Leonard Dickson, Maria's uncle, was standing with him now, as were Sidney Sharpe, the cousin on his mother's side who was closest to Justin in age, and Bevin Ormsbury, Aunt Augusta's eldest son, also close to Justin in age. Doris Haig, Sidney's sister, had just wandered up to join them.

"The children are settled for the night?" Justin asked her. Eliza and Edward were seven and five years old respectively.

"They were excited by the presence of *your* children, Bevin, and inclined to be mutinous despite Martin's dire threat of *consequences* if they made one more excuse for rising from their beds," Doris said, grinning. "But then Megan Chandler poked her head around the door of the room they are sharing and offered to read them a few stories if it was fine with us. It was *perfectly* fine with us. What a very sweet niece you have, Mr. Dickson."

Megan, the youngest child of Maria's aunt Patricia and Irwin Chandler, her husband, was fifteen. It was a frustrating age, Justin remembered. Not a child, not an adult. She had been allowed to join the family for dinner, but afterward, despite a halfhearted plea to her father, she had been sent back to the nursery floor by her mother.

"I do, indeed, Mrs. Haig," Dickson said. "She is a lass any uncle would be proud of. Always willing to help out wherever she can. Did you put a limit on the number of stories? Any self-respecting child would insist upon at least ten before admitting to being sleepy."

"Oh dear," Doris said. "I did not. Poor Megan."

She joined in Dickson's hearty, booming laughter. He was the owner of a textile mill and undoubtedly a wealthy man. Irwin Chandler, his brother-in-law, was a prosperous banker, portly and a bit self-important, but not unlikable. Their aunt, Lady Maple, did not share their broad Yorkshire accents. She spoke, rather, with an almost exaggeratedly upper-class voice and, it seemed to Justin, looked with some condescension—often through her long-handled lorgnette—upon her provincial relatives. The late countess, Maria's mother, had spoken similarly to her aunt. Her voice had never betrayed her origins.

His aunt Betty was sitting some distance from the fireplace, surrounded by Margaret Dickson and Patricia Chandler from the late countess's side of the family and Justin's aunts Augusta and Felicity on the late earl's side. They were engrossed in what looked like a comfortable conversation.

The Lamarrs must be finding this gathering of people a bit confusing, Justin thought. Most if not all must be strangers to them. These people also belonged to three distinct family groups. The brother and sister were not showing any sign of confusion, however. They were clearly adept at mingling at their ease with all sorts of people, even strangers, even those of the middle class.

"How different Everleigh seems now, Justin, than it did when we used to come here as children," Doris said. "I remember it as all twists and turns, a positive maze of corridors and staircases. I was constantly getting lost and panicking."

"I remember loving it for just that reason, Dor," Sidney

said. "We could hide all day and then pretend we had got lost. Mama used to hug us and cluck over us instead of scolding, while Papa looked skeptical but would not accuse us of lying."

"*You* might have loved it, Sid," his sister retorted. "But part of your glee—yours *and* Ernie's—came from deliberately losing me. Remind me never to forgive you."

"I do recall being put in the west wing, as we have been now, when we came for Lilian's wedding to your father, Brandon," Dickson said, "and ending up lost somewhere in the east wing when I ran up to my room for something. I had to beg for directions from a passing servant."

"I was very young when I came here last, Justin," Bevin said. "I scarcely remember it at all even though Mama and Aunt Felicity like to talk about growing up here. I look forward to the grand tour you have promised."

"I look forward to giving it," Justin told him.

Maria was over by the pianoforte with some of the young people, a promising sight. Lady Estelle was with them. Rosie Sharpe, his young cousin, was sitting on the pianoforte bench, her back to the instrument. The others were standing in a semicircle around her. There was a burst of laughter from their direction even as Justin looked.

"Maria is really quite lovely, Justin," Doris said, following the direction of his gaze. "She is on the pale side and a bit thinner than she ought to be, but losing her mother must have been a terrible ordeal for her. Apparently she nursed the countess almost single-handedly throughout her lengthy illness until she died."

"It need not have been that way," Leonard Dickson said, clearly annoyed. "And so I have told my niece. If Lilian had written to us or got someone else to write to us, we would have been there, Margaret and I, and I daresay Patricia and Sarah too, as fast as horses could gallop. If Lilian was alive at this moment, I would be hard put to it not to give her a good shake. Poor Maria. She could certainly do with some meat on her bones. I absolutely agree with you, Mrs. Haig. Though girls these days seem to have the daft notion that the thinner they are, the more the boys will like them."

Irwin Chandler, Justin's uncle Rowan Sharpe, and his uncle Harold Ormsbury were in conversation together. Lady Maple was seated on the side of the room farthest from the pianoforte, alone until Viscount Watley took a seat close to her and engaged her in conversation. Everyone else was either part of a group or moving from one to another.

Yes, it was all working out as Justin had hoped it would and feared it might not. Though it was early days yet, of course.

Uncle Rowan, tall and thin, with a narrow, kindly face and bushy eyebrows turning gray to match his unruly hair, came to join Justin's group, bringing young Nigel Dickson with him.

"You have an impressive library, I saw this afternoon while you were busy greeting new arrivals, Justin," his uncle said. "I remember that about Everleigh. Though you have added to it since I saw it last."

During the past six years, yes. He had traveled light before that, but books had been his one indulgence since inheriting the title and having a fixed home again—and money to spare.

"I have," Justin said. "Though I am always open to recommendations."

His uncle, a gentleman with a modest private fortune, was something of a scholar and spent much of his time immersed in his studies, mostly of astronomy and mathematics. He had always been a family man too, however, interested in and involved with his children—and now his grandchildren—and proud of them all. Justin, as his only nephew on his wife's side, had always been included in that group.

"If you have a sheet of paper long enough, Justin," he said, his eyes twinkling, "I will make a list for you."

"With the heading *Books to Make You Snore*," Sidney said, grinning and slapping a hand down on his father's shoulder.

"Oh, please, sir," Nigel said in all earnestness. "Would you make a list for me too?" The boy was at Cambridge and was apparently a serious student.

Lady Estelle had linked an arm through Maria's and was leading her toward Lady Maple. Ernest Sharpe joined them there, and soon a small cluster of young people was gathered about the old lady, who was holding court, her lorgnette waving about in one hand, looking rather pleased with herself. Viscount Watley meanwhile had given up his seat to Maria and then moved away to talk with the older ladies gathered about Aunt Betty.

"Ernie is such a dreamer," Sidney said, indicating his younger brother with a jutting of his chin. "Lady Estelle Lamarr is far beyond his orbit. And that is not just because she is the daughter of a marquess."

"You think you would have a better chance with her, then, Sid?" his sister asked.

"That was not my point, Dor," he said, but he did look a bit abashed.

"Lady Estelle Lamarr is a true lady," Leonard Dickson said, beaming with hearty approval. "As is my niece. *Lady* Maria Wiley. I am only sorry we never saw her while she was growing up or during the years when she had it so hard nursing Lilian. No young person should have to do that alone. Young people should be able to enjoy their youth— with plenty of support from their families, aunts and uncles and cousins as well as just parents. Like my boys, even if Nigel here *did* turn out to be bookish and not at all interested in kicking up his heels for a year or three. Sebastian at least is interested in the mill. Although, come to think of it, he has never kicked up his heels either. Margaret and I have been blessed with good boys. But no daughters. Thank goodness for nieces."

"Studying is how I enjoy my youth, Pa," his younger son said. "And you and Ma have always encouraged me even if you do not quite approve of the path I have chosen."

"Well," his father said, beaming. "I do, I must confess, like making mention to my colleagues and competitors of my son the Cambridge scholar."

Lady Estelle Lamarr was almost certainly in her midtwenties, Justin thought. Why the devil was she not already married? Everything about her—*everything*—made her into surely one of the most eligible ladies in England. Just as her brother must be one of the most eligible bachelors. Of which number he was probably one too now, he supposed. He had not really thought of himself that way. Of course, he was almost an unknown to the *ton*. Though that very fact might actually enhance his eligibility. The elusive earl and all that nonsense.

For a moment he longed to have his old life back, the one he had lived for the six years before his father died and still did whenever he could get away for a few weeks or longer. He missed his friends. He had had women during that time too. Three of them in total, two for just a few months apiece, one for longer. In fact, he still saw Gertie occasionally, though it was strictly a friendship now. She had insisted from the start that she did not want anything permanent, and that had suited him. She had had one husband, she had told him. He had died, and she was happy to run with her good luck for the rest of her days. When word had reached him of his father's death and she had learned that he was now an earl, she had laughed with what had seemed like genuine amusement and told him he had better go away before her customers started calling her *countess* and getting themselves clipped about the ear for their cheek. Gertie was the widow of a publican and since his death had run the tavern he had owned. The tavern where Justin had acquired his broken nose.

His father's death had forced him to return to the life of a gentleman, or, rather, to that of an *aristocrat*. And let no one try to tell him that birth and position and money gave a man freedom. They gave him a lot, admittedly, but freedom was not part of it. Six years later he was still adjusting to life as the Earl of Brandon. Sometimes it seemed almost as though Juss Wiley, his alter ego, had ceased to exist.

He *did* miss the old life, dash it all. And he resented this life and the responsibilities it had brought him. Including Maria. But there were other duties too, and some of them he had still not faced. He gazed at Lady Estelle Lamarr while conversation flowed around him, and he found himself resenting *her*. For whenever she looked at him, she saw a dour barbarian. And that was at least partly his fault. He *was* dour. He had not always been so. He had learned dourness and silence and self-containment as a defense against a world that was often hostile and sometimes downright dangerous to vagrants, especially vagrants with soft hands and fine linen and fastidious ways and accents that inspired ridicule at best, violence at worst.

He had taken on some of the burdens of his position in the past six years. There were others he had been avoiding.

He stepped away from his group and approached the one around Lady Maple. She was in the middle of telling the young people how she had been considered a rare beauty when she was a girl and how she had caught the eye of Sir Cuthbert Maple at an assembly in Harrogate and nothing would do for him but he must have her. He had proposed to her that very night and married her, by special license, one week later.

"What a very romantic story, Great-aunt Bertha," Gillian Chandler said with a sigh.

If Justin had the rights of it, Lady Maple had been barely eighteen when she married, while her groom had been sixty. She had been a wealthy widow at nineteen and had remained single ever since.

"You introduced my mother to my father," Maria said. "And they married one month later."

"Five weeks," Lady Maple said, pointing her lorgnette at her great-niece. "Your papa insisted upon having banns read."

Rosie Sharpe, Justin's youngest cousin, had seen him standing slightly behind her chair and turned to look up at him.

"I could have died, Justin," she told him, "when you walked into the drawing room with the other men after dinner. Of all my accomplishments, none of which will ever win me widespread acclaim, pianoforte playing is the most dismal."

"Then the others cannot be bad at all," he said. "What is your *best* accomplishment?"

"Baking, actually," she said. "Cakes and scones and éclairs and biscuits. But Mama complains that I am making her fat." She laughed and looked very pretty. She still had the freckles across her nose that he remembered from when she was a young child. "And Papa complains that I am not making him fat enough."

He could remember hugging her that morning more than twelve years ago before he left to ride off into the unknown. He had pretended she was Maria, whom he had not been allowed to hug at all. Or even see.

"And what are some of *your* main interests?" he asked Gillian Chandler.

"Carpentry," she said without hesitation. "Papa is trying to get Wallace interested in it, for he says it is a worthy career if one has the skills. My brother is just not *interested*, however. I am and I have even made a few things, which are not terribly good but would be very much better if only I had a proper instructor. Papa says a girl cannot be a carpenter. It is very provoking."

Chandler did not follow his brother-in-law's practice of allowing his children to follow their dreams, then? But Dickson did not have daughters.

"It is," Justin agreed. "Why should you knit or paint with watercolors when you would far prefer to be sawing and pounding nails?"

"Exactly! Oh, Cousin Justin—*may* I call you that though you are not, strictly speaking, my cousin?" she said. "Cousin Justin, I *like* you. How fortunate Maria is to have you for a brother. Perhaps I can exchange you for Wallace."

She and Rosie and Paulette Ormsbury, Aunt Augusta's youngest child, went off into peals of laughter while Maria bit her lower lip and Lady Estelle smiled and looked amused.

"A young lady's foremost duty to herself is to secure a husband who can support her well during his life and leave her independently established when he dies," Lady Maple said, drawing everyone's attention back to herself. "*Then* she may think of doing something as cork-brained as learning carpentry. If she is wise, however, she will always leave the cooking to the servants. Otherwise, they may come to look down upon her, and that is never a desirable thing."

Lady Estelle was looking even more amused when Justin caught her eye. But her smile quickly faded.

Only a barbarian, he supposed, would encourage a girl to make a cabinet rather than knit a scarf or paint a landscape.

The following morning was cloudy but warm with no noticeable wind. Although everyone was eager for the promised tour of the state apartments, it was a pity to waste a fine morning indoors, it was agreed at breakfast. It might be raining by this afternoon. Maria spoke up with a suggestion. She offered to take anyone who was interested to the lake to see it and the Chinese bridge and the waterfall, though she warned it was a longish walk.

Now, half an hour later, Maria was outside under the portico with an eager group of the young cousins. Estelle and Bertrand were out there too. It was getting a bit crowded. A few of the older couples were strolling among the parterres, having decided to stay closer to the house in case it rained, as it very well might.

Estelle, looking across the formal gardens to the river and the rock gardens and wooded slope beyond, down which they had traveled yesterday, thought that surely a lovelier stately home could not exist anywhere. What a pity it was not also a happier place. Though perhaps it would be in time. Certainly all the guests here seemed to be a congenial lot, and it must be remembered that it was the Earl of

Brandon, stiff and humorless as he seemed to be, who had invited them all here—for the sake of his sister. And he *had* sympathized last evening with young Gillian's dream of being a carpenter.

The group of young people began to make its noisy, chattering way down the marble steps to the terrace, led by Maria. Bertrand went with them. He had offered his arm to Angela Ormsbury, one of Maria's cousins on her father's side, perhaps because she seemed shier than any of the others. He was smiling at her and drawing her into conversation. Estelle held back until last. She was here to give her support to Maria, it was true, but she did not want to stifle her friend's ability to manage on her own. Mr. Ernest Sharpe, her brother's cousin, had given her his arm and Maria was smiling at him, apparently pleased to have his escort. Mr. Sidney Sharpe was hovering in Estelle's vicinity and would offer his arm in a moment, she supposed. His young sister had just plucked his sleeve, however, to point out something across the valley before turning away to run lightly down the steps in pursuit of the others.

At the same moment one of the main doors opened and someone else stepped outside. The dour earl himself, Estelle saw with a glance over her shoulder. He was coming too, was he? He drew to an abrupt halt.

"Ah, Lady Estelle," he said just as Sidney Sharpe was turning back to her. "May I show you the summerhouse? I am on my way there."

"Oh, I say, Justin," his cousin protested. "Pulling rank, are you? Cutting the ground from under my feet?"

"Pulling the age advantage, Sid," the earl said. "I always was two years older than you, if you will recall. I still am. But *had* you already asked the lady to walk to the lake with you?"

"I had not," his cousin admitted. "But I was about to, as must have been glaringly obvious. Perhaps we ought—"

"Excuse *me*," Estelle said, bringing the eyes of both gentlemen to her person. "The lady is standing right here. She has ears. She also has a tongue."

"She is also a lady of some spirit," Sidney Sharpe said, his eyes laughing into hers before he grinned more fully at his cousin. "Lady Estelle, the choice is yours. You may walk to the lake with my humble self, or you may admire the summerhouse with Justin. Or you may do something quite independent of both of us, I suppose, and go stalking off alone to walk the maze or explore the greenhouses. But before you decide, may I point out that if you reject my offer as an escort, I may be doomed to walk with my own sister?" He pulled a forlorn look.

Estelle laughed. The others, she could see, had crossed the terrace and were descending the wide stone steps to the formal garden and making their way to the fountain at its center, where Maria and Mr. Ernest Sharpe were awaiting them.

"That does sound like a sad fate, Mr. Sharpe," she said. "However, when a lady has a choice of escort, good manners dictate that she accept the one who asked first."

She heard the words that came out of her mouth rather as though someone else had spoken them. There was a measure of truth to them, but . . . She had agreed to walk to the lake before she had been asked to go in the opposite direction. So why . . .

"Run along, Sid," the earl said.

And his cousin ran along, laughing and calling to the others to wait for him.

"You are on the way to the summerhouse, Lord Brandon?" Estelle asked, wheeling on him. "Alone?" *When you have guests to entertain?* She did not say it aloud, but her tone implied it.

"I often spend time there," he told her. "I thought to steal a private hour or two there this morning while everyone else is happily occupied. Lady Maple informed me last night that she never leaves her room before noon. My aunt and uncle are in the nursery with Doris and Martin and their children."

"You do not like children?" she asked him.

"Doris's two are of that alarming breed of youngster that awakes at the crack of dawn every day, bursting with energy and demanding to be entertained," he said. "I took them out to the stables this morning, where they made Captain's acquaintance—I am not sure who was the more ecstatic, he or they—and then came riding with one of my grooms and me. After that they helped brush the horses down and chased Captain around the stable yard before feeding him. I brought them home in plenty of time for their nurse to make them look and smell respectable before the other children, who all slept until a decent hour, were ready for breakfast. I believe I have done my duty by them for one morning."

Well. She had had her answer.

"Perhaps," he said, "you will not mind if we collect Captain on our way to the summerhouse. He does not take kindly to being in residence at the stables and thus relegated to an inferior status, on a level with the horses. He usually occupies the house with me, but it occurred to me that some of my guests may not enjoy his company. You, for example?"

They descended the marble steps together and turned to walk along the terrace. He did not offer his arm.

"Oh, you will not make me responsible for your dog's

misery in being put out of his own home, Lord Brandon," she said. "I believe I have already conceded that he is not the vicious hound I took him for at first."

Why, she wondered, did he often spend time at the summerhouse when he had this vast and splendid mansion in which to live?

Eight

Captain was sitting out in the stable yard, watching one of the grooms exercise a horse in the paddock, but he scrambled to his feet and turned when he saw them approach. He did not come dashing toward them, however, until he was summoned by a single word from his master.

"Come," the Earl of Brandon said.

The dog came at a run then, panted up at the earl when he arrived, and sat to offer a paw to Estelle. As she shook it and bade him a good morning, she found herself smiling and wanting for some inexplicable reason to hug the dog. His brown ears were soft and silky, his black jowls, nose, and eyes mournful looking. Fleshy folds curved above his eyes, like eyebrows, and extended down the sides of his face, making it seem as though his eyes slanted downward. He was not so terribly fierce after all. Perhaps he was not sad either. Looks could deceive.

"I can remember," she said, smoothing one hand over the dog's huge head and down along one ear, "that Bertrand desperately wanted a dog when we were seven or eight. There was a litter of collie pups at a neighbor's house. He begged and pleaded and moped, but our aunt was immovable. Dogs were dirty, in her opinion, and they shed and jumped on furniture and beds and frightened visitors and servants. Worst of all, they were useless. Except, perhaps, to warm a little boy's heart."

"You did not want one of those puppies too?" the earl asked, and Estelle looked at him in some surprise— surprise at herself, that she had confided such a distant and personal memory to him of all people. Good heavens, she had probably not even thought of that incident for years.

"I was not desperate for one," she said. "But we are twins. We feel each other's pain. I can remember wrapping my arms about him and weeping on his shoulder when I found him huddled in a corner of the attic after he had finally understood that he was not going to have his dog."

"Your aunt had great power in your home, did she?" he asked.

"She and my uncle raised us," she explained. "Our mother died in an accident before we were even a year old, and her elder sister and her husband and their two children came to Elm Court to care for us. They stayed for the funeral, and then somehow they stayed for the rest of our childhood and youth."

"Your father . . . ?" he asked.

"He went away," she told him. "He came home a couple of times each year, but it was our aunt and uncle who raised us."

"They did an excellent job," he said.

She looked at him in surprise again.

"They are good people," she told him. "I did not mean

to imply by the dog story that my aunt was some sort of cruel and unfeeling tyrant. She was not and is not."

"Shall we walk?" he suggested, and she fell into step beside him. What had he meant by that? *They did an excellent job.* He did not know either her or Bertrand. But even a slight acquaintance was often enough to give one a firm impression—just as she had formed one of him. She did not really *know* him, though, did she?

The dog loped along ahead of them.

The summerhouse was built on a steepish slope above the greenhouses and was largely hidden from them by a band of trees and bushes. It was slightly above the level of the house too and was angled to face away from it, toward the southeast.

"Someone was using his head when it was built," the earl said as they approached it. "My great-grandfather again, I suspect. The lower level has windows from ceiling to floor, as you will see in a moment. The upper level too has large windows. Most people would choose to have the building face full south to get all the sunlight and then discover the heat of a summer day unbearable. This way the house gets all the gentle morning light, but more slanted rays in the afternoon."

It was an attractive building. The lower level was all one room and furnished for relaxation with a number of comfortable-looking chairs and sofas and low tables to hold refreshments and books and newspapers. There was even a long, low bookcase against the back wall, its shelves filled with books. Two of the windows that made up the front wall could be slid back to open the room to the outdoors. They could also be kept closed to hold the warm air inside on a cool or rainy day. The view was unexpected and lovely.

The summerhouse did not look over any part of the formal gardens or flower beds but rather over fields and meadows to the east and the low hedgerows that divided them and gave them the appearance of a patchwork quilt. There were sheep grazing in one large field. The view stretched into the distance over a widening valley and low, undulating hills. The river meandered through it.

"All your land?" Estelle asked.

"Yes," he said.

It had indeed been an inspired idea to build the summerhouse to face this way. There was an impression of rural peace here. One could be happy here for days at a time, Estelle thought. She no longer wondered that the earl chose to spend time here despite the fact that he lived in that vast and magnificent mansion out of sight behind them.

"I started to spend a lot of time here after my mother's death," he told her.

"How old were you?" she asked.

"Ten," he said. "One week shy of my eleventh birthday, actually. She was a superb horsewoman, but she had a fall that day and hit her head. She lived for another five days, but she never regained consciousness. The light went out of my life with her."

Estelle felt her stomach muscles clench, for that one sentence spoke volumes. She carried the pain of never having consciously known her own mother. He had the pain of having known his for more than ten years. Which was worse? Or were there no degrees of pain in the loss of a mother? She wondered if the light had ever come back for him, and what it would say about him if it had not. She had worked out his age to be thirty-four. His mother had died twenty-four years ago, then. About the same time as *her* mother. Both by accident, the result of a fall.

"Come and see the upstairs," he said, and his dog scrambled eagerly up ahead of them, though he had to wait on the top stair. There was a door, which the earl had to unlock with a key he drew from his pocket.

It was also one room. This one had two large windows, though not as large as the ones below. There was a big desk against the wall between them and reaching halfway across each. It was strewn rather untidily with paper and pencils and quill pens and an ink bottle. There were bookshelves here too, all of them filled, and two easy chairs and a bed pushed against the back wall, covered with a fawn-colored quilt and bright cushions and books. There was a book on the seat of one of the chairs too. Both sides of the ceiling sloped with the shape of the roof.

It was not a tidy space, but there was something very cozy about it. It looked lived in. Estelle wondered if he had ever spent a night in that bed. As a boy, perhaps, mourning his mother, wondering if his life would ever be the same again—and knowing at heart that it would not be.

"This was always just a storage space," he told her. "I asked my father if I could clear it out, and he raised no objection. One of the grooms and a couple of gardeners helped me move the junk out and the furniture in, and it became my retreat. No one has ever been here but me. And Maria a few times when she was a child."

And now her, Estelle thought. What was she to make of that?

She approached the desk and all the papers spread across it. "Do you write?" she asked.

"I do," he said. He was standing in the middle of the room, where the ceiling was high enough to accommodate his height, his hands behind him, looking at her with a slight frown between his brows.

"What do you write?" she asked him. "Or is that an unpardonably intrusive question?"

"Hardly," he said, "or I would not have brought you up here. I am trying my hand at a novel. If it can be called that. I am beginning to realize that a novel must have some . . . *shape*, some point, some meaning, something to bind beginning, middle, and end together in a unified whole. I do not even know the word to describe what I mean, if there is such a word. But whatever it is, I suspect my book may lack it. It is the picaresque story of a young man's adventures as he travels about the country without any idea of where exactly he is going or why he is going there or what he will do when he gets there or how he will survive when he has no money in his pockets or friends upon whom to lean."

The words were out of her mouth before she could stop them. "It is autobiographical, then?" she asked. She could feel her cheeks turn hot as his stillness seemed to intensify. She knew nothing about the years before his father's death, though the gossips had made much of them even as far away as Elm Court. But even if she had known anything . . . Oh, her wretched mouth.

"I suppose," he said after an uncomfortable pause, "I can identify with my main character sufficiently to make him convincing, Lady Estelle. But he is not me. He is far more heroic. *Accidentally* heroic, I ought to add. He stumbles into adventures and challenges and dangers and often makes matters worse with his clumsy attempts to deal with them and help people who neither need nor wish for his help. Despite himself and against all odds, however, he invariably wins the day and comes out on top before moving on."

She felt herself smiling. "He is a bit of a comic hero, then?" she asked. "A bit of a Don Quixote?"

He was still frowning. "Quite by accident," he said. "I

wanted him to be a serious adventurer, someone who would vanquish all the demons at loose in the world and teach the reader a thing or two about courage and virtue and the truly important things in life. Someone epically heroic. But I have made a disturbing discovery about writing. My characters, especially my hero, are of course my creations. They have no existence outside my imagination. Yet no one seems to have told *them* that. They will insist upon living their lives their way no matter how often I tap them on the shoulder with a timid sort of *'Excuse me?'* They simply stare at me before continuing to carry on as they please."

She smiled as she tipped her head to one side. Oh, *this* was a revelation. "Unlike Captain, who is obedient to your every command," she said.

The dog, hearing his name as he lay in a very temporary shaft of sunlight from one of the windows, opened his eyes, thumped his tail twice on the floor, and returned to his somnolent state.

"Well," the earl said. "Captain is not a figment of my imagination. I really believe the imagination is not even in the brain, you know, but is something far larger and more powerful that the brain has access to when one quiets the mind sufficiently to relinquish control. And if you believe this is the rambling of a madman, I would not necessarily disagree with you."

He went abruptly to look out through the other window.

"Why did you bring me here, Lord Brandon?" Estelle asked.

"To Everleigh?" He turned his face toward her.

"Here," she said. "To the summerhouse. You brought me to *Everleigh* to keep Maria company. I was in her company when I left the house this morning. We were going to the lake together. Why did you ask me to come here instead?"

"When I stepped outside myself," he said, "you looked like more of an observer of the lake party than a participant in it. And Maria had plenty of other company. It occurred to me that you might like the summerhouse."

"I do," she said. But she was feeling very uncomfortable. Why had he singled her out and asked no one else? And why *here*, to the upstairs, which he had admitted was very much his private domain? It even had a door that locked, though it was open now. And why, for that matter, had she agreed to come here with him when she had had a perfect excuse not to do so? No, it was not even an *excuse*. She had had a *reason*. She had been a part of that other group, and she had really wanted to see the lake and the bridge and waterfall.

"You would have come here eventually, of course," the earl said. "Everyone will. We will arrange to have tea out here a time or two, preferably when the weather is at its best. I will enjoy being here with all my guests. Downstairs. I thought you might like to see this quiet retreat, however."

Her and no one else?

"And to hear about your accidental hero?" she said.

"I did not intend for you to meet him," he said. "I ought to have hidden all evidence of his existence before I brought you here. But then I did not expect to be bringing you. Perhaps I have more in common with my hero than I realized."

"You write with a pencil rather than a pen?" she said. It was not really a question. She could see that he did. He had bold, sloping handwriting.

"When he embarrasses me too much or gets himself into a scrape I cannot think him out of or becomes tedious for more than one page in a row," he told her, "I can simply erase what he said or did and send him off in a different direction to do better."

"As you cannot do in your own life," she said. But that sounded insulting. "As none of us can do."

"Being a writer does give one certain power," he agreed. "The power to play God. But only on paper, alas. And only with people who do not even exist. Perhaps that is one of the attractions of writing fiction. It is therapeutic."

She wished he would look away. His eyes were very direct on hers, very dark, quite unreadable. His voice was deep. Oh, what did that have to do with anything? He was not a comfortable man to be alone with. Not that she felt she was in any sort of danger. Just . . . uncomfortable. He was giving her glimpses behind the stark exterior that had so repelled her. She preferred to be repelled. She did not want to know him. For there was something about him that . . . disturbed her. She could not even put words to the unease she felt whenever she was in the same room as him.

"Why did you leave home?" she asked. "Before your father died, I mean. You *did* leave, did you not? Several years before?" She wished fervently then that she had not asked. She had just told herself she did not want to know anything more about him—especially about those years. Darkness lurked there, and it was *none of her business*. But her questions had not been written in pencil, alas. They could not be erased.

His eyes continued to bore into hers for a few uncomfortable moments before he turned his head away to look through the window again. His hands, clasped behind him, beat a slow, rhythmic tattoo against his back.

"All the gossip and wild stories have not satisfied you, Lady Estelle?" he asked her. "I assume there have been plenty of both in the neighborhood of Prospect Hall since the late countess and Maria went to live there after my father's death."

Because he had sent them there, apparently, despite the fact that the house just behind here was vast and he might have avoided them if he had so wished without sending them away.

"One cannot help hearing gossip when one is part of a community," she told him. "Though I try not to give it too much credence unless I can confirm the facts for myself. But I do beg your pardon. I have no right to the facts in this case. They are not my business."

His clasped hands continued the tattoo. "But you are my invited guest here," he said, "and have a right to some knowledge of the man who persuaded you to come. I left here six years before my father's death. He sent me away. *Banished* me, if you prefer the more dramatic but very accurate word. I was banished on a moment's notice, with time only to gather the personal possessions I could carry with me. I was told not to return. Ever. *Ever*, of course, expired with my father's life, for he could not disinherit me, only disown me while he lived. I learned of his passing four months after it happened when I checked at the place letters were sent me occasionally by two persons I trusted. No one else knew where I was or how to find me or communicate with me. So far I daresay the facts match closely with the gossip. It is probable that none of the others do. I did not, for example, spend a couple of years or even one day in chains or walking a treadmill or at hard labor in jail."

One thing stood out in Estelle's mind. His father had been dead for *four months* before he even knew it. The late earl would not have been able to rescind the sentence of banishment even if he had wished to do so. He could not have summoned his son home to his deathbed. Neither he nor anyone else—except two persons—had known how to contact him. No one had been able to find the new Earl of

Brandon after the old earl died. What on earth had happened to lead to such severe circumstances?

"Did you always have an adversarial relationship with your father?" she asked. What sort of father, no matter how difficult his son, his *only* son, would *banish* him and tell him never to return? And cut off all lines of communication.

"On the contrary, we had an extraordinarily close relationship," he said. "Until I was twenty-two years old, that is." He looked at her again, his face harsh and forbidding. "Do *not* ask me what I did that was so heinous that he would cast me off forever. I daresay you have heard theories, each more hair-raising than the last. Perhaps one of them is Maria's. I will confirm or deny none of them. Only two living people, apart from me, know the truth, and they will never divulge it because I asked them not to and they are honorable people."

Two people. His uncle and aunt came to mind. Mr. and Mrs. Sharpe. They seemed extraordinarily fond of him and he of them. Mrs. Sharpe was his mother's only sister. Were they also the only people who had been able to write to him at a prearranged place?

"That is fair enough," she said.

The dog had got to his feet and gone to stand by his side. He nudged the earl's hand with his nose until he smoothed his palm over the dog's head and the dog whined and pressed close against his leg. It was almost, Estelle thought, as though Captain had sensed distress in his master. Or perhaps it was more than just *almost*. The Earl of Brandon had been very close to his father, but he had lost him—*on a moment's notice*—six years before his actual death.

Oh, she did not want to know these things about him. Yet she was not being quite honest with herself. She had asked the questions, after all. He had not forced the information on her.

"Perhaps we ought to return to the house," she said.

"Something occurred to me last evening," he said, turning abruptly but ignoring her suggestion. He crossed to the bed, picked up one of the books there, and fitted it into an empty slot on a shelf of the bookcase. He stayed in front of it, his back to her. "It occurred to me that I hate Everleigh. It was once my home but ceased to be a dozen years ago. Even though it has been my property for six of those years it has never again been my *home*. It just looks vaguely like it. As though someone had re-created it but omitted the soul."

"But it is beautiful," she protested. "I have lived in or stayed at a number of stately homes, Lord Brandon, and none have been lovelier than Everleigh, either inside or out. I have not seen more than a fraction of it all yet, it is true, but it strikes me that it comes close to being paradise on earth."

. . . but omitted the soul.

Perhaps she saw it her way because she had no emotional history with the house. He did, and that made all the difference. Whatever had happened when he was twenty-two must have shattered his world. Perhaps he was bowed down with guilt now. His father had never seen him again. There had been no chance for forgiveness or absolution. Oh, what if her father had died before they could talk things through with him, she and Bertrand, and so forgive him and begin a new life of love and happiness with him and their stepmother? It was unthinkable. Their lives would be so very different—and impoverished. And lacking in wholeness.

"I have looked at my aunt, my mother's sister, and her

family during the past couple of days," he said, "and remembered all the visits I have made to their house, which
is *perhaps* one-tenth the size of Everleigh but is ten times
the home Everleigh is. This is not a home at all."

"But it could be made into one again. It is people who
make a home," she said. But she stopped there. That was
precisely the point, was it not? *It was once my home but
ceased to be* . . . "Everleigh once *was* home?"

He reached out and half removed a book from a shelf
before pushing it back. "When my mother was alive," he
said. "When we were a family."

"You have a sister," she reminded him. "And you have
just insisted that she return here. To a place you hate. To a
house that is not a home."

"That was the very thought that occurred to me last evening," he said. "That I have held back from making Everleigh my own. That I have neglected to make the earldom
fully my own. There are responsibilities that come with
being who I am, not the least of which is caring for my
sister, whom my father loved. Whom I both loved and
love. It is probably time I stopped resenting what I have
inherited."

Resenting? There was a whole world of meaning behind
that one word, Estelle thought. How could anyone resent
inheriting an earldom and a property like this and—
probably—wealth untold? But it was very clear there were
heavy burdens from his past that he had shared with no one
except two unnamed persons, possibly his aunt and uncle.
And there was the fact that he had never had the chance to
set things right with his father. There was the fact that he
had sent his stepmother away to Prospect Hall before coming back here himself. There was the fact that Maria hated
him and was seemingly unwilling to forgive him for what-

ever he had done to her and her mother. Had he sent them away just because they were not his blood relatives? But that would have been ridiculously petty, and Estelle could not believe it had been as simple as that.

It was becoming a bit tedious to keep telling herself that she really did not want to know, that apart from a natural sort of curiosity she had no wish to understand him better. But oh, she really did not want to like him. She really, *really* did not want to start finding him attractive. The very thought gave her the shivers. There was no warmth in him. Oh, but yes, there was. There was no *light* in him, though. He had admitted it himself.

The light went out of my life.

Twenty-four years ago, when his mother died.

Had he resented his father's second marriage, which, if Maria was to be believed last evening, had been a sudden one and one in which there had been a great disparity in age?

"What I need," the Earl of Brandon said abruptly, half drawing the same book out of the bookcase once more before yet again pushing it back into place, "is a countess."

A *countess*. Not a *wife*. Even his chosen word was a bit chilling.

"But even in that choice," he said, "there is little freedom. Only more responsibility. To choose someone of suitable birth and breeding. Someone who will know how to make a home of this place and be a welcoming hostess for visitors both here and in London. Someone who will be kind to my sister and help settle her into a meaningful life either here or in a marriage. Someone who will bear the children I am duty bound to beget. Particularly a son, of course. Preferably more than one."

Estelle was feeling decidedly uncomfortable. "That can

never be guaranteed," she said. "Some women bear only daughters. Some are barren." *Sometimes the man is incapable.* But she did not say that aloud.

"*Nothing* is certain," he said. "Even an apparently settled life can change totally and without warning within an hour. Within a *moment*. But when one has great responsibility, Lady Estelle, one really ought to make a serious attempt at organizing oneself, doing one's duty, planning a future as well as one is able for the security of one's dependents."

"Yes," she agreed. "It is all very well, is it not, to consider the lilies of the field, which neither toil nor spin, as the Bible urges us to do, and conclude that we ought to model our lives upon their example and do nothing but enjoy life and allow fate to carry us along as it will? People are not lilies. People do need to plan."

"I wish you would marry me," he said.

For a moment she did not trust her ears. He *had* spoken rather softly. Also quite distinctly.

"*What?*" She stared, wide-eyed, at his broad back until he turned to look across the room at her. Or, rather, to *frown* across the room.

"I wish you would marry me," he said again. "We are equal in birth. We are not very far apart in age. We are both unattached. At least, I assume you are, though it surprises me. You are past the first blush of youth and must have received any number of eligible offers. Your beauty alone would make that inevitable, but you have far more than just beauty to recommend you. Perhaps you have waited for love. If so, it would seem to have eluded you until you are past the age at which you can continue to expect it. I wish you would consider me, then."

She had listened to a few proposals of marriage when

she had not been able to avert them. She had never heard anything remotely like this one. And never before had a marriage proposal been so totally unexpected. She had always been able to prepare herself, plan something to say that would soften the blow of her refusal. This time, however . . .

"Lord Brandon," she said, "I cannot think of anything whatsoever that would induce me even to *consider* marrying you."

They gazed at each other for what seemed a long while before the pencil Estelle did not realize she was holding snapped in two and he nodded briskly.

"Then it *is* time I returned you to the house," he said, striding toward her and taking the two pieces of pencil from her nerveless hands and tossing them onto the desk.

He looked into her eyes, his own dark and hard, the frown line still between his brows. He hesitated while Captain pranced and panted at the head of the stairs.

"Accept my apologies for insulting you," he said curtly, and kissed her hard right on the mouth.

It was not just a brief peck of a kiss. It must have lasted for several seconds while Estelle stood in shock, burned by the heat of him, smelling some combination of shaving soap and leather, and somehow feeling the kiss from her mouth to her toes, but *inside* her body rather than outside, with a hideous awareness that threatened to rob her of both breath and control of her knees. She was aware of her hands dangling uselessly by her sides and of a ghastly temptation to set them on either side of his waist or on his shoulders or on either side of his face.

Then his mouth was gone from hers and he took half a step back and indicated the staircase with one hand, his eyes still holding her own. "After you," he said, his voice still curt, just as though he had not recently stopped the world and set it spinning again in the opposite direction. And otherwise discomposing her. And outraging her. And . . .

And *why* had it not occurred to her to use her hands to push him away—and maybe slap his face for good measure?

She preceded him down the staircase, Captain panting at her side, and outside into a light drizzling rain.

Nine

It was not far from the summerhouse to the main house. Right now, however, it seemed an endless distance to Justin, though they hurried along, heads down against the light rain. Too late he remembered that there was an umbrella at the summerhouse. He doubted he would have brought it anyway, though. He would have had to offer her his arm and hold her close to his side so they could share it. As it was, there was a space of three or four feet between them. Captain was loping along in front of them.

Could he have orchestrated a worse disaster if he had tried? He very much doubted it. The idea had come to him last evening. *Ideas*, rather. Plural. First that Maria was going to need a respectable and socially connected female to present her to society next spring, but he did not have a candidate in mind. His aunts on both his mother's side and his father's rarely went to London, and had their own families to occupy them anyway. Maria's aunts were not members of the *ton*. Her great-aunt was too elderly. His second idea had been that he could solve the problem—and a few others for good measure—by marrying and letting his wife sponsor Maria. The third idea was that he was looking at the perfect candidate. Except that she was an impossibility.

And he had realized that last evening.

Lady Estelle Lamarr, that was.

She *was* perfect. She was poised and charming, not to mention gorgeous. In company she knew how to take the lead when it was necessary, retreat into the background when it was not. She could talk with ease to anyone, listen with interest, smile with what looked like genuine pleasure. She never drew attention to herself yet somehow commanded it. She was elegant and graceful. She would be the perfect candidate for his countess in every imaginable way. Except one. She disliked him.

She had never made any bones about it, though she had, of course, always been polite. Courtesy under all circumstances had been bred into her very soul, it would seem. But even if they could have got past their first unfortunate couple of encounters, she would still never recover from her hostility toward him. For she had been poisoned against him by local gossip long before she even met him, despite her assurance that she believed it only when it could be proved with facts. Maria had probably supplied some of those facts, or what she had believed to be facts, courtesy of her mother. And he had done nothing to help Lady Estelle change her perception of him. Even after six years back in society as the Earl of Brandon he was still stiff and gauche and uncomfortable and inclined to hide behind the morose armor he had built around himself after he was banished.

Last night he had struck Lady Estelle Lamarr from his mental list of prospective countesses. Not that there was anyone else on the list.

And what had he done this morning? He had mistimed his departure from the house and found that a few stragglers from the lake party were still up under the portico—including Lady Estelle. It had been perfectly clear that his cousin Sid was about to take her in pursuit of the others, but he had not yet done so. Justin had offered *his* escort instead—to the summerhouse. And she had accepted.

He might have known there and then that disaster was looming. The summerhouse was *his* domain, especially the upper level. It was the only place on Everleigh land where he felt fully at home and relaxed. And private. He had wanted the privacy this morning in particular because he had a very personal letter to write.

But, he had thought as they made their way there, he would not need to take her to the upper level. He had had a door and a lock installed at the top of the stairs. He could sit downstairs with her, let her see the view, relax for half an hour. So of course he had taken her up. He had even been glad about it for a while. She had liked it. She had been interested in his writing. She had asked him about his reason for leaving here twelve years ago and about his relationship with his father, and he had felt that she was genuinely interested in knowing the truth, even though he had not told her a great deal of it. And then . . .

Well, then he had made an ass of himself.

I wish you would marry me.

And as though that idiocy were not enough to embarrass him for the rest of his natural life even if he lived to be ninety, he had proceeded to explain his reason for asking . . . *You are past the first blush of youth . . . Perhaps you*

*have waited for love. If so, it would seem to have eluded
you until you are past the age at which you can continue to
expect it. I wish you would consider me . . .*

The memory was enough to make him break out in a
cold sweat. The drizzling rain did not help.

The lake party was hurrying back to the house from the
other direction, he could see. Fortunately, he had an excuse
not to encounter them or have to mingle with them for a
while.

"Captain," he called. "The stables."

And his dog, after turning to look at him as though to
say, *"What? Again?"* nevertheless obediently changed direction. Justin followed him without a word to his companion, who held her course for the house.

*Lord Brandon, I cannot think of anything whatsoever
that would induce me even to* consider *marrying you.*

Her rejection had been cutting in its brevity. And clear
in its meaning beyond the shadow of any doubt.

So he had kissed her. Hard. On the mouth. With no fi-
nesse whatsoever.

He owed her an apology. *At the very least.* He had made
one, in fact, but that was just before he kissed her. He owed
her another. The trouble was that he did not want to get close
enough to her for the next eternity or two to say anything at
all. And he did not doubt she felt exactly the same way.

He settled Captain back at the stables, rubbing him
down with a towel and cleaning his paws and underbelly.
He fed him, though it was the wrong time to do so, and
changed the water in his bowl, though what was already
there had looked fresh.

His letter remained unanswered.

He was as far as ever from finding a countess. That list
of his was quite blank. He did not *know* anyone.

He wanted desperately to go home. Which was laughable when he considered that the home for which he yearned was half of a poky, drafty loft in a small, dilapidated old cottage with a dreary view over a stone quarry through its windows.

Through one of its windows—the tiny square one under the eaves in the loft—Ricky was perhaps gazing at this very moment, watching for Justin even though July had come and gone and Justin had not come with it. Ricky understood simple facts. What he could *not* understand was *changed* facts or the reasons for them. He could not understand the difference between cancellation and postponement. One always had to be very specific with what one told him, for as far as Ricky was concerned, the things one told him were then facts written in stone. If they changed, he was not only disappointed; he was also distraught and quite inconsolable.

"It's something you need to keep in mind next time you say you are coming here, Juss," Wes Mort had dictated to Hilda, his woman, who had written the letter for him. Wes could both read and write—Justin had taught him by candlelight through one cold winter and beyond—but he was embarrassed by the slowness with which he read and the large, childish appearance of his handwriting.

> *Don't tell Ricky you are coming back in July after you have finished all your stuff in London and then write to say you can't come then after all but will come in the autumn instead, after harvest. Ricky don't understand things like that, Juss. You said July but you didn't come in July and now he is mortal down in the dumps. He don't want to eat or sleep or even wash. He drags about, driving us mental, and he*

*don't smile no more. Hildy is threatening to leave me.
(This is Hilda here, Justin. I am NOT threatening to
go, how would my men do without me and where
would I go anyhow, but poor Ricky is in a bad way.)
In future when you are leaving here tell him goodbye
and you will see him sometime when you can. I'm
ready to pop you a good one and put another bend in
your nose. Perhaps it will improve your looks. Come
when you can, but make it soon or you may find
Ricky looking after two lunatics here.*

For four years Justin had lived in half that loft above
Wes's cottage. Ricky, Wes's brother, lived in the other half.
He was thirty years old now, a few years younger than Wes,
and a big man, but he still had the mind of a four- or five-
year-old. He was sweetness itself except when something
frustrated him. Then he tended to mope and sulk and sigh
and sometimes throw a tantrum. He had taken a liking to
Justin from the start and considered himself Justin's protector from all ills, real and imagined. Leaving him after a
visit was never an easy thing to do.

Wes was a great bruiser of a man, all brawn and muscle
and big heart—and sometimes big mouth. It was Wes who
had broken Justin's nose in a tavern brawl that had been
more of a massacre than a fight between equals. Wes had
jeered at him when he lay on the floor, blood pouring from
his nose, eyes unfocused. He had spit to one side of him and
commented that if Mr. La-di-da wanted to toughen up a bit
so he could give a better account of himself in the future, he
could come and work for *him*. In a stone quarry. His mouth
had fallen open in astonishment when Justin had turned up
on his doorstep two days later to inform him that here he
was, reporting for work. Wes had grinned at him then.

"I did a good piece of work on that face, Mr. La-di-da," he had said. "There is not a single part of it that is not still swollen. Except maybe your eyeballs. Even your ma wouldn't know you."

Justin had still been marveling that he had all his teeth. "If I can last out for a whole week of working for you," he had told Wes grimly, "you can drop the *La-di-da* label. It is the way I talk. It is not going to change. My name is Justin. Justin Wiley."

"Juss." Ricky had been smiling sweetly from behind his brother's shoulder. "Did you fall down and hurt yourself? Come in the house. Hildy has made some soup. Hildy's soup is always the best. It will make you all better again."

Wes was a foreman at the quarry. He had given Justin a job, and Justin had kept it for four years. For at least the first of those years he had been given all the hardest jobs, though that was merely a matter of degree. There was no easy job at the quarry.

And that was the home and the life for which he still sometimes found himself yearning. He had proved himself worthy of that life. He had gritted his teeth and refused to accept defeat and made himself fit in—until he no longer had to make the effort.

And now he had to find a way of sending a message that would comfort Ricky. And reassure him that he had not been forgotten. That he was still loved. And that Justin was safe even though Ricky was not here to protect him.

All the way back to the house, Estelle had been desperately hoping she would not meet anyone before she reached her room. She needed time to get her teeming thoughts and her battered emotions in order before she could even think of putting on her social face. She had just been proposed to *and kissed* by a man who gave her the shivers. And it was entirely her own fault. A cool *No, thank you* outside the house earlier when he had asked if she would like to see the summerhouse would have averted all of this. So why had she not said it?

But she had not done so and that was that. And she was not going to escape, it seemed. Even before the Earl of Brandon turned away toward the stables with his dog she both heard and saw the approach of the lake party. They were hurrying back to the house, apparently in great high spirits despite the lowering sky and the discomfort of the drizzle. So she had to don her social manner after all and greet them with answering smiles and laughter as they all dashed up the marble steps to the shelter of the portico and on into the great hall.

"You are not half as wet as we are, Lady Estelle," Gillian Chandler observed, shaking droplets of water from her skirts. "We had that horrid rain in our faces all the way back. It did not have the courtesy to go around us." She found her own words funny. So did everyone else.

"Those of us who wagered that there was rain in those clouds," Mr. Frederick Ormsbury, one of the Cornish cousins, said, "ought not to have allowed ourselves to be overruled by those who insisted there was not. How much did we wager?"

"I believe that was nothing. The rain deniers were afraid to take us on," Bertrand said to the loud amusement of all.

"Thank heaven for bonnets, I say," Rosie Sharpe said. "Though I do wish I had not worn one of my favorites."

"What we ought to have done," her brother Mr. Ernest Sharpe said, "was jumped in the lake and gone for a swim. We were going to get wet anyway."

"Ugh!" Maria said to more laughter.

Estelle, smiling brightly as she shook out her skirt, met her brother's eyes. He held her look for a moment and raised his eyebrows. Was she in for a scold? For going off alone with the earl instead of staying with the main group? But he was their host. They were all at his home. She was *twenty-five years old*.

"You were wise, Lady Estelle, to go only as far as the summerhouse," Angela Ormsbury said. "And you were even wiser to remain at the house, Mrs. Sharpe. Though we were all enjoying the walk exceedingly before the drizzle came on. That waterfall is *breathtaking*, just as Mama has always said it is."

Mrs. Sharpe, the earl's maternal aunt, had been waiting for them in the hall with her husband and was clucking and fussing over them and urging them to run up to their rooms to change their clothes before they caught their deaths. She had taken the liberty, she told Maria, of asking for hot chocolate and hot cider to be sent to the drawing room in half an hour's time.

"I am so glad you did, Mrs. Sharpe," Maria said.

"Fresh Chelsea buns straight out of the oven too," Mr. Sharpe added. "Or so your housekeeper promised us, Maria."

"And, Maria, dear," Mrs. Sharpe said, "you must please call us Aunt Betty and Uncle Rowan. We are, after all, your *step*aunt and -uncle, if there is such a relationship. Now, off you go. All of you."

Even then Estelle could not fully escape. Maria slipped an arm through hers and they climbed the east staircase together while Bertrand came up behind them.

"I am sorry you felt obliged to go off to the summer-house, Estelle, and missed the walk to the lake," Maria said. "It was a lovely outing even if it *did* end prematurely with the rain. It was bad of Brandon to take you away."

"You are enjoying the company of your guests, then?" Estelle asked.

"I have little choice," Maria said. "They are here at my home, and it would be shockingly bad mannered of me to ignore them or treat them with disdain. And it is really not difficult to be civil. They are all very amiable. I do wonder, though, if I am being disloyal to Mama. They treated her dreadfully, you know, disowning her merely because they were jealous of her. She was *so* alone after Papa died and Brandon sent us away. None of them came to see her or even wrote to her."

Estelle wondered if the late countess had written to *them*. But it was a subject best left alone.

"They have come now," she said. "And it is surely a good thing that you are giving them a chance to make your acquaintance. They are your family, after all. Even Lord Brandon's relatives on his mother's side want to draw you into their fold and show some affection to you. They have asked to be called uncle and aunt."

"Even Lady Maple turned against Mama," Maria said, stopping outside her door while Bertrand went by with merely a smile for them and disappeared into his room.

"Maria," Estelle said, taking one of her friend's hands in both of her own. "Is it perhaps time you *talked* with your relatives? Asked them about what happened? It was all a long time ago, was it not? More than twenty years? They have come now to see *you*, and they all seem delighted to be here. Why not take the opportunity to mend some bridges, if it is possible? They are not even *your* bridges, are they? *Talk* to them. A great deal can be accomplished through frank, honest conversation. I know from personal experience. Bertrand and I were virtually estranged from our own father from the time of our mother's death before we were one until we were seventeen. I will not burden you with details, but the whole thing got cleared up when we talked with one another eventually, honestly and from the heart."

Maria smiled at her. "Perhaps I will do it," she said. "Otherwise I fear we will all have a wonderful time here for a couple of weeks, and then everyone will go home, and nothing more will ever happen. Nothing will have been resolved, and nothing will have been accomplished. Though it does seem a bit disloyal."

She shrugged and went into her room and closed the door. And finally Estelle was able to shut herself inside her own room. She set her back against the door and closed her eyes.

She had been kissed a number of times by a number of men. Some kisses had been pleasant. A few had not. But none of them—not one—had disturbed her as had that brief one in the summerhouse half an hour or so ago. None of them had shaken her to the core. And never before today had she realized that revulsion and attraction could be so similar that it was virtually impossible to distinguish the one from the other. The very look of him repulsed her. His touch made her shudder. But she was so powerfully attracted to him that she felt as though she might well be going out of her mind. He was not even handsome. Or charming. Or refined in manner. Or . . .

She shook her head and opened her eyes. She was damp and uncomfortable, and the thought of hot chocolate and even of a Chelsea bun, close as it must be to luncheon, was very tempting even though getting them would mean stepping into the drawing room with her social face back on.

But she was going to have to do that soon enough anyway. She could not hide out here for the next two weeks.

Olga was in her dressing room and helped her out of the wet clothes and into dry ones. She also brushed and coiled Estelle's hair, which had remained largely dry beneath her bonnet. Estelle was soon ready to leave her room, though she hoped fervently the Earl of Brandon would not be in the drawing room. Why would he not, though, when he had been away from his guests all morning so far?

Before she could leave, there was a tap on the door of her bedchamber and Bertrand let himself in without waiting for a summons. Estelle joined him there and shut the dressing room door.

The scold was not to be avoided, then, was it?

He stood against the door, his arms crossed over his chest, and looked steadily at Estelle while she smiled brightly.

"The lake and waterfall are lovely, are they?" she said. "I look forward to seeing them. The summerhouse is lovely too. There is a magnificent view to the southeast."

He continued to gaze at her.

"What is it?" she asked a bit crossly.

"Just exactly what I was about to ask you," he said. "What *is* it, Stell?"

Oh, that wretched twin connection.

"Nothing at all," she said. "This is all going very well, is it not? I believe Maria is going to be fine without too much help from us."

"Stell," he said. "Did he say something or *do* something to upset you?"

"No, of course not," she said. But naturally she went on to confess. "Oh, Bert, he asked me to *marry* him. And he *kissed* me." She closed her eyes. "And a fine one I am for keeping my private business to myself. Why did there have to be *two* of us? Why not just one, like everyone else? Just me. Or just you."

"It would not feel right, would it?" he said. "There would be something missing. Like half of oneself. Most people do not seem to feel it, of course. Only twins, and not even all of them. We are stuck with it. Tell me, do I need to slap a glove in his face?"

"No-o-o," she said, and her voice came out on a bit of a wail.

"He *is* the Earl of Brandon," he said. "He owns all this, and my guess is that there are pots of money with which to sustain it and a lavish lifestyle to boot. He is probably . . . what? Thirtyish? Not very much older than you. I saw him once at White's Club in London when I went there with Papa. He was dining alone with Avery—the Duke of Netherby—and they seemed to be on the best of terms. Avery does not strike me as the sort who would dine with a villain or a boor."

"Are you telling me that I ought to have accepted his proposal?" she asked.

"I take it you did not," he said. "He is not your perfect someone, Stell?"

"He had a whole litany of very sensible reasons why I should accept his proposal," she said. "The equality of our birth, et cetera. Oh, and my advanced age, which suggests I have been holding back for love but have not found it. Therefore, I ought to see the wisdom of forgetting about love and marrying for more sound reasons. Or something to that effect."

"No!" His eyes laughed for a moment. "He is not a romantic, then?"

"Poof." She made a gesture of disgust.

"But he kissed you."

"It was horrible," she said.

"Was it?" He tipped his head to one side and looked closely at her again. She hated it when he did that. She felt as though all her insides were laid bare to him. She felt sometimes that he knew her better than she knew herself.

"It was," she assured him. "It was horrible." She set the back of her hand over her mouth.

"Don't start crying," he said softly. "We are going to have to go down pretty soon or there will be no Chelsea buns left."

"I am not going to *cry*," she protested, and punched him in the chest.

"Good." He stood back to open the door and offer his arm. "But I will say this for him, Stell, even if you *are* my sister. He has good taste."

She laughed a bit shakily.

Ten

By the time Justin returned to the house and changed into dry clothes, his guests were gathering in the drawing room for hot drinks and light refreshments. Luncheon, his butler informed him, had been moved back half an hour at Lady Maria's direction. The refreshments, Justin guessed, were not very light at all.

It seemed a merry enough gathering, he thought as he stood on the threshold of the room. Although almost all the younger people had fallen victim to the drizzle, which had now turned to rain, their spirits did not appear to have been dampened.

Chelsea buns, he saw as soon as he went to the sideboard to pour himself a cup of chocolate. Plump and fresh and glistening with a liberal glazing of some sugary substance. Definitely *not* light refreshments. Irresistible, nonetheless. He put one on a plate and looked around for a group to join. Lady Maple was up, he saw, despite the fact that she had announced quite firmly last evening that she never rose before noon. She was in the same armchair she had occupied last night. He crossed the room and seated himself close to her. He set his cup down on the table between them.

"Good morning, ma'am," he said. "I hope you slept well."

"When you are my age, Brandon," she said, "you are happy if you can say you *slept*."

"Ah," he said, realizing that the bun was sticky and he had forgotten to pick up a napkin from the sideboard. He pulled his handkerchief from a pocket. "I hope you *slept*, then, ma'am."

She inclined her head regally.

Everyone else seemed to be part of a group, though there were still a few people missing. Lady Estelle Lamarr and her brother, for example. Justin wondered if she was pouring her complaints into her brother's ear. He wondered if he would be facing pistols at dawn tomorrow.

Cousin Miriam Rogers-Hall, Aunt Augusta's married daughter, had apparently skidded on the wet grass on the way back from the lake and had been saved from falling by two of the men, neither of whom was her husband. She was telling the story rather loudly to her group.

"It is quite a while," she was saying, "since I had *two* handsome men—Viscount Watley and Mr. Ernest Sharpe—with an arm about my waist and a hand clasping each of mine."

"My ears are still ringing from the shriek you let out, Mrs. Rogers-Hall," Nigel Dickson said, slapping a hand against the side of his face as though to restore his hearing.

Gillian and Megan Chandler, on either side of Maria, each had an arm linked through one of hers. They were strolling about the room with her as she made sure everyone had had enough to eat and drink. It was a promising sight, the three young cousins together, apparently in perfect amity with one another. Maria was looking flushed and very pretty.

"I suppose," Lady Maple said, setting down her unfinished mug of cider beside Justin's cup, "you want me to take your sister next spring and fire her off onto the marriage mart as I did her mother. She should take well. She has the looks and the refinement of manner, not to mention the eligibility, which is more than her mother had. It always helps to be *Lady* Someone. Lady Maria Wiley in her case. Daughter and sister of an Earl of Brandon."

It had crossed Justin's mind, especially as he could think of no one else. But he certainly would not want Maria's great-aunt to *take* her. His sister would live with him at his town house, as would be both proper and appropriate. He had thought that perhaps Lady Maple would come to stay with them for a few months or at least agree to chaperon Maria to the various social events that would fill her days once the Season began in earnest. He would have to attend many of those events himself too—perish the thought. However, he had seen since her arrival here that Lady Maple was really quite elderly. While she was not infirm, it seemed unlikely she would be up to the demands of chaperoning a young lady through her first Season.

"I do plan to take her to London next spring," he said. "She will be twenty-one. It is rather late for her to be making her come-out, I suppose, but her mother's illness and passing have made the delay unavoidable. I do not believe it will matter, however. She is, as you have just remarked, the daughter of an earl. I would be happy if—"

"With her mother it was more difficult, of course," Lady Maple said, cutting him off. "Even though she was younger and twice, even three times, as beautiful and alluring as Maria is. I had to hire a voice coach to rid her of that appalling accent you can hear now from my nephew and niece and their families. I had to teach her manners and proper etiquette and a thousand and one other things before I could even consider turning her loose upon society, the daughter of a mere cit. Before I took her to her first *ton* party I had picked out two perfectly eligible young bucks for her to choose between. I had them each to a smallish party in my own home. And both fell head over heels for her. But they were not good enough for *her*. I suppose she was the cause of your quarrel with your father?"

"I—" Justin was dumbfounded for a moment at the abrupt change of subject. "I do not ever talk of that, ma'am. It is old history."

"Oh, pshaw!" She made a dismissive gesture with one heavily ringed hand. "I knew it as soon as I heard about the rift. She would have denied it if she had still been on speaking terms with me, of course, just as she always did. It was absolutely not her fault, da-da, da-da, da-da. Just as it was not *her* fault she and your father got locked accidentally together inside that little anteroom in the middle of her first ball when they were total strangers and were discovered an hour later, after I had raised a hue and cry and everyone was searching for her. Just as it was not *her* fault that she had become so overwrought at being stuck there alone with a strange gentleman that she had torn the bosom of her gown and pulled half the ringlets out of her hair."

Justin was very thankful for many years' practice at confining his feelings to a place deep within and presenting an impassive face to the world. Even so, he wished he could reach out a hand to clamp over her mouth or even just urge her to keep her voice down. Fortunately there was enough buzz of conversation going on around them that it was unlikely anyone had overheard.

Viscount Watley and Lady Estelle Lamarr had just come into the room together and turned toward the sideboard.

"She quarreled with me just after her wedding," Lady Maple continued. "Told me I was a cruel, heartless woman, or words to that effect, for suggesting that she would descend to paltry trickery to satisfy her ambitions, which is something I never did myself, for all the fact that I landed Maple. I came here for the wedding and I had a good look at your father and took a good look at you—you were just a boy at the time—and at those relatives of yours, and I knew Lilian had done a wicked thing. Never in a million years would your father have married her under normal circumstances. I was not sorry when she told me she never wanted to see me again. I never wanted to see *her* again. I blamed myself, though, and I *was* sorry when she quarreled with her brother and sisters too. None of us ever got to see Maria. Until now."

Justin felt a little as he might if he were trying to chase down a runaway horse on foot. And what *was* all this? It was appalling. Could any of it be true?

"Until I went to Prospect Hall a couple of weeks ago to fetch her home, I had not seen her either since she was a child," he said. He kept his voice low, willing Lady Maple to lower her own too. Or to speak of something else. "I am very pleased that she is back home and that—"

Where was Maria? He had lost sight of her. And of her two cousins. Perhaps they had left the room?

"It always consoled me that that child had her father," Lady Maple said, cutting him off again—and she had not taken the hint to lower her voice. "He was a good and honorable man. And that she had you. You were just a lad when I came here, but you were a polite boy and good-natured, which was more important, and I thought you would probably be kind to a little sister."

"I adored her from the day she was born, ma'am," Justin told her. "She almost fit in the palm of my hand."

Watley and his sister were drawing nearer. One glance at their faces was enough to convince Justin that they had heard every word. And was it his imagination, or had most conversations around him ceased?

"I knew as soon as I heard about the rift between you and your father that my niece must be behind it somehow," Lady Maple continued, leaning forward in her chair to tap Justin's hand with her lorgnette. "It was no ordinary quarrel, was it? It did not blow over with the cooling of tempers as most quarrels do. Your father was very proud of you when you were a lad, and you clearly adored him just at a time in your life when many boys begin to rebel. I remember the way you scarcely removed your eyes from him during the marriage ceremony. I thought it was good of him to have you as his best man. No, it could have been no ordinary quarrel, Brandon. Nothing—*no one*—could have come between you and your father but my niece. I have never doubted it for a moment. If I have one regret in life, it is that I agreed to bring her to London to introduce to the *ton*."

"I prefer not to talk about—" Justin began.

He was interrupted by Maria herself, who had stepped up behind his chair without his noticing. Her cousins were still with her, though she had freed her arms from theirs. What had she heard? But how could she not have heard everything?

"Oh," she said, her voice soft and tight. "It is not true. You are a wicked, evil woman. It is not true that Mama trapped Papa into marrying her in such a *despicable* way. It is a *lie*. He saw her dancing at her very first ball, and he fell in love with her even before they were introduced. He asked her that very evening to marry him, and when she protested that she was not even a lady by birth while he was an *earl*, he told her that when a man fell in love, nothing else mattered. He would have married her if she had been a scullery maid, he told her. Theirs was a great *love* story."

"Oh, my dear child." Lady Maple reached out with her lorgnette, but Maria pulled her arm out of its reach.

Justin closed his eyes briefly and inhaled slowly.

"You quarreled with Mama," Maria said, "because you were jealous that she had married an earl while you had been able to snare only a baronet."

She was still speaking softly, but there was no doubt now that everyone in the room was listening.

"This is neither the time nor the place—" Justin said far too late, getting to his feet.

"And Mama had *nothing* to do with your quarrel with Papa," Maria said, rounding on him, her eyes blazing. "It is . . . *despicable* even to suggest such a thing. *You* know why he sent you away and told you never to return. Those jewels you stole were Mama's, gifts from Papa, costly in themselves but many times more precious to her because they were tokens of his love. You *took* them and broke both their hearts. I hope you lived well on what you got for them during the years you were away."

What the devil?

"Well, Aunt Bertha," Leonard Dickson said in his hearty, booming voice, "you have opened a Pandora's box right enough. Margaret and I need to go and change for luncheon. We probably all do. Though who will be able to eat anything so soon after those delicious Chelsea buns I do not know. Your cook is doing us proud, Brandon. I daresay my aunt has misremembered the events of that evening when my sister met your papa. It was many years ago, and whose memories can bear up for that long? I know I would rather believe the romantic version Maria heard. And whatever happened between you and your father, Brandon, was your business and is none of mine or anyone else's. Tempers sometimes flare, as I know all too well from the mill, and people say things they wish afterward they had not said. It's always best to pretend that indeed they were not said aloud. I am looking forward to seeing the state apartments this afternoon. I am sure they are grand, just as the rest of the house is."

Everyone began to disperse.

Lady Estelle was approaching with a smile. "Come, Maria," she said. "Let us go up to that sitting room between our two bedchambers, shall we, and relax until luncheon? I always love looking out upon rain, though it is not as pleasant to be caught out in it. "

Maria allowed her arm to be taken. Within a minute or two Justin was alone in the room with Lady Maple.

"What was your purpose in gathering us all here, Brandon?" she asked. "All are family to either you or Maria or both of you except for those handsome Lamarr twins. Did you intend that we all merely smile at one another and talk nicely and let old quarrels caused by a dead woman fester below the surface as though they had not caused lasting damage? I am sorry Maria overheard me. The feelings of the very young are tender things, and it is only just over a year since she lost her mother. I am sorry other people seem to have overheard me too. I suppose I was speaking too loudly. But if this family gathering is to have any real meaning, and if *you* ever hope to have a real relationship with your sister, there needs to be some plain speaking, and it might as well be done by me. Did you take those jewels?"

"No." Justin spoke curtly and frowned down at her.

"I would have been surprised if you had," she said. "I think your father would have been surprised too. It would have been a silly thing to do and pointless, since I daresay your father kept you in funds and I never heard of your being an expensive young man. There needs to be some plain speaking in this family, Brandon."

Justin felt rather as though he were in the throes of a nightmare. Disaster had struck—for the second time in one morning—and he had no idea how he was going to face his guests in just an hour or so to eat luncheon. It was altogether possible they did not know how they were going to face him either. Maria would quite possibly refuse to face any of them or even talk with anyone except her particular friend. And thank goodness for Lady Estelle, who had persuaded her to leave the room before she could become quite hysterical.

Beneath all his distress, one revelation thrummed in his head like a heavy drumbeat.

His father had been *tricked* into marrying Maria's mother. He had not, after all, been just a foolish middle-aged widower of close to fifty who had been dazzled by the looks and charms of a girl only four years older than his son. Where, Justin wondered, had she hidden the key of that anteroom after locking the door? How had she lured his father there? He did not for one moment doubt that Lady Maple's version of that story was the true one, though he had heard Maria's version numerous times from his stepmother while his father had listened and smiled but neither corroborated her story nor contradicted it.

"Give me a hand and help me to my feet, Brandon," Lady Maple said. "I was up early today. It must be the country air, though it is reputed to make a person sleep longer. I will go to my room and summon my maid—*if* I can find my way to the west wing and the right room, that is."

"I shall give myself the pleasure of escorting you there myself," Justin said, offering his arm after he had helped her up. "This house can be confusing until one gets to know it."

Estelle settled Maria in a comfortable chair in the sitting room and chafed her hands.

"I believe I missed the first part of what Lady Maple was saying," she said. "I did understand, though, that she had upset you dreadfully by telling a different story than the one you have always been told of how Lady Brandon, your mother, met your father."

Estelle had not missed much of it. She and Bertrand had been the last to arrive in the drawing room. After pouring two cups of hot chocolate, she had given her brother his, taken his arm, avoided his look of surprise—they usually went their separate ways after they entered a crowded room—and drawn him in the direction of Lady Maple. The Earl of Brandon was sitting with her, and it had seemed to Estelle that the very best thing she could do was go right up to them and make conversation. It would be far better than tiptoeing around him for the rest of the two weeks here. But she *had* needed her twin to give her the necessary courage. Poor Bertrand had not even had a chance to take a Chelsea bun.

Hence they had both heard almost everything. So had everyone else. Estelle's personal discomfort over the Earl of Brandon had been forgotten in the greater disaster that had been unfolding before her.

"She is a wicked, evil woman, and I told her so," Maria said as Estelle sat down beside her. "She told Brandon that

Papa was forced to marry Mama after she trapped him inside a small locked room with her during a *ton* ball until they were discovered sometime later. By then her dress was torn and her hair was disheveled. It is *not true*. Papa fell in love with Mama when he saw her dancing with someone else."

"I daresay," Estelle said, "Lady Maple misremembers the details of what happened that evening. She is rather an elderly lady." She did not for a moment believe Lady Maple *had* misremembered. It was a very distinct story, not the sort of thing one would get confused about in one's memory. And she had not detected any sign of senility in Maria's great-aunt.

"She *does* misremember," Maria said. "But she is a guest here. I behaved badly, did I not? Melanie would scold me if she were here now. *'A lady owes unfailing courtesy to her guests, even when she has not personally invited them and they have been ill-mannered.'* I can almost hear her say the words. I owe Lady Maple an apology."

Estelle patted her hand.

"She also said it was Mama who quarreled with *her*," Maria said, frowning as she gazed through the window at the rain. "But it was the other way around. She said it was Mama who quarreled with her brother and sisters, but again she got it backward. She said it was Mama who caused the rift between Papa and Brandon—the present Brandon."

She never used her half brother's given name, Estelle had noticed.

"That last was mean and cruel and absolutely untrue," Maria continued. "She knows nothing about that rift. She had been estranged from Mama for years before it happened. It was Mama who was the greatest victim. She suffered the most, and she suffered dreadfully. She had loved him as a son and had trusted him utterly, just as I had, yet he *stole* from her. All her most costly jewels, all her *personal* ones, the jewels Papa had given her. She always said it was not so much their monetary worth that grieved her as their emotional value. To her they were irreplaceable. And he took them. Then he showed not a glimmering of remorse, though he had broken her heart and Papa's. It was why Papa banished him. It is downright cruel to say it was all Mama's fault when *none* of it was. She even pleaded with Papa not to be so harsh with him."

Estelle patted Maria's hand again while the words echoed inside her head. *And he took them. Then he showed not a glimmering of remorse.* She remembered his cold unconcern when his dog had frightened her half to death by the riverbank. And his stiff, reticent manner when she and Bertrand had called at Prospect Hall soon after his arrival there. She thought of his strange, abrupt, passionless proposal of marriage earlier this morning. And his brief, hard kiss. Was it all of a piece? *Then he showed not a glimmering of remorse . . . It was not so much their monetary worth that grieved her as their emotional value.*

No. No, somehow it did not ring quite true. She had no idea *why* not. It was not as though she felt kindly disposed toward the man. She would gladly believe the worst of him if only the worst were credible. Somehow it was not.

"Your brother seems to be trying to make amends, Maria," she said. "He has brought you home and invited Bertrand and me to come too so that you will have familiar people with you for a while. He has arranged this house party to give you and your relatives a chance to get to know one another, to turn a page in your family history, perhaps, so that they may be a part of your life in the future."

"Do you believe, then, that I owe *him* an apology too?" Maria asked.

"Oh, I will not tell you what you ought to do," Estelle said.

Maria sighed. "Melanie would not hold back," she said. "She would instruct me to remember that a lady always thinks first before she speaks, especially when she has a potential audience of more than one person. I condemned him very publicly. Melanie would say it is no excuse that I was severely provoked."

Estelle smiled at her.

"But perhaps it is a good thing everyone now knows him for the thief he is," Maria said. "I can never forgive him. Not only was he not sorry he had taken Mama's precious treasures, as she always called her lost jewels. He also banished *her* as soon as he was able. He did it while she was still almost prostrate with grief over the loss of Papa. Even while *I* was. For a time after Papa died, I wanted to die too."

She ran her hands over her face before clasping them in her lap.

"You have never spoken much about your papa, Maria," Estelle said. "I would like to know more sometime. One's father is very precious. One's mother too. I always regret that I was too young when my mother died to have any memory of her. But I love my father dearly. Losing him would seem unbearable."

"I am so sorry for having behaved badly in the drawing room," Maria said, looking up after a while. "For making you listen to all my bad temper now. For being so self-absorbed. I am going to have to face everyone soon. At luncheon. I am going to have to think of something to say, since it will be impossible to behave as though nothing has happened, despite what Uncle Leonard said. Thank you for being my friend. For listening and not lecturing me. How did you enjoy your morning? What did you think of the summerhouse?"

"I love it," Estelle said. "I can quite understand why Lord Brandon spends so much time there. It is . . . peaceful."

"He used to take me there when I was a child," Maria said. "But never just to sit downstairs. He used to take me upstairs, where all his things were—pictures and books and his private hoard of sweetmeats and biscuits the cook used to slip to him. He used to cuddle me next to him on an old armchair if it was a chilly day, a blanket from the bed around me like a cocoon, and tell me stories. His own stories, not anything from any of his books. They were always thrilling adventures, and he always used to leave them off abruptly at an exciting point and make me wait until next time before he continued. All my wheedling and pleading would not shift him. Those were *such* good days." Her face had lit up at the memories.

And now he wrote a continuing story of the adventures of a young man turned out upon the world without a penny or a friend or an ounce of life experience. An accidental hero who vanquished all the demons that threatened destruction.

But had the author also been turned loose upon the world *without a penny*? Or had he had a considerable fortune, amassed from the sale of a treasure trove of precious jewels belonging to his stepmother?

Maria was frowning with her eyes closed. "How can I possibly go down for luncheon?" she said. "Or join in the tour of the state apartments this afternoon? Or leave my room until after everyone has left Everleigh?"

"When something that needs to be done is impossible to do," Estelle said, "I have always found that the only possible course of action is to do it anyway."

Maria looked at her and pulled a face.

"Boldly and without delay," Estelle added.

"I called Lady Maple *evil* and *wicked*," Maria said. "I called Brandon a thief in front of all his family and mine. In front of you and Viscount Watley."

"You did indeed," Estelle said, and smiled.

"All of which was true," Maria added. "I think I am going to be sick."

"If that is so," Estelle said, "you had better hurry over to your dressing room, Maria. If it is not literally true, you had better go there anyway. It is almost time for luncheon and your hair needs combing."

Estelle let herself into her own room after Maria had rung for her maid. What an unbelievably eventful morning it had been. And there was no knowing what lay ahead. This gathering of family to welcome Maria home had seemed very successful until an hour or so ago. But now?

Perhaps, she thought, this upset was very necessary if there was to be any lasting reconciliation. Yet all the trouble, she suspected, had been caused by a dead woman, a woman who had been too beautiful, too conceited, and too immature and morally bankrupt for her own good. She could be wrong, but she did not believe she was.

Yet Maria had had a deep attachment to her mother and still did.

But really it was not her concern how it would all play out, was it? She was not a member of the family.

She might have been.

A couple of hours ago the Earl of Brandon had asked her to marry him.

And kissed her.

Eleven

Justin made his way down to the dining room for luncheon, wondering as he went if he would be presiding over an empty table. It had been a disaster of a morning, and that was a bit of an understatement. It would not be at all surprising if even now every last one of his guests was busy packing bags and summoning carriages, intent upon putting as much distance between themselves and him as they could before the day was out.

Everyone turned up for luncheon. Without exception.

It was a somewhat subdued gathering, it was true, with bursts of conversation that were halting and self-conscious at best, overhearty at worst. The soup, a simple beef broth, was lavishly praised as though there had never been a soup to match it for taste and substance.

Then Maria spoke up, and silence fell upon the table just as if someone had hit a gong with a mallet.

"I owe everyone an apology," she said.

There was a halfhearted murmur of dissent, but it lasted only a moment.

"I have observed, before today," she said, "that people often remember events differently. If you were to ask ten people to give an account of something they had all witnessed, you would surely get ten different stories, some of them varying only in small details, others quite different from one another. Yet all ten people would believe quite sincerely that the event happened just as they remembered it. My mother had vivid and very fond memories of her first meeting with my father, and he always smiled at her when she told the story in his hearing. He never once contradicted her. Lady Maple remembers that evening differently. I was startled in the drawing room earlier when I heard her tell the story as she recalls it, and I reacted without consideration. It was very ill-mannered of me. No, it was worse than that. It was offensive. I did not intend my words to be heard by anyone except Lady Maple herself, but they were in fact overheard by most if not all of you. I insulted her and I embarrassed everyone else, myself included. Inadequate as an apology is, I do apologize. Especially to you, ma'am."

She looked directly at Lady Maple, who was seated to Justin's left at the head of the table. There were two spots of color high on Maria's cheekbones. Otherwise her face was as pale as parchment.

"Handsomely said, Lady Maria," Sidney Sharpe observed.

"It was my fault, child," Lady Maple said, picking up her lorgnette from beside her plate before changing her mind and putting it back. "I ought not to have said what I did without first making sure you were nowhere near being within earshot. And that no one else was, for that matter. And I believe that sometimes I speak more loudly than I intend."

"It is not a normal day with any family," Leonard Dickson said in his booming voice as he beamed genially about the table, "if there is not at least one crisis to set everyone on their heads. You and Aunt Bertha must kiss and make up after we have eaten, Maria. This is excellent soup, by the way, Brandon. Your cook is to be commended."

That had taken great courage on Maria's part, Justin thought, looking at her appreciatively. Not just a private apology to her great-aunt, but a public one to everyone. She was certainly not the timid little thing he had taken her for when he arrived at Prospect Hall, and he was glad of it.

"That is not all," Maria said, and the footmen who had been about to remove the soup bowls glided back to stand beside the warming dishes with the butler. "I also heard my mother being accused of causing the . . . the unfortunate *rift* between my father and my half brother. I spoke out in anger and said things I ought never to have said. I am deeply ashamed and beg everyone's pardon. I beg *Brandon's* pardon for the public nature of my accusations."

Not for the accusations themselves, Justin noticed, but for making them *publicly*.

"We all speak out in anger sometimes, Maria, and regret it almost before the words are out," Uncle Rowan Sharpe said in his usual kindly way. "Not all of us, though, have the strength of character to say we are sorry."

"Thank you, Maria," Justin said. "I hope the air has now been cleared and we can move on to enjoy the rest of our luncheon. Good though the soup was, there is, I believe, more substantial food to come." He signaled Phelps with a raising of his eyebrows as several people laughed.

"How can any of us be hungry," Cousin Ernest said as a footman removed his bowl, "when we ate those excellent Chelsea buns no longer ago than a couple of hours?"

"Speak for yourself, young man," Uncle Harold Ormsbury said.

"You are always hungry anyway, Ernie," young Rosie said. "You ought to be the size of a house. There is no justice in this world that you are not."

"I only have to *look* at food," Mrs. Chandler said, "and my stays grow tighter."

"Mama!" fifteen-year-old Megan said on a gasp. "You said *stays* aloud. In *company.*"

"What was that you said, Miss Chandler?" Watley asked, cupping one hand about his ear. "I had fallen into a dream for a moment. I do beg your pardon. Did I miss something?" He grinned at young Megan, who blushed and giggled.

"Suffice it to say," Mrs. Chandler said, "that I have to watch what I eat."

It seemed, Justin thought as he proceeded to make conversation with Aunt Betty on his right and Lady Maple on his left, that his house party had been saved. Though everyone doubtless now believed, probably rightly, that his father had been trapped into marrying the ambitious Miss Lilian Dickson more than twenty years ago. And that he, Justin, had stolen her jewels several years after that and been banished as a result.

Lady Crowther and her sister, Lady Felicity Ormsbury, had grown up at Everleigh Park as daughters of a former earl. They did not wish to traipse through the state apartments but chose rather to spend the afternoon with their husbands in the library. Lady Maple announced that she would rest in her room and join the party for tea later. Everyone else gathered in the entrance hall half an hour after luncheon for the promised tour. The rain had more or less stopped outside, but the clouds had still not moved off. An indoor option was the perfect choice for the afternoon.

Estelle was looking forward to it. It would perhaps take her mind off other matters, even if the tour guide *was* unfortunately the Earl of Brandon. She wanted to put the memory of his marriage proposal and kiss out of her head, and she wanted to forget what Maria had said about his stealing her mother's jewelry. She wanted just to enjoy herself.

The earl had joined them in the hall, and they were about to move off. Mr. Ernest Sharpe, who had informed Estelle just before luncheon, one hand over his heart, that he had been devastated at being cut out of escorting her to the lake this morning by his own cousin, made sure of her this afternoon by offering his arm as soon as the earl appeared. Bertrand, she could see, was between Maria on one side and Angela Ormsbury on the other. He could be relied upon to see Maria through any residual embarrassment she felt after this morning. He had her arm drawn through his now and was smiling, his head bent toward hers as he said something.

The state apartments were rarely used but were opened to visitors on public days or by private appointment, the earl explained. They extended the full length of the north wing and were all connected to one another—with the result, Estelle soon saw, that anyone sleeping in the state bedchamber could have little expectation of privacy. But then, the grand bed looked more like a throne than a sleeping place. It stood on a platform that required three steps to reach it. Intricately carved spiral posts supported an ornate canopy decorated with gilded cherubs and gold and scarlet velvet curtains.

"No doubt when a king sleeps here," Mr. Martin Haig, Doris's husband, said, "he hangs his crown on the bedpost and exchanges it for a scarlet nightcap."

"With a gold tassel," Mr. Chandler added.

"And his courtiers gather around him in the morning for the levee," Mr. Bevin Ormsbury said.

"But not too early," Ernest Sharpe said, looking down at Estelle and winking. "Never before noon. One can only hope that none of them have arthritic knees when it comes to climbing those steps."

"One must hope the present king never sleeps here," Mr. Dickson added. "He has arthritic *everything*, does he not?"

"Oh, do hush, Leonard," his wife told him, laughing. "You will end up in a dungeon deep beneath the Tower of London."

"And I will carry forever the shame of having had a brother beheaded for treason," Mrs. Chandler added.

There was a great deal of such quipping and laughter. Oh, she *did* like silliness, Estelle thought, when it drew a group together and caused general amusement without any suggestion of malice.

"If King George ever does decide to honor my humble abode with his presence," the earl said, "I daresay I will have to have a sling lift installed to convey him to bed at night and out of it the following morning—*afternoon*."

He had a sense of humor too, Estelle admitted grudgingly. But of course he did. He had invented that accidental hero, had he not?

"It is all really quite *magnificent*, Justin," Mrs. Sharpe, his aunt, assured him. "I never tire of seeing these rooms."

They all looked avidly about them as they moved from room to room, oohing and aahing at the splendor of it all. There were three connected rooms in the center of the wing, a grand, square, high-ceilinged reception room in the middle, with half-square sitting rooms on either side. The latter were mirror images of each other in both decoration and furnishings. Young Rosie Sharpe and Nigel Dickson and Paulette Ormsbury ran several times across the central room to peer into each smaller room in turn to confirm that yes, they really were mirror images, down to the finest detail—even the arrangement of the furniture.

All three rooms had coved gilded ceilings with painted scenes from mythology and crystal chandeliers, the ones in the sitting rooms exactly half the size of the one in the reception room in the middle. The floors were covered with Persian carpets rimmed with highly polished wood. All three rooms were furnished in the slightly faded elegance of the previous century.

The Earl of Brandon was a good tour guide. He gave enough information to draw everyone's attention to features of each apartment they might not otherwise have noticed and to set it all in historical context. He pointed out to them, for example, that two of the cherubs in the mythological scene on the ceiling of the large square reception room had the faces of the young sons of the earl who had built the house. And one of the cherubs in each of the twin rooms on either side had the face of a daughter of his. The guests all acquired stiff necks from gazing up at the likenesses. Yet the earl did not drone on about every little detail as some guides did until their listeners were ready to scream with boredom.

Even so, Estelle's mind was feeling close to bursting by the time the group moved on to the state dining room, all chatting merrily. She slid her hand unobtrusively from Ernest's arm and let him go ahead with everyone else while she wandered to the window of one of the smaller sitting rooms—though *smaller* was a relative term in a wing of the house that was designed to convey the impression of size and grandeur.

A grand house's kitchen gardens were usually behind it. That was not so here. The hill against which the house had been built sloped gradually upward. It was largely covered with trees, though near the house was mostly low bushes— azaleas, rhododendrons, others she could not immediately identify—and there were flowers planted among them to give the appearance of their being wild though they were not. It was a clever piece of gardening, contrasting pleasingly with the cultivated formality of the parterres and lawns and walking paths at the front—and the fields and meadows to the east of the summerhouse. She had still seen only a fraction of the whole park during the twenty-four hours she had been here. She had not even seen the lake yet, except off in the distance while she and Bertrand were descending the hill opposite.

She might have been mistress of all this, she realized suddenly. Ah, but at what a cost.

"This hill looks at its absolute best," the Earl of Brandon said from behind her shoulder, making her almost jump with alarm, "when the bluebells are blooming among the trees. They form a carpet of blue just when the leaves on the trees are at their freshest spring green."

Estelle hunched her shoulders for a moment. She did not turn. He had a deep voice, a bit gravelly. A rather attractive voice, she conceded—if one had never seen the man or had any dealings with him or if one did not know that he had done something so villainous as a younger man that his father had banished him from his home . . . *this* home—and never reprieved him. Jewel theft, perhaps? She really did not know if she believed that story. But even if it was not that, it was *something*.

She had already conceded, though, had she not, that she might be attracted to him? Whatever did that say about her?

"I love bluebells," she said.

"Sometimes," he said, "one could wish to grasp time within one's two hands and hold it there for a good long while before releasing it. The bluebells bloom all too fleetingly."

"But there are the snowdrops and primroses before them," she said, "and the roses and so much else after. Everything is precious in its season. Perhaps we would be less appreciative if we had the bluebells with us all year long."

"The voice of good sense," he said. "But you are right. If we could find a way to manipulate time or weather to suit our preferences, can you imagine the wars that would have to be fought against people with different preferences?"

"Farmers with their pitchforks wanting rain for their crops against the idle rich with their dress swords wanting sunshine for their spas and seaside promenades?" she said.

They both laughed.

It was a horrible moment. She had no wish to enjoy any moment of shared amusement with this man.

"I owe you an apology, Lady Estelle," he said.

Two robins had landed on a frail branch of one of the trees near the house. It swayed beneath them, like a swing. They did not fly away to a steadier perch, though, and it occurred to Estelle that perhaps they were enjoying themselves. *Could* birds enjoy themselves? But why not?

Had there not already been apologies enough for one day? This was at least to be a private one.

"I do not believe it is necessary," she said. "If you refer to your offer of marriage, that is. You asked; I said no."

"For kissing you," he said. "Without permission. *After* you had refused my offer and it was unlikely you would welcome a kiss."

She drew a breath and released it without saying anything.

"I was fortunate," he said, "not to have my face slapped."

"How did you get your broken nose?" she asked, and was appalled as she heard the words come out of her mouth. She had not even been *thinking* them.

"You are imagining that perhaps someone else *did* slap me?" he asked her. "And very hard?"

"Please ignore the question," she said. "It was impertinent." The vegetable garden was not at the back of the house, but she could see now over to her left what looked like a knot garden close to the house. An herb garden, perhaps?

"I was unwise enough," he said, "to suggest to a loud-mouthed yokel in a village tavern that perhaps the barmaid did not enjoy being fondled as she delivered his ale. Another patron, altogether larger and more formidable than the loudmouth, took exception, not so much to what I said, but to *how* I said it. *Mr. La-di-da*, he called me among other, less complimentary things. I made the mistake of inviting him to stay out of my business. I would like to say that I gave a good account of myself in the ensuing fight or that at least it lasted an hour while we slugged it out. Alas, it was not so. I went down within moments to ignominious defeat—and a face swollen beyond recognition. And a broken nose."

She turned to look at him. "You were not an accidental hero in that particular incident, then?" she said.

"Neither accidental nor heroic, alas," he said.

"Did you at least have the man arrested for assault?" she asked him.

Something happened to his very dark eyes. They *laughed*. Just for a moment, but she was sure she had not been mistaken.

"I realized sometime afterward," he said, "that he quite purposely avoided damaging my teeth. It had to have been deliberate. Nothing else above my neck was spared. I do not believe I would have been so fortunate had I provoked a second fight—at that point in my history at least. Perhaps not even later. No, there was no official complaint and no arrest. He became my best friend."

Oh.

"Lord Brandon," she said. "I have the feeling that if you were to write your own story, it might be twelve volumes long. Perhaps longer."

"Ah," he said. "But would you wish to read it, Lady Estelle?"

His eyes were no longer laughing or even smiling. They were fathoms deep. It would be awfully easy to lose herself in them, Estelle thought, a little horrified. Whatever *that* meant.

"It would have to be written first," she said.

"By which time you would be an old lady seated by your fireside, your grandchildren gathered about your knee," he said. "But perhaps it would not be suitable reading for them."

She drew a breath. "Did you steal the countess's jewelry?" she asked him.

"Ah," he said, and his eyes narrowed somewhat. "You are picturing me living a life of luxury for six years at the very best inns on their proceeds, are you? Perhaps simply *buying* the inns so that I would not have to share them with lesser mortals?"

His hands were clasped behind his back. He stood with his booted feet apart and leaned slightly toward her. And she could not tell whether his dark eyes were now intense with anger or . . . laughter. Certainly there was no smile on his face.

"*Did* you?" she asked him.

He moved back to stand straight. "None of those things," he said.

She nodded and was aware of voices and laughter coming from the adjoining room. They seemed very alone together here in contrast.

"But do you believe me?" he asked.

"Yes," she said. She somehow could not see him as a thief. She did not like him. At least . . . No, she did not like him. He had done *something* terrible, though it was long ago and was really no concern of hers. But whatever it was, it had turned him into a hard man who found it difficult to smile or to relate to others with any degree of amiability. He would be a difficult man with whom to live. And that was *true*, despite the frisson of attraction and sexual awareness she felt suddenly, standing here looking at him. She had never looked at any other man and wondered what it would be like to go to bed with him. She had thought of kisses and romance, but not of *that* except in vague terms associated with wedding nights. It was a bit horrifying that she was thinking of precisely that now.

"It is not my business *what* you did or how you spent those years or what you lived on," she said.

"It would be your business," he said, "if you had agreed to be my countess."

"Yes," she said. "But I did not." Those large, powerful-looking hands. That broad-shouldered, broad-chested body. Those powerful thighs. That harsh-featured, almost craggy face and those intense dark eyes. No, it would be impossible. Too intense. Too far beyond her control. "The state apartments are all on the lower level of the north wing, are they not? What is on the floor above?"

He accepted the abrupt change of subject without comment. "The portrait gallery," he said.

"It must be a very large collection," she said, "if it stretches the whole length of the wing."

"The room was designed as a long promenade for the family during inclement weather," he told her. "And as a place to take guests too fearsome of slopes and steps and what the outdoors might do to their hair or their complexions. As a play area for children to roar along. As a retreat for anyone wishing for some quiet exercise and solitude. And, incidentally, as a family portrait gallery. I will not show it today. People who visit the state apartments have their heads stuffed with what they have seen and heard by the time they reach the last room. I believe all my guests are very ready for tea in the grand reception hall. I will show you the gallery another day."

You as in her, Estelle? Or a collective *you* as in all his guests? He did not say and she did not ask.

"Shall we?" He gestured with one hand toward the dining room, and she walked there beside him. He did not offer his arm.

It was a long room, quite breathtaking in its size and splendor, as were all the apartments. The sound of voices now came from the room beyond it. There was no one else left here. They walked slowly but did not stop, and he did not point out any features of the room. Estelle was sure she had never seen such a large table. It looked as if it would accommodate at least fifty diners without any clashing of elbows.

The rest of the party was in the ladies' withdrawing room beyond the dining room, some sitting, some standing. They looked expectantly at the earl when he appeared in the doorway.

"What does it *feel* like to be the owner of all this, Lord Brandon?" Gillian Dickson asked. "I cannot even *imagine* it."

"Oh, I can, Gill," her brother, Wallace, said. "I would feel like a *prince*."

"When one inherits something like this," the earl said, "one realizes that one has done nothing to earn it, that one owes it all to an accident of birth. It is an enormous privilege and a weighty responsibility. Is anyone ready for tea?"

Everyone was, it seemed. Energy was instantly restored and they were all on their feet in moments.

The earl crossed the room to a closed door and spoke to the footman who was standing beside it, waiting to open it. The young man hurried away, back through the state apartments, and the earl opened the door himself and stood back to let them through.

And so they entered the room with the dome, which Estelle had been longing to see since her arrival yesterday. It was a vast round hall with a tiled mosaic floor and a high balcony that ran all about the circumference and that was held up by marble pillars and made safe by a marble balustrade, which must be at least waist-high. The great glass dome above it filled the room with light. Even as Estelle looked up, clouds must have moved off the sun and a shaft of sunlight beamed downward, to be fractured into all the colors of the rainbow as it caught walls and balcony and pillars and floor.

"Now *that*," the earl said to the whole group, "was perfect timing. This is sometimes a grand reception hall, occasionally a ballroom. Today it will be a tearoom."

"A ballroom," Estelle said, looking up and about her at the fractured light. She spread her arms wide and turned once about. "It would surely be the most wonderful place in the whole world in which to dance."

Maria laughed. "Oh," she said, her voice filled with delight. "I had a birthday party here once. It was my eighth birthday. How could I have forgotten until now?"

Perhaps, Estelle thought, because not long after there had been a great upset in the house and her brother had vanished. She wondered what it had been like here then, after he had gone. How upset by it all had Maria's father been? And her mother? And Maria herself? It must have been a life-changing event for all of them.

"I remember it well," the earl said, looking at his sister with what was surely fondness. "The room was filled with squealing little girls, and I had been put in charge of organizing games and entertainment for you all."

"I can just picture it," Mrs. Sharpe said, clapping her hands once before clasping them to her bosom and beaming at her nephew. "I suppose you performed your magician's act, Justin? You were always so good at it. I never knew how you could produce an endless stream of ribbons from an empty hat or gold coins from behind people's ears."

"It was pure magic, of course," the earl told her. "Maria, this is your tea, I believe? You are the hostess."

The center of the room had been set up with several square tables covered with crisp white cloths and laid with gleaming china and crystal and silverware. Maria moved toward them.

"Ah, and here comes Lady Maple," the earl said.

She was being ushered into the room from the entrance hall by the young footman the earl had sent upon an errand a short while ago. The Ormsbury uncles and aunts came in behind them.

"A private showing of the summerhouse this morning, complete with a marriage proposal," Bertrand murmured, coming up behind Estelle and setting his hands upon her shoulders. "A private moment in one of the sitting rooms this afternoon while everyone else moved on. Do I smell a romance after all, Stell?"

"If you do," she said, "there is something drastically wrong with your nose. But, Bert, have you ever in your life seen anything more splendid than all this?"

"Yes," he said, grinning at her. "Elm Court."

She laughed. *"Splendid?"*

"It is a sizable manor house," he said. "More important, it is home. This is a magnificent showpiece, though. I was particularly impressed with the half-square rooms with their perfect mirror imaging. Twin rooms."

"We are an imperfect example of the type, alas," she said. "We are not quite mirror images of each other."

"Sometimes," he said, squeezing her shoulders, "imperfection can be more interesting than perfection, Stell. It is something you may wish to keep in mind, actually, when you continue your search for your Mr. Perfect."

"Continue?" she said. "Have I started?"

Maria was approaching them. She had already seated most of the other guests. "Lord Watley," she said, "would you care to sit beside my aunt Margaret at *that* table?" She indicated it. "And, Estelle, will you sit with my cousin Megan? She admires you greatly but is also a bit in awe of the fact that you are the daughter of a *marquess*."

Servants were bringing in plates of sandwiches and scones and various dainties. Others were carrying in teapots and hot water jugs.

They took their places and Estelle spread her linen napkin across her lap. She turned to make conversation with the very young, blushing daughter of Mr. and Mrs. Chandler.

The Earl of Brandon's best friend had been—and still was?—a man from a tavern somewhere who had taken exception to his cultured accent, got into a brawl with him for no other reason than that, and broken his nose.

Really?

Estelle would be willing to bet the earl had not been so large and well muscled at that period of his life. So what had happened during those years? Where had he gone? What had he done? What had he lived on? What had he been like before? He had told stories to his young sister out in the summerhouse. He had entertained her and other little girls with a magic act at a birthday party. He had told a man at a tavern not to molest the barmaid.

Who exactly *was* the Earl of Brandon?

"Which was your favorite room?" she asked Megan, and determinedly gave the girl the whole of her attention.

Twelve

The weather remained fine for the next few days, and Justin found that his guests did not need to be entertained at every moment. There was much to explore and much to do, both indoors and out, and most of them were content to do it all in small unstructured groups.

The disaster that had happened in the drawing room on the first full morning of their stay seemed to have had no serious consequences. Maria's apology at luncheon afterward had undoubtedly helped, and everyone's determination to put the embarrassment out of their minds made it possible to carry on as though none of it had happened.

But almost everyone now probably believed he was a thief, Justin thought, and a cruel one at that. There was nothing he could do about it, though, since he was certainly not going to tell the truth. All he could do was continue regardless. As for what Lady Maple had said about his father having been trapped into marrying her niece . . . Well, that also must be set aside for now and pondered at some later date.

If her story was true, though, it would change a great deal. *Everything*, in fact.

Meanwhile the house party continued.

The children's early-morning ride and playtime with Captain became a daily event and sometimes included more than just the original two. There were also Olwen and David Ormsbury, aged five and three, children of Justin's cousin Bevin and Esme, his wife. All of them enjoyed the usual activities as well as trudging out to the sheep pens to watch the sheep and lambs being released and led out to their pastures. They all enjoyed being taken to the smithy out behind the stables to watch the blacksmith at work at his anvil.

And at other times of the day the children never tired of running through the maze and getting hopelessly lost. Even when by sheer accident they arrived at the center, it was still difficult to find their way back out. Some of the young people tried it too and fared no better. Even Watley got lost when Gillian Chandler and Rosie Sharpe persuaded him to go in with them because they were scared to go alone. They had giggled and clung to his arms and looked anything but scared.

Justin took a party of youngsters up over the wilderness walk behind the house one morning. Some of them had pulled faces at the initial suggestion, and he had agreed with them that they might indeed be wise not to come. It involved the climbing of a few steep slopes that might tire them needlessly, after all, and even a bit of a scramble up a rocky series of steps that were not for the faint of heart. Also there was a tall lookout tower near the top with dark stone stairs spiraling about the inside of it that might be too scary for some. And there was a hollow dragon amid some dark, dense trees that one could climb right inside if one could get up the courage. Then one could roar to create deep, hollow echoes that would scare birds and wildlife and unwary passersby for miles around. There was one lookout point that offered a view of a church spire all of twelve miles away down the valley, if one could imagine being able to see such a distance. He would take a telescope for anyone who wished to verify that it was indeed a spire with what looked like a miniature church below it. At the end of the walk, he told them, there was an easy way down a gently sloping path, and there was a dangerous, scary way down a sheerer, grassy slope. They would doubtless consider rolling down it beneath their dignity, of course. They were undoubtedly right to turn up their noses and go find some safer, more sedate amusement elsewhere.

Everyone below the age of thirty joined the walk, as did Justin's cousins Ernest and Sidney, who remembered persuading Doris to climb those steps inside the tower when they were all children, though they had had to half carry her down again. She might otherwise have stayed up there for the rest of her life.

Captain went too, and the children enjoyed making him bark and bare his teeth at the roaring dragon.

They all gazed wistfully at the long, steep slope down one side of the hill, which provided a superb sledding run when it snowed.

Almost everyone went to church on Sunday morning, and during the following days Maria received several neighbors, who came to pay their respects to her and the guests. A few of the older ones remembered Aunt Augusta and Aunt Felicity and were happy to reminisce with them while their children listened and laughed. One of those visitors, Lady Jemima Hodgkins, had been a particular friend of Justin's aunts when they were all girls—they both called her Jim, while they were Gussie and Fliss. Her call had to be returned, and the aunts went off to visit her one afternoon, taking Maria and Paulette Ormsbury with them.

It pleased Justin to think that his sister would not be entirely alone after all the guests had returned home but would be a part of the community as mistress of Everleigh and could be a social leader in the neighborhood if she chose to be.

They all occupied themselves in the evenings with conversation and cards. Once they engaged in a spirited game of charades. Often there was music, though none of them pretended to any extraordinary talent.

And just occasionally it was possible for Justin to steal an hour or so to be alone out at the summerhouse without feeling that he was neglecting anyone. He varied his destination one afternoon, however, after he had spent the morning leading a group through the portrait gallery in the north wing and then taking those who had a head for heights up to the balcony that surrounded the base of the dome. After luncheon he collected Captain from the stables and took him for a walk to the lake.

He had written a letter to Ricky a few days before and sent it by special messenger. Hilda would read it to him. Justin had explained that he had not come during July because he had needed to go in search of his sister to bring her home. *"But it hurts my heart that I will be unable to see you in person for a while,"* he had written. *"I will come as soon as I possibly can, Ricky, but I cannot say exactly*

when. I think of you every day and miss you every hour."
He had sent his love and asked Ricky to tell Wes and Hilda
that he sent love to them too.

It was not a fully satisfactory explanation. Ricky had a
very literal mind. When one told him one would come in
July, he expected that one would make an appearance on
one of those thirty-one days—and somehow he always
knew what month it was and what day of that month. He
could not think in abstractions. *For a while* and *as soon as
I possibly can* would very likely mean to him that Justin
was not coming for a long time, that therefore Justin did not
really love him. Perhaps the mention of a sister would
wound him more than it would console, suggesting as it
might that Justin's sister meant more to him than Ricky did.

Justin did not know quite why Ricky had grown so at-
tached to him during those years. Perhaps it was because
he had always believed he was the protector and Justin the
one in need of protection. It had been a novel role for him.
He was the one who had first invited Justin inside Wes's
house. It was he who had offered—with a huge, anxious
eagerness, lest Wes and Hilda forbid it—that Justin share
the loft with him, with a curtain between the two halves to
mark their territory. Ricky had loved the fact that they
could talk after they went to bed at night and that Justin
would actually listen to him—and respond. He had loved
settling in his bed and telling Justin about the new duck-
lings on the village pond or how Hildy could not believe he
had chopped so much wood all in one morning or how the
village baker had given him a currant cake all for himself
after he had swept off the step of the bakery without being
asked but how he had brought half the cake home for Hildy
because she was always giving *him* food and it was nice to
give back. He had assured Justin very kindly that he did not

look *very* ugly with his broken nose even though Wes had said he did that very evening. Ricky told Justin he would love him forever and ever even if he *did* have a bust nose.

When he had left Wes's house and his job at the quarry to return to Everleigh, he ought perhaps to have said a firm and final goodbye to them all, Justin thought as he picked up a broad stick Captain had brought and deposited at his feet and hurled it as far as he could. His dog tore after it. It would have been ultimately easier on Ricky, easier on him.

But an idea had been forming in his head ever since he read Wes's letter. He did not know how workable it would be, or how desirable to his elderly blacksmith, whom it would involve. It was not always wise to try playing God with other people's lives, after all. Sometimes it was necessary, as with his forcing Maria to leave Prospect Hall to return here. At other times it was not. And it was never wise to act impulsively. Just consider his marriage proposal, as a case in point. He stood on the bank of the lake, gazing out across it, occasionally stooping to pick up the stick, wrestle with a playfully snarling Captain for possession of it, and then hurl it into the distance.

He needed to ponder his idea carefully before acting on it and perhaps regretting it for the rest of his life.

It was a large natural lake, fed by the waterfall, which cascaded down the steep hillside to his right. Its waters emptied into the river that flowed through the valley below the house. His grandfather had had a wooden mock-Chinese bridge constructed over the narrow part of the lake just below the falls. It had steps leading up to it and down at the other side. It had a bend in the middle, taking it across the other half at a different angle. There was a roof over the central part, pointed like a cone but with four corners that were curled upward. It was fanciful and brightly painted and probably did not resemble any bridge that had ever been constructed in China. On the far side was a boathouse.

Justin went to stand on the bridge. He gazed at the waterfall and let the sound of rushing water fill his ears and shut out the rest of the world. Captain, minus his stick, trotted across the bridge behind him and sniffed about the boathouse.

Justin looked up at the grotto—the cave in the hillside to one side of the waterfall. Someone had once called it a grotto, because the word was more evocative than *cave*, he supposed, and the name had stuck. It was far larger inside than it looked to be from here and used to be a favorite boyhood haunt of his. He had been a bandit of the Robin Hood variety and a marooned sea captain and a spy hiding out from his enemies there and a thousand other heroic characters. A boy's imagination was limitless, after all. He wondered if blankets and cushions were still stored in the boathouse and—if they were—when they had last been laundered.

They were still there. They also looked and smelled clean and free of mildew. He took a few with him and climbed to the grotto. It was not far up the hill or difficult to reach, but one definitely felt cut off from the world when one was inside it. He spread a blanket on the stone floor, sat close to the entrance, a cushion at his back, and made room for Captain, who had scrambled up after him. The dog sniffed every inch of the cave, panted in Justin's face as if to ask if they were *really* going to stop here for a while, turned in a few circles when he guessed the answer to be yes, and then plopped down on the blanket to gaze out at the lake.

There was surely nothing quite as blissful as solitude,

Justin thought. Of course, one did tend to bring one's teeming thoughts along with one, but a few minutes of stillness, during which one concentrated upon one's breath and nothing else, usually helped quell them. Maria—how was he going to secure a proper come-out Season and a happy future for her? His father—had he really been trapped into marrying Lilian Dickson? Ricky—how could he atone for letting him down? Lady Estelle Lamarr—how could he have been so gauche as to rush into proposing to her? The Season in London next year—how was he going to find a countess soon enough to help with Maria? Could the Duke of Netherby help—or the duchess? Lady Estelle Lamarr— why did she have to be so dashed beautiful and so dashed . . . vibrant and . . . Argh!

Finally his thoughts stilled enough that he could close his eyes and be lulled by the sound of the waterfall.

After luncheon Estelle went with several of the other guests to look inside the greenhouses. Maria was with them. She had explained ahead of time that she was not at all knowledgeable about the plants within them, though she did intend to learn. Fortunately it did not matter. One of the gardeners was there, and he cheerfully agreed to walk about with them and identify all the plants and answer all their questions. They spent a very agreeable hour there.

"You will not mind, Maria, if Leonard and I go and sit in the summerhouse for a while with Patricia and Irwin?" her aunt Margaret Dickson asked when they came outside at last into the relatively cool air of an English summer afternoon. "We feel too lazy to do anything else even remotely strenuous, but it would be a pity to return to the house so soon."

"Of course I do not mind," Maria assured all four of them. She stood and watched them go while everyone else was dispersing, a few to the house, others to different outdoor activities.

Mr. and Mrs. Sharpe were making their way toward the fountain at the center of the formal gardens, where the Ormsbury aunts and uncles were gathered. Bertrand was going to go riding with a group of the cousins. Another group was going to walk along the path on the other side of the river. Estelle decided she would walk to the lake, since she still had not been there. She turned to see if Maria wished to go with her, but Maria spoke first. She was still watching her aunts and uncles make their way toward the summerhouse.

"Estelle," she said, "I am going to go and speak with them. Will you come with me?"

She did not mean just social chitchat. Estelle could tell that from the pinched, determined look on her face and the tone of her voice.

"Of course," Estelle said. That embarrassing scene in the drawing room a few days ago had not ruined the house party, as it might very well have done. Maria's apology had gone a great way toward clearing the air, and they had all been enjoying themselves since. The three distinct family groups were mingling well despite the social differences between them, and Maria appeared to be increasingly comfortable in her role as hostess. The Earl of Brandon did his part as host.

That scene had had a lingering effect, however, and Estelle guessed that it haunted Maria. If the earl's aim in inviting them all here had been to restore his sister to her family and make her feel comfortable even with his own, then Estelle was not sure he had succeeded. What would happen after they all returned home? Would that be the end of that? Would there be any future such visits here? Would Maria make any future visits to any of them?

And now it seemed that Maria herself was ready to confront the issue. Estelle could not help but admire her—if that, indeed, was her intention.

"Ah, there you are, Maria," Mr. Leonard Dickson said in his usual hearty manner when they all arrived at the summerhouse at the same time. "You decided to come too, did you? And you as well, Lady Estelle? This is grand."

Estelle was not sure Maria's aunts and uncles were truly happy to see them. Perhaps they had been looking forward to relaxing for a while, just the four of them. But they all smiled and made a fuss. They were pleasant people. Estelle liked them.

They left the long windows wide open and sat gazing out at the view for a while, exclaiming a little self-consciously about the beauty of it all. But Estelle had been right about Maria's intention.

"Tell me about Mama," she said at last—and caused a sudden, uncomfortable silence.

"Well," Mrs. Chandler said. "She was the third of the four of us—younger than both Leonard and me, older than Sarah. She was by far the loveliest. Aunt Bertha—Lady Maple—took her to London when she was seventeen, and she met and fell in love with your father and married him, all within a month. It was a happy love story, Maria."

"It was grand," Mr. Dickson agreed, rubbing his hands together and beaming at his niece.

"Why just Mama and no one else?" Maria asked. "Why did *you* not go to London, Aunt Patricia? And why not Aunt Sarah?"

"I already had my eye on Irwin," Mrs. Chandler said, laughing. "And Sarah was only fifteen at the time."

"You have it the wrong way around, lass," Mr. Chandler said to his wife. *"I* had my eye on *you.*"

"I believe," Mrs. Dickson said, "it was mutual. We were all wondering why it was taking the two of you so long to recognize the truth and announce your betrothal."

Maria was looking at the palms of her hands. "I want to know," she said. "I *need* to know. All I know of Mama I learned from her. She never spoke of any of you except to say that you had all quarreled with her after she married Papa because you were jealous of her. She never spoke of her childhood or girlhood. And she did not say any more about Lady Maple than that she introduced Mama to the *ton* and Papa saw her and fell in love with her at her first ball. And that Lady Maple quarreled with her afterward because she was jealous that Mama had done so much better than she had herself. Lady Maple married a baronet while Mama married an earl. I loved Mama. I adored her. But . . ."

Her voice trailed away, and Mr. Chandler shifted in his chair, causing it to creak alarmingly, and cleared his throat.

"Why was Mama the only one to go to London?" Maria asked. "And please . . . Please do not spare my feelings. It is only recently that it has seemed a bit odd to me that everyone was so jealous and everyone quarreled with her. I expected mean, nasty, *evil* people. But I cannot see any of those things in you. Or in any of my cousins. Or even in Lady Maple despite what she said a few days ago. *Tell* me about my mother."

"Eh, lass," Mr. Dickson said, sitting back in his chair. "You loved her, and that is as it ought to be. And you loved your papa, I daresay. The last thing we want to do . . ."

"Leonard," his sister said. "She needs to know some things from our point of view. It is *only* a point of view,

Maria. People can have vastly different views of the same set of facts. So I will tell you this. Lilian was indeed very beautiful. She was also restless, and she was obsessed by the story of Aunt Bertha, who met Sir Cuthbert Maple at an assembly in Harrogate when she was a girl, and so took his fancy that he offered her carte blanche then and there. He intended to make her his mistress, in other words. She was not a *lady*, after all, and no one could have expected him to marry her. But Aunt Bertha held out for marriage anyway and got it. This is the story as the family knows it, at least. It may not be true in all its details. She turned herself into a lady and distanced herself from her family in Yorkshire. She did not cut herself off entirely, however. She used to descend upon us once in a while. Her visits were legendary. She always brought us gifts. Do you remember, Leonard? During one of those visits, when Lilian was barely seventeen, she begged to be taken to London and made into a lady. Our father tried to forbid it, but he was a bit intimidated by his sister and gave in without much of a fight."

"My grandfather?" Maria said.

"He was not a well man," Mr. Dickson told her. "He did not come here for your mother's wedding. He died just before you were born. Your grandmother died six years before him."

"I did not know that." Maria was still examining her hands. "Whose version of the meeting of my mama and papa is the correct one? The version Mama always told me and everyone else? Or the one Lady Maple told a few days ago?"

"Oh, Maria," Mrs. Dickson said, and she leaned forward in her chair as though to cover one of Maria's hands with her own. It was out of reach unless she got to her feet, however. "None of us were there. Except Aunt Bertha and Lilian herself, that is. But it was a long time ago—more than twenty years. Does it really matter who was right? Your mama and papa were very fond of each other, weren't they?"

Maria said nothing for a while but continued to frown at her hands. Her aunts and uncles were looking quite distressed, Estelle could see. It was obvious to her that they did not want to speak freely. Maria was their niece, after all, and they were clearly fond of her.

"Tell me about the quarrel," Maria said.

Mr. Dickson sighed audibly before drawing breath again. "Lilian's task when she married your father was . . . colossal, Maria," he said. "Our aunt had taught her to speak like a lady and to behave like one. But suddenly she was a *countess*. She had so much else to learn. After the wedding she took us all aside—Patricia, Sarah, Margaret, and me—and explained that it would be best if we kept out of the way for a while. She—"

"She was ashamed of us, Leonard," his sister said bluntly. "She did not want her new associates to see what she had come from. Or to *hear* what she had come from. I beg your pardon, Maria, but—"

"I did ask for the truth," Maria said. "So, according to your perception, it was *Mama* who quarreled with *you*?"

"Let us not call it a quarrel," Mrs. Dickson said. "It was more of an *agreement*."

"Margaret the peacemaker," her sister-in-law said, shaking her head. "There was nothing *agreeable* about it. We were given our marching orders, and we marched."

"There was no further communication?" Maria asked.

"Your father wrote a very kind letter to each of us when your grandpapa died," Mr. Dickson said, "and then again when you were born. His solicitor informed us of his demise. We all wrote to commiserate with the new Earl of Brandon, his son, and with Lilian, your mother. We did not hear back from either one. I learned just this week that Brandon—your brother—was gone from home for years before his father died and for a while after. That would explain why he did not answer our letters."

"Because he stole all of Mama's most precious jewelry," Maria said sharply.

"Perhaps," Mrs. Chandler said with a sigh. "We know nothing about that, Maria. And we did not know of your move with your mother to that other home. She did not inform us. We did not know of her illness or of her passing until Brandon wrote to us. We would not have let you bear the burden of all that alone, my dear. Our letters of commiseration came to you very late, I am afraid. We just did not know that our own sister had had a lingering illness and died." Her voice shook a little and she blinked away tears as her husband took out a large handkerchief and handed it to her.

No one spoke for a while.

"Papa wrote to you but Mama never did?" Maria asked at last.

"The earl your father was a very kind gentleman, Maria," Mrs. Dickson said, evading the second part of Maria's question.

"And a very honorable man," Mr. Dickson added. "He never for a moment made us feel during the week we were here for the wedding that we were inferior in any way. He was interested in our lives. I can remember him shaking my hand and calling me brother after the wedding."

"His son, your brother, is like him in a number of ways," Mrs. Chandler said. "Maria, are you quite *sure* he took Lilian's jewelry? He must have been a very wealthy young man. One cannot imagine *why* he would have done such a spiteful and *wrong* thing. And he seemed a very pleasant boy when we were here. He was only thirteen or fourteen, I seem to recall."

"Of course I am sure," Maria cried. "And of course *Papa* was sure. He sent him away, never to return. He never mentioned his name again."

"Your father gave *theft* as the reason for what he did?" Mrs. Chandler asked.

"I was eight years old," Maria said. "Papa said *nothing*. He would not say why Jus— He would not say why his *son* was gone. And Mama would not say in his hearing. But I think it killed him. He changed after that. He was sadder. And thinner. He spent more time than ever with me, and he smiled a lot and was always kind. But he was not . . . *fun* any longer. He did not laugh."

"Oh, Maria." Mrs. Chandler got to her feet, closed the distance between them, and drew her niece up and into her arms. "I am *so* sorry you lost your papa when you were so young. And that you went through all you did with your mama without any of us to help you. I am so sorry."

They were weeping then in each other's arms, and Mr. Dickson was blowing his nose loudly into his handkerchief while Mr. Chandler stood and went to stand in the gap between the windows and looked out.

"You loved her all the time, then?" Maria asked when she could. "You love *me*?"

"Aye, lass," Mr. Dickson said as he stuffed his handkerchief back into his pocket. "You are our niece. Our flesh and blood. We won't let you be all alone ever again, even if you go and marry a duke. You are stuck with us from now on, whether you like it or not."

Maria was laughing through her tears. "Oh, I like that,"

she said as her uncle got to his feet to enfold her in his arms.

It was not happily-ever-after, Estelle thought as she stood quietly and moved to the doorway and through it, past Mr. Chandler. Maria had genuinely loved her mother and still did. It was perfectly clear that the late Countess of Brandon had been a thoroughly disagreeable woman. It was not to be expected that Maria would fully accept that, however. So perhaps she would always be a bit suspicious of the version of events her aunts and uncles—and her great-aunt—had given. And they understood that and sympathized with her. And loved her. They would have a relationship with her going forward, and she with them. The Earl of Brandon had been right to invite them.

She was not needed here any longer, Estelle decided. Maria had not needed her at all, in fact, except as moral support. She drew a few deep breaths of the summer air and thought that after all she would have time to walk to the lake. She did not need company. Indeed, the chance of an hour or so of solitude seemed quite blissful.

She turned her steps in that direction.

Thirteen

Justin did not know how long he had been sitting in the grotto—he had not brought a watch with him—but he did not think it was important to hurry back. However, it seemed that his peace was in danger of being shattered. Captain had scrambled up onto his haunches and was panting while he gazed intently outward.

"Quiet, Cap," Justin murmured.

A lone figure had come into sight, strolling along the bank of the lake in the direction of the bridge. His first instinct was to withdraw farther back into the cave until she went away. But if she should decide to sit on the bank as she had beside the river north of her home a few weeks ago and remove her shoes and stockings and lift her skirt up over her knees and *then* look up and see him anyway, she would be horribly embarrassed, and he would feel like a Peeping Tom. He stayed where he was. His dog was still alert and watching, but he was no longer panting.

Lady Estelle Lamarr, Justin suspected, liked solitude as much as he did. Else why had she been alone that day by the river? Why was she alone now? And why was she still unmarried and presumably content to live with her twin in a modest manor in the depths of the country when she could probably marry very eligibly anytime she chose?

He did not want to be alone with her. He had made a thorough ass of himself at the summerhouse with his proposal of marriage and the subsequent kiss—after she had refused his offer. He had felt an inconvenient attraction to her later that same day when he stopped for a private conversation with her during the tour of the state apartments. That had been unwise. He had kept his distance from her as much as he could during the days since then.

She did not sit on the bank. She strolled all the way to the bridge and halfway across it before stopping under the roof, just at the bend, to gaze at the falls as he had done earlier, her arms crossed on the balustrade before her and pushing up her bosom as she leaned on them. With just a slight turn of the head she would be looking right at him. Would she see him in the shadows? Or his dog?

Why wait to find out?

"It is one of the loveliest sights in the park," he said, raising his voice so she would hear him above the sound of rushing water.

She looked both ways, startled.

"Over here," he said. "To your left."

She surprised him by smiling when she saw him. "That looks like fun," she said.

"I always thought we should have a resident hermit here," he said. "But it might be considered a little eccentric."

"Counting his beads and plaiting his beard?" she said.

"It would be very picturesque. Who would bring him food, though? Or her. Are there female resident hermits? It would be a great injustice to women if there were not."

"I thought they lived on air," he said. "Hermits of both genders, that is."

"Oh dear, their lives must be very tedious, then," she said. And laughed.

"It would be a long walk from the kitchen three times a day," he said. "The servants would start handing in their notice en masse. Perhaps it is as well we have never had a hermit."

His mother and father used to talk nonsense sometimes. He could remember one time becoming helpless with giggles as he listened until they turned to him and his father pounced upon him and tickled him while his mother urged him to stop before he made Justin ill. Where the devil had that memory come from?

"Come and see," he said. "It is just a cave, but it has always been known as the grotto."

"And why not?" she said, walking to the end of the bridge and descending the steps to the grass. "*Grotto* is a far more romantic word. How do I get there?"

"Go and fetch her, Cap," he said, and his dog bounded out and down to her.

There were rocks. Big, smooth, flat boulders like giant steps. It was neither a difficult nor a dangerous climb and really the grotto was not far above the level of the lake anyway. He stepped out to offer his hand, but she did not need it. She made her way carefully toward him, one hand on Captain's back, while Justin wondered why on earth he had invited her inside the cave.

"The blankets and cushions are *not* damp and moldy," he assured her when she lowered her head and peered inside. "They are stored in the boathouse with towels for swimmers."

"Is there a boat too?" she asked.

"Yes, there is," he told her.

"It is quite splendid," she said of the cave, "and far bigger than it looks from the outside. Did you use it as a place to hide when you were a boy? I bet you did."

"You would not lose your wager," he said.

She came right inside and sat on the blanket he had spread earlier. She arranged a cushion behind her back, then took off her bonnet when she discovered that she could not lean her head back with it on. She set it down beside her. They sat across from each other, their knees drawn up, not quite touching.

"I thought you were with Maria," he said.

"I was," she told him. "One of the gardeners gave a large group of us a very interesting tour of the greenhouses. He knows everything there is to know about all the plants, including the countries from which they all came. Everyone went their own way after that. Maria's Yorkshire aunts and uncles went off to sit in the summerhouse. I was going to suggest that Maria come here with me to relax for a while, but before I could say a word she decided to go after them and wanted me to go with her. She asked them about her mother and insisted upon the truth as they knew it. It was an uncomfortable conversation for them all, but I believe it is going to help enormously. I left them hugging one another and shedding tears."

"Ah, reconciliation," he said. "It is what I hoped for. Though there was always the chance the opposite would happen and they would all part forever after a bitter quarrel."

"I do not believe that will happen now," she said. "I believe Maria has discovered a family who will stick with her in the future. Poor thing. She loved her mother very dearly. But I think she is beginning to understand that the countess was not always perfect."

He gazed at her while Captain nudged at his hand in the hope of being petted. Justin obliged him.

"I did not meet her," Lady Estelle said, her eyes steady on his. "But I think she must have been an unpleasant woman. I cannot imagine any other mother refusing help from professional nurses who had been sent to her, no doubt at considerable expense, and insisting instead that she be tended exclusively by her very young daughter. Maria was barely nineteen when she died."

What could he say? He chose to say nothing.

"I am sorry," she said, smiling fleetingly. "It is none of my business—as usual. But I have interrupted your musings. I ought to leave you to them and continue my walk."

"I made it your business, Lady Estelle," he said, smoothing his hand along Captain's back, "when I asked you to come here as a companion for my sister. I will say this much. I was badly hurt when my father remarried. Perhaps children always are under such circumstances, but—"

"No, not necessarily," she said. "How old were you?"

"Thirteen," he said.

"I was seventeen when my father married my stepmother," she said. "There were complications in their courtship and they broke off their betrothal and went their separate ways. Bertrand and I had to work very hard to bring them back together and get them to marry each other on a Christmas Eve. We did it because it was obvious to us that they were painfully in love with each other, and because our father would never have been happy without her. And because his happiness mattered to us. I will always love my mother, though I have no conscious memories of her. But I adore my stepmother. Children are not *always* resentful of the second marriage of their surviving parent."

"My father and mother were very close," he said. "There was affection and laughter in the house when I was a child, and I was included in it. They made me feel that I was their most prized treasure. I thought my father would go insane after she died. I thought he would never be happy again. After three years he was just beginning to pull himself back from the brink. But when he went to London for the parliamentary session and came back with a . . . a *girl* not quite five years older than me and announced that he would be marrying her within a month, I thought I must be in the middle of a bizarre sort of nightmare. I was biased against her, of course. I will admit that. But no matter how hard I tried, I could not understand *why* he was doing it. Apart from the fact that she was extraordinarily lovely, that was. But it seemed so unlike my father to be bowled over by *just* that. It seemed to me that she lacked character and . . . and anything else that could possibly interest him. I was terribly hurt. We had been closer than ever since my mother's death. He had promised to return from London just as soon as he possibly could. We were going to go to Cornwall, he to spend time with his sisters and brothers-in-law, I to frolic with the cousins. We had been planning it since Christmas. But . . . Well, I felt abandoned, forgotten, pushed aside for someone who was more important to him, though I could not for the life of me understand why. It hurts to lose faith in a parent you have always looked up to as perfect in every way."

"The story Lady Maple told a few days ago about the first meeting of your father and stepmother was new to you?" she asked.

"Entirely," he said. "But it explained . . . everything."
And he did mean *everything*. Even the way it had all ended
between him and his father. For before all else, his father
had been an honorable man. An honorable man married a
woman whose reputation he had compromised, even if he
had been tricked into doing so. And an honorable man defended his wife at the expense of all else. Even his only son.

"Yes," she said. "I suppose it did." She moved as though
she intended to rise.

"Stay awhile," he said.

She settled back against her cushion.

She was wearing some perfume. Something floral. Gar-
denia? It was not a harsh scent, though, as many women's
perfumes were. It was soft and subtle. It seemed part of her.
He had not consciously noticed it in the summerhouse or
when he stood with her in one of the twin sitting rooms in
the state apartments, but he must have done so unconsciously.

"When you were banished from here," she said, "you
did not take a fortune in jewels with you. Presumably you
had nothing or next to nothing. You were gone for a number
of years. Where did you go? What did you do?"

He had never mingled his worlds. Wes and Hilda had
known nothing of his life here. They had not even known
until he got word of his father's death that he was heir to
an earldom. All they had guessed was that he was a gentleman by birth, down on his luck. No one in this world, not
even his aunt and uncle, knew about his other life. They
knew only that he had survived and that three or four times
a year he had gone to pick up the letters they had written
or forwarded to him and had sent them a brief note to
acknowledge their receipt. He had been thinking earlier of
a plan that would bring his worlds together, but it had not

yet taken definite shape in his mind and perhaps never would. It might be preferable to leave well enough alone.

Was he now to bring those two worlds together simply by answering the questions this woman had asked him? This woman who less than a week ago had refused his offer to make her his countess? This virtual stranger?

"I went," he said. "I had a choice of four directions and infinite subdirections within each. I went west. I stayed at inns and ate at taverns for a week or so while reality set in. There was no going back home. Ever. Not while my father lived. There was no home. There was no replacement for the little money I had. There was no income."

"You had no friends to go to?" she asked. "You would not—or could not—go to any of your relatives? There was no chance of genteel employment—perhaps in London?"

There had been possibilities. He had had a few friends who might have helped. His uncle Rowan would have recommended him to some employment suited to his education and background. His aunts and uncles in Cornwall would almost certainly have taken him in and pointed him in the right direction if he had told them he wished to earn his way. He had chosen instead to go his own road—quite literally.

"There was a matter of pride and some stubbornness," he said. "And despite all the pain I was feeling, I had an image of myself as a young adventurer striding off into the world and into the future to make his fortune."

"And did you succeed?" she asked.

"I made my future," he said. "One really has no choice over that, short of ending it all. I never considered taking my life. I worked wherever I could, and pride—as well as necessity—led me to take anything I was offered. It was never anything even remotely attractive. The respect with which I had been treated as a matter of course for the first twenty-two years of my life meant nothing when I stepped out of my own . . . bubble. It was in fact a cause of ridicule at best, of vicious hostility at worst. I was considered good for nothing—and was told so. I swept out taverns and cleaned latrines. I fed pigs and mucked out their pens. I worked in a coal mine until there was a cave-in along one of the underground tunnels—I was in the other at the time. I worked on a dock, loading and unloading freight. I could go on and on. Some jobs lasted a few days, others a few weeks. I slept wherever I could, sometimes under a solid roof, sometimes in a barn or beneath a hedgerow. After two years I met the man who was to become my best friend."

"The one who broke your nose," she said.

"Yes. Wes," he said. "Wesley Mort. He was and is a foreman at a stone quarry. After he had knocked me to the tavern floor and I was only semiconscious, he voiced his contempt for me and all men of my class and told me that if I wanted to be a real man I could come and work for him. Which I did two days later, much to his astonishment. I worked for him for four years, until I heard about my father's death and came back here. He was not easy on me. Quite the contrary. He gave me all the most brutal tasks during the first year or so and kept me at them for longer hours than he kept anyone else—because I was slower and worse than useless, in his stated opinion. I earned nothing for the extra time I put in."

"But he became your best friend?" She had set an elbow on her knee and had her chin propped on her hand. She was looking slightly amused, Justin thought.

"He kept his end of our bargain and stopped calling me Mr. La-di-da after the first week," he said. "Ever after I was Juss. He worked as hard as I did, I must explain, and con-

siderably harder until I toughened up. I lived with him and
Hilda, his woman. I shared a loft with his brother, Ricky. I
taught Wes to read and write, though he still gets frustrated
at the slowness with which he does both. I used to tell Ricky
stories, and Wes and Hilda would often listen, though Wes
pretended not to. It was beneath his dignity to take delight
from an imaginary world. We made a wagon between us,
and both Wes and Hilda had the use of my horse to pull it."

"Ricky was a child?" she asked.

"He is a few years younger than I am," he said. "But his
mind is that of a child. When I went to Wes's house to get
work, it was Ricky who invited me inside for a bowl of
Hilda's soup to make me feel better. Then he showed me his
loft and decided it was large enough for the two of us. Hilda
put up a curtain to divide the space in two."

"And that is where you lived for four years," she said.

"And for a couple of months each year even now," he
said. "The Earl of Brandon becomes Juss Wiley, stone
hewer, twice a year and is happy again."

He gazed at her, his eyes and his whole face deliberately
blank. He had not told anyone else these things.

"You love them," she said.

"Yes," he said curtly. "There were no deductions from
my wages, by the way, for room and board."

"And I suppose," she said, "you did not charge for the
reading and writing lessons or for the use of your horse."

"It did not occur to me," he said. "Perhaps I ought to
send a bill."

She had a way of looking. It was not exactly a smile. It
was a . . . warmth. As though she smiled inside but chose
to keep most of it to herself. But some spilled over into her
eyes and onto her face nonetheless. She was looking that
way at him now.

"What?" he said.

"I bet his bill would be larger," she said.

"Undoubtedly," he said. "Wes is as hard as nails. Or as a boulder. But yes, I love him."

"And this," she said, "is why you are so . . . large?" She seemed to have taken herself by surprise with her question. Even in the shadowed light of the cave he could see that color had flooded her cheeks.

He opened his hands and looked at his palms. There were still calluses at the base of each finger. His badges of honor. And the hands themselves were larger than they had once been. No longer the hands of a gentleman. He closed his fingers into his palms.

"I am sorry," she said. "It was not intended as an insult. You looked very . . . frightening the first time I saw you. It did not help, I suppose, that I was sitting on the riverbank and you were on horseback and Captain looked as though he was coming for my throat."

Captain woofed.

"You ought not to have been there alone," Justin said.

"Now you sound like my aunt," she told him.

"Not your brother?" he asked her. "Did he not scold you?"

"I did not tell him," she said. "He *would* have scolded, and I would have been forced to quarrel with him and accuse him of sounding like our aunt."

"The one who raised you," he said. "What is she like? Apart from the fact that she did not approve of dogs as pets."

"She was very strict," she said. "Very proper. Very pious. Very a lot of upright, moral things. She has a strong sense of what is right and how a house should be run and how all the people in it ought to behave, both family and servants. She ruled my uncle and my two cousins and Bertrand and me. Bert was brought up to be a gentleman. I was raised to be a lady. We were raised to value church and prayer and morality. We were *never* told that our father was a rake and a ne'er-do-well. We were taught to respect him. But whenever he came to visit, he felt his sister-in-law's disapproval and agreed with her unspoken condemnation. He has told us so since then. He thought we were in the best possible place with the best possible people, and he never stayed for longer than a few days at a time. He did not want to contaminate us with his presence. It did not help that we were taught to be quiet except when spoken to. We stayed quiet when we were with him, waiting for *him* to speak with *us*, but he never spoke except to ask a few stilted questions that could be answered with a monosyllable. Our father believed we hated him and wanted him to go away. So he went."

"I am sorry," he said.

"You need not be," she told him. "We did have an excellent upbringing. And we were loved, as I believe I told you before. Strict discipline does not necessarily preclude love, you know."

"But you longed for your father," he said. It had shrieked through every word of her account of her childhood. Or perhaps more through the look on her face and the tone of her voice than through her actual words. She and her brother had been reconciled with him, but much damage had been done them anyway.

"I am so *thankful*," she said, "that he did not die before we had a chance to get to know him properly, to understand him and why he behaved as he did, to be fully . . . restored to him."

He patted his dog's head and gazed at her. Captain turned his head to pant in his face. His breath was not exactly sweet.

He watched Lady Estelle swallow. "I ought not to have said that," she said. "It was insensitive. You were not as fortunate as we were."

"My father was ailing for several months before his death," he said. "I do not believe he ever asked for me or tried to send word to me."

"Would there have been any way for him to contact you?" she asked.

He shook his head.

"How did you hear of his passing, then?" she asked.

"My aunt and uncle knew where to send letters," he said. "Though it was often weeks or months before I got them."

"Mr. and Mrs. Sharpe?" she said.

He nodded. "They wrote me of his death."

She clasped her arms about her legs and lowered her head until her forehead touched her knees. "Is that where the worst of your pain is?" she asked him.

It was not perfectly clear what she meant by *that*. But he understood her to mean the fact that his father had apparently stuck by the decision he had made that day when he banished his only son. Even when he was dying he had stuck by it. There had been no olive branch, no offer of reconciliation.

It was a pain so deep that he never, *ever* thought of it. It would, he knew, be unbearable if he allowed it to intrude upon his conscious mind and take up residence there.

"You are mistaken, Lady Estelle," he said. "That was all a very long time ago. There is no pain." He set his head back against the stone wall. The sound of the waterfall somehow sealed them in here as though the rest of the world no longer existed. "I suppose I am neglecting my guests. Is it teatime? Past teatime?"

"I have no idea," she said, lifting her head. "But I believe everyone can fend for themselves. And Maria is probably back at the house to see to it that no one starves."

He got to his feet anyway, careful not to straighten up and bang his head on the low rocks above it. He held out both hands to help her up. She looked at them before setting her own in them. Hers were slim, long-fingered, smooth-skinned. A lady's hands, half lost in his own. Hands that aroused his masculine protective instincts, though she did not strike him as the sort of woman who craved or even welcomed male protection. She was no one's typical image of a helpless female. Generalizations were useless things anyway. Not many people fit into them once one scratched the outer surface they presented to the world and took a good look at the person within.

She raised her eyes to his, her eyebrows slightly arched upward, as though to ask him why he was holding her hands if he was not intending to help her get to her feet. Why indeed? But their faces were suddenly uncomfortably close.

"You did not tell me if I was forgiven," he said. "For kissing you," he added when her brows rose a little higher.

"Did I not?" she said. "You were. You are."

"I regret," he said, "that I was so gauche. And so impetuous. Such a blockhead. I went about it all wrong."

"The kiss?" Her voice was almost a whisper.

"That too," he said. "But I was referring to my proposal of marriage. I have always despised bended knee and rose-buds and poetic speeches and hand over heart. But there is surely a large range of possible behaviors between that and *'I wish you would marry me.'* I believe those were my very words, or something similar. I am glad you had the good sense to refuse me."

"Are you?" she said. "Then we are in perfect agreement." But there was a thread of amusement in her voice.

"Watch your head." He drew her to her feet and released his hold on her hands. Captain was on his feet too, eager to return to the outdoors.

"The blanket and cushions?" she said as he stepped out and turned to offer her a hand back down to the level bank beside the bridge.

"I will put them away later," he told her.

"Why not now?" she asked, and bent to pick up two cushions after tying the ribbons of her bonnet and linking them over her arm.

They put everything away neatly inside the boathouse. After Justin shut the door securely behind them, he turned and saw Estelle standing a few feet away, between him and the bridge, in full sunlight. Her pale blue dress was the exact color of the sky. She was looking directly at him, that inner smile lighting her face. And . . . oh, God.

He took a step closer.

"I want you," he said.

Fourteen

She ought to have turned and run without stopping—over the bridge and all the way back to the house. There she ought to have grabbed Bertrand, dragged him up to the east wing to pack their bags, and then dashed down to the stables with him, retrieved their carriage, and sprung the horses all the way home to Elm Court.

That is what she ought to have done.

Instead she stood her ground. And swallowed. And frowned. And dropped her bonnet to the grass.

For she wanted him too. Though she did *not* say so out loud.

He was searching her eyes with his own. "Is it possible to pretend the summerhouse debacle did not happen?" he asked her.

"The proposal with all your very sensible reasons for making it?" she said. "My refusal in all its starkness? The kiss that followed despite it all?"

"No," he said. "I did not suppose it could be done."

"But perhaps it is possible to put it behind us," she said. "To dismiss it for the idiocy it was."

"It *was* idiotic," he said. "That proposal."

"It was," she agreed. "So was my response."

"You could not think of anything whatsoever that would induce you even to consider marrying me?" he said.

"I believe those were my exact words, or close enough," she said.

"It was idiocy?" He raised his eyebrows.

"Yes," she said.

"And the kiss?" he said. "Idiocy?"

Idiocy under the circumstances, yes. She shrugged.

And he took one more step closer, set his large hands on either side of her waist, and drew her forward until she was pressed to him all the way from her bosom to her knees. She looked into his eyes the whole time and saw depth there, not just the usual hard blankness. There was uncertainty too, perhaps. Yearning, maybe. Desire, definitely. She raised her hands and set them on his shoulders. And was shot through with such a charge of lust that she almost lost control of her knees. At least, she assumed it was lust. She had never before felt anything quite like it. It was more than just desire.

And he kissed her.

His lips were parted, and soon hers were too, and he ravaged her mouth with his tongue. She was no idle spectator while he did it. She sucked his tongue deeper, made inarticulate noises when he stroked the tip of it over the roof of her mouth, pressed herself closer to him, twined one arm about his neck, and pushed the fingers of the other hand into his hair. One of his hands spread over her upper back while the other went lower and pressed her to him.

She could feel the hardness of his desire through the layers of their clothing, and it half frightened, half excited her.

He was so terribly large. The whole of him. All breadth of shoulders and chest, all hard muscles and masculinity. Powerful arms, large hands, firm thighs. And he smelled enticingly musky with a cologne her brother did not use, or any other man she had ever been close to.

Both hands were now below her waist and pressing her to him. His head had moved back from hers and they were gazing into each other's eyes again.

"Estelle," he murmured.

"Lord Brandon, I—"

"Say my name," he said softly. "Let me hear you say it."

"Justin," she said, and watched him inhale slowly.

"You agreed to come here for two weeks," he said. "A little more than a week remains. At the end of your stay I will make a new offer. In quite different words. Unless, that is, you stop me before I can even launch into speech. It is my hope that by then your answer will have changed."

"You intend to *court* me?" she said.

"One of the genteel arts," he said. "I never learned how it is done. But I hope to change your mind . . . Estelle. How that will happen, I do not know. I must think of a way."

"Why?" she asked. He was still holding her to him. She still had her arms twined about his neck. A thick, powerful neck. He had the body—and the hands—of a laborer, she realized. And she lusted after him. She would not even pretend to herself that she did not.

"I want you," he said again, returning his hands to either side of her waist. "But I know I cannot have you outside of matrimony. And there. I have opened my mouth and stuck a large foot inside it again. I have given the impression that I would marry you for sex alone—which, by the way, I did not even mention in the summerhouse. I do indeed want you. But I also want *you*. And there *is* a difference, the one purely physical, the other more . . . But I am stuck for a sentence ender."

"Emotional?" she suggested.

He considered. "Is that what I mean?" he asked her.

In her case the wanting was entirely physical. It could not possibly be anything else. She had believed him when he denied stealing his stepmother's jewelry. But he had done *something*. And it had been so dreadful that his father, who had loved him dearly and with whom he had always been close, had banished him for life. There was, surely, only one possibility. And it was just as bad as theft. No, it was worse.

She could not want such a man in any but the most base physical way. She certainly could not marry him.

He had spent four years living and working with people he loved as dearly as he loved his own family members. He still spent time each year with them. That cottage by the stone quarry and the coarse laborer with his woman and his simpleminded brother were from a world that was alien to her. Not inferior, just . . . different. That made *him* different. How could she ever be close to him when half his life was lived in a world so different from her own that it might as well be a distant planet?

He kept vast swaths of himself to himself and presented a granite exterior to the world—at least to *her* part of the world. When she married, it would have to be to a man who welcomed her with open warmth into the very depths of his being, just as she would welcome him into the depths of hers. That could never happen with this man. His years away from home and the reason he had been sent away had deeply damaged him. She could neither mend nor heal him.

No one could. His father had died and stranded him in a life of guilt and probable regret. She could not, would not, take that on.

She slid her hands down to his shoulders.

"I believe it would be best for you, Lord Brandon," she said, "if you abandoned your . . . courtship now. For my answer at the end of next week if you asked the question again would surely be the same as it was the last time. I want a happy, light-filled marriage when the time comes. I— Ah, pardon me. That sounded like an insult and that is not what I intended. But . . . I feel no joy at the prospect of being your countess."

"Then it is a good thing you are not being asked to be my countess," he said, releasing his hold on her and bending to pick up her bonnet and hand it to her after brushing off a few blades of grass. "Not yet, anyway. Perhaps over the next week I can cause you to feel a little more joyful at the thought. No. A little would not suffice, would it? I shall see if I can fill you to the brim with light and joy at the idea of marrying me."

And suddenly she wanted to weep. The light had gone from his life when his mother died, he had once told her, but he had remained close to his father, who sounded like a kind, honorable man from what she had heard of him. He had been planning a summer holiday in Cornwall with his son just before he had married his second wife instead. Had joy deserted Justin forever after he had committed some heinous sin at the age of twenty-two and broken his father's heart? Was he grasping for a return of it now—with her?

It could not be done.

She put on her bonnet and tied the ribbons beneath her chin before turning without another word. Captain was lying at the bend in the middle of the bridge, his head up, watching them. He scrambled to his feet, waited for her to come up to him and run a hand over his huge head, and then went trotting off ahead of her.

Estelle made her way back to the house. The Earl of Brandon fell into step at her side but did not offer his arm. Or any conversation. They walked beside the river in silence, and she wondered if despite herself she was in love with him.

Justin settled Captain in the stables and paused to have a chat with a few of the cousins who had returned from a ride half an hour or so before and were gathered at the rail of the paddock, watching one of the grooms put a new horse through its paces. On his return to the house he went to the library to check the day's mail.

The library, normally a quiet haven, had been invaded. His uncle Rowan was in there facing one of the bookcases, his nose in a book he had drawn from one of the shelves. Nigel Dickson was standing not far from him, a sheet of paper in his hand. Viscount Watley was sitting in one of the leather chairs by the fireplace, reading. Angela Ormsbury, Aunt Felicity's daughter, sat on the companion chair at the other side of the fireplace, frowning down at the book she held, though it was not clear if she frowned because she was deeply absorbed or because she disapproved of what she was reading.

"I say," Nigel said eagerly when he saw Justin. "Mr. Sharpe has been as good as his word, Lord Brandon. He has made lists of recommended books for us. Yours is on the desk. This is mine." He waved the page he held. "I cannot wait to get Pa to take me to my favorite bookshop in

York. I daresay I will spend the whole of my allowance there and not even make a dent in the list."

"Those books do not all have to be read in a month," Uncle Rowan said with an affable smile for the young man. "It takes a lifetime to get to the end of a good reading list. More than a lifetime, in fact, but a lifetime is all any of us has. And what a horror story it would be if we *did* run out of everything worth reading. What would we do then? Your list is a bit different, Justin. I tried to avoid adding books I can see are already here."

"Thank you." Justin took a quick look before putting the list away in a top drawer. "I shall take it with me the next time I go to London."

He sat down at the desk and had a quick look through the pile of mail stacked there, mostly official estate business his secretary had already dealt with. There were two personal letters as well, though, one of them from Maria's aunt Sarah, addressed to him. She and her husband were enjoying their tour of Scotland, she had written, but they were very sorry it had coincided with the house party at Everleigh. She hoped it would be convenient to him and her niece if they invited themselves there sometime after their return. She would write again later.

"It would be so wonderful to meet Maria and to see you again," she had written. *"I remember that you were very kind to me when I was at Everleigh for Lilian's wedding to your father—who was also extremely kind, by the way. I recall being quite terrified because you were aristocrats and lived in a vast mansion, and I was just fifteen. But you befriended me, although you were only thirteen yourself, and made sure I relaxed and enjoyed myself."*

Despite the fact that he had been horribly bewildered

and upset at the time of that wedding, Justin could remember liking his new stepmother's family, who were all very different from her. They had been hearty and warm and genuine and comfortable in their own less-than-aristocratic identities—and yes, a bit awed by their surroundings and in need of some reassurance.

"A letter from your aunt Sarah you may be interested in reading," he said, handing it to Nigel. "She seems to be enjoying herself in Scotland."

His other letter was addressed in Hilda's handwriting. Justin wondered as he picked it up and broke the seal if his own letter had reached them before she wrote. Was Ricky *still* upset that he had failed to come in July?

It was a brief note. His own letter *had* arrived, and Hilda had read it to Ricky and he had run from the house. *"And that was the last we have seen of him, Juss. He is gone and we are frantic,"* she had written. There was no sign of him anywhere, and no one had seen him. He had never been farther from home than a few miles in any direction, but where could he be? He had no money on him that they knew of, or anything else except the clothes he was wearing. But he was gone without a trace. The *only* thing they could think of now—Hilda had both capitalized and heavily underlined the one word—was that he had gone to see Justin since Justin had not come to see him.

"But how would he know where to go?" she had written. *"How would he get there even if he did know? How would he manage without any money? And without someone to look after him? He won't be able to manage, and that is that. But it is all we can think of, Juss. We are at our wits' end. Wes is beside himself. He is running around in circles. And all the men from the quarry and all the neighbors are out looking."*

"It is grand that they intend coming here later," Nigel said, setting his aunt's letter down on the desk. "Aunt Sarah and Maria will surely like each other. I'll go find Pa and Aunt Patricia and tell them the Scottish tour is going well."

Justin smiled vacantly as the boy left the room, still clutching his precious book list, all youthful exuberance.

Justin's hands were tingling as he set down Hilda's letter. He could remember once when he had gone to the grotto by the waterfall without telling anyone and had fallen asleep there after playing for a while. It had been after dark when one of the gardeners had found him and carried him home to his parents, both of whom had been outside while search parties went in every direction. They were both so frantic that even Justin's five-year-old self had recognized the blind, helpless panic that consumed them. That was what Wes and Hildy would be feeling now for Ricky. It was what *he* was feeling. He felt sick to his stomach and wanted to dash off . . . But where?

Good God, could they possibly be right? But they would not have written to him until they had exhausted all other possibilities. And they had not searched alone. Friends, neighbors, fellow workers—*everybody* would have turned over every stone and forked over every haystack and searched every barn.

Ricky had listened to what Justin had written him and then promptly disappeared. Wes and Hilda had concluded that he was coming to find Justin. Mad as it seemed, it was possibly true. *Probably* true. Had he ever mentioned Everleigh Park in Ricky's hearing? Justin could not remember. Had he mentioned Hertfordshire? But even if he had . . . Well, Hertfordshire was a whole county. It covered a sizable area. How was Ricky ever going to find him? Without a man's mature understanding? Without company? Without money or belongings? Would he even know how to find his way home if he changed his mind? Did he *know* where he lived? Did he know it was in Gloucestershire? Justin's first instinct was to go dashing off there himself to help Wes with the search. But what end would that serve? None whatsoever. What *could* he do, then? *Anything?* His throat was dry. His tongue felt thick. His stomach churned.

"Bad news?" someone asked.

He looked up, frowning. His uncle and Angela were no longer in the library, he realized. Only Watley remained, still reclined in his chair by the fireplace, a finger holding his place in the book he was reading.

"A bit of a bother," Justin said, setting a still-tingling hand down on top of the letter. "It will sort itself out. I hope you had a pleasant ride. The landscape around here is quite scenic. Have you had tea? I am sorry I was not here myself. I have just returned to the house."

"I believe Lady Maria was having tea brought to the drawing room for whoever wanted it," Watley said. "I came here instead for a bit of quiet. Yes, the ride was very pleasant. Good company, lovely countryside."

"I have been showing your sister the grotto beside the waterfall out at the lake," Justin said. "I daresay she told you I offered her marriage a few days ago and she refused."

"Yes," Watley said. "She did tell me."

"I beg to inform you," Justin told him, "that I will be renewing the offer before you leave here next week."

"I see," Watley said. "And does Estelle know this too?"

"She does," Justin said. "Her answer would have been the same if I had asked again today. At least, I am almost certain it would have been. I hope to convince her over the next week that it will be worth her while to change her mind."

He was aware of the stilted nature of his words. And of the possible offensiveness of some of them. *I hope to convince her . . . that it will be worth her while to change her mind.* But his heart was still thumping and his head was still buzzing with the knowledge that Ricky was out there somewhere, wandering about England, or even Wales if he had got himself turned about the wrong way, in the hope of finding his friend Juss. Did he even know Justin's last name? Or his title name? Or that *Juss* stood for *Justin*?

"You plan to woo her, then?" Watley said. He had closed his book and set it down on the table beside him.

"That word makes me cringe," Justin said. "*Woo.* Is that what I will be doing? I do not know. But you ought to know that I hope to marry your sister."

"I am not her guardian," Watley said. "Neither is my father. Estelle is her own person."

"But you are her twin," Justin said. "The bond is close, I believe."

"It seems to be closer than any I have seen between mere siblings," Watley told him. "I will not say we read each other's mind. That would be ghastly. But we sense each other's feelings. Well, we more than just *sense* them. We feel *with* each other or *for* each other. I have often tried to verbalize just what the bond is, but have always found it impossible to do, even in my own head. We do not interfere with each other, though we sometimes intervene. There *is* a difference. If through bringing up this subject you hope to enlist my help in convincing Estelle that the title Countess of Brandon would be a good one for her, I must disappoint you, I am afraid. The choice, whether yea or nay, will be hers to make."

"If I cannot . . . woo my own woman, I would be a sorry excuse for a man," Justin said. "Whether I succeed or fail

will be all on me—and on your sister. I merely wanted you
to know my intentions. If you believe that I am taking unfair advantage of her in my own home when I invited her
here for another purpose entirely, then you may feel free to
say so."

He picked up Hilda's letter, unfolded it, folded it again
without reading any of it, set it on top of Sarah's letter, picked
it up once more, and slid it *beneath* her letter. He felt nauseated. *Where are you, Ricky? Are you frightened? Have you
been taken up as a vagrant somewhere and locked up in
a jail?*

He became aware of the silence and looked at Watley,
who was looking back.

"If you take unfair advantage of Estelle, she will tell you
so," Watley said. "If she chooses to marry you, she will do
so. If she chooses not to, that will be that. I will neither
intervene nor interfere unless your wooing should turn into
harassment. I do not expect it. I am not going to turn into
the heavy-handed brother either with her or with you. But I
wish you would believe me when I say I am a good listener.
Something in the letter you have shoved out of sight is con-
suming your mind and your emotions. I know whatever that
letter says is none of my business, and as soon as you have
told me so I will leave the library and never refer to the
matter again. If I may be of some assistance to you, however, I will sit here and listen."

It was not in Justin's nature—or had not been for the
past twelve years, anyway—to confide anything to any-
body. He bore his burdens alone. He buried his feelings
beneath the armor of tough stoicism he had erected
about himself soon after leaving home. But earlier this
afternoon—and to a certain degree at the summerhouse a
few days ago—he had let the sister beneath his guard. Was

he now to confide in the brother too? The man he hoped to make his brother-in-law?

"I have a friend who is missing," he said. "There is no trace of him close to home. His brother and . . . sister-in-law are frantic and believe that perhaps he is trying to come to me."

Watley was looking steadily at him, his eyebrows slightly raised.

"Ricky is thirty years old with the mind of a very young child," Justin told him. And he went on to explain the situation as briefly and clearly as he could.

"And you are not sure," Watley said when he was finished, "if he knows your full name and title. Or the name of your estate or what county it is in."

"But I cannot imagine Ricky setting out to come to me if he did not have at least one or two of those answers," Justin said. "Even if he knew all four, though, how could he possibly find me here? He has nothing with him. He has no money. And my fear is that even if he has changed his mind and decided to return home, he will not be able to find it or tell anyone exactly where he lives. I blame myself for saying I would go to see him in July and then not going."

"What you really blame yourself for," Watley said, "is letting him love you and loving him in return. Life can be damnable when one opens oneself to love. It can be even worse when one does not."

"Damned if you do, damned if you do not?" Justin said. He closed his eyes and set his hand flat on top of the two letters on his desk.

"But this is not the moment for either panic or philosophy," Watley said. "Let us think of what we can *do*."

"*We?*" Justin opened his eyes.

Watley shrugged. "I am your guest," he said. "If you

have your way, I will be your brother-in-law in the foresee-able future. More to the point, I am a fellow human being. You are going to have to get out the word throughout the county—a full description of Ricky and an emphasis upon his great importance to *you*, the Earl of Brandon. Titles and influence can be useful things at times. Fellow landowners. Magistrates. Clergymen. We need to make a list. And offer a reward—but only if he is detained without violence and treated with kindness."

"If he *gets* as far as Hertfordshire," Justin said.

"We must at least consider the possibility that he will," Watley said. "For the rest of the country we must consider notices in newspapers, among other things."

Justin sat back in his chair, drew a deep breath, and let it out slowly through his mouth. "Perhaps," he said, "they will yet find him fast asleep in the hay inside someone's barn close to home that they have not thought to search yet."

"It would be the best possible outcome," Watley agreed. "Though it does seem unlikely. May I make another suggestion? Will you send for my sister? You said you told her about those years you spent living with Ricky's brother. She may have some ideas. A woman's perspective and all that."

Justin got to his feet and pulled on the bell rope beside the mantel. He sent the footman who answered his summons to find Lady Estelle Lamarr. "Ask her if she would be so good as to join me and Viscount Watley in the library," he said.

They waited in near silence.

"I am making a mental list of everyone I know in this county," Justin said after a few minutes. "It is not a long one. My steward and my secretary will be able to help.

They have both been here a long time. They worked for my father before me."

The same footman opened the door ten minutes after he had been sent and admitted Lady Estelle. She stood just inside the door and looked from one to the other of them, her hands clasped at her waist.

"I hope there is a reason for this odd summons that is not going to have me exploding in wrath," she said.

"I am *not* about to order you to marry Brandon forthwith, Stell," her brother said. "Nor am I about to forbid you to marry him and order you to pack your bags and be ready to leave within the hour."

"Well, that is a relief," she said. "You get to keep your head, Bert."

"Ricky is missing," Justin told her, and her eyes came to him and remained upon him while he told her about Hilda's letter.

She *did* have ideas in addition to those her brother had suggested.

"Involve women and servants," she said. "If you wish to spread any news as fast as wildfire, those are the people to tell. Men will spread the word in official ways and be very thorough and methodical about it. Women and servants will just *talk*. And the people to whom they talk will talk to others. Those others will talk to yet more. Soon scarcely anyone, either upstairs or down, will *not* know that a man of Ricky's description and mental slowness is wandering around lost and—most important—that he is *very precious* to the Earl of Brandon, who will pay a handsome reward to whoever finds him and treats him with kindness while he or she brings him here to Everleigh."

"*If* he finds his way to this county," Justin said. By now Lady Estelle was sitting on the chair across from her brother's and Justin was standing between them, his back to the fireplace.

"Well, you know, gossip does not stop at county borders, Brandon," Watley said.

"But you must be prepared for much of that gossip being about *you*, Lord Brandon," Lady Estelle warned him. "You have kept your secrets locked up tight and your two worlds very separate until now, have you not? The initial story will explain that Ricky is trying to find you here and that he is very important to you. You can control that explanation at the source of the story, but once it starts spreading you will lose control of the details, and the story will grow and swell like a hot-air balloon. Everyone will be very eager to fill in the *why* and the *how*."

"You can control that too if you wish by getting ahead of the rumors with solid fact," her twin added.

Lady Estelle set a hand on Justin's arm, whether unconsciously or deliberately he did not know. He could feel the warmth of it and the comfort of it through his coat sleeve and shirtsleeve. "You can do a great deal more than his brother can to spread the word and find Ricky," she said. "You have power and influence."

He turned his head to look at her, and she seemed to realize where her hand was. She removed it after patting his arm a couple of times.

"Thank you," he said. "To *both* of you. I do not know why you would be willing to help me. This is supposed to be a house party primarily for your relaxation and enjoyment."

"We actually enjoy helping friends, do we not, Stell?" Watley said.

"Like you, we have a large extended family," she said. "On our mother's side and our father's and our stepmother's. Hers includes all the Westcotts, and there are dozens of them. Or am I exaggerating? But they include powerful people, like the Earl of Riverdale and the Duke of Netherby."

"Netherby is a friend of mine," Justin said.

"We will write to them all if it should become necessary," Lady Estelle said. "He will be found, Justin. You must believe that he will."

His panic was beginning to recede just a little. *We actually enjoy helping friends.*

She had called him *Justin.*

He wondered if she had noticed. Or if her brother had.

Fifteen

When Estelle was called away from tea in the drawing room to the library, Maria had been talking with Mrs. Sharpe, her son Ernest, and her elder daughter, Doris Haig. Mr. Sharpe had just joined them too. Maria reported on what Estelle had missed of the conversation before the two of them went down for dinner that evening.

"I asked them straight-out if they had resented my mother," she said. "I even told them it would be perfectly understandable if they had. Mrs. Sharpe told me Papa had always been very good to her sister while she lived, but that she had thought him entitled to find happiness with someone else after she was gone. They did not blame him for marrying Mama. Though Mrs. Sharpe did add that it gave her a pang of sadness anyway since she had worshiped the ground her sister walked upon, to use her words."

"I am glad you brought the subject up with them," Estelle said. "They are very pleasant people. And honest too."

"Mrs. Sharpe explained that losing her sister was the

greatest, most painful loss she has suffered in her life," Maria said. "Greater even than the loss of her parents. They were very close. But she had never expected that Papa would mourn her for the rest of his life. She told me some things about her sister after I asked, and Mrs. Haig and Mr. Ernest Sharpe added a few memories of their own. I think she must have been a warm and charming lady. When I asked why none of them had ever come here after Mama and Papa's wedding, they told me they had considered it more tactful to stay away than to make Mama uncomfortable with the reminder of Papa's first wife. I think . . . Maybe there was no actual quarrel? Maybe they did not hate Mama. Maybe it was a mere misunderstanding and she simply *thought* they did."

"I am very glad you had a frank talk with them, then," Estelle said. She was not so sure there had been any such misunderstanding—or that any of the fault lay with the Sharpes. But she had not known the late countess personally, and it would be unfair to judge.

"I asked Mrs. Sharpe if she resented *me*." Maria sounded breathless. "I asked if she hated the fact that I am the daughter of the house but not her sister's daughter. She simply said, *"Maria!"* in a shocked voice, while Mr. Sharpe called me a goose, and then they all *hugged* me."

"Well." Estelle hugged her too when she saw tears brighten her friend's eyes. "I believe this family gathering is turning out to be a very good thing for you, Maria. It is helping you discover that you *do have* family and that they are all disposed to love you."

"Mrs. Sharpe told me," Maria added, "that Papa always adored me and that Jus— She told me that Brandon did too. They both talked about me a great deal whenever they went to the Sharpes' house to visit. She told me *they* had always loved me too even though they had never met me. She begged me again to call her Aunt Betty, and I am going to do it."

This gathering was also enabling Maria to separate her own identity from that of her mother and become her own person, Estelle thought as they made their way to the dining room together. Maria sat between Mr. Dickson and Mrs. Chandler, her maternal uncle and aunt, at the foot of the table, and she conversed with each of them in turn with some animation and a becoming flush of color in her cheeks. Estelle wondered if she had admitted to herself yet that she owed all this self-discovery and reconciliation with her family to her stepbrother, the Earl of Brandon.

Even as she thought it he began to speak from his position at the head of the table. He was addressing everyone. Estelle turned her eyes his way. She had avoided looking at him throughout the meal, lest he catch her at it. *Justin.* She had called him that in the library earlier, quite inadvertently. She hoped he had not noticed. Bertrand certainly had, of course. He did not miss much. Sometimes she wished he were anyone's twin but her own.

"Justin?" Bertrand had murmured as they made their way up to their rooms in the east wing after making a list in the library and assuring the earl, without any evidence to support their confidence, that all would be well and Ricky would be found safe and sound and restored to his brother.

She had not misunderstood her brother for a moment. "Well," she had said, very much on her dignity. "That *is* his name, is it not?"

The conversation had ended there.

"I am spreading word of a missing person as far and as wide as I possibly can," he said now—Justin, that was. The Earl of Brandon. The man who had warned her this afternoon that he was going to harass her for the rest of her stay here, though, to be fair, he had not actually used the word *harass*.

His words drew everyone's attention. And he told them about Ricky and his own connection with the man and with his brother and . . . sister-in-law. There was always a pause before he indicated Hilda that way, for of course she was not married to Ricky's brother. Inevitably he told part of his own story, something he had not done with anyone before he had told her, Estelle, today out at the grotto. She could guess how much this telling was costing him. It must make him feel as though the armor he had built about himself with such painstaking care were being ripped away, leaving him exposed to view and to censure.

"I do not even know if he can find his way anywhere close to here," he said at last. "I cannot even know for sure that he *is* trying to find me. But I must do all in my power to spread the word so that if he is seen, he will be taken home or brought here, whichever is closer. I let him down in July by not going to see him when I had promised I would. I will not let him down now. I will make every effort to find him."

"Including letting us all know things about yourself and the missing years that you would otherwise have kept to yourself for the rest of your life," Mr. Sidney Sharpe, his cousin, said. "I honor you, Justin." He held up his empty wineglass.

"So do I," Lord Crowther, his aunt Augusta's husband, said. "Though why you did not come to us in Cornwall when you had to leave here, I do not know, Justin. Family and all that."

"It is my hope," Lord Brandon said, "that you will all keep your eyes open for a strange young man, though it seems too much to hope that he will find his way here on his own."

"But why is it you had to work at a stone quarry and live in a laborer's cottage?" Maria asked. "Had you squandered all the money from Mama's jewels?"

There was a sudden uncomfortable silence. Estelle had the impression that several of them would have slid under the table to avoid further embarrassment if they could.

Lord Brandon looked directly at his sister, whose face had turned pale except for two spots of color high in her cheeks. "The first I heard of stolen jewels, Maria," he said, "was when you mentioned them while I was talking with Lady Maple several days ago. I do not know what happened to them, but I do assure you I did not take them."

"Then why did Papa banish you?" Maria cried, regardless of the appallingly public nature of this exchange. "Why did he send you away and never relent for the rest of his life?"

"It was a private matter between him and me," Brandon said after a brief pause. "But it had nothing to do with theft or your mother's jewelry, Maria. And absolutely nothing to do with you either. I loved you dearly, as your memories of childhood will perhaps confirm for you. How could I have done anything to hurt you? You have my word on this, if my word is good enough for you."

"I daresay, Justin, your pa thought you were an idle young buck who stood in need of some toughening up in the real world," Mr. Dickson said in his usual hearty York-shire voice, breaking what threatened to be an awkward silence no one else would have had the courage to fill. He was also patting Maria's hand on the table beside him. "So he pushed you out the door like a bird from the nest and you found your wings and your backbone and stayed out until after he was gone. It was a pity he never saw you again. I daresay he regretted that at the end. He would surely have been proud of you for making your own way, even if it was at a stone quarry. Any father would."

"Strict love," Mr. Harold Ormsbury said. "It sometimes works, though I have never approved of it or even considered it with my own son. And we never heard that Justin was running wild as a young man, did we, Felicity? You should indeed have come to us, Justin. But forcing you out the door does not sound quite like your father. I do not know what could have—"

"Estelle and I have helped Brandon make a list of people in the vicinity who may help in the search for Ricky Mort," Bertrand said. "Men, women, servants—they are all on it. The more the merrier. We all know how news and rumor spread. I daresay the poor young man will be spotted in no time at all once the word is out. I will fetch the list to the drawing room if I may, Brandon. Someone may be able to suggest names we missed, or other ideas altogether. Two heads are said to be better than one, and three better again. How many of us are there? I have not stopped to count. But all our heads together will be vastly better than three."

Maria took that as her cue to get to her feet and lead the ladies from the dining room.

There followed a spirited discussion in the drawing room over what could be done to help find Ricky. Viscount Watley led it, the list in one hand, a pencil in the other. Almost everyone participated, as though they were playing a parlor game. It was a cause and a story that seemed to concern and animate everyone. They were all nearly enjoying themselves, Justin thought. He took himself off to the library for a while to write to a few people on the list and left everyone else to it. He felt a bit as though he were standing on his head rather than his feet. Or as if the whole of his world had been turned upside down while he had not.

He felt bruised, disoriented, exposed. He had worked hard to keep his two worlds separate, and his two lives and his two persons. Now he did not know how he would cope with having everything merged. It had happened all of a rush in the course of one day, and he was aware that there would be no going back. He had made the decision after Watley had asked his questions in the library this afternoon to put Ricky first, the consequences to himself be damned, and now everyone knew. *Everyone.* His butler and four footmen had been present in the dining room while he told his story. He had been aware of them and had briefly considered dismissing them. But what would have been the point when part of the strategy was to involve servants as well as everyone else?

He did not doubt that well before the gentlemen joined the ladies in the drawing room everyone belowstairs was buzzing with the news that their master had lived for a number of years after his father kicked him out of here with the foreman of a stone quarry and his daft brother in a cottage and had earned his living in the quarry.

Did it matter that everyone now knew how he had spent those missing years? Did it matter that they knew he had not relied upon privilege or the charity of relatives or friends? That he had worked for a living at the most menial and brutal and backbreaking of tasks? That he loved the people who had taken him in and given him work? That he was frantic over the fact that one of them was missing— and did not have the mental capacity to look after himself?

It did *not* matter, he decided as he dipped his quill pen into the ink bottle to continue one of his letters. He was not ashamed of those years or of those people. He could have stayed with his aunt and uncle Sharpe after running to them. He could have crawled off to Cornwall to throw himself upon the charity of his aunts and uncles there. He could have tried a number of other options more suited to his status and upbringing. Instead he had gone alone into the world to make his own way.

It was not his pride that mattered now, but Ricky. And Wes. And Hilda. His first letter, which he would send off early tomorrow morning with a groom rather than with the regular mail, was to Wes and Hilda.

Would his father have been proud of him? Leonard Dickson thought so. Or had his father gone to his grave believing what he had believed that day—the worst day of Justin's life and possibly of his father's too? No, not quite the worst. The day his mother died had that honor.

When he returned to the drawing room a number of the young people were taking sides for charades while most of the older ladies had gathered in a circle to talk. Angela Ormsbury was playing the pianoforte softly while Ernie Sharpe stood behind the bench and turned the pages of her music. Lady Maple was seated in her usual chair. Maria and Lady Estelle Lamarr were with her, though Maria had been picked for one of the teams for charades and was being summoned to join it. Lady Estelle was rising with her. Four of the older men had made up a table for cards.

Watley removed his list from an inside pocket of his coat when he saw Justin and waved it in his direction.

"We have lots of new ideas and suggestions," he said. "Poor Ricky does not stand a chance against us, Brandon.

Tomorrow we will spring into action. But for now . . . ? My team has a game of charades to win." He returned the list to his pocket.

"Or to lose," Sid Sharpe said. "You are not on my team, Watley. Jolly bad luck, old chap."

"Ah, but we have Lady Maria," Watley said, grinning.

"And I am about to acquire your sister," Sid told him. "Lady Estelle?"

"I am going to escort Lady Maple to her room," she said. "She is tired. Please proceed without me."

"Dash it all!" Sid exclaimed. "Who is that hiding in the corner? Wallace Chandler? Get over here, young man. You are on my team as of this moment."

Justin strode toward Lady Maple's chair. "You are ready to retire for the night, ma'am?" he asked her. "Allow me to join Lady Estelle in escorting you. You may have two arms to lean upon instead of one. I shall have your maid sent up."

"I am not *old*, Brandon," she said rather tartly. "Merely a bit on the elderly side. However, I never was able to resist the escort of a handsome man. And I like Lady Estelle. She does not fuss or treat me like a doddering old thing."

He helped her to her feet and gave her his arm before taking her cane in his free hand. Lady Estelle went ahead of them to open the door. They walked at a sedate pace along a wide corridor, up one flight of stairs to the west wing, and along another corridor to Lady Maple's room. She talked most of the way.

"She looks like a frail, timid thing, that great-niece of mine," she said. "But she has backbone. No thanks to Lilian. She is beginning to understand that all the members of her family on both sides *plus* those on your mother's side, Brandon, are not the collective enemy. One is not supposed to speak ill of the dead, but really there is just one villain in this whole situation. I am not sure Maria has got quite there yet, but she surely will. She is beginning to talk to her relatives and to listen to them. Bless her heart."

"Your niece was only seventeen when she married the late Earl of Brandon, I believe, ma'am," Lady Estelle said. "She had not been raised in his world or even the world of the lesser gentry. She came from a wealthy middle-class family and had a very brief training in the manners of the upper classes when you took her to London. She was little more than a child. Perhaps it would be kinder to see her not so much as a villain but as a bewildered girl whose insecurities must have been enormous. I suppose she did the best she could to cope with a situation that must have almost overwhelmed her."

"I suppose you are of the sort that has always felt sorry for Cinderella," Lady Maple said.

"Well." Lady Estelle laughed. "I have. The dazzlingly glamorous life of a princess she must have expected was probably neither as dazzling nor as glamorous in reality as it appeared in anticipation. Even the romance of falling in love with a prince would not have helped her beyond a certain point. The late Lady Brandon—Maria's mother—was probably no more villainous at heart than anyone else. She just did what she believed must be done to help her adjust to the new world into which she had been thrust."

As *he* had done under totally different circumstances, Justin thought. Except that he did not believe he had ever hurt anyone in the process—except Ricky. He had made a careless promise to a man who did not understand that promises could not always be kept, and the consequences might well be catastrophic.

"What you mean," Lady Maple said, "is the new world into which she thrust herself with her lying and scheming and determination to better herself."

Fortunately they had reached her room. Justin opened the door and was thankful to see that candles were burning within and Lady Maple's maid already awaited her there.

"Maria wanted me to tell her more about her mother tonight," Lady Maple said. "So I did. I told her how she had been spoiled and flattered throughout her childhood and girlhood because of her looks. I told her how she wheedled and pestered me until I agreed to take her to London and let her attend a few parties. I told her that Lilian's one goal in life was to marry a prince, or as close to a prince as she could get."

"Ah," Justin said. "Your maid is here, ma'am. I am sure she will see to it that you have everything you need."

"I hope you sleep well," Lady Estelle said.

"I still believe," Lady Maple said, "that she caused that rift with your father, Brandon. And I disagree with you, Lady Estelle. She was not a normal human being, that one. She was a wicked puss. My one consolation for having agreed to take her to London is that Maria is in this world as a result and that she seems to have more of her father in her than her mother."

"Good night, ma'am," Justin said. "Sleep well."

And he shut the door firmly and turned toward Lady Estelle. They stared silently at each other for a few moments in the flickering light of a candle in one of the wall sconces.

"You do not need to be playing charades in the drawing room in order to become involved in high drama here," Justin said. "I do beg your pardon for dragging you into it. It was *not* what you bargained for when you agreed to come here."

"Sometimes," she said, "days and even weeks go by and one has no memory afterward of what one did during them. And then there are days like today. You do not need to apologize. You could not have predicted any of this."

"I must lack something of imagination," he said. "I hoped that gathering our families would draw Maria into the fold and help her feel less alone in the world now that both our father and her mother are gone. I ought to have guessed that if that was to happen there would need to be a few confrontations or at least a bit of plain speaking and truth telling."

"A writer admitting to a lack of imagination?" she said. "Your poor hero. Will he ever slay his final dragon? Will he ever find his way back home?"

"I really and truly do not know," he said, wondering if she was asking about him or just his silly hero. "Do you want to return to the drawing room immediately? Or will you come and stroll in the gallery with me?"

She gazed at him for what felt like a long time. He had almost decided to walk away so that she would not have to reject him openly.

"The gallery," she said. "I am not ready yet for more socializing."

Sixteen

Justin was not sure he was ready to be alone with her again. He had given her due warning earlier—was it really just today, just a few hours ago?—that next week he would be asking her again to marry him. He had warned her that in the meanwhile he would be trying to change her answer from the no she had given in the summerhouse to the yes he hoped for in the end. But was he ready—was she?—for them to be alone together again today after their encounter down by the lake? And after everything that had happened since then?

He had rarely felt more out of control of his life. Which was saying something when he considered all he had lived through during the past twelve years.

They walked side by side and in silence to the north wing and the long gallery. He lit a taper from the wall sconce outside its doors and walked the whole length of the gallery and back, lighting all the candles in their sconces while Lady Estelle waited quietly just inside the door. Justin was very aware of the hollow sound of his heels on the wood floor, of the gradual lifting of the darkness, of their aloneness here. He blew out the taper and set it down on a brass tray on the bureau inside the door.

"I did not come here when Lady Crowther brought a group a few days ago," she said. "It is quite breathtaking, even at night."

"It stretches the full length of all the state apartments below us," he said. "But with no intervening walls. I used to love coming here with my cousins—Ernie and Sid and Doris. Rosie had not yet been thought of in those days. And, less often, with the cousins from Cornwall—Bevin and Miriam, Angela and Frederick. Paulette came later. There was never anyone up here to tell us to slow down or be quiet, except when the occasional parent or nurse poked a head in to make sure we were all alive with no broken arms or bloody noses. My parents were of the firm belief that children ought to be allowed to be children, and there was nothing much here with which we could harm ourselves. Interestingly, they never seemed worried that we might damage the paintings. Even more interestingly, it never occurred to any of us to draw mustaches or horns or freckles on any of the ancestors."

"This is not the best time to look at the paintings, is it?" she said. "I must come back when there is daylight. Is there a portrait of you? And of your father? And your mother?"

"Yes," he said. "Close to this end. They are hung in chronological order, starting at the far end."

He showed her first the painting of his grandparents with his father and his aunts. His father, aged about eighteen at the time, slender and smiling, stood at his seated father's shoulder. Aunt Augusta, aged about twelve, stood gracefully beside her mother's chair. Aunt Felicity, about six, stood on her mother's other side, her elbows on her mother's lap, her chin in her hands.

"My grandmother once explained to me the rather wide gap in their ages," he explained. "The other children—four of them—did not survive infancy. Or even birth, in one of those cases."

"Ah," Lady Estelle said. "Life is sometimes cruel. But it is a charming painting."

He led her to the next portrait, a solo one of himself, painted when he was nine years old. He was standing beside his pony, one arm draped over its neck, the other hand holding a riding crop like a cane, propped on the ground. His booted feet were crossed nonchalantly at the ankle. A child pretending to be a man, like his father.

"My mother had the painting hung in her bedchamber," he said. "She said the moment she saw it that it was her favorite painting ever. Not that she was biased in any way." It had been moved here to the gallery before his father's second marriage.

"Oh," Lady Estelle said. It was all she said for a while. But she stood directly in front of the painting and stayed there for some time.

And then the portrait of the three of them: his father seated on a chair with gilded back and curved gilded arms; his mother on a low stool beside him, her arm, bent at the elbow, resting across his lap; he, Justin, standing behind her, one hand on his father's shoulder. All of them were smiling, which was unusual for a family portrait.

"I was ten," he said.

She looked at the painting, and then turned her head to look at him. "Ten?"

"The painter delivered the finished portrait two weeks after my mother's funeral," he said.

His father had wept—for the first time since her death.

He could not see Lady Estelle's face clearly. One of the candles was in his direct line of vision, behind her head. But he was aware of her eyes brightening—with tears?—before she dipped her head and brought her forehead against his chest.

"Oh, it is awful, *awful*," she said, "to lose one's mother. It is not right. It is not *fair*. I do not even have a portrait of mine. Or any conscious memory. But it hurts. It hurts more than *anything*. She was nothing like Aunt Jane. Both my aunt herself and my father have told me that. And she was nothing like my stepmother. She was nothing like *anyone*. No one ever is. Everyone is unique. I never knew the unique person who was my mother. You did know yours. You have a portrait. You have memories. But it does not matter, does it? You lost her far too soon. You felt the immediate pain of her death, which must have been unbearable. I did not feel that with my mother because I was *too young*. And people assume that therefore there has been no pain at all, for either me or Bertrand. How can there be? We are twenty-five, and she died twenty-four years ago. Oh, I am sorry."

She tried to raise her head, but he wrapped his arms about her and drew her close. Not tightly. She could have drawn free if she had wished. He heard her inhale deeply and exhale with a puff as she relaxed against him. He rested his chin on the top of her head.

"I do not spend my days moping and mourning for my mother, you know," she said.

"I do know," he said. "The people who have been central to our lives are always there in us and always will be, even when they are no longer alive and we are not actually thinking about them. We are fortunate if our memories of them, conscious or unconscious, are happy ones. If we know and can feel deep down inside ourselves that they loved us constantly and unconditionally."

He looked at the portrait over her head. None of them had had any inkling of what was facing them so soon after they had posed thus for the painter and laughed at the absurdity of staying still for so long—laughter the painter had chosen to use in his painting. What a blessing it was that one could not see into the future. When they had laughed— he had started it by announcing in a frantic sort of agony that he had an *itch*—they had been utterly happy. If one discounted the agony of his itch.

"And then you lost your father," she said.

"I was twenty-eight by then," he said. And he did *not* want to pursue this point.

"Did you hate him?" she asked.

"No," he said.

"*Do* you hate him?" she asked.

"No."

She drew back her head to look into his face. She had the advantage over him that the closest candle was behind her. He had hated *himself*. For not asserting himself more forcefully after returning home to live full-time when he came down from university and declaring once and for all that he was absolutely not interested in . . . Well, that he was not interested. He hated himself for dashing unheeding into a room he had thought empty without ascertaining first that it *was* empty—*that* of all rooms. For not telling his father the truth. Though he would have hated himself more if he had. He hated himself for withholding the truth and putting that look of raw pain and barely leashed anger on his father's face.

She raised one hand and set her fingertips against his cheek.

"The only way I could retain my soul," he said, "was to keep on loving him. To keep on knowing that he was an honorable man."

She searched his eyes with her own and nodded slowly. *Please do not ask,* he begged her silently. *Please do not ask what happened.*

She did not. She turned her hand and brushed the backs of her fingers over his cheek before taking a step away.

"I will look at the other portrait another time," she said, nodding toward the remaining painting at the end of the line. She must have realized that it was of his father's second family, which had included him—until he was twenty-two. "In the daylight. Have you thought of having new portraits done? Of the adult you as Earl of Brandon? Of Maria? Perhaps of the two of you together?"

"I have not thought of it," he said. "Perhaps I will wait until I have a countess. And children. Though I would like a portrait of Maria. She was four years old when that one was done." He inclined his head toward the last painting.

"I know a portrait painter who would do a wonderful job of it," she said. "He is my sort-of brother-in-law."

"Is that a legal designation—*sort-of brother-in-law*?" he asked her.

She laughed and the breath caught in his throat. There was a great deal of joy in Lady Estelle Lamarr, even if she had not shown much of it directly to him. When she smiled or laughed, she seemed to be lit up from within.

"Camille is my stepsister," she said. "We did not grow up together. She was already married with children when my father met her mother—or rather met her *again*. But we love each other. Joel Cunningham is her husband. He has been growing in renown as a portrait painter to a point at which I believe it is a matter of great distinction now to be able to boast that one has secured his services."

"And you believe I might be one of the chosen few?" he asked her, feeling a bit amused.

"Well," she said, "you would have his stepsister-in-law to speak up for you. And his stepbrother-in-law too. Joel is very talented. But that is not a strong enough word. He is—*amazing.* You would have to see for yourself. He always explains that he does not paint what he sees with his eyes. He points out that the eyes are such a small part of one's entire being. He has to observe and converse with his subjects long before he starts to paint them. He has to find the core of their being and then paint from that deeply held knowledge."

"It sounds like a slow process," he said.

"I believe," she said, "that is why he is so much in demand. He does not produce a dozen or so paintings every week. Or even one."

"Has he painted you?" he asked.

"No." She shook her head.

"Perhaps he will paint you," he said, "when you are my countess."

She smiled, though she did not laugh this time. "I do not believe he enjoys painting groups," she said.

"I will commission him to paint my countess on her own, then," he said.

She did laugh then. "You, Lord Brandon, are presumptuous," she said.

"Persistent," he said. "Consistent. An optimist. Do you want to stroll along the gallery and back? Or would you prefer to watch the charades?"

She thought about it. He expected that she would choose to return to the drawing room.

"The stroll," she said, and when he offered his arm she took it. "Why specifically do you want a countess, Lord Brandon? You have had your title for six years. Why now?"

"Sometimes the stars align," he said. "It was time to fetch Maria home. She has come without her longtime governess and companion. It makes sense to offer her a sister-in-law instead of a new companion. It is also time to consider the full responsibilities of my position—as I told you at the summerhouse. And I met you."

"The perfect candidate," she said. "Daughter of a marquess. Not too young for your thirty-four years, but not quite in her dotage either."

"Yes," he said. "But not *just* for those reasons."

"You fell in love with me at first sight," she said. "By the riverbank."

"Hardly," he told her. "If I did any falling on that afternoon, it was *in lust*."

"Because my hair was loose down my back and my legs were dangling in the water?" she said. "And my skirts were up about my knees?"

"I *am* a man," he told her.

"Yes," she said. "I had noticed."

Was she flirting with him? There was a lightness in her tone. Was *he* flirting with *her*? He had a feeling that he was smiling and discovered that yes, he was. But no, they were not flirting. They were teasing each other. Was it the same thing? Either way it was a bit astonishing and felt rather good.

"So you wish to marry me not *just* because you need a countess and I am eligible," she said, "but because you are in lust with me. You are improving. That sounds a little less impersonal and offensive."

"But only a little?" he asked.

"Is lust a good enough reason for marrying someone?" she asked.

"I believe sex is an important part of marriage," he told her. "It would—it *will*—certainly be an important part of mine."

"And lust will be good enough for that?" she asked.

He could not see her clearly. He had lit all the candles along both sides of the gallery, but their flames had to compete with vast expanses of darkness. Even so, he was almost sure she was blushing rosily. This, he thought, was not a very proper conversation for a lady to be having.

"It will be a start," he said as they came to the end of the gallery and turned to walk back.

"Oh?" she said. "And what will come after it? Boredom? Duty?"

"Shall we wait and see?" he asked her.

"We?" She turned her head to look at him. "Are you assuming that I will say yes, Lord Brandon?"

"I am trying to think optimistically," he said.

"And I am thinking of what a huge risk I would be taking if I married you for lust and hoped for some vague future that might *not* be boredom or dreary duty," she said.

"You do lust after me, then?" he asked her.

She laughed again. "You are trying to discompose me," she said. "You are expecting me to be shocked and deny that I feel any such unladylike thing. I beg to disappoint you. Yes, I lust after you, Lord Brandon. I have *no* idea why. I think . . . making love with you would be an interesting experience. Now I wish to return to the drawing room if you please."

An interesting experience.

"Are there many new names and ideas on that list of your brother's?" he asked as he led her from the gallery a couple of minutes or so later.

"Yes," she said. "Mr. Chandler has suggested having posters printed and pinned up in all sorts of public places between here and Ricky's home in Gloucestershire. He is willing to travel to the closest place where there is a printing press and use his influence as a Yorkshire bank owner to make a rush order. He insists that he will pay for it all himself."

"Dash it all," he said. "I wonder where Ricky is tonight. At this very moment. And I wonder how Wes and Hilda are feeling. He has to be found, Estelle. He must be terribly bewildered and frightened. He will not know how to cope . . ."

Her hand, which was linked through his arm, pressed his arm to her side for a moment. "He will be found," she said. "Mr. Ernest Sharpe suggested the Bow Street Runners. Hiring them seems a bit of an extreme step to take, but it is a possibility. They have a great deal of experience in tracking people down."

"Poor Ricky," he said. "Ah, poor Ricky. He is the sweetest person I have ever known, Estelle. I hate the thought of his being *tracked down*. Like an animal."

She pressed his arm to her side again and turned her head to smile at him while a footman opened the doors of the drawing room for them. Justin sent him to extinguish the candles in the gallery before they turned to enter.

When Estelle stopped to think about it the next day, she was amazed at how the plight of one simpleminded man of no social significance whatsoever could animate a whole gathering of both gently born and middle-class guests at an aristocratic home, as well as all the indoor and outdoor servants there.

Nobody lingered over breakfast—and no one was late for breakfast either except Lady Maple, who rarely put in an appearance before noon. Even she was up before half past ten, however. She wished to find Mr. Chandler, her niece's husband, before he went off to have his posters printed and distributed. She wanted to make sure he worded them correctly and effectively, and she wanted to offer to help with the cost of them.

"He owns a *bank*," Doris Haig murmured to Estelle before rolling her eyes. "He is probably as rich as Croesus. But it is good of her to offer, I suppose. The decision has already been made, however, to hold off for a couple of days before hanging up posters or sending out leaflets or dashing off to London to engage the services of the Bow Street Runners."

The guests fanned out through the neighborhood, calling upon people who had paid their respects to them at church on Sunday and those who had called at Everleigh to welcome Maria back and greet the earl's guests. Coachmen and footmen who conveyed them undertook to mingle with their fellow servants and engage in unrestrained gossip. Bertrand went with Mr. and Mrs. Peter Ormsbury to call upon the vicar and his wife. Several of the young people went off riding in a largish group, though they did intend to split off into smaller pairings as they stopped at inns and taverns to imbibe ale or lemonade or tea while talking with landlords and other patrons.

Estelle and a number of others settled at desks and tables in various rooms, writing letters to everyone of any significance from Hertfordshire whom the Earl of Brandon

had been able to think of yesterday when Bertrand started
the list in the library. That list grew during the day as other
suggestions came from the vicar and a few of the neighbors, some of them people who lived farther west in bordering counties.

The earl went to call upon the local magistrate, who
might have had something to suggest by way of help from
law enforcement officers.

"Though I do hate to set the law on Ricky, as though he
were a common criminal," Estelle overheard him saying to
his uncle, Mr. Sharpe. "I really do not know if he would
look upon constables and sheriffs as friends or see them as
threats."

"If they can but find him, Justin," his uncle said, patting
his shoulder and then squeezing it, "we or his brother will
soon be able to reassure him."

At the end of a busy day they were all weary. Nevertheless, everyone at the dinner table wanted to tell one
another about their experiences, about what they had said
and what the people to whom they had said it had had to say
in return.

"I was very proud of Wallace, I must say, even if he *is*
my brother and a whole sixteen months younger than I am,"
Gillian Chandler told them all, grinning impishly at that
young man. "Even when a few men at one tavern where we
stopped jeered at him for ordering lemonade, he was not
bothered. *'I am seventeen,'* he told them. And when they
laughed and nudged one another after we had told them
about Ricky because we spoke in Yorkshire accents and
were all upset over a man from the lowest of low classes
who was also simple in his head—those were *their* words—
Wallace stood up and looked them all in the eye, including
the landlord himself, and said, *'Do those facts make him*

less of a human being? Do they make him less worthy of love and care?' And they did not know *what* to say."

"Gill!" Her brother blushed mottled shades of scarlet. "They were *laughing* at me."

"But they did not know what to say," she said.

"Thank you both," the Earl of Brandon said. "Thank you especially, Wallace. It was brave of you to speak up in the face of ridicule. But you can be sure that if any of those men should by chance set eyes upon Ricky, they will know instantly who he is and see to it that he is brought here. People are not always as heedless or as heartless as they pretend to be."

"I am proud of you too, son," Mr. Chandler said, beaming. "That lad will not be able to set one toe over the border into Hertfordshire without being spotted."

"My main fear, though," the earl said, "is that he is not headed this way. There could be nothing rational about his travel plans, after all, assuming that his desire to find me really is the reason for his disappearance. He might well be wandering about Wales at this moment or heading for the Lake Country or merely moving in circles, unable to find his way forward or back."

He looked directly at Estelle for a moment and she saw utter bleakness in his eyes. *Or he might well be dead,* that look seemed to say.

"He will find his way," she said. "Either back to his brother's house or here."

Soon after, Maria got to her feet to lead the ladies from the dining room and leave the men to their port.

"Brandon," she said before she went. "May I have a word with you later? In my sitting room? Perhaps Lady Estelle will come there with me. Perhaps Viscount Watley will come with you."

There was an unnatural silence for a few moments while everyone looked at her in collective surprise, the earl included.

"Of course," he said then. "Aunt Augusta, perhaps you would preside over tea in the drawing room after the men join you there? Maria, perhaps you would give the order to have a tea tray delivered to your sitting room in . . . half an hour's time?"

She inclined her head and swept from the room, trailed by all the ladies.

Seventeen

"I spoke with the Cornish aunts and uncles this afternoon after we had all returned from our visits," Maria told Estelle while they waited in her sitting room for the two men to join them.

"Yes," Estelle said. "You were even laughing with them when I saw you. I do admire the way you are going about getting to know all your relatives. You are forcing the issue with each group of them and showing a strength of character I always knew you had. Bertrand and I are happy to be here, but you really do not *need* us, I have been happy to observe."

Maria was fussing with the folds of the curtains, which had already been drawn across the window when they came here. She turned to look at Estelle.

"Oh, there you are wrong," she said. "You have no idea how lonely and even frightened I have been feeling, Estelle. Although I am related to almost everyone here, they are all strangers. They all hated my mother—or so she believed. I

assumed they all hated me too, or at least were not interested in claiming me as one of their own. Yet they all came
here when they were invited. Even Aunt Sarah, who might
have used her plans to go to Scotland as an excuse to avoid
me, wishes to come later. The others have all come and
have been . . . amiable. Just as I have been in return. But
amiability was not going to be enough."

"No," Estelle said.

"I needed to know why none of them have been in my
life until now," she said. "I needed to know what their relationship with my mother was and why everyone quarreled
with her—or she with them. I needed to know how they felt
about me, my mother's daughter. I have provoked those
conversations. No one bears any grudge against me, Estelle. And I bear none against any of them. I really *like*
having cousins who are close to me in age. I believe some
of them, perhaps even most, will be real friends even after
they have gone home. We will be able to write to one another. Some of them want me to visit them. I think some
will visit me here again. And my aunts and uncles, even Mr.
and Mrs. Sharpe, who are now Uncle Rowan and Aunt
Betty, have affection to give. It makes me happy. I have
always envied you your large extended family and all the
things you do with them."

"I am happier for you than I can say," Estelle said, smiling
at her. "You have been very brave in taking the initiative as
you have."

"But it is only because you are here," Maria told her,
plumping the cushions on the sofa before sitting down.
"You and Lord Watley. I have tried hard not to cling to
either of you. Or to hide in your shadow. It has been tempting, for you are both so confident and poised in manner. But
you cannot know the sense of relief I feel every time I see

either one of you. You look . . . *familiar.* You look like *friends.* You give me courage even without a word spoken. I will never forget that you came here for my sake even though I strongly suspected you did not really *want* to come. I think perhaps you did it because you knew Melanie was leaving me."

"You had a letter from her this morning?" Estelle said.

"Oh, yes," Maria said. "I did not have a chance to read it until after luncheon. She is very busy helping with all the children. Her mother is not at all well after her last confinement. Oh, and Mr. Sheridan is still unmarried, and he has called at the house every second day since Melanie's return—to see how her mother does." She laughed.

"Mr. Sheridan?" Estelle raised her eyebrows.

"The gentleman farmer Melanie refused when she was eighteen," Maria explained. "She thought he had asked out of pity then because her papa does not have a great fortune and there was already talk of her having to seek a position as a governess. But he has not married in the meanwhile, Estelle, and now he is *back.*"

"You think you smell a romance," Estelle said, and they grinned at each other.

"Even from this far away," Maria said. "She says—"

But Estelle was not to hear what Melanie Vane had said concerning Mr. Sheridan. A tap on the sitting room door preceded the arrival of the tea tray. It was Lord Brandon who had opened the door for the footman who carried it. He waited at the door to admit Bertrand and then close it after the footman left.

None of them spoke while Bertrand came to sit beside Estelle on a love seat and Maria poured the tea. Lord Brandon, predictably, took up a stand before the fireplace, his back to it, his hands clasped behind him.

"I will set your tea here," Maria said without looking at her brother. She put his cup and saucer down on the small table beside an armchair close to him.

"Thank you," he said.

She sat on the sofa and looked at him. "All the aunts and uncles—mine, yours, ours—remember you as a cheerful, kindly boy," she said. "It is how I remember you too, though you never seemed like a boy to me. You always seemed like a grown-up."

"That was all a long time ago," he said.

"Yes." She picked up her own cup but changed her mind and set it back down on the saucer. "You have denied taking Mama's jewelry. The Sharpes and our Ormsbury relatives believe you. So does Lady Maple, Great-aunt Bertha. None of them think it would have been in your nature to do such a thing. Uncle Peter, Lord Crowther, said it would have been unkind, even cruel, as well as dishonest, and he did not believe you to be capable of any of those three."

She looked at him briefly, but he made no comment.

"I have not asked my own aunts and uncles, as they met you only briefly at Mama and Papa's wedding," Maria continued. "Though they all—except Uncle Irwin, who was not yet married to Aunt Patricia at the time—remember you as a kindhearted boy who went out of your way to make them feel welcome here."

"But what do *you* believe, Maria?" Lord Brandon asked.

"If it was not theft, then what *was* it?" she cried in a sudden passion. "What *happened*, Brandon? I want to know the truth. I *need* to know. I have observed you yesterday and today, distraught over the disappearance of someone most men of your rank would not even *notice*, any more than they would a worm at their feet, let alone care about and get upset over. I have seen that you care deeply, both for him and for his brother and the woman with whom he lives, presumably *not* his wedded wife. I have seen you willing to bare your soul to all the relatives and neighbors. Even to the servants. All for the sake of a man with the mind of a child and for that of his relatives, who are frantic because he is missing. You have been behaving, in fact, as I would have expected you to do all those years ago. You have been behaving like a man of conscience and kindness."

There was a silence none of them seemed prepared to break.

"But there was that theft and its consequences," Maria said at last. "And I want you to tell me what happened. I want you to tell Viscount Watley and Lady Estelle so there can be no chance of any misunderstanding between the two of us. Tell me."

He inhaled deeply and let the breath out with a ragged sigh. "It was something very personal between my father and me, Maria," he said. "It had nothing to do with—"

"*No!*" She cut him off, and her eyes were flashing. "That is *not* good enough, Brandon. Papa was *my* father too. He was not *your* father. He was *ours*. You were *my* brother. Whatever it was that happened, it concerned my mother. I was only eight years old at the time. I understand why no one explained to me immediately what had happened. I was a *child*. But I am twenty years old now and can no longer be shut out of knowing what happened to *my* family. Something did, and it broke everything apart. Even my childhood self knew that."

He sighed again. "I was playing with you that morning," he said. "Hide-and-seek. It was always one of your favorites, though you could never keep quiet when I was drawing close to your hiding place. You would start to giggle and I would pretend not to know from where the sounds were coming. Then you would burst out into the open just as I was about to pounce and run away, shrieking, while I took my time about chasing you down. It was all part of the game." He sighed. "On that particular morning you dashed into your mother's room, and after a few moments I dashed in there too—without knocking. I had seen your mother not long before at the escritoire in the morning room, reading a letter and preparing to answer it. But . . . she was in her room after all. You were not. You had darted into her dressing room and back out into the corridor and away, I suppose. I was horribly embarrassed and apologized profusely and would have left the way I had come without further delay, but our father came through from his dressing room and saw me there and was furiously angry that I had intruded upon your mother's privacy without even knocking. He sent me down to the library and followed me there. He said my behavior was inexcusable, and he . . . sent me away."

The Earl of Brandon, Estelle thought as the silence following his words lengthened, was not a convincing liar.

Maria had moved to the edge of her seat and was gazing incredulously at him. "You expect me to believe that Papa, who had always so openly adored you, *banished* you and never relented for the rest of his life because you had committed the indiscretion of chasing after me and bursting in upon Mama without first knocking on her door?" she asked.

"Yes," he said after a pause. "It is what happened."

It probably *was* what had happened, Estelle thought. It was undoubtedly not *all* that had happened, however.

Her hands were pressed flat against the cushions on either side of her. Bertrand's hand came down to cover one of hers, and she leaned her shoulder against his. They did not turn their heads to look at each other. They did not need to. They were feeling the same things, and they were taking comfort from each other. Or, more accurately, Bertrand was giving comfort and Estelle was taking it. She felt a bit nauseated.

"I believe you are lying," Maria said. Her voice was shaking.

He nodded slowly without saying anything. He was gazing at her, his eyes dark and bleak.

He would have been twenty-two at the time, Estelle thought. His stepmother had been seventeen to his thirteen when she married his father. She was twenty-six by this time, then. And still very beautiful, no doubt. Perhaps more so than she had been at seventeen. Perhaps irresistibly attractive to her stepson. He must have been a handsome young man, slighter of build than he was now, more open of countenance, his nose unbroken. A cheerful and kindly young man, according to his relatives. Adored by his father and by his young half sister. Irresistibly attractive, perhaps, to his father's young vain wife, who might have grown bored and restless with her older husband.

Who had seduced whom? Or had it been mutual?

"I do not believe you," Maria said again. "Papa would have given you a thundering scold, even though it would have been mainly *my* fault really. But he would not have *banished* you. Or never let you come back home. That story does not even make *sense*."

He continued simply to gaze at her while Bertrand clasped Estelle's hand tightly in his own.

"I was an idle, careless young man in those days," Lord Brandon said. "It did me good to be sent off to cool my heels, though what was intended as a brief sort of punishment for careless behavior stretched into six years. I was too busy exploring the country and enjoying myself to come home. Unfortunately I left it too long. I hope our father forgave me for that before he died."

When a first lie was unconvincing, a second rarely improved upon it.

"He spent more time with me after you left," she said. "He smiled more. He was sadder. It was strange how both those things happened. He was always so very sad, and always smiling and smiling. Everything was broken. You took those jewels, Brandon. And now you add lies to theft. Mama's heart was broken. She loved those jewels, but I never saw them again after you went away. They were gone."

The Earl of Brandon tipped back his head and closed his eyes. When he opened them he was looking at *her*, Estelle. And at Bertrand.

"I am sorry you have been exposed to the discomfort of this conversation," he said. "At the same time, I thank you for giving my sister the comfort of your friendship. She is very young to have lost both her mother and her father and to have been left with only a half brother she does not trust."

"I have aunts and uncles and cousins too," Maria said.

"Yes." He looked at her with such desperate fondness that Estelle had to turn her eyes away.

"Both of you can rest assured that what has been said here will be safe with Estelle and me," Bertrand said. "It has been our pleasure to be here at Everleigh. Your family reminds me a bit of our own—large and diverse, blood relatives and those more loosely related by ties of marriage. But all happy to mingle with one another and to offer support and help wherever it is needed. And affection. Such bonds never break, even when sometimes they are stretched almost to a breaking point."

Estelle squeezed his hand and they both got to their feet.

"Shall we join your family in the drawing room, Maria?" Estelle suggested. None of them, she noticed, had touched their tea.

They led the way out, leaving the men to follow them.

"I so desperately want to believe in him," Maria said. "I doted upon him when I was a child. I cannot remember him ever being impatient with me or unwilling to play with me. And last night and today I have seen the old Justin in him and want to believe that at heart he has never changed or been cruel or dishonest—or a liar. But the story he told when I *begged* him to tell me the truth was just ridiculous."

Yes, Estelle thought. He *was* kind and caring at heart. He had loved his father and his half sister. Theft *would* have been out of character. So would seduction of his father's wife, of Maria's mother. Oh, it would *not* have been that way around. Everything she had heard about the late countess, however, had revealed a woman of vanity and ambition and little conscience. His only sin, surely, was in not telling his father the truth but taking the blame upon himself so that he would not hurt his father beyond bearing. Though perhaps he had done that after all.

"I so want to love him again," Maria said. "If he would just tell me the truth."

"I am very certain he loves you," Estelle said.

Two days went by during which nothing of any great significance happened except that Justin received another letter from Hilda. She was at home alone. Ricky was still missing and now Wes had gone too, to search for him. It was madness, Hilda had written, for neither they nor anyone else had any idea where Ricky had gone—if he had gone anywhere. Perhaps he had drowned somewhere, she had written with stark frankness—and Justin could only imagine the terror behind that admission. But Wes had had to believe that Ricky was trying to find his way to Everleigh Park and that somehow he was headed in the right direction. Wes had accepted the loan of a horse from the owner of the quarry—*"Everyone has been awfully kind, Juss. People are even bringing food to the house as though I had suddenly forgotten how to cook"*—and a loan equivalent to a month's wages, though the owner was insisting that Wes did not have to pay it back. And he had set off to find his brother.

It rained all of one day and the guests entertained themselves in the house in varying ways, a few in the library, several in the drawing room or the morning room, others in the billiard room, a crowd of young people in the gallery with the children playing vigorous games, blindman's buff and three-legged races among them.

Justin had invited them all here for Maria's sake so that she could get to know the various branches of her family and perhaps establish an ongoing relationship with them. But he was happy for his own sake too. He had hated being back at Everleigh—so large, so magnificent, so cold and silent, so lacking in soul. But now, wherever he went, with the exception of his own apartments, he came upon relatives or steprelatives, all of whom were genial, all of whom were happy to talk to him and draw him into their groups.

Even the children. Doris's two had found him after breakfast when they had escaped from the nursery undetected. There had been no ride that morning because of the rain. They had appropriated one of his hands each and dragged him off to the nursery to—

"Play horsey, Cousin Justin," Edward had demanded, though he was already five and might have been expected to have outgrown such an infantile game. "Papa says he has bad knees, and Mama says we are too heavy. Grandpapa says if he gets down he will never get up again, and Grandmama is too old."

So for half an hour Justin was a horse, bucking and neighing and plodding and occasionally galloping while four children—Cousin Bevin Ormsbury's two as well, aged five and three—bounced and shrieked and squabbled over whose turn it was and drummed their heels against his sides and gripped his hair and urged him to "Gee-up!"

The vicar and two neighbors made brief separate calls to the house to report that several sightings had been made of men who might have been Ricky Mort but had turned out not to be. One had been a fourteen-year-old lad running an errand for a local butcher. Another had been a seventy-two-year-old former farm laborer, out for an afternoon stroll with his grandson. None of the others had been simpleminded or from the West Country or lost. All had been indignant at being mistaken for the missing man. One of them, indeed, had been out and wandering only *because* he was looking for the unfortunate young man himself.

Justin went out despite the rain. He was too restless to remain indoors all day. He took Captain and went walking off to the lake and across the bridge and a mile or so beyond it before climbing the hill on the house side and gazing about in all directions. There was, of course, no sign of Ricky. Visibility was not good anyway in the rain. He was terribly afraid Ricky would never be seen or heard from again. Which would be worse in a way than finding . . . his body. And he would always blame himself. Ricky loved him. He had waited all of July for Justin to come and it had not happened.

He was reminded of how Lady Estelle and her twin had waited for their father to come home during the years when they had lived with their aunt and uncle, and of how, even when he did come, he did not stay. However had they brought themselves to forgive the man eventually? Yet they seemed to have done so.

Could he ever forgive his father?

He shook off the thought, as he always did when it somehow sneaked under his guard and popped into the forefront of his mind.

His father was dead.

Would Maria ever forgive *him*? Had she suspected the truth after he had told that wholly inadequate story? Would she ever believe it, even if she had? Or would she cling to what her mother had told her?

It *had* been his fault, that incident.

Throughout the year following his return home to stay after his university years he had been careful to avoid being alone with his stepmother. He had learned during the last few vacations while he was still a student that it was necessary to do so. He had become quite adept at it, even while she was just as busy maneuvering chance meetings or deliberate tête-à-têtes it was difficult for him to avoid. If she had wanted to walk to the village, for example, on some drummed-up errand and had deliberately chosen a day when she knew Justin's father would be unable to accompany her, she would pout playfully and tell him she would forgive him this once and take his son instead. Justin would declare himself happy to oblige and would suggest bringing

Maria with him. She would be delighted to have an outing, he had always said. And of course she *was* delighted.

But then had come *that* morning. He had seen his step-mother about to settle to some letter writing in the morning room, but that had been an hour before he went dashing into her room in pursuit of Maria and had found his step-mother there. Instead of continuing through to her dressing room as his sister had obviously done just moments before, uttering some abject apology as he went, he had pulled to an abrupt halt, somehow incapable of moving either forward or back, and quite unable to think of a thing to say. Though of course she had just seen Maria, shrieking and giggling, and must have understood the situation at a glance.

She had stepped into his path, set one arm about his neck, lowered her dress from the other shoulder, grasped his nerveless hand and pressed it against her bared breast, and breathed his name into his mouth. All that in a few seconds.

He had not even begun to react—his mind had been stupidly reeling—before his father stepped into the room, presumably having come through his own dressing room and then hers. She must have heard him coming, for her amorous advances had suddenly turned to struggles and sobs and admonitions and finally hysteria.

And Justin had stood there like a prize idiot, his mouth agape, his heartbeat drowning out all else for the first fateful minutes. No, not minutes. Just seconds really. They had felt like years.

She was lonely, she had once told Justin. His father did not pay her enough attention. He was old. He did not really love her. Justin on the other hand was so *young*. And vigorous. So *handsome*. They could have so much fun together.

Fun.

In an affair with his father's wife. Whom he did not even like. Whom he actively disliked, in fact, because the only person in the world Lilian Wiley, Countess of Brandon, cared about was herself. Because she had made his father unhappy—though he never, *ever* gave any outer sign that it was so. Because she neglected Maria, who doted upon her. Because she had driven away everyone whom she deemed a threat to her consequence—her own relatives, her husband's relatives, her husband's former in-laws. Justin disliked her because she had had the portrait of him with his mother and father removed from the gallery, having protested tearfully one day that it was disrespectful to her to have it hanging there for all to see—even though everyone told her she was far prettier than the first countess.

His father had banished him because he had seen—*with his own eyes*—his son attempting to seduce his wife over her protests and hysteria. Because Justin had refused to defend himself except with a simple denial. How *could* he have defended himself? She was his father's *wife*. If Justin was not guilty, then she was. How could he have told his father that? How could any son tell his father that? His father was an honorable man. He had taught his son the importance of honor above all else.

Perhaps his father would not have believed him anyway even if he had fully explained what had happened. Or perhaps he would have. Perhaps, even, he had believed his son's simple denial. But what could he have done? Called his wife a liar? Banished *her*? He had married her and made sacred vows to her. They had a daughter.

Perhaps on that morning he had had as little choice as Justin had had.

So things had been as they had been.

And were as they were.

The countess had told her daughter that Justin had stolen from her and been banished as a punishment.

Perhaps, Justin thought, he did not need to forgive his father. His father had been as much a victim as he had. Perhaps more so. He, Justin, had had a chance to make a new life—and had taken it. His father had not had that chance.

It did not rain on the following day, though clouds remained overhead and made the weather rather dreary. Most of the guests stayed indoors, enjoying the company of several visitors, all of whom brought stories of sightings that had turned out not to have any significance. Some of the guests ventured outdoors, a few to stroll as far as the lake.

Justin once more took Captain and went walking across the Palladian bridge and up into the wooded hills on the other side of the valley. This time, though, a few of the young people went with him—his cousins Ernie, Sid, and Rosie Sharpe, Frederick and Paulette Ormsbury, Gillian Chandler, Maria, and both the Lamarrs.

The wooded hills had always been a favorite playground of Justin's when he was a boy. They were less contrived than the hill behind the house, with its ironically named wilderness walk, though he had always loved that too. Here he had been free to let his imagination run wild. Today he could think only of getting free of the trees, somewhere close to the lake and at a higher elevation than the hills opposite, where he had stood yesterday in the rain. Visibility was better today too. The cloud cover was unbroken but high.

The others were more interested in climbing straight up the hill so that they could descend the other side and walk into the village for refreshments at the inn—and perhaps for some news.

"I'll keep going this way," Justin said, pointing off to the west, when they were halfway up. "But do not let me stop the rest of you. Perhaps there *will* be some news."

He looked at Lady Estelle, but he had been avoiding her—or she had been avoiding him—since the night they had met in Maria's sitting room. He had been embarrassed by what had occurred, and doubtless she and her brother had been too. Any plans he had had to court Lady Estelle seemed to have evaporated. And she would be leaving here soon. They had promised two weeks, she and her brother, and there were only a few days left.

She was looking back at him now while Ernie was chatting with her on one side and Paulette was hovering at her other side.

"I will come too," Lady Estelle said. "I want to see the view from higher up."

Captain woofed, impatient at the delay.

"I will come—" Paulette began. But Watley had moved to her side and was offering his arm.

"The hill is a bit steep straight ahead of us," he said, giving Paulette his most charming smile. "Allow me to assist you. Or, if worse comes to worst, perhaps *you* can assist *me*."

Paulette blushed and giggled and slid her hand through his arm, any idea of following where Lady Estelle went forgotten.

Had that been deliberate? Justin rather thought it had been—which was interesting in light of what Watley had heard the other night. He gazed at Lady Estelle as she crossed the hill to join him. The others were already trudging onward toward the top.

"I will look with you," she said. "Perhaps my eyesight is better than yours."

"I hope it is," he said. "I hope you can see all the way to Gloucestershire."

Captain went bounding off ahead of them.

"Thank you," Justin said after a few moments, and she turned her head to smile at him.

Eighteen

Estelle had sat for a while in the morning room with Maria while Mrs. Sharpe, at Maria's request, told them stories of growing up with her beloved elder sister, the Earl of Brandon's mother. Doris Haig and Sidney Sharpe had joined them, bringing fresh coffee. They had added their own stories of their aunt as they remembered her, fond memories, full of humor and nostalgia.

Maria had listened quietly and smiled and even laughed, especially when Mrs. Sharpe had recalled how her sister always used to wince at the bright mismatched jewelry she loved to wear, in the form of rings and bracelets, necklaces and earrings and brooches, and tell her that she positively *jangled*—on the nerves if not always on the ears. Her sister in contrast had always been quietly and faultlessly elegant, and Mrs. Sharpe had envied her good taste.

Yesterday Maria had asked her Cornish aunts to tell her about their childhood here with her papa and their parents, her grandparents. The memories had come spilling out, of games they had played, of mischief they had got into, of squabbles, of one horror of a governess who had left finally—and abruptly—the day after their brother had accidentally on purpose capsized the boat and spilled her into the lake after she had refused to let him take the oars because he was only fifteen. Their children too had gathered about them to listen and laugh.

Last evening Mr. Leonard Dickson and Mrs. Patricia Chandler, his sister, had become the focus of attention with a sizable group in the drawing room after Maria had asked them to tell her about her mama as a child and about her aunt Sarah and their family life generally. Their voices had grown louder and more boisterous, their Yorkshire accents more pronounced, as one memory provoked another and their children and spouses egged them on. After the busy day of making plans to find the missing Ricky Mort, the laughter their sometimes outrageous stories provoked had felt very good.

It was all making Estelle miss her own family—her mother's side, her father's, her stepmother's. And it struck her that when she and Bertrand returned to Elm Court within the week, she might not be as contented with their solitude there as she had been for the past couple of years. Family, all those people who had some connection with one another, however slight, was of such huge importance to one's well-being. It gave one identity and a sense of belonging. It was the answer to loneliness and any sense of disconnection with the world one inevitably felt at times. There were all sorts of exceptions to that ideal, of course, but . . . Well, she was going to value her own family more than ever after being here. And Maria was coming to see how much she had missed all through her childhood and girlhood because she had been cut off from her own family.

Estelle was mulling these thoughts as she walked diagonally up the hill with the Earl of Brandon. His thoughts
must have been moving along similar lines.

"How did you bring yourself to forgive?" he asked her.

The question was not specific. But she knew what he
was asking.

"My father?" she said. "It was not terribly difficult, you
know. We *always* longed to do so. At any point in our childhood we would have forgiven him if he had given us the
smallest opening."

"He *deserted* you," he said.

"Yes," she agreed. "He did. He blamed himself for our
mother's death. He was the one who had opened the window from which she fell. And they were bickering at the
time. He had just got us both to sleep after a difficult night
when she came storming into the nursery, angry with him
for staying up with us when they paid a nurse to do just that.
After her death he did not trust himself to raise us. Then
Aunt Jane turned up, confirming him in his beliefs, taking
over very ably and very forcefully."

"So he slunk off," he said, "and left you to her for . . .
what? Sixteen, seventeen years?"

"Sixteen," she said. "Yes, he did. He punished himself
with a life of riotous . . . debauchery. I make no excuses for
him. He makes none for himself. Forgiveness does not con-
sist in making excuses for the transgressor, Lord Brandon.
It consists in acknowledging the facts, understanding the
reasons for them—not the excuses—recognizing the pain
it all caused both the one who was wronged and the one
who did those wrongs, and admitting that forgiveness is not
something given by the innocent to the guilty. No one is
innocent. We all do stupid things, even when we *know* they
are stupid, and even when we know we are causing unhap-

piness for someone else and for ourselves. Forgiveness is given despite all those things."

"It sounds like pious nonsense," he said harshly as their climb took them up clear of the trees. Captain was waiting for them. His ears flopped and his jowls shook as he came toward them and nudged Estelle's hand with a cold nose. She patted his head and smoothed a hand along his back.

"That way, Cap," the earl said, pointing off to the west. "I beg your pardon. Those were ill-mannered words."

"The point is," she said, "that if we had not forgiven our father, or at least *listened* to him and given him a chance to listen to us at last, we would have carried the hole in our hearts where he ought to be for the rest of our lives. For the sake of pride. And righteousness. Forgiving him was not just about making *him* feel better. Indeed, for a while I was more furious with him than I had ever been in my life. I had planned a surprise fortieth birthday party for him—when I was *seventeen*. I was so proud of myself. And he simply did not come. When I went halfway across England to find him— Yes, I did, even though I had never asserted myself before. *Nothing* was going to stop me. I went, taking Bertrand and our aunt and our father's brother with me. And when we found him, he was with a *woman*. He had run off with her instead of coming home to us." She laughed quietly, almost to herself. "She is now our stepmother. Oh, forgiving him was not about making him feel better, Lord Brandon. It was for *us*, for Bert and me, so that our hearts would finally heal and be whole. If that is pious nonsense, then so be it."

The lake was below them on their right. Behind them, to the left, the village was half hidden behind trees and some lower hills. They walked past the lake until the only way to go was down on one of three sides or back the way they had come. They took the fourth alternative and stopped.

"This has not been all about me and my father anyway, has it?" Estelle said after they had been silent for several minutes. "Are you unable to forgive *your* father, Justin?"

She heard the echo of his name on her lips. She did not know if he had noticed. He was gazing ahead, his eyes squinting against the rather chilly breeze.

"Why would I need to forgive him?" he asked her. "I was the transgressor. He punished me with banishment."

"For something you could not possibly explain to him," she said. "Not without accusing your stepmother. Your father's wife. Maria's mother. That is the truth of it, is it not? You sacrificed yourself so that his life would not be impossibly wrecked. So that Maria's would not be."

"You would make a saint of me, would you?" he said. "I was furious with him. For not seeing the truth himself. For having married her—after he had been married to *my mother*. They were not just different sorts of women. They were more like different *species*. But he married her, and he always—*always*—treated her with unfailing courtesy. Forgive me, Lady Estelle, but I have said enough. More than enough. He was my *father*. Maria is *my sister*."

"I think perhaps," she said, "you were and are very like your father."

He did not reply.

"Do you think he probably suspected the truth?" she asked. "Even knew it? Do you think he expected that you would go and live with one of your aunts? Or find some respectable employment with their assistance? Was his intention to remove you from a place and a situation that were intolerable to you—and to him? Did he never expect that he would lose all communication with you?"

"How *the devil* am I supposed to know what he expected or intended or *thought*?" he asked her.

"But instead," she said, "you went off on your own and worked at any menial job you could find until you ended up at the stone quarry and made your home there. And your family. I suppose your aunt and uncle had promised to say nothing of your whereabouts or of the place where they sent you letters. Was it your way of punishing your father?"

He wheeled on her. Beneath the brim of his tall hat his eyes looked black and bleak. Just a few weeks ago Estelle would have been frightened. She might have taken a step back.

"Yes," he said. "Yes. That is *exactly* what I was doing. Thank you for making me understand that. I had not realized it until this moment. And you were quite right a few minutes ago too, Lady Estelle. No one is innocent. But how can I forgive my father now? He is dead. How can he forgive me now? *He is dead.*"

They stood facing each other for several moments, his breathing labored as he glared at her, and she gazed back. He reminded her a good deal of her father as he had been during those weeks after Viola had broken off their betrothal and he was at home with her and Bertrand, determined to be there for them at last but still bearing the burden of his guilt and loneliness. Wanting to let them in but not knowing quite how to do it. Wanting forgiveness. Wanting Viola but punishing himself by not going after her.

Lord Brandon turned away first, and they stood side by side, gazing out over the countryside mapped out below them stretching west, south, and north. There was little to see except fields and pasture, sheep, a few cattle, some huddles of farm buildings. Almost no people. There was a cart in the middle distance, driven by a man with a woman at his side. It looked as though she was holding an infant on her lap. There were three children standing on the bars of a gate not far off, watching the sheep on the other side.

"Ricky," the Earl of Brandon murmured. "Where are you?"

Estelle touched his hand, and without turning to look at her he set his arm about her waist and drew her to his side. She did not believe he was even fully aware that he was doing it. His dog had settled, panting, at their feet.

"He was always the peacemaker," Lord Brandon said. "You must not imagine that life in that cottage was some sort of rural idyll. Wes and Hilda used to quarrel occasionally, and quite noisily at times. Wes sometimes bickered with me and I bickered right back. Ricky would say things like *'You weren't nice to Hildy, Wes. She didn't mean to burn the crust on the pie. You ought to say sorry.'* Or *'You needn't get cross with Wes, Juss, because he can't read those words. He's trying. You ought to say sorry.'* And dash it all, we always did. No one ever lost their temper with Ricky. Or got impatient with him. Or made fun of him. There was a great deal of love in that house too."

"It was a family," she said. For four years it had been *his* family. It still was.

"Please, God," he muttered a while later, and his eyes were closed and his head tipped back, Estelle could see when she turned her head. "Let him be found. Let him be safe."

Estelle leaned her head to the side and rested her cheek against his shoulder.

The next day the sun was shining, the air was suddenly almost hot again, and Maria suggested they cheer themselves up with a picnic at the lake after luncheon. They all went, even Lady Maple, who rode there in a gig with Mrs. Chandler, her niece, while Mr. Chandler carried a chair for her, having brushed off the services of a footman. A whole fleet of servants carried their tea out there in large hampers, however, and spread big colorful blankets on the grass for them to sit upon.

It was a lovely occasion, Estelle thought, and surely something that ought to have been happening every summer for years past. The three distinct family groups had mingled well from the start of this visit and were enjoying one another's company today. One person had kept them apart until now—the late countess. What an unhappy woman she must have been. And what unhappiness she had spread around her.

The boat was brought out of the boathouse, and rides were given in relays, the various rowers being the earl, Ernest Sharpe, and Bertrand. Estelle stayed away from it, having always been of the opinion that water was best appreciated from the safety of firm land beneath her feet, or beneath some part of her person, anyway. A few of the younger people—Paulette Ormsbury, Megan and Wallace Chandler, Nigel Dickson, and Rosie Sharpe—went swimming, though they did more splashing and shrieking and laughing than actual swimming. The young children surprised their parents by being more interested in playing in the grotto than in frolicking in the water.

Some people strolled along the banks of the lake, on both sides of the bridge. Maria stood right on the bridge for a long time, gazing at the waterfall, her cousins Angela and Frederick Ormsbury on either side of her. Gillian Chandler and Sidney Sharpe climbed partway up the steep hill on the other side of the waterfall from the grotto while both their mothers kept anxious eyes upon them, though neither—to her credit—called out to them to come down. A few people simply sat and soaked up the heat and the sunshine and chatted with whoever happened to be close.

Captain, reclining upon a flat rock outside the grotto, kept watch over the children.

Estelle strolled between Mr. Rowan Sharpe and Mr. Harold Ormsbury, enjoying their conversation though not participating in it a great deal. She was too busy watching everyone else and appreciating the whole scene. And feeling—paradoxically—a bit melancholy. Everyone belonged here in one way or another, except her and Bertrand.

"Your brother is going to have blisters on his hands tonight, Lady Estelle," Mr. Ormsbury said, nodding in the direction of the boat, where his wife and her sister, Lady Crowther, were being rowed by Bertrand. All three of them were laughing. Bert did not seem to be feeling any lack of belonging. He was being sociable and kind and charming to all, and Estelle knew he was actually enjoying himself here, despite his misgivings before they came.

"I doubt it," she said. "He was on a rowing team when he was at Oxford, and I never once heard him complaining of blisters."

"Complaining to his *sister*?" Mr. Sharpe said. "I should jolly well think not. A man has to have *some* pride."

Estelle laughed.

She felt her lack of belonging, something she never felt when she was with the Westcotts, her stepmother's family, though she had no blood connection with them either. Most of them were not even really her stepmother's family. Viola had been married to Humphrey Westcott, the head of the family, for twenty-three years, but the discovery had been made soon after his death that, unknown to her, it had been a bigamous marriage and her three children were illegitimate. The Westcotts had simply refused to let her and her children go. They had *rallied*, something at which they excelled. They were always more willing to give love a chance, to ignore differences and forgive wrongs, than to bear grudges or stubbornly maintain old hurts. As *this* family was perhaps more prepared to do than either Justin or Maria had given them credit for.

When Viola had married Estelle's father at a family Christmas, the Westcotts had gathered Estelle and Bertrand into the fold too. *Honorary Westcotts*, Alexander Westcott, Earl of Riverdale, head of the family, had told them at the wedding breakfast, his eyes twinkling.

She could have been drawn into this family too, Estelle thought—if she had said yes instead of no at the summerhouse. She could still belong—*if* he made good upon his warning that he would offer for her again before she and Bert left here within the next few days. And *if* she said yes.

Would he?

Would she?

There was still so much darkness in him. And it would be very much worse if Ricky Mort was never found. Was she willing to take on a man's darkness? It would be madness.

But was she willing to walk away from the only man who had ever stirred her deepest emotions?

Bertrand was holding the boat while the Earl of Brandon handed his aunts out. The two men turned the boat over on the bank, and all four of them came across the bridge to the picnic site for tea. The earl stopped on the way and offered his arm to Maria. She hesitated a moment, but then she slid her hand through it.

An hour or so later they straggled homeward in small groups after the gig had arrived to take Lady Maple. This time it was Lady Crowther who went with her. Bertrand helped the earl put the boat away in the boathouse while Estelle and Maria gathered up the wet towels from beside the lake and the cushions from the grotto. They heaped the towels into a hamper in the boathouse to be collected later and put the cushions on their assigned shelves. Bertrand set out for the house with a few other people while Estelle and Maria followed. The earl waited on the bridge for his dog to finish sniffing around the boathouse.

"What a lovely day it has been," Maria said. "I hate to see it come to an end."

Estelle chuckled. "Yet just a couple of weeks ago you were dreading coming," she said.

"I know." Maria thought for a moment. "Estelle, I *loved* my mother. I will never stop doing so. But I think perhaps she may have been oversensitive about some things. She easily felt threatened, probably because she was of humble origins socially—though the Dicksons have been wealthy and influential in Yorkshire for several generations, I understand. They have also always been unabashedly middle class, except for Great-aunt Bertha and Mama, who wanted something they considered better. And then there is the fact that Mama was very young when she married Papa—good heavens, she was three years younger than I am now. She saw criticism and jealousy and quarrels where none were intended, and walled herself off from further threats that simply did not exist. It is all very sad. She could have been far happier if she had had her family about her, and she could have found consolation with them after Papa died. So could I. I do not believe I am being disloyal to her in allowing myself to be restored to them now. Am I?"

"Oh, absolutely not," Estelle said. "You need your family, Maria. You have been so very alone. Now they will always belong to you."

"Rosie wants me to go home with her for a while," Maria said. "And Aunt Betty and Uncle Rowan are willing to take me if it is all right with Brandon. Gillian and Megan and Wallace want to come back here later when Aunt Sarah and Uncle Thomas come. They do not believe Aunt Sarah will mind. According to Wallace she is a brick—whatever *that* means." She laughed. "And Aunt Augusta and Aunt Felicity have told me Brandon and I simply must come to Cornwall next summer—if I do not meet someone and marry him during the spring. Or if Brandon does not."

"Goodness," Estelle said. "It sounds as if you have a busy year ahead."

Or if Brandon does not. Meet and marry someone during the next Season, that was.

Fortunately there was some sort of distraction up ahead. "But what is *this*?" Estelle asked.

This was a ragged beggar standing in the middle of the drive just on the house side of the Palladian bridge, looking hesitantly toward Lord Crowther and his eldest son and daughter-in-law. They had been distracted for the moment by the two children, who were gazing intently into the river and pointing and demanding to know what sort of fish *those* were.

"Oh dear God," Estelle said, hurrying past the others until she was just a few feet from the beggar. *"Ricky?"*

He looked at her warily, a tall, solidly built young man with pleasant features more or less disguised by a scruffy growth of beard and a few layers of dirt, and dirty fair hair that stood in stiff, untidy spikes on his head. He had no hat. His clothes were not so much ragged as filthy and grass-stained with clumps of straw clinging to them in places. The sole of one of his boots was bound in place with what might once have been a handkerchief. Even from several feet away Estelle could smell him.

"I don't know you," he said slowly.

"I am a friend of the Earl of Brandon," she told him. "Justin Wiley. Juss."

"You know Juss?" he said.

"I do." She smiled at him. "He will be *so* happy to see you, Ricky. Let me take you to him."

But he was looking suddenly anxious and agitated. "Did he find his sister?" he asked.

"His sister?" Estelle said. "Maria?"

"Did he find her?" He took a step toward her. "She is lost. He is looking for her. I come to help."

Oh. In his letter explaining why he could not go to see Ricky as planned during July, the Earl of Brandon must have explained that he was going to find his sister and bring her home.

"I'll look too," Ricky said. "We'll find her, me and Juss."

"She has been found and brought home," Estelle said. "Here she is, Ricky. Maria is Justin's sister, and she is back home safe and sound."

Maria was gazing at him, both hands pressed to her mouth. The others had turned from the river and were gawking.

"Good God," Lord Crowther said. "Here he is. He found his way."

"She is back?" Ricky said. "I'm happy. I come to look with Juss, but now I can go home to Wes and Hildy. Maybe Hildy will make my favorite soup. I'm hungry."

"Let me take you to Justin first," Estelle said, stepping up to him and taking his large hand in hers. "Come. I believe he will be at the stables by now."

He was not. He had walked home, not beside the river as Maria and Estelle and the others had done, but closer to the house. He was up on the terrace now, looking toward the bridge. Captain was looking too, and then bounding down the stone steps and streaking through the formal gardens and across the lawn to jump up on Ricky, both large paws against his shoulders while he licked his face.

"Cappy," Ricky complained, laughing. "You mustn't do that. Your paws may be dirty. Juss will be cross with you. Hildy would be cross if she was here."

But Estelle was not looking at either the dog or the man. She was looking at Lord Brandon, who was still up on the terrace, a wide, sun-filled smile on his face as he took off his hat and dropped it at his feet. He strode down the steps then and down to the bridge, his eyes never leaving Ricky's face.

"Well, it's about time," he said as he drew close. "What kept you so long, Ricky? I thought you would never get here."

And he caught Ricky up in his arms, heedless, it seemed, of either the dirt or the smell, and laughed.

And oh, the realization hit Estelle low in the stomach like a real physical blow.

Oh, she loved him.

Nineteen

R icky launched into excited chatter, much of it incoherent, though Justin did understand some of what he said. He had come to Everleigh, it seemed, *not* because Justin had failed to go to him but because Justin had lost his sister and was going to look for her and bring her home and Ricky wanted to help in the search.

He had remembered the name of the house because when Justin had said it, he had also said, *Everleigh is mine for everly and everly after, Ricky*. And he knew the house was in a big place with a long name, but Juss had told him it was often shortened to sound like a place where hearts (or *Herts*) belong because it is home. He had found his way by asking stagecoach drivers when they were stopped outside inns. They refused to give him a ride.

"Though I never did ask, Juss," he said, "because you can't do that without money and I didn't take any from Hildy's jar because she buys stuff with it to make dinner."

But they would wave off in the direction of hearts belonging because it was home and told him that was where it was but it was too far off to be walked.

He did get some rides, usually on farmers' carts among hay or vegetables or even manure, once for a whole afternoon standing up behind the vehicle of a wild young man whose name he could not remember. But they had moved like the wind, and when Ricky had laughed, the young man had laughed too and they had gone even faster. He sometimes got food, but only when he could do something to earn it. Not otherwise. He would not let that young man buy him a meal even though it was going to be beef and potatoes and gravy and other things. It was wrong to beg unless you were starving and he was never starving, just hungry. He was very, very happy now.

"That lady told me you found your sister, Juss," he said. "She is nice. I wouldn't've talked to her because she is a stranger, but she said she is Juss's friend and that's you. And she said she'd bring me to you."

"She *is* my friend," Justin told him, looking at Lady Estelle, who was flushed and bright-eyed and smiling at the two of them. "She is Lady Estelle Lamarr. Ricky, you stink."

"That's not a nice word, Juss," Ricky said. "I don't stink, though Hildy would tell me time to wash my hands and Wes would tell me time to shave. The sole come almost off my boot, but I used my handkerchief to keep it on. Look!" He raised his foot for Justin to see. And he was off again, recounting some of his adventures and how yesterday a few men had shouted after him. "They even guessed my name, Juss. That was clever, wasn't it? But they was strangers so I ran and hid and then they went away."

Word had spread fast in the last few minutes. There was a crowd on the terrace, Justin could see. A few of the guests had come closer. There was a little huddle of servants under the portico.

"And this, Ricky," Justin said, "is my sister, Maria. She is home now and quite safe, as you can see."

And Maria, who had come to stand beside Lady Estelle, smiled with warm sweetness. "Thank you for coming all this way to help search for me, Ricky," she said. "Maybe Justin would have found me sooner if you had been with him. But he did find me and bring me home."

"Ah," Ricky said with a big smile. "You must be very happy."

"I am," she said, and transferred her gaze to Justin for a few moments. "It always feels good to be home."

She was, Justin realized, speaking to him.

"And on the subject of home, Ricky," Justin said, "Wes and Hildy are worried."

"No!" Ricky said, and shook his head vigorously. "They'll know I come to help you, Juss. I'm good at finding things. Remember when I found Mrs. Klebb's cat when it didn't come home for two days that time? And remember how I found the button that come off Wes's shirt when Hildy was ironing it and it rolled and no one else could find it?"

"I remember. But come," Justin said, setting an arm about his shoulders. "It is time for a bath and a change of clothes, Ricky. I know you hate baths and like to wear your own clothes, but there will be no arguments today, please. You stink. Afterward you will smell like a rose."

"Like a rose." Ricky laughed. "Do I want to smell like a rose, Juss?"

"You do if the alternative is this," Justin said firmly. And he led Ricky off toward the house while his sister and all his guests inexplicably applauded. The servants too.

"Have hot bathwater and shaving gear sent to my dressing room," Justin told Phelps as they climbed the steps to the portico. "And a pot of chocolate with extra milk and sugar and a few sweet biscuits immediately. A full meal can follow half an hour after the bathwater."

He had no idea where he would put Ricky until Wes found his way here too—and even perhaps after that. But for now it was going to be his own room, even if his valet quit without notice.

His valet did not quit. He brought shaving water and a new razor within minutes of Justin's arrival in the dressing room with Ricky. A footman came behind him with the chocolate and biscuits. The valet's nose twitched only slightly at the smell before he went into action, stripping Ricky from the waist up and wrapping a towel about his shoulders while he seated him and lathered his face and shaved him. Ricky sat very still and stopped grinning when he was told to.

He ate his biscuits and drank his chocolate while the valet dug out some of the plain clothes Justin always took with him when he went to spend a few weeks with his friends at the stone quarry. Fortunately, he and Ricky were of similar enough size that the clothes would more or less fit him.

By then the bathwater had arrived and Justin's valet stripped Ricky of the rest of his clothes and the sorry boots, directed one of the footmen who had brought the water to take everything away, and soon had Ricky immersed in the water and being thoroughly scrubbed. He shut his eyes tightly while his hair was being washed.

Justin sniffed the air when Ricky was finally standing on a towel beside the bathtub, being vigorously dried off. "Soap," he said. "Not roses, but plain soap. A much better smell for a man. Hildy would be proud of you, Ricky. Clean from the top of your head to the tips of your toes." His valet had set a new toothbrush and tooth powder on the wash-stand, but the meal would come first.

And thinking of Hilda, he must write to her without delay, send one of his grooms across country again to deliver the letter in person and set her mind at ease—about Ricky, anyway. Wes would be less of a worry to her. He could look after himself. Though as for that, it had turned out that Ricky could look after himself too.

A hot meal was awaiting Ricky in Justin's bedchamber, where it had been set out on a table. He devoured every morsel.

"That soup was good, Juss," he said when he was finished. "Almost as good as what Hildy makes." And he yawned hugely and noisily.

There was a room adjoining Justin's own, separated from it by his dressing room and another, empty one. It would be his countess's bedchamber after he married, Justin had always thought, though this was not the suite of rooms his father and mother—and then his stepmother—had occupied. Those were in the west wing, while this was in the corner of the east wing. He took Ricky through to the other room, which his valet had prepared by drawing the curtains across the window and turning back the bedcovers. Justin helped him off with his coat and cravat and then with his boots—a bit of a tight fit—after Ricky had sat on the side of the bed, yawning again.

"We ought to have put you straight into a nightshirt, I suppose," Justin said. "But no matter. You can sleep here for the rest of the day and all night too if you wish, Ricky. You must not be frightened if you wake up and I am not here. I am going to leave a candle burning once it gets dark. And that door into the dressing room is going to be left open, as well as the one on the other side that leads into my room. You can call for me during the night if you need me.

If I am not there, then you must pull on this bell rope and someone will find me and I will come up to you. Just wait here for me."

"Call for you if I am frightened," Ricky said. "Pull on that rope if you do not answer. I'll remember. Pull on that rope. I'm awful tired, Juss." He yawned again to prove it.

"I know," Justin said. "Lie down now and I will tuck you in. And, Ricky? Thank you for coming. I know you would have helped me look for my sister. You probably would have found her too, long before I did."

"I'm good at it," Ricky said as he lay down and Justin tucked the covers around him.

Justin stood by the bed looking down at his friend. He had been privileged in his life. He had been given the chance, as so few were, to live with people of all sorts and stations in life, to find friendship in unexpected places. Even family. And love.

But he really must go and write to Hilda.

The library was empty, he thought at first when he got there. Perhaps everyone was getting dressed for dinner. Perhaps they were *at* dinner. Perhaps they had already eaten. He really had no idea what time it was. But the room was not empty. Lady Estelle Lamarr was standing at one of the windows looking out, and she turned her head to see who was coming into the room. She turned fully when she saw it was him. She was dressed for the evening and looking stunningly beautiful in emerald green. She made him conscious of the fact that he had not changed, or even combed his hair, since he had returned from the lake.

"I thought perhaps you would come here," she said. "I waited awhile to see if you would."

"I need to get a letter on the way to Hilda," he said.

"Yes, I know," she said. "I took the liberty of writing

one myself. It is on the desk. I thought it might save you some time if it meets with your approval, though you will no doubt wish to add a more personal message to assure her that I am who I say I am. I do not know her address or her last name, I am afraid. I had to call her Hilda. I hope she will not be offended by the familiarity."

He raised his eyebrows and crossed to the desk to pick up the letter lying there. She had neat, stylish handwriting. She had written Hilda that Ricky had arrived safely at Everleigh Park an hour or so before and was at this very minute abovestairs with the Earl of Brandon—Justin—having a bath and shave and a meal. He had found his way, she had explained, by remembering jokes Justin had once told him as memory prompts for the names Everleigh and Hertfordshire. He had asked directions of the drivers of stagecoaches and got a few rides with farmers and one young gentleman. He had insisted upon performing odd jobs in payment for food. He had come here under the mistaken impression that the Earl of Brandon's sister was missing. He had intended to help search for her. Everyone at Everleigh had been happy to welcome him, especially the earl himself, who would keep him safe until Mr. Wesley Mort arrived.

She had signed the letter and added the explanation that she was a friend of Lord Brandon.

"Thank you," Justin said, looking up from the page.

"He is resting?" she asked.

"I believe he was asleep almost before his head hit the pillow," he said. "Which was a blessing. Ricky's yawns when he is very tired are enough to drive anyone within range of the sound of them to the brink of insanity."

She smiled. "Oh, Justin," she said then, her face lighting up. "He did not come here for selfish reasons, because *you* did not go there to see *him*. He must have misunderstood something you wrote in a letter and thought Maria was missing. He came to help you look for her."

"I know," he said. "One has to be very precise about what one says to Ricky."

"He is lovely," she said.

"He even smells sweet now," he told her. "I will just add a postscript to this and a signature and get it addressed and sent off. The poor woman is probably close to losing her mind. She always says that the men in her life will be the death of her sanity."

"I will leave you to it, then," she said.

But she did not immediately move, and he did not immediately sit down at the desk. He crossed the room toward her until he was almost toe to toe with her.

"Thank you," he said again.

And he took her mouth with his own and lingered there for a while. She did not resist. She did not even remain passive. Her lips parted beneath his, and her mouth pressed back against his. They did not touch anywhere else.

He gazed at her for a few moments after he had lifted his head. She smiled slightly and moved away to let herself quietly out of the room.

She had stepped close enough to Ricky to take his hand in hers. She had not flinched from either the sight or the smell of him. Yet she was *Lady* Estelle Lamarr, a marquess's daughter.

Who he rather suspected was the light of his life.

Everyone was busy again the following day, writing letters, paying calls, doing everything in their power to spread the word that the young man who had been missing was lost no longer but was safely ensconced at Everleigh Park. Everyone was thanked for their efforts in keeping an eye out. Irwin Chandler was a little disappointed that the poster he had planned would not after all be printed, but he was very glad there was no longer any need of it.

"One is always afraid, though one does not speak a word of one's fears aloud," he confided to Justin, "that someone who is lost will never be seen alive again."

"Yes," Justin said. "It is what I feared most."

No one appeared to find the renewed activity a chore. They threw themselves into it with enthusiasm. None of them seemed to feel that Ricky was simply not worth all the fuss. Indeed, some of them had been a bit disappointed yesterday to learn that he was asleep and very likely to remain asleep until this morning. A few had been disappointed when he was not at the breakfast table. He *was* awake, however. He had risen early, Justin explained, as he always did at home. Justin had taken him and Doris's children out to the stables to see the horses and take Captain for a walk. The children had held Ricky's hands and chattered with him while they led him over the Palladian bridge to walk along the path on the other side of the river. They had not made their usual demand to be taken for a ride. Ricky had chattered right back. Justin might as well not have been there at all, he had thought in some amusement.

Later in the day when Justin had taken Ricky outside again for a breath of air, Nigel Dickson and Wallace Chandler took him through the maze. Everyone within earshot smiled at the sound of his excited laughter. Ernest and Sidney Sharpe, Frederick Ormsbury, and Martin Haig, Doris's husband, made private bets upon how long he would remain in there and whether or not the three of them would reach the center. Neither Nigel nor Wallace had had any luck with doing that yet. Ricky had confidently predicted he would find it.

"I am good at finding things that are lost, missus," he had told Mrs. Dickson after she had suggested to her son that perhaps it was unwise to confuse Ricky by taking him in there.

The three of them emerged eight minutes after going in—the most optimistic bet had predicted twelve minutes, with no success at reaching the center. Ricky was still laughing.

"There's a big stone there in the middle with writing on it," he said. "It says, *'You found it,'* and another long word."

" *'Congratulations!'* " Nigel said. "In large letters. With an exclamation point."

"Nige and Wally read it to me," Ricky said.

"You found your way to the center?" Sid Sharpe asked with a grin.

"Nige and Wally kept wanting to go the wrong way," Ricky said. "It was funny. Sorry we were so long. I kept having to call them back and wait for them so they wouldn't get lost. It was funny."

And of course throughout the day everyone kept an eye on the road over the bridge and up the hill, watching for the arrival of Wesley Mort. There was no real anxiety over him, however. He would come eventually, but his search for his brother along the way would slow him down.

Justin did not take Ricky to the dining room at mealtimes or to the drawing room. He sat with him while he ate his meals in the room next to Justin's, which was his temporary home. And he showed him parts of the house and park that were unlikely to be crowded. He took him to the stables again and out behind them to the smithy, where the blacksmith welcomed him and explained a few things to him while Ricky listened and watched with rapt attention. Justin took him up through the wilderness walk and stood for a long time by the tower and again by the dragon, while Ricky amused himself and Captain yipped and barked. Viscount Watley went with them. He explained to Ricky that he was the brother of the lady who had met him yesterday after he had stepped over the bridge.

"Brothers are good," Ricky said, beaming at him. "I got a brother. Wes. He looks after me. And Hildy does too. Hildy is a good cook."

And inside the house Justin decided to take Ricky up to the balcony beneath the dome in the grand reception room. They met Maria and Lady Estelle in the entrance hall on the way there. The two had just come in from outside.

"That's Maria," Ricky said, pointing. "Your sister, Juss. And that's your friend with her, the lady who was kind to me when I come yesterday. We went up to that dragon with her brother. Brothers are good. I got a brother. Wes."

"I believe he is on his way here," Maria said, smiling. "We will be happy to meet him."

"He is nice," Ricky said. "And this lady's brother is nice too."

"We are going up to the gallery under the dome," Justin said. "Ricky liked the tower on the wilderness walk. I believe he will like this as well."

"Oh," Maria said. "May we come too? I have not been up there since I was a child. Y-you took me. You held my hand and I was not at all afraid. Children are so ready to trust in the invulnerability of the adults they l— Of adults."

"I will hold your hand again, if you wish," Justin said. "Lady Estelle, will you come too?"

"Yes," she said. "I have been hoping to do it before we leave here."

And so the four of them climbed the stairs that wound their way through a narrow corridor outside the domed room before emerging onto the balcony. It was wide and solid and supported by the sturdy marble pillars that surrounded the floor below. The marble balustrade about the outer edge was solid and slightly more than waist-high, even against Justin's height. The small marble pillars that held it up were spaced closely enough that not even the thinnest child would be able to squeeze between them. The whole thing had been built with safety in mind, though it was beautiful too. Above them the dome soared. Below them the mosaic floor was laid out in all its splendor.

Maria was holding very tightly to his hand, Justin noticed. Lady Estelle was standing to one side of them, Ricky at the other.

"This is *fun*, Juss," he said. "But if this is Everleigh—for everly and everly—where is your *house*?"

"This is it, Ricky," Justin said. "This is my house."

Ricky turned to stare at him. "No-o," he said. "How do you keep it clean?"

"I have a lot of people to clean it for me," Justin said.

"That's silly," Ricky said.

"Those people earn their living working here instead of hewing stone in the quarry," Justin explained. "Lady Estelle, are you all right?"

She had moved forward to grasp the top of the balustrade with both hands, though she stood back from it the length of her arms. Her knuckles were white. Her head was tipped back and she was gazing at the dome.

"My stomach feels as if it may be standing on its head,"

she admitted. "And I believe I must have misplaced my knees while I was outside with Maria. But yes, thank you. I am perfectly fine. Provided I do not look down. The balcony seems far higher from up here than it looks from down there."

"This rail is made of stone," Ricky said, moving toward her. "Stone is ever so strong. We could all of us push at this all day long and it wouldn't budge. Even if Wes was pushing too. That floor down there looks pretty. Hold my hand and have a look at it. I'll keep you safe. Won't I, Juss? I kept Juss safe when he come to our house after Wes had hit his face raw and bust his nose. Wes didn't ought to've done that."

"I will take your hand if I may, Ricky," Lady Estelle said, suiting action to words. "Thank you. I remember from yesterday how strong it feels. And I will look down."

"If you tried to fall you couldn't," Ricky said. "I wouldn't let you, and this stone rail wouldn't let you."

"You are quite right," she said. "The floor does look pretty from up here. And the dome takes my breath away."

"You got to breathe," Ricky said. "Or you will faint. I'll carry you down the stairs if you do—don't worry—but there's no need. You got to breathe."

"There." She inhaled audibly and exhaled. "This is a lovely room. The very heart of the house. At the center of it and very beautiful. Oh, look, Ricky. The sun must be coming out. Look at how the whole room is lighting up."

"It's the prettiest thing *ever*," Ricky said.

Maria turned her head to look up at Justin. "I feel as safe as I always used to," she murmured. But instead of smiling, as she might have done, her eyes filled with tears, and she bit her upper lip and turned her head away.

Love was no soft emotion that brought endless bliss, was it? Why, then, did one allow oneself to feel it at all? Because the alternative was unthinkable?

"Shall we walk around the gallery?" Justin suggested.

His guests had been here for two weeks, Justin realized the following day. All were planning to leave within the next few days. He hoped no one would go away disappointed. He had not organized any grand activities for them—excursions beyond the confines of the park, for example, or parties or even a ball that included his neighbors. If he had had a countess, she might have thought of that and the necessity of *entertaining* their guests.

If he had had a countess . . .

The days were running out, and soon, if he was to keep the promise he had made to Lady Estelle out at the lake, he was going to have to propose marriage to her again. Would she accept this time? Sometimes he thought she might. At other times he could not imagine why she would. What did he have to offer her except all *this*—Everleigh, a title, wealth? And his heart, for whatever that was worth. He did not have any of the . . . the *light*, for want of a better word, that filled her and surrounded her like an aura. It was the word she herself had used, now that he came to think of it. It was something she had said he lacked.

He did not even know how he was going to go about asking her. How did one make a proposal of marriage in such a way that it would tip the scales in one's favor?

But he was distracted from that problem by Wes's arrival, two days after Ricky's.

Unlike Ricky, Wes did not come at a time when there were other people outside. And he did not come to the front doors or even to the kitchen door. A groom brought word from the stables that Mr. Wesley Mort had come for his brother and would be obliged if someone would bring him to the stables so that they could be on their way and not trouble anyone any further.

A typical Wes sort of message.

Justin was having tea with his guests at the time in the square reception room in the state apartments. The butler came discreetly to his table and murmured in his ear.

Justin set his napkin beside his plate and got to his feet. "Excuse me," he said loudly enough for everyone to hear. "Wes Mort has just arrived at the stables. No, please." He held up a hand to discourage those of his guests who had also begun to get to their feet. "Wes is nothing like his brother. He would be mortified beyond belief if he were to see anyone but me coming from the house. It sounds as though he intends to leave here as soon as Ricky joins him. He would leave sooner than that if he could. I'll go alone."

Wes was frowning darkly when Justin strode into the stable yard. Captain was sitting beside him, panting in ecstasy. "Good God, Juss," Wes said. "You didn't say anything about living in a palace. And just look at those clothes you are wearing. And all those fobs and watches and whatnot. And that quizzing glass. Good God!"

Justin grinned and reached out his hand. "And good day to you too, Wes," he said. "Ricky found his way here two days ago, hungry, tired, unshaven, and dirty, but unharmed and undaunted. He came to help me find my sister, who, according to his interpretation of my letter, was lost."

Wes stared at him. "I didn't even notice that," he said. "But you ought to know, Juss, not even to whisper the word *lost* to Ricky. He thinks of himself as some sort of super finder of the missing. But I knew he was here. A tavern keeper about twenty miles away told me. I loosened a few of his teeth after he told me the raving lunatic was safely confined at Everleigh and everyone could sleep safe in their beds again."

"Did you?" Justin grinned again. "I wrote to Hildy, Wes. Or at least, one of my guests wrote and I signed my name and sent it with one of my grooms so that she would not worry longer than necessary."

Wes set a hand in his at last and shook it with what might have been a hearty grip if he had not looked so uncomfortable. "This is all deuced embarrassing, you know, Juss," he said. "Good God! You live in a palace! And Ricky walked into it, I daresay, as though he belonged here. Where is he? I'll take him and get going. You're a real nob, aren't you, Juss? Mr. La-di-da."

"He is having a sleep after spending the morning with the blacksmith," Justin explained. "And you will stay here tonight, Wes. I daresay your borrowed horse needs a good, long rest even if you do not. And I have a proposition to make to you."

"What?" Wes asked warily.

"A job," Justin told him. "Something you once told me would be your dream come true. And a home to go with it. For you and Hildy and Ricky."

Wes's eyes narrowed on him. "A dream come true," he said. "What do you think I am, Juss? A wide-eyed girl waiting for her prince like in that one story you used to tell that so thrilled Ricky and Hildy?"

"The story you never listened to?" Justin said, grinning once more. "I value my personal safety too much ever to call you Cinderella, Wes."

"Ricky isn't sleeping in that palace, is he?" Wes asked.

"In the room adjoining my own," Justin told him. "Like old times."

"Oh, God in his heaven," Wes said in disgust while Captain got to his feet and licked his hand. "Sometimes, Juss, I wish you had another nose to bust."

Twenty

Most of the family and guests were gathered in the drawing room again that evening, though Bertrand and Mr. Sharpe had wandered off to the library, and Nigel Dickson and Angela Ormsbury had followed them. There was a group of people clustered about the pianoforte, though they were doing more talking and laughing than actual playing. A few of the men were playing cards. Mrs. Dickson, Mrs. Chandler, and Mrs. Sharpe were sitting with Lady Maple. Maria and Estelle were listening to Lady Crowther and her sister reminiscing about their courtship by brothers and the early days of their marriages. The Earl of Brandon was standing behind Maria's chair, listening too.

He looked tired, Estelle thought. He had had a busy couple of hours before dinner. His friend Wesley Mort had been persuaded to stay for at least one night before taking Ricky home, but it had not been easy, apparently. He had been quite adamant about not staying anywhere in the house—and upon Ricky's not staying here for another night either. The blacksmith had offered them a room in his cottage up in the laborers' village on the other side of the hill behind the house. That was where they both were now. Estelle had the feeling there had been an argument. They were best friends, the earl had once said. They also butted heads now and then, she believed. She also suspected they were similar sorts of men, both very proud.

The sisters' memories had turned to their mother, Lord Brandon's grandmother. They were laughing over how she had loved the slightest excuse to dress in all her best finery and deck herself out with as many of the family jewels as she could comfortably drape about her.

"Or uncomfortably, for that matter. If she had had more than ten fingers," Lady Felicity Ormsbury said, "she would have worn more than ten rings."

"But she *did*," Lady Crowther said. "She always wore her wedding ring and her diamond on the same finger."

"But no rings, surely, on her thumbs," Maria said.

Her aunts looked at each other.

"Well, perhaps not on her thumbs," Lady Crowther conceded. "But there were all the other pieces too, most of them heirlooms. Papa used to threaten sometimes to call out the militia to guard her because she was carrying around a fortune on her person."

"Mrs. Sharpe reminds me of Mama a little, Augusta," her sister said. "Always jingling and jangling with necklaces and bracelets and bangles. We would stay awake in the nursery despite all of Nurse's threats and scolding on evenings when Mama was going somewhere or expecting guests here. She would always come to say good night, sometimes long after our bedtime, and we would gaze at her, speechless with awe."

"You might have been speechless, Felicity," Lady Crowther said. "I always used to jump up and down on my bed with excitement until Mama threatened that if I fell off and broke a leg, she would positively not come up and see me ever again."

"She was *such* a liar," Lady Felicity said, and they both laughed.

"I have not seen the family heirlooms for years," Lady Crowther said. "Of course I have not. I have not *been* here for years. Neither have you, Felicity. And we will be leaving here the day after tomorrow. Justin, may we see them before we go? Where do you keep them?"

All eyes turned his way. Maria looked over her shoulder at him.

"That is a good question," he said. "I have no idea."

"What?" Lady Crowther half shrieked.

"Where were they usually kept?" he asked.

"In the safe," Lady Crowther said. "In Papa's bedchamber. In *your* bedchamber."

"I am not in the room Grandpapa and then my father slept in," he said. "I have rooms in the corner of the east wing. I . . . do not go into those rooms."

His aunts both stared at him.

"Indeed," Lady Felicity said. "Well. That is understandable, I suppose. But you have not given a single thought to the family heirlooms and where they all might be? One can tell *you* are not a married man. They are probably still there in the safe."

"They are probably *not*," Maria said sharply. "They probably disappeared with Mama's jewels."

There was an awkward silence, during which Estelle wished there were a way to get up and move somewhere else without drawing attention to herself.

"Perhaps we should go and see," Lady Crowther said.

"How are we to get into the safe?" the earl asked. "I must confess I never even knew of its existence. I do remember once seeing the heirloom jewelry with my mother. I must have been quite young at the time. I do not believe she ever wore any of it. Or Maria's mother. I suppose I would have assumed it was all in a bank vault somewhere if I had ever thought of it at all."

"If he had ever thought of it," Lady Crowther said to her sister.

They gazed at each other and spoke in unison.

"Men!"

"You never even knew of the existence of the safe, Justin?" Lady Crowther asked, sounding dismayed. "You do not have the key, then? Maria?"

She shook her head. "Papa used to keep Mama's jewels in his room," she said. "But I never knew where. I never saw the family heirlooms. Mama said they were ugly."

"Our father, your grandpapa, was not so secretive with his children," Lady Crowther said. "We were always fascinated by the safe, hidden away as it was, and by all the jewels our mother used to wear whenever she had an excuse to do so. But who *would* know where the key is? Our brother surely would have left that information with *someone*, Justin."

"He left a whole lot of information with his lawyer and his man of business," the earl said stiffly. "I have not encouraged them to share any but essential business with me."

They stared at him, frowning, and Estelle realized, not for the first time, how badly his father had hurt him.

"Well," Lady Felicity said, looking a bit shamefaced, "I know where the key used to be kept. I watched Papa open the safe once and then close it, and I memorized just what he did and where he got the key from and returned it to. I crept back in there one day to make sure I was right, and I was. I got it open. But that was *years* ago. I must have been eleven or twelve."

"And you still remember it, Aunt Felicity?" the earl asked.

"I still do," she said. "It is amazing what sticks in one's head from childhood, while something I take particular care to memorize today will in all likelihood be gone without a trace by next week. The human mind is an odd thing."

"Then let us go," Lady Crowther said, getting to her feet. "Justin, you had better come too. Those heirlooms are, after all, your property now. Your countess will wear them one day, and I hope that will be sooner rather than later."

"I am coming too," Maria said. "Estelle, please come with me."

Estelle held up one hand. "I believe I had better not," she said.

"Please do," the Earl of Brandon said.

"Oh, by all means, Lady Estelle," Lady Crowther said, linking her arm through Estelle's. "I hope my brother did not do the sensible thing after our papa died and change the lock or hide the key elsewhere or both. And I hope Felicity's memory has not become decrepit with age. Otherwise this is going to be very anticlimactic."

The suite of rooms that had always been the earl's until six years ago was at the south end of the west wing. The earl's bedchamber was magnificently decorated in deep shades of wine and gold. The furnishings were heavy and old-fashioned and stately. It was a grand room, Estelle thought as the earl lit candles until the darkness and the shadows receded. Yet it had an air of being unlived in.

The Earl of Brandon's face, she noticed, looked as though it were carved out of granite.

Maria came to a stop just inside the door. Estelle remained at her side. Lady Crowther pointed to the ornately carved fireplace, and she and her sister made their way toward it. The earl, having finished lighting the candles, stood and watched.

"It was one of those knobs down there," Lady Crowther said, pointing to the paneling to the left of the fireplace. "This one, I believe." She bent and pressed and poked at the carved leaves there with no result until her sister bent across her and twisted an acorn. A panel above them slid back. "The safe is still there, at least. Now we just need to get into it. Felicity? Here, I will stand back out of your way and cross all my fingers. And my eyes too. And I will hold my breath for good measure."

Neither Maria nor her brother moved at all. Estelle found that she was also holding her breath. It somehow seemed terribly important that the family treasures be intact. What would happen if the safe was empty? Or if some of the pieces the earl's aunts remembered were missing? Or if the safe could not be opened at all?

Lady Felicity went to the other side of the fireplace, reached up to a carved leaf just below the mantel, and pulled outward on it, pressing on the inside of it at the same time. The leaf opened on some sort of hinge to reveal a small dark cavity. She reached inside with two fingers and her thumb and brought out a small metal key.

They all, it seemed, exhaled at the same moment.

She crossed the fireplace again and bent to insert the key in the lock of the safe and turn it.

The door swung open, the key still in the lock.

"Oh," Lady Felicity said, and stepped back. Her sister crowded forward to join her and peer inside. "It is not empty."

"Let us take everything out and spread it on the bed," Lady Crowther suggested. "Come and see, Justin. Come closer, Maria. And you too, Lady Estelle. Oh, this *is* exciting. I would have *kicked* myself if we had gone home the day after tomorrow and *then* I had remembered the family heirlooms. Oh, look, Felicity. The ruby brooch. It was my *favorite*."

Soon the bed was half covered with jewelry that must surely be worth a king's ransom, Estelle thought. But while the sisters were exclaiming over remembered items and declaring that absolutely nothing was missing, the Earl of Brandon was picking up a folded document or letter that had been tossed out with everything else but had not drawn anyone's interest. He slipped it into an inner pocket of his coat.

Maria meanwhile was reaching out with a trembling hand to pick up a bulging white silk drawstring bag.

"Oh," she said when she had opened it and peered inside. She closed her eyes and swayed on her feet. "Oh, dear God."

Estelle set a steadying hand on her arm, and the earl strode across the room to stand behind her and grasp her by the shoulders.

"Mama's jewels," she said. "Papa always kept them for her. In this bag."

"Look through it," the earl said. "See if everything is there."

She emptied it onto the bed and spread out the items. She set one hand over her mouth before removing it to speak.

"Everything," she said. "Oh, I think everything is here."

"My dear Maria," her aunt Augusta said, "they were here all the time. Your mama was mistaken."

Or she had lied. No one said that, though.

"Or I could simply have put them back in there," the earl

said, lowering his hands from his sister's shoulders. "I told the truth, Maria, when I said downstairs that I did not even know of this safe. I certainly did not know where it was or how to expose it or where to find the key. But I could be lying."

"No," she said, running a shaking hand over the jewels. "No, Justin. I think I have known for some time that there was no theft, that Papa had some other reason for sending you away. Mama made up that story, did she not? Just for my ears. I do not remember Papa ever saying anything about any theft or Mama mentioning it in his hearing. My mind is weary. I do not want to think about why you were really sent away. You are not a thief. And I am glad."

She turned to look at him, her eyes troubled.

"She never wore any of them after that day," she said. "It must have been very important to her that I believe you had stolen them, for she always loved wearing them. She did not take any of them to Prospect Hall with her when we left here. Perhaps she was afraid I would see them. She was very eager to blacken your name and preserve her own name. Did she not understand that I *loved* her? That I always would have done, no matter what? Perhaps she simply did not know how to get them from the safe," she added wearily.

Her brother drew her into his arms and kissed the top of her head.

"Some things are best left in the past, where they belong," he told her. "I have always loved you, Maria, past and present. I will love you as long as I live. Perhaps you will come to love me again in time. I will try to be patient."

"Come," Lady Crowther said briskly. "We will put everything back and go join everyone else. Perhaps Felicity and I can come back for another look tomorrow, with your permission, Justin. We will bring our daughters with us."

"Do you want your mother's jewels to go back into the safe for now?" the earl asked Maria.

"Yes," she said.

Everything was put away—except the document or letter that was in the earl's pocket. It seemed to Estelle that she was the only one who had noticed it. The safe was locked, the key removed, and the panel closed. The key was returned to its little nook behind the carved leaf. Lady Felicity led the way to the door while her sister linked an arm through Maria's and followed. Estelle went after them, leaving the Earl of Brandon alone in his father's room.

Everyone had returned to the drawing room, Estelle could see when they arrived there. The late-evening tea tray had been brought in, and Esme Ormsbury, Lady Crowther's daughter-in-law, was pouring. She looked up and smiled at the returning party.

"Was Aunt Felicity able to find and open the safe?" she asked.

"She was," Lady Crowther said. "And everything was there. We spread it all out on the bed. It felt almost like having Mother back for a few minutes. All the pieces looked *so* familiar."

"This is very exciting," Angela Ormsbury said. "The Wiley family treasures. We must all go and look tomorrow. May we, Mama and Aunt Augusta? But you are not the ones to ask, are you? *May* we, Justin? Oh, has he not come back yet? Ah, here he comes. *May* we see the jewels tomorrow, Justin?"

He was standing inside the door, Estelle saw when she turned her head. He was looking like what she thought of as his granite self, his hands at his back.

"Of course," he said. "I will bring them down for every-one to see."

"Come and get a cup of tea while it is still hot," Esme said to the new arrivals.

"My mother's jewels were there too," Maria said, and though she did not speak loudly, there was something in her voice that silenced everyone. "They were in the bag where she always kept them. Everything was there. At least, every-thing I could remember was there."

"But that is wonderful," Paulette Ormsbury said, beam-ing at Maria while everyone else remained silent. "Well . . . is it not?"

"I daresay your mama was mistaken, then, Maria," Lady Maple said. "So all is well that ends well. If there is any tea left in the pot, Mrs. Ormsbury, I will have—"

"No," Maria said. "She was not mistaken. She lied. She knew her jewelry was in the safe in Papa's room, where it was always kept. She lied to me about why Papa sent Justin away because she did not want me to know the truth. And if anyone is now thinking that Justin must have been . . . *dallying* with Mama and Papa discovered them together, then I feel compelled to say that I am as certain as I can be that that is not the truth either. I was only eight years old, but I knew my brother better than that. That is all. Brandon is *not* a thief, and I apologize for having accused him in front of you all."

Estelle took a step closer to her friend. Bertrand too was drawing nearer from one side while Sidney Sharpe was coming from the other side. But someone else forestalled them all. Mrs. Sharpe was sitting on a sofa close to Maria. She lifted one arm jangling with bracelets and bangles.

"Come, my love," she said in her comfortable voice. "Come and sit here."

"Aunt Betty," Maria said, sitting and snuggling close while Justin's aunt set an arm about her, just like a bird with her chick. "I loved her so much."

"Well, of course you did, my love," Mrs. Sharpe said. "And of course you *do*. Here, look. Rosie has brought you a cup of tea."

Rosie Sharpe sat on a footstool before the sofa and gazed up at her new friend with anxious concern. She held Maria's cup and saucer in both hands. Mrs. Chandler had come to sit on Maria's other side and was patting her thigh.

Everyone else launched into determined conversation.

Mr. Dickson was asking Lord Brandon about his years at the stone quarry and his acquaintance with Wesley Mort. The earl, Estelle could hear, instead of answering evasively, was telling the story of his broken nose.

"And just to think, Stell," Bertrand said, coming to stand beside her, "that one of our main concerns in coming here was that we might be facing an unbearably tedious couple of weeks."

"We will be home again soon," she said.

"Is that what you want?" he asked softly. "To be home?"

She shrugged, and his arm came about her for a moment and hugged her to his side.

"Well," he said, releasing her. "Maybe we need to think about where home really is."

Estelle was sitting on the side of her bed, pulling a brush through her hair though her maid had done it for her just a short while ago in the dressing room before leaving for the night.

She was thinking of Bertrand's questions. *Is that what*

you want? To be home? . . . Maybe we need to think about
where home really is.

Home was Elm Court, where she could be quiet and
safe. Where she could have just her beloved twin for company. Where they had gone two years ago to find out who
exactly they were and what it was they wanted of their
lives. Had they discovered the answers? Had Bert? Had
she? She would have said no—until with a single sentence
her brother had revealed a truth to her. *Maybe we need to*
think about where home really is. And she had found herself yearning for her father and her stepmother and . . .
home. Redcliffe Court. The very heart of her family. For
that was who she was—a member of a family, or, rather, of
a group of families. And it was what she wanted of her life.
Family. Belonging.

But being a twin had taught her about two halves of a
whole. She would always need Bertrand to complete herself. But over and above that connection, she would need
two families. Two *sets* of families. She had not even left
Everleigh yet, but already she knew she would miss the
Ormsburys, the Sharpes, the Dicksons and Chandlers.

She wanted Justin Wiley, Earl of Brandon.

Oh yes, she wanted him in *that* way. Of course she did.
She *yearned* for him, or, rather, for *it.* For it with him. But
it was not the *only* way. She wanted him with all his darkness, with all his contradictions. She wanted him with all
his complexities, with all the dizzying array of experiences
that had shaped him into who he was now.

A man in deep pain. Possibly a man with no way out of
that pain ever. For his pain centered about his father, who
was dead.

He was a man who could perhaps never be happy. Not
even in those brief snatches of joy that comprised happiness

for most people. No one, surely, ever lived happily ever after. Even her father and stepmother. Even Camille and Joel or Abigail and Gil, her stepsisters and their husbands. Or Anna and Avery, Duke and Duchess of Netherby. Or any other couple she could think of whom she considered happily married. But for most people there *was* happiness to be found.

Perhaps Justin could never be happy. Could she live with that?

Would she be given the chance to live with it? Most of the guests here were planning to go home the day after tomorrow. She and Bertrand were planning to leave too.

Would he offer her marriage again before then?

Would it matter if he did not?

Perhaps it would ultimately be a huge relief. She would not have to make the momentous decision.

Or perhaps she would be heartbroken. *Really?* Just a couple of weeks ago she had disliked him intensely. She had been repulsed by him—*but only because you did not recognize that what you were really feeling was attraction, Estelle. An attraction that horrified you because you did not believe he was the sort of man to whom you ought to be attracted.*

He was not at all the man she had thought he was.

She had a sudden mental image of him standing on the terrace outside the house here, gazing toward the Palladian bridge, his face lit up with a smile like sunshine as he gazed at Ricky. She saw him laughing and catching Ricky up in his arms, dirt and smell notwithstanding.

A man filled with sudden and total joy. He *was* capable of happiness.

She sighed.

There was a light tap on the door of her bedchamber.

She stopped brushing her hair. Her maid? No, Olga would have let herself into the dressing room if she had forgotten something. Bertrand? Normally he would just come on inside after tapping on the door to warn her. She crossed the room and opened the door a crack.

Ah. She was suddenly aware of her nightgown and bare feet and flowing hair.

"I am going out to the summerhouse," the Earl of Brandon told her, his voice soft.

Now? At this time of night? It must be close to midnight.

"I need to . . . read it," he said. "You saw?"

"The document from the safe?" She spoke as softly as he and opened the door wider.

"It is addressed to me," he told her. "In my father's handwriting."

"Oh," she said. In the flickering light of the candles on her dresser he looked very pale. She reached out and set a hand on his arm, forgetting her appearance for a moment. He was wearing a greatcoat and boots and looked even larger than usual.

"I need to read it," he said. "But not here. Not in this house. I am going to take it to the summerhouse. Will you come with me?"

She closed her eyes. The letter might say nothing of any significance. On the other hand, it might be full of bitter recriminations. Or it might offer a final word of forgiveness. It might be everything. Or nothing. Whatever it was—or was not—it might break him. She opened her eyes.

"Yes," she said. "I will get dressed."

"I will wait here," he told her before she shut the door and stood for a few moments, her eyes closed again, her hand still on the doorknob.

She hurried into her dressing room.

Twenty-one

Justin sat on the top stair while he waited, a lantern beside him. He tried to still his thoughts, something at which he was generally good. He did not want to consider the fact that he normally kept to himself all that was deeply personal and shared it with no one. Solitude was his preferred state, especially when something was weighing upon him. It had all started, he supposed, on that day twelve years ago when he had made the decision not to defend himself to his father. It had not been absolute then, for he had fled to his aunt and uncle and poured out the whole of it to them. But he had felt almost instantly the burden he had put upon their shoulders and had resolved never to do that again.

So why the devil had it seemed important—even essential—to him that Lady Estelle Lamarr be with him when he read his father's letter? And why tonight, now, close to midnight? At the summerhouse, rather than here?

He tried not to think.

He did not time her. But fewer than ten minutes must

have passed between the shutting of her bedchamber door
and its opening again. She was wearing a long dark cloak
with the loose hood pulled over her head. He took hold of
the lantern and got to his feet.

Her eyes were on him as she approached, large and
steady and calm, and he took her hand in his and led her
down the stairs. He released it in order to unbolt the main
door and open it. She stepped out beneath the portico ahead
of him and waited while he shut the door. She raised her
hand and set it in his again.

It was not a dark night. The lantern was hardly necessary. It was not cold either. He hesitated for a moment when
they reached the corner of the house. Normally it was to
Captain he turned for company and comfort. One did not
have to confide in a dog. A dog sensed when it was needed.
But tonight it was a person to whom he had turned. Tonight
he kept on walking.

They did not talk. Neither of them had uttered a word
since she closed her door to get dressed and accompany
him. But Justin did not believe he had ever felt closer to any
other person. The letter—paper? document? The whatever-
it-was in the inside pocket of his coat had a physical weight
and heat out of all proportion to its appearance. It might be
no more than a list of what Justin would find in the safe. It
might be anything in the world. At the very least, though,
it was paper upon which his name was written in his father's
distinctive hand. It was ridiculous, perhaps, to take comfort
from that single fact. Perhaps what was inside that sealed
paper would break his heart, or what remained of his heart.
And perhaps that was why he had not immediately broken
the seal and read what was inside. And why he had not
done so when he went to his own room. Maybe it was why
he needed her with him.

He led the way up the stairs inside the summerhouse to unlock the door at the top, holding the lantern in such a way that she could see her way up behind him. He set the lantern down inside the door, found the tinderbox, and lit a few candles. She closed the door and stood inside it until he was finished and turned to her.

"Thank you," he said.

She looked at him with that smile of hers that was not really a smile but a beaming outward of some warmth or light. And let no one ever try telling him that he was good at expressing meaning in words.

"Everyone ought to have a twin," she said. "Since you do not, you may borrow me."

Her words might have sounded flippant, but they did not come across that way. She was offering something priceless. The sort of close connection she normally felt only with her brother. Though he wanted more than just to *borrow* her.

"Come and sit down." He indicated one of the chairs, the one without books on it. It was not cold in the room. It must have been trapping sunlight all day and was still holding on to it.

She removed her cloak, sat, and relaxed back into the chair. "I have been trying to imagine," she said, "that I had suddenly discovered a letter addressed to me in my mother's handwriting. I would recognize it. My aunt once very generously gave me a letter my mother sent her after she learned she was expecting Bertrand and me, though she did not know at the time that there would be two of us. I am trying to imagine discovering a new letter. I know that breaking the seal and reading it would be the hardest thing I had ever done."

He stood looking down at her, his hands at his back. "It feels like a very last chance," he said. "But chance for what? I do not know. It is a one-way communication with no way of replying. And perhaps it is nothing anyway. Or further condemnation. It is foolish, is it not, to let the possibilities roll around in my head while I have the answer, whatever it is, in my pocket?"

Those large, calm, fathomless eyes looked steadily into his. Understanding him. Knowing how he felt. Feeling with him. What the devil was she doing with a fellow like him, with his workman's hands and muscles, with his broken nose and dour manner? With a man who had made a mess of his life and was only just beginning—perhaps—to set it on some sort of course for the future?

"Sit down to read it," she said softly.

But he could not sit. He went to stand at one of the windows, where the light from a candle would shine down upon anything he held in his hands. He took off his greatcoat and tossed it over the back of the desk chair, and he drew the letter from his pocket. His father had once held this. He had put it into the safe on top of the jewelry and shut the door. And Justin had been the next person to touch it. He held it to his nose for a moment, but nothing of his father lingered there. He broke the seal with his thumb, and his heartbeat drummed in his ears in such a way that he thought he might faint. She had *known* that. She had suggested that he sit down. He concentrated on his breathing— on the feel of the air coming in and going out. And he unfolded the letter.

My dearest son.

He stared at the words for what might have been a minute or ten before he had the courage to let his eyes move lower.

There are times in life when one's God-given freedom to choose good over evil at all times, no matter the circumstances or consequences, is snatched away, and one is left only with the choice between two evils. It is what is meant by the term "hell on earth," I have come to understand.

I was faced with such a dilemma, as I hope you will never be. As I hope all those dear to me and even my worst enemies will never be. I chose one of the evils and sent you away. Perhaps I hoped the choice would not be irrevocable. I expected, perhaps, that you would seek help, and even maybe shelter, from your mother's family or mine. I hoped they would set your feet on a good and prosperous path until I could somehow claim you again.

Alas, it was not to be. Whether by chance or by design, you disappeared, and put yourself beyond my reach. I believe—I must believe—that your steadiness of character has enabled you to make a decent life for yourself. It is my fervent hope that you have found some happiness with friends and even made a family of your own. It is the consequence of my own choice that I do not know and will never know.

I make no excuses. When a man marries, he has a great deal of power over his wife. Both the Church and the law see to that. It is unfair, even unjust, but it is the reality. He must compensate by offering her his unyielding support and protection, by treating her always with gentleness and courtesy. If in doing those things he must treat his own flesh and blood unjustly, then so be it. I made my choice. I honored my wife and disowned my son.

Ah, but not in my heart, Justin. If the words of a man who has somehow sullied his honor are of any importance to you, then know this. I did not for a moment doubt you. I have never, even for a single minute, stopped loving you. It would not be possible. You are the son of my ever-beloved first wife. You are my son.

Although I will be dead when you read this, and though I can never deserve or earn your forgiveness, I would ask for it. Not so much for myself—I will be dead, after all. But for yourself, Justin. If you still think bitterly of me, let the wound heal. And if you cannot love me, then love my other child, your sister. Love Maria.

Live a good life, my son. You were always good at loving. You lit up my life and your mother's. You lit up Maria's life. You were loved wherever you went. Do not allow bitterness and the injustice with which you were treated change you forever. Live a life filled with love. It is, ultimately, all that matters.

And his signature. Not his name or his title. Just one word.

Papa

Justin folded the letter neatly and deliberately, put it back into his pocket . . . and drew it out again. He turned.

Her head was against the back of the chair. But her eyes watched him. He strode toward her, handed her the letter, and went back to look out through the window onto darkness.

He concentrated upon his breathing as he had never done before, ignoring thought, quelling emotion. In, cool.

Out, warm. I am breathing in. I am breathing out. *Papa.* No. In, out. *My dearest son.* No. In, cold. Out, warm. *You lit up my life and your mother's.*

He did not know how long he had been standing there, breathing in, breathing out, before his concentration was broken. Arms had come about his waist from behind, and her body rested against his, the side of her head against his shoulder. She said nothing.

He crossed his arms over his waist, curling his fingers about her slender arms. And he took her warmth, her relaxation, into himself. He turned eventually and held her to him until he stooped down to scoop her up into his arms. He strode over to the chair where she had been sitting, sat down with her, grabbed her cloak from the arm of the chair, and wrapped it about her though there was no chill in the air. He held her tightly. A few minutes passed.

He felt the tremor first with his stomach muscles. Then there was the ache in his throat and down in his chest. He sniffed once. But it was no good. She nestled her head between his shoulder and neck.

And he wept.

With great, hideous gulps and sobs. With an almost total loss of dignity. And control. The armor he had built so painstakingly about himself was shattered. Gone without a trace.

"I am s-so s-s-sorry."

"I am not," she said. "I am not, Justin."

His name on her lips destroyed what little control was left.

And he wept on until there was nothing left.

He fumbled about in his pocket for his handkerchief, swiped at his eyes, and blew his nose. "Devil take it," he said. "I am so sorry. Whatever will you think?"

She tipped her head back against his shoulder and looked into his face. "*Can* you forgive him?" she asked.

He thought about it a long time, until his breathing fully calmed.

"She was vain and conniving," he said. "She destroyed his life and very nearly mine too. And probably her own. She lied to Maria and depleted her happiness. But she was essentially a helpless woman, out of her element, only seventeen when she trapped him. And he chose to honor and protect her. Until doing so led him into hell itself. *The choice between two evils.* He chose the one he had to choose, being the man he was, the man I admired above all others. Yes, I forgive him. I just wish I could tell him so. And I wish I could tell him that I would not wipe out the last twelve years and everything that happened during them even if I could. There would be no Ricky, no Wes, no Hilda."

"No broken nose," she said.

"And no broken nose."

He closed his eyes and rested his head against the chair back.

"Life is a funny thing," he said. He surprised himself by laughing then. "A profound observation indeed. Someone should include it in a book of wise quotations for the ages. *Life is a funny thing.*"

They sat quietly for a while.

"Stay here with me?" he said then. His voice made a question of it.

There was another stretch of silence.

"Yes," she said.

Estelle heard the echo of her response and waited for guilt, panic, denial, moral outrage, *something* to rush at her in protest. Nothing did. She had said yes, and yes was what she meant.

He stood up with her and set her on her feet before tossing her cloak back over the chair arm. He reached for her hands and curled his own about them at their sides. Then he moved his hands up her arms and along her shoulders and cupped her face in his palms. There were the marks of tears still on his own cheeks. His eyes were luminous. And she marveled over the fact that this was the same man she had first seen on horseback, dark and dour, huge and menacing, while she sat on the riverbank. She set her own hands on either side of his waist.

"You will be marrying me," he said.

Her eyes smiled into his. "That is a proposal?"

"No," he said. "That is a statement."

"The proposal is still to come?" she asked. "Are you busy composing a sonnet?"

For a moment—ah, for a precious moment—laughter flashed in his eyes. She thought he was about to say something. But he kissed her instead, lightly and gently, and she felt all his need for her, all his yearning for a human touch, for connection. She felt his barely leashed passion. This was something she would not have considered herself capable of doing in a million years—lying with a man to whom she was not wed or even officially betrothed. But there were no doubts in her mind. He needed her now, tonight, and she . . . ? Ah, she needed him too. His father's letter had affected her deeply. If only . . . If only her mother had had enough warning of her death to have written to her and Bertrand. Surely she would have done it had she known. And surely she would have written something similar at the end—*Live a life filled with love. It is, ultimately, all that matters.*

She wrapped her arms about Justin's waist, leaned into him, and kissed him back. Not just with desire, but with everything that was herself.

He drew back from her after a while and went to extinguish the lantern and all the candles except the one on the bookcase. The single flame flickered dimly over walls and ceiling while he tossed a few of the cushions from the bed onto the chair with the books on it. He drew back the covers to expose crisp white sheets and pillowcases.

"It is narrow," he said, turning to her again. "But we will make it wide enough."

"Yes."

He turned her to face away from him and undid the buttons at the back of her dress, which she had so recently done up without the help of her maid. He folded the edges back and over her shoulders and down her arms until the whole dress slid down her body to pool at her feet. She was not wearing stays. She turned for him to roll down her stockings one at a time and remove them with her shoes. Only her shift remained.

Desire hummed in her now. It pulsated low in her abdomen and along her inner thighs. His eyes gazed into hers as his hands were in her hair, which she had pinned up earlier into a simple, rather untidy knot. After a few moments it all cascaded down her back and over her shoulders. She heard the tinkle of a few hairpins as they hit the floor.

He took off his coat and waistcoat then, and his neckcloth. He pulled his shirt free of his pantaloons, crossed his arms, and drew it off over his head to join her dress on the floor.

She had known that his great size was due to muscle more than fat, but she had not guessed quite how magnificent he would look without his shirt. All solid, rippling muscles and broad shoulders and powerful arms. A light dusting of hair on his chest tapered in a V shape to disappear below the waistband of his pantaloons. He was masculinity personified.

He sat down on the side of the bed to pull off his boots and stockings before standing and setting his hands on either side of her waist and looking her over slowly, from her head to her feet.

And she realized that he was intentionally moving slowly and deliberately rather than tearing in a frenzy at their clothes. It was part of the lovemaking. She guessed he was experienced and was strangely thankful. She was twenty-five years old and really knew nothing beyond a few unsatisfactory kisses.

He was looking into her eyes again.

"I always knew you were beautiful," he said. "I just did not realize that you were . . . perfect. I wish I could be perfect for you."

"Idiot," she said, and he raised his eyebrows. "You *are* perfect. And even if you were not . . . you are *Justin*. That is all that matters."

His eyes brightened again for a moment with what might have been tears. Though in truth the light from the single candle was very dim. He grasped the sides of her shift and lifted it over her head as she raised her arms. He turned her, and she lay down on the bed and watched as he unbuttoned his pantaloons at the waist, lowered them, and stepped out of them. He lay down beside her, sliding an arm beneath her and turning her onto her side so that there was room on the bed for the two of them. But only just. And only when they were pressed together.

Estelle, feeling him along the naked length of her body, wondered if she would ever be able to catch her breath again. Now she could believe that he really was that man astride his horse who had so frightened her beside the river. But she was not frightened tonight. For she had spoken the truth just now. Nothing about him mattered more than that he was Justin.

"Let me make it good for you," he murmured against her lips.

"Yes," she whispered into his mouth.

He pushed back the bedcovers, and his hands moved over her. His mouth too, after it had left hers. And for the next while he did indeed make it good for her, touching her everywhere with those large, callused, sensitive hands of his and with his mouth, his tongue, his teeth, caressing her and arousing her until she ached and tingled with desire and longing. She touched him too, tentatively at first, with more assurance when he drew in a hissing breath and murmured encouragement. She explored him with one hand, kissed him, and reveled in the breathtaking carnality of it all, the feel of him, the smell of his soap, of his cologne, of *him*. And at every moment she was aware of the size and hardness of his arousal, of his intent, of where this was all leading.

But where there ought perhaps to have been fright, there was only the eagerness of anticipation and the wondering realization that this was *Justin*. The Earl of Brandon. The man of all men she had least expected to love with her whole heart and her whole body.

And then his hand was *there* in her most secret place, his fingers stroking, parting, going inside her. She was wet, she realized. She could both feel it and hear it and was curiously unembarrassed.

"I want to come there," he murmured into her mouth. "You are ready?"

"Yes," she said.

And he lifted himself over her and lowered himself onto her with all that glorious size and weight. His hands slid down between her back and the mattress to spread over her buttocks as his knees came between hers and pushed her legs wide. She could feel him at her entrance and twined her legs about his.

He pressed inside her.

There were no words. There were not even thoughts. Only sensations. Hardness, size, stretching, discomfort that was not really uncomfortable, pain that did not really hurt, thoughts and words that would not form in her head with any coherence. The conviction that there could not possibly be room enough or depth enough. The sudden sharpness of a pain that was only too real, and a deep penetration that somehow banished the pain. The joining of bodies.

"I have hurt you," he murmured.

"No. Yes. *No*," she said. And *"No"* again when he withdrew slowly. But only to the brink of her.

He pressed deep again. And withdrew and pushed deep. And she knew—*of course she knew*—that this was what happened between man and woman. This was the act of love. She tilted her pelvis slightly, the better to accommodate him, and learned his rhythm and matched it with her own and rotated her hips because it felt even better that way. She could feel his hardness better, catch it at different angles inside.

"Witch!" he said, a note of sudden urgency in his voice. "Oh, God, you witch, Estelle."

And if he had been trying to be gentle because he knew he had hurt her, he gave it up, knowing it to be unnecessary, and drove hard into her, over and over again until nothing existed except him and her. Them. *There*. Panting, labored breath. Sweat and rocking movement and the rhythmic sound of wetness. And the growing sensation that they were nearing the edge of some cliff or the peak of some mountain or the heart of some volcano. But no, there were no real words.

He found her mouth with his own as he thrust deep into her again and held there, poised on the precipice and somehow, suddenly, over it. But not to destruction. To its opposite, whatever that was. The hot flow of his love deep within her. The leftover throbbing as he lay still in her. The heavy weight of him. The sweaty heat of their bodies. The peace—ah, the peace. And the sense that for a moment they had become one and were now settling gently back into their own bodies. But forever linked by the fact that they had known that unity.

"I am probably crushing the life out of you," he said.

It was not quite that dire, but he was very heavy. And large. Deliciously so. "I do not want you to leave yet," she said, tightening her arms about him.

But after a few moments longer he withdrew slowly from her and moved to her side, holding her to him as he did so. Somehow he got hold of the bedcovers and pulled them up over them. And Estelle sighed against him as warmth upon warmth enveloped her. The candle flickered on. Her legs were twined with his. Her arms were trapped against his hard, muscled chest. Her head was nestled between his shoulder and neck. One of his arms was beneath her, the other over her hip while his hand was spread over her back. It was a night she did not want to end.

You will be marrying me, he had said earlier. Not a question. A statement. Which ought to have made her bristle a bit with indignation but actually made her smile. A man who knew what duty and responsibility were. And love.

And he *would* ask. She would insist upon it, though she was sure she would not have to. Her smile deepened.

And she realized he was sleeping. It was somehow the loveliest moment of the night. He had loved her and relaxed into sleep, holding her close.

Estelle closed her eyes and breathed in the sweaty, musky smell of him. Sleep. It was an enticing idea. She was so very weary and so very relaxed. A wonderful combination. Especially when she lay in her lover's arms.

Twenty-two

J ustin was conscious of a feeling of great well-being that went bone deep, even soul deep. But he must not let himself sleep late or even to a normal getting-up time. Wes would probably rise with the dawn or before it, and he would rouse Ricky too, and they would be on their way back to Gloucestershire. With a single horse and without saying goodbye.

Wes had been mortified to see Justin here in his own world. He had been mortified too by Ricky's enthusiastic accounts of being bathed and shaved by Justin's own special servant and of sleeping in a great big bed that felt as though it were made all of feathers. And of Justin's sister thanking him for coming and telling him that he would have found her sooner than her brother had if he had only been here in time. And of a lady who had held his hand to take him to Justin when he first came, and whose hand *he* had held tight because she was frightened up high on the gallery right in the middle of Justin's house, just under that great dome of glass Wes could see if he looked. And of how his food was fetched on a tray with real china plates and real silver forks and spoons and how it tasted almost as good as Hildy's food.

Wes had patted Ricky's shoulder while muttering, "Bloody hell."

"You didn't ought to say that, Wes," Ricky had said. "Hildy would be cross with you."

He ought to have made Wes promise not to leave without saying goodbye, Justin thought as he reluctantly forced himself up to full consciousness—and the realization that he was on the narrow bed in the summerhouse, his body entwined with Estelle's, both of them naked. She was sleeping.

Good God. What time was it? He had not intended to sleep. His watch was out of reach. He must get her back to the house before she was missed, and before she was seen by any early-rising servants.

He moved the hair back from her face with one finger and lowered his head to kiss her brow, her nose, her lips. She made a low sound of protest or appreciation—it was impossible to tell which—and opened her eyes. The single candle was still burning, but it was guttering a bit, as though it was close to burning itself out.

"Oh," she said.

"I must take you back to the house," he said. "I do not want you to be seen."

She raised one hand and laid a finger along the top of his nose. "You must have had two black eyes as well," she said.

"Black, purple, blue, green, puce, lavender. Name a color and my eyes were it," he said. "Wes knows how to use his fists. Did I tell you what he did after he knocked me to the floor in that tavern?"

"I do not believe so," she said.

"He turned to the yokel who had been pawing the bar-maid," he said, "and told him to take a good look at me. He warned him he would look twice as bad if his hands ever again came within six inches of that barmaid or any other."

She smiled slowly at him. "Will I meet him tomorrow?" she asked. "Or *today*, I suppose I mean."

"He probably hopes to leave here before I am out of my bed," he said. "I will take you back to the house and then go up and talk to him."

"Up?" she said.

"He and Ricky are staying at the blacksmith's house," he told her. "Up on top of the hill behind the house. All the laborers' cottages are there in a village of their own. There is a shop too, and a school. Most of the farmland is up there. I'll go and talk to Wes before he can sneak away."

"Take me with you," she said, running her fingers through his hair and kissing him on the lips.

"That is not a good idea," he said. "You will be seen."

"That would be dreadful," she said, and even in the dim light he could see laughter in her eyes. "Do you still want me to be your countess?"

"Yes," he said.

"Do you not want your best friend to meet your future countess?" she asked him.

"Estelle—"

"I want to say goodbye to Ricky," she said. "I love him, and I think he loves me."

"Are you trying to make me jealous?" he asked her.

She smiled radiantly at him and he swore under his breath. He heaved a sigh.

"Did I hurt you terribly?" he asked.

"Not terribly," she said. "It was lovely beyond belief.

And if that look on your face means that you are about to feel qualms of conscience, forget them and refrain from being tedious. It was fully consensual, Justin."

"Not just sympathy because I wept?" he asked her.

She shook her head. "It was joy," she said. "Because you were finally able to forgive your father and yourself. And were free to be yourself again. Justin, the darkness is gone."

At which moment the candle died without further warning and they were plunged into total darkness.

She laughed, a sound of pure glee. And he laughed with her, hugging her tightly to him and rolling with her until he could kiss her properly and silence both her and himself.

"You must not miss them," she said after a while. "Take me with you."

"Stay there," he said as he turned and swung his legs over the side of the bed. "I'll find the tinderbox and give us some light. If you do not hear from me within the next five or ten minutes, send out a search party."

"I will convene the family committee again," she said. "They have had some recent experience."

Was this how their life together would be? he wondered as he felt his way to the tinderbox on the bookcase. Full of light and laughter—and passion? As his mother and father's marriage had been? Would the lives of their children be as joy filled as his own had been? And was it true, what she had just said?

. . . you were finally able to forgive your father and yourself. And were free to be yourself again.

Justin, the darkness is gone.

It had not been quite as late as Justin had feared. There had been time after they dressed to return briefly to the house for Estelle to run to her room to tidy up before a mirror and make herself comfortable and change her shoes to stouter ones.

This was not the best of ideas, he thought as she joined him again in the hall and they left the house together. The likelihood of her being seen with him when it was still really just the middle of the night was strong. And it would take only one groom or servant or laborer—or house guest for that matter. Nevertheless, it felt good to know that she wanted to be with him, that she wished to meet Wes. It promised well for the future. He took one of her hands in his.

They went to the stables first, where Captain greeted them with the usual ecstasy and a sleepy groom was able to assure Justin—with a sidelong glance at Estelle—that the horse Wes Mort had brought with him yesterday was still in its stall. Then they walked up the road to the top of the hill, Captain prancing along beside them. Estelle exclaimed in the lessening darkness over the beauty of the cluster of cottages around a village green and the farm buildings and cultivated fields, meadows, and garden plots stretching off into the distance.

No one appeared to be stirring in the village. But when Justin knocked softly upon the door of the blacksmith's house, Wes himself opened it and Justin stepped inside, while Estelle remained out by the garden gate, with Captain sitting on his haunches beside her.

"They are both still sleeping," Wes whispered, frowning and none too happy to see his friend.

"Get your boots on and we will go outside, then," Justin whispered back.

Wes looked even less happy when he saw Estelle. He frowned ferociously even as he patted a panting Captain on the head.

"Wes," Justin said, keeping his voice low. "This is Lady Estelle Lamarr. My friend."

Poor Wes looked as though he did not know whether to bow, pull on his forelock, or flee back inside the house. Estelle stepped forward, her right hand extended.

"Mr. Mort," she said. "I am very pleased to make your acquaintance. Your brother is an absolute delight."

Wes looked at her hand, visibly hesitated, and then grasped it and pumped it once before releasing it. "Ma'am," he muttered.

"Let us walk back toward the stables," Justin said, "before we wake everyone up. Ricky is still sleeping," he told Estelle.

"I left him where he was until I was ready to go," his friend explained. "I was about to get him up. I'll just fetch the horse, Juss, and we'll be on our way."

They did not talk again until they were back on the road down the hill.

"You enjoyed Bill Slater's company last evening?" Justin asked. He had placed himself between his friend and Estelle, but he was holding her hand. "And at the smithy yesterday?"

"The blacksmith?" Wes said. "He's a pleasant fellow. Easy to talk to. He's good with Ricky."

"He is also very eager to retire," Justin told him. "His only son went off years ago and joined an infantry regiment. His daughter and son-in-law want him to stop working and go live with them and their three young girls, all of whom adore him. But he does not want to hand the smithy over to just anyone." Justin glanced sideways at his friend. "I remember you telling me once that as a boy you were apprenticed to a blacksmith and thought the job was like a dream come true."

"A long time ago," Wes said.

"But you left," Justin said, "because your father was making life impossible for Ricky."

"He was brute and devil all rolled into one, that man," Wes said. "And I say so even though he *was* my father. After I was twelve I was able to stand up to him on my own account, but Ricky couldn't. I wasn't able to turn my back without the poor lad getting cuffed around. I used to take him to the smithy with me whenever I could, but it wasn't always possible. And then . . . Well. Ricky got his arm broken and I took him away and we stayed away. He's safe with me—except when he takes it into his head to run away and help a man who is too daft to choose his words more carefully to look for his sister, who was not even lost. You've taken ten years off my life with that one, Juss."

"It was like a dream come true, that apprenticeship of yours," Justin said. "It could still happen, Wes."

"No, it couldn't," Wes said. "If you are suggesting . . ."

"Well, I am," Justin said, and his hand tightened about Estelle's. He desperately wanted to find the right words to use with a man whose pride was prickly, to say the least. "Hear me out, Wes. You gave me a job years ago when I could not have been more unsuited for the work if I had tried. You gave me a chance—and a home. You are not destitute now as I was then. But I can offer you the job of your dreams and a home all three of you might like. You could complete your apprenticeship here and then take over the smithy. I have talked to Slater about it, and he is all in favor. I pay my workers well, Wes, as my father did before me. I keep their homes in good repair and give them good pensions when they retire. I give pensions to their wives if they are widowed. I see to it that there is a doctor to tend all of them when they are ill or hurt. I see to it that their children, boys and girls, go to school. I did not earn any of all this, Wes, but I can and do take my responsibilities seriously. All this is mine so that I can make it possible for a whole lot of other people to live decent, productive lives with the security of knowing that neither they nor their families will ever starve or be homeless."

"Bloody hell," Wes Mort muttered—probably loudly enough for Estelle to hear.

"Give it some thought," Justin said. "Talk it over with Hilda and with Ricky if you wish. Wes, you are my friends, all three of you. You are too far away there in Gloucestershire. Give it some thought."

They had stopped walking not far from the stables.

"Damn," Wes said. "Ah, I beg your pardon, ma'am. Juss, I'm set to marry Hildy at the end of next week. The oddest thing has happened after all these years. There's going to be a little one. She used to cry every month when it didn't happen, but then she got used to the notion that it wasn't going to happen at all. Then suddenly it did. Are you going to stand there grinning like a fool, or are we going to the stables to get the horse?"

"I am grinning like a happy man," Justin said. "And because you are squirming with discomfort. Wes! I am delighted for you both." He was too. Hilda would be an excellent mother. And Wes would be a good father. Consider the way he had always looked after Ricky, never losing patience with him, never belittling him, always loving him. Even though he had had to give up his dream job to keep him safe.

Estelle was smiling, Justin could see.

"If it's a boy," Wes said, "I don't want him doomed to working all his life in the quarry. And if it's a girl, I want her to live in a place where there's green grass and trees and where her hair and her dresses aren't always gray with dust. I want her to have . . . prettiness in her life. It's what I've always wanted for Hildy too. But wanting isn't always getting. And there's a school here? For girls as well as boys? Girls are often brighter than boys. Hildy is brighter than I am. Which wouldn't be difficult, I suppose."

"You will give this job some thought, then?" Justin asked, almost holding his breath and aware that he was squeezing Estelle's hand only when she winced slightly.

"Damn you, Juss," Wes said. "Beg your pardon again, ma'am." His eyes came to rest upon her, quite accidentally, it seemed to Justin. "Damn, Juss, but you know how to pick the pretty ones. Begging your pardon, ma'am."

Justin was laughing then, as was Estelle herself. It was novel to see his large friend squirm with discomfort. He released her hand in order to hug Wes. "You and Hilda getting *married*," he said. "Next week. I am going to find a way of being there, whether I am invited or not. How does Ricky feel about it all?"

"Oh, good God, we haven't told him yet about getting married," Wes said. "He would be asking twenty times every day if this is the day yet. When he knows about the little one, he'll be pestering poor Hildy all day every day about her health and whether she ought to be lifting that pot or poking the fire. He will drive us both out of our heads."

"He will be a wonderful uncle," Estelle said.

"That's what I'm afraid of, ma'am," Wes said. "He'll be forever shushing me and keeping me away from my own baby." He laughed suddenly then. "There will never have been a more doting uncle."

"Stay another day," Justin said. "Have a good talk with Bill Slater. Let Ricky say goodbye to all his friends—there must be dozens, in the house, in the kitchens, in the stables.

Get some rest. I will see you on your way early tomorrow. And next week I will see you at your wedding."

"Ah, bloody hell," Wesley said before apologizing to Estelle yet again. "We don't want no fuss."

"*You* do not," Justin said. "I'll wager Hilda would not mind a bit of one. Go on back up to the cottage. Get some sleep. I bet you have not had a wink all night."

"I was afraid of sleeping in," Wes said. "I—" He gave Justin a hard look, shook his head, and turned to make his way back up the hill.

"I believe he will return and bring his wife and Ricky to live here," Estelle said as they watched him go.

"His *wife*," Justin said. "It seems strange to hear Hilda referred to that way. They had already been together a year or two when I went to live with them ten years ago. I often wondered why there were no children. Neither of them ever spoke of it."

"Which is hardly surprising," she said, sounding amused. "I think your offer of employment came at the perfect time. But it was not made just out of kindness, was it?"

"Kindness?" He shrugged. "Wes has a steady job, and he is good at it and well respected by his bosses and his fellow workers. Ricky has work. They have a home, though it is in a bleak place. They can manage, even with a family. No, not kindness. I want them here because they are my friends," he said.

"Because they are your *family*," she said. "And because you knew of his dream."

He took her hand in his again. It was still early, but it was definitely morning now and any number of early risers might be looking out through a window and see them in the gray predawn light. A servant might step outside at any moment. The sound of their voices, even though they had kept them low, had probably woken a few people up in the village. *A groom had already seen them in the stables*. Setting a decorous space between themselves as they walked back to the house would have been a bit ridiculous. Rather like shutting the stable door after the horse has bolted.

In fact . . .

"The sun is going to rise soon," he said, nodding at the eastern sky, already streaked with pale pink. "Shall we go and watch it from the bridge?"

"I have crossed it a few times since we came here," she said. "But I have never stopped and actually looked at it—or from it. It is beautiful, just as the Chinese bridge at the lake is in a different way. Yes, let us see the sunrise as we stand upon the bridge."

Twenty-three

They crossed the valley, Captain trotting after them, and walked halfway along the Palladian bridge before stopping. Estelle looked up and about at the intricately carved stonework overhead and on either side. It was like a small Roman temple with pillars and large openings on either side to afford views over the river. They stepped up to the side that looked east. The sun had not yet shown itself over the horizon, but both the sky and the water now were alight with varying shades of pink and gold. Her free hand, slim and delicate, was resting on the broad stone balustrade. Her eyes squinted as she looked out into the brightness.

"I am reminded of standing with you on another, far more modest stone bridge," she said. "Was it really only a few weeks ago?"

"Somewhere between Prospect Hall and Elm Court?" he said. "But just as lovely as this one."

At the time he had been happy to know she was coming here—for Maria's sake. He had been trying to convince himself that it was in no way for his sake too that he was glad. He had been aware of her dislike, even revulsion.

"Oh, look!" she cried suddenly, awe in her voice. "Look, Justin."

The sun, unnaturally huge, exaggeratedly orange, was coming over the horizon, and the river turned color with it.

"Why, oh why, do we not get up early enough every morning to watch this?" she asked.

He watched her instead, sunlight on her face, sparkling in her eyes, her dark hair pinned high on the back of her head, but inexpertly, even a bit untidily. She looked breathtakingly lovely. "Why indeed?" he said, and she turned her head to smile at him.

"You are not even *looking*," she said.

"Oh, yes," he assured her. "I am. Estelle . . ."

She turned to face him fully then and took her hand off the balustrade to set it in his. He clasped both her hands and raised them one at a time to his lips.

"Yes?" she said.

He had had two weeks to prepare a speech that would improve upon the one he had given at the summerhouse. It ought not to have been hard. It would be difficult, after all, to compose one that would be more disastrous than that had been. He had procrastinated, however, and now his mind was quite blank. He had so wanted the perfect moment, and he had it. They both turned their heads to watch the sun clear the horizon and begin its daily journey across the sky. He heard her inhale as she watched it. And he had so wanted the perfect words.

"I am not going to talk about the equality of our birth or our relative age parity," he said. "Or about duty. Or the fact that you must allow me to make an honest woman of you, though of course you must."

It was *not* a good start.

"Thank you," she said, and she was gazing into his eyes again. "What *are* you going to talk about? How is that sonnet coming?"

He grimaced. "I believe the sonnet was your idea," he said. "But I have been working up something. How about *Shall I compare thee to a summer's day?*"

"Hmm." She tipped her head to one side. "It has promise. Depending, of course, upon the type of summer day to which you mean to compare me."

"Thou art more lovely and more temperate," he said.

"Well, thank you," she said.

"Rough winds do shake the darling buds of May," he said.

"I like that phrase—*the darling buds of May,*" she said. "That was clever of you. But shame upon the rough winds."

"And summer's lease hath all too short a date," he said.

She frowned and pursed her lips. "Do you know?" she said. "This is beginning to sound vaguely familiar."

"I suppose," he said, "some dastardly poet has already stolen it from me. That Shakespeare fellow, for example."

"Maybe you should forget the poetry and speak to me in plain prose," she said. "I believe I would rather you not go on to tell me that *every fair from fair sometime declines.* But oh, Justin, you should always smile like that. You do not need to cower behind that granite facade any longer, do you?"

"Cower?" He raised his eyebrows.

"Hide," she said. "You do not need to *hide* any longer. You can be the Justin Maria remembers and all your relatives and hers. The Justin your father knew and loved. But with the added experience and fellow feeling that have grown in the twelve years since you left here. You can be the Justin I have come to know in the past couple of weeks, and so much more."

"I love you," he said.

She smiled, and the light from the sparkling river flickered against the side of her face. "The best poetry of all," she said.

"I want you in my life," he told her. "Forever. Or at the very least until I die. I do not want to have to live without you. You are the light of my life. Will you make me happy and marry me?"

"Oh," she said, and her eyes were bright and she was blinking them, but one tear trickled down her cheek anyway. "Am I, Justin? The light of your life? Do I make you happy? You were quite right in the summerhouse that first time, you know. I have been waiting for love and wondering if it would ever happen for me and if I would recognize it if it did. I am glad I have waited, for I have found it at last—and recognized it. I do love you so much."

"Broken nose and all?" he asked.

She tipped her head to the side again and regarded it with a frown. "Would I love you more if it were straight and ordinary?" she said. "No, I think not, though I never saw it that way, of course. I like it extraordinary. It adds character." She looked up into his eyes and smiled with exaggerated radiance, and he laughed.

Captain, stretched out on the bridge beside them, chin upon his paws, woofed but did not move.

"It was ignominiously acquired," he said.

"No, it was not," she protested. "You had spoken up in defense of a woman who could not speak up for herself."

"Actually," he said, "the landlady of the tavern was already on her way to the offender to box him about the ears before evicting him. Wes was on his way too, to help him out faster with a boot to his rear end. I got in their way."

"The accidental hero," she said. "*My* hero."

And they gazed at each other while the humor receded—the lovely humor that promised light and laughter down the years of the future, however many were allotted them.

"Estelle," he said, raising her hands to hold them palm in against his chest. "Are you really going to marry me?"

"I really am," she said while Captain woofed again and raised his head.

And the reality of it hit Justin. She was going to be his wife, his countess. His lover. The mother of any children with whom they might be gifted. He moved his head closer to hers. But her eyes had gone beyond him, and it occurred to him that Captain did not woof for no reason.

"We have company," Estelle said.

The twin, Justin saw when he looked over his shoulder. Standing at the end of the bridge, looking steadily at them.

"Tell me," Watley said. "Is this a very late-night walk or a very early-morning pilgrimage to watch the sunrise?"

His room was next to Estelle's. And they had that odd twin connection even though they were not identical. They were different *genders*, for the love of God. He had no doubt heard the soft knock on her door last night. His room faced east. He had probably seen them making their way to the summerhouse. Perhaps he had stood in his window all night waiting to see them return. Justin would not have put it past him.

"Tell me," Justin said. "In what way is the answer any of your business?"

Estelle gave a little huff of what might have been laughter.

"It is not," Watley said amiably. "I just thought it a more

original conversation opener than a comment upon the weather."

"Was any conversation opener necessary?" Justin asked. "Have you ever heard the one about three being a crowd?"

Rather than look abashed, Watley grinned. "You are going to have to get used to it, old chap," he said. "That is my twin whose hands you have trapped against your chest. Whom you were about to kiss, if I am not much mistaken. In what is now broad daylight. For every servant and house guest to see."

"They are all very welcome," Justin told him. "So would you have been if you had kept your distance. I have asked Estelle to marry me. She has said yes. I was indeed about to kiss her. I am curiously unashamed of the fact. I take unkindly to having been interrupted."

"Are you quite sure, Stell?" Watley asked, looking beyond Justin. He was still grinning.

"I am quite, quite sure," she said. And she, Justin saw when he looked at her, was grinning back at her brother.

You are going to have to get used to it, old chap.

"Then you must allow me to congratulate you," Watley said, striding onto the bridge and drawing his sister away from Justin and into a tight hug. He turned then to offer his hand to Justin. "I believe she will be happy with you, Brandon. She would not have said yes if she was not quite certain she would be. Nor would she have made this such a late night—with the sun already up on a new day."

"*Not* your business, Bert," she said.

"I suppose," he said, "I had better make myself scarce now."

"Oh, Bert," she said. "There was a letter in the safe with all the jewelry. Addressed to Justin. From his father."

"Ah," Watley said.

"I needed to read it in private," Justin said. "I took it to the summerhouse last night after everyone had gone to bed. I persuaded Estelle to go with me. Because I needed her, Watley. Because I love her."

Watley nodded and patted his shoulder. "I am glad," he said. "Stell and I were fortunate that our father was still alive when we were ready to confront him. We were able to have it out in person. I suppose she has told you."

"Yes," Justin said. "I look forward to meeting him, though I do have an acquaintance with him from the House of Lords. I will write to him later today."

"Really?" Estelle said. "To ask for my hand?"

"I know it is unnecessary," he said. "But yes."

"Oh." She smiled warmly at him. "Thank you. He will like that. *I* like it."

"We are going to Redcliffe tomorrow," Watley said, his eyes upon Estelle. "It is home, after all—for a short while longer for Estelle, that is. And there will be no point in trying to organize a wedding from Elm Court. I would not be given a moment's peace. Our stepmother is good at organizing. She has all the weight of the Westcott ladies' committee behind her. They are a formidable lot, Brandon. Be warned."

"We *are* going to Redcliffe?" Estelle asked her brother. "Oh, I am so glad. It seems forever since we saw Papa. And Mother. The Westcott ladies' committee is not too successful, though, is it? When they were planning a grand wedding for Avery and Anna, he simply went and got a special license and took her off one afternoon to marry her in an obscure little church in the middle of London, with only his secretary and Elizabeth, Lady Hodges, as witnesses."

"The Duke and Duchess of Netherby?" Justin asked.

"Yes," she said. "And most recently, this past spring, the committee planned a thirtieth birthday party for Harry Westcott at Hinsford and took along three prospective brides for him to choose among since everyone thought it was high time he married and lived happily ever after. He foiled them all by marrying Lydia Tavernor, the late vicar's widow, on the morning of his birthday."

"Good old Harry," Watley said, laughing. "But by the law of averages, Brandon, they are almost bound to succeed one of these times, are they not? If I were you I would do what Netherby did."

Justin looked at Estelle and took one of her hands in his again. "I suppose we are stuck with this twin of yours until we have a few matters settled," he said. "Like the sort of wedding you want."

Watley folded his arms and leaned back against the balustrade.

"*Not* one like Avery and Anna's," she said. "Though I am sure it was perfect for them. As I see it, a wedding can be considered in one of two ways. It can be seen, quite justifiably, as something for the bride and groom. It can also be seen, though, as something for their families too. A chance to celebrate. Together. A mingling of families, which can be a beautiful thing. We have seen it in the last two weeks. Your family is not a single entity, Justin. There are your father's relatives and your mother's, and even Maria's. She is your sister, so in a sense her family is your family too. And there are Wesley and Hilda and Ricky. On my side there are my mother's sister and her family, and my father's brother and his sister and her family and a few cousins, children of the late marquess. And there are all the Westcotts, who are related to me in much the same way as

Maria's relatives are to you, not by blood but by a marriage connection. They have been wonderfully welcoming to Bert and me. They treat us as honorary members. When you and I marry, these two large, diverse groups will become our larger family. I want to celebrate that at our wedding."

"It will have to be at Redcliffe, then, if you hope to squeeze all those people in," Watley said. "Or in London, where everyone can find their own accommodation. That would be the easiest solution. I'll wager Netherby would offer his ballroom at Archer House for the wedding breakfast."

Justin was gazing at Estelle, and she was gazing back.

"The wedding will be here," he said. "Unless you have another firm preference, Estelle. In October, when autumn will have turned the valley into something so beautiful you will run out of superlatives in your first sentence and then be doomed to repeating yourself or merely gazing in silence. You have only to look over your shoulder to the house to remind yourself that it is big enough to accommodate an army with room to spare."

She smiled.

"But there is another reason," he said. "Do you remember on the afternoon when I took everyone through the state apartments and then directly into the grand reception hall for tea?"

"The domed room?" she said. "I will never forget seeing it for the first time."

"Do you remember what you did and what you said?" he asked her. "When the sun shone through the dome and made rainbow colors of light all about the room? I had just told everyone that it is occasionally used as a ballroom. You looked up at the light and spread your arms and twirled once about. And you said it would surely be the most wonderful place in the whole world in which to dance."

"Oh." Her face was glowing. "I do remember. And I still think it."

"You, my love," he told her, "are going to dance there. You are going to *waltz* there on our wedding day."

Everyone was already expecting a busy day even before they sat down to breakfast. For they were all leaving tomorrow, and there were bags to be packed—though, of course, it was the servants who would do the actual work of filling trunks and hatboxes and valises and bags. There were also favorite places to be revisited while there was still time—the lake, the wilderness walk, the gallery, the maze, the rock gardens, among others. There was to be a tea out at the summerhouse during the afternoon. Lady Crowther and her sister wanted to pay a farewell call to their old friend Lady Hodgkins.

There were future meetings to discuss—and it seemed that they all *did* want to meet again and wished to talk about it at breakfast. Maria would go with the Sharpes tomorrow to spend a few weeks with Rosie. But the Dicksons and the Chandlers were eager for her to come to Yorkshire later. She still had her aunt Sarah and uncle Thomas to meet, after all. And the Ormsburys hinted at Christmas in Cornwall, certainly for both Maria and Justin, but also perhaps for the Yorkshire families and the Sharpes if they did not have other plans.

"And you and Lady Estelle would be very welcome to come too, Lord Watley," Lady Crowther added. "If your company is not already spoken for, that is. But we must not all go years again without seeing one another. Families ought not to allow themselves to drift apart just because of the great distances that separate their homes."

"Maybe next spring when Maria goes to London to mingle with all the other titled nobility for the social Season," Mr. Dickson said, beaming at his niece, "she will take the eye of some handsome gentleman and fall in love and we will all be invited back here for a grand wedding in the summer."

"Leonard!" his wife scolded. "You are putting the poor girl to the blush, not to mention Justin, inviting us back here like this."

"No, he is not embarrassing me, Aunt Margaret," Maria said, laughing. "But my bridegroom is going to have to be *very* special. I refuse to settle for anyone just because he is handsome."

"Maybe you have a chance yet, Ernie," Sidney Sharpe said.

That was when Justin spoke up from his place at the head of the table. They were all present, except for Lady Maple.

"I am about to invite everyone back here anyway," he said, his eyes meeting Estelle's along the table. "Long before next summer. Even before Christmas. In October actually, when the valley will be at its absolute loveliest. There is to be a wedding here. My own to Lady Estelle Lamarr, who accepted my offer this morning and agreed to be my wife. My countess."

He smiled at Estelle, and she smiled back. How very different he looked when he smiled, when the darkness had gone from inside him.

Everyone seemed to be speaking at once. For several moments Estelle let the sound wash over her without attempting to sort out individual voices or what exactly they were saying. She was just simply happy.

"How much was that wager for, Sid?"

"*Estelle?* You are going to marry *Estelle*, Justin?"

"It was not hard to see which way the wind was blowing, was it?"

"Not a single pound or guinea. No one was willing to bet against you."

"Oh, Justin! I was never happier in my life. Well, except when Martin offered for Doris and she said yes."

"Never mind winds. I told you it was sure to happen any day now, Irwin."

"She is going to be *my sister*?"

"Ernest is right, Sidney. No one would take you up on that bet. It was as clear as the nose on your face."

"How splendid, Justin. But we all guessed, of course."

"I say, Lady Estelle. You are going to be the *Countess of Brandon*. How grand it sounds."

"*A wedding? In October?* Ma? Pa? Say we may come back for it. I will die if you say no."

"A wedding? That soon? And you are going to be here alone after tomorrow, Justin? Without even Maria? However are you going to plan a whole wedding? Do you have *any idea* of all the work involved? But how could you? You are a man. You need help. *Female* help, and it would be unfair to put it all on poor Mrs. Phelps. Some of us are going to have to put our heads together today and make some plans."

"I will help, Augusta. We had a lovely wedding for Doris. Not a single thing went wrong. Well. Except that Rowan left his shoes to put on until the last minute and then could find only one black shoe and one brown. And I had gone off to the church already. What we need is a few lists."

Estelle looked into the laughing eyes of her betrothed and came back to herself. "Bertrand and I will be going to Redcliffe Court tomorrow," she said. "Our stepmother will be happy to take charge of some of the planning, but I am sure she will appreciate any lists you can all draw up today. I think it might be a good idea, Justin, if instead of writing to Papa today, as you planned, you actually come with Bert and me tomorrow."

"Do you, my love?" His eyes were still laughing. "Then I will come."

And since everyone had more or less finished breakfast, the table was soon abandoned and Estelle was engulfed in hugs and kisses and exclamations while Justin was being hugged and was having his hand pumped and his shoulder slapped and it all started to feel very real indeed.

She was *betrothed*, Estelle thought. In two months' time she was going to be marrying Justin, Earl of Brandon—of all people. She tried to think of him as she had seen him that first time by the riverbank and a couple of days later at Prospect Hall. Just a few weeks ago. If anyone had told her then . . .

Maria was hugging him, and he was hugging her back, rocking her in his arms and drawing back his head to say something to her. She listened earnestly to him and then smiled and nodded. And he hugged her again.

Well, if anyone had told her, Estelle thought, she would simply not have believed that person.

Bertrand squeezed her shoulder and hugged her again. "I feel duty bound to remind you that you are making a ghastly mistake," he murmured into her ear.

"What?" She drew back her head and frowned at him.

"He is not your perfect someone," he said. "He does not have blue eyes."

She gasped. "And *now* you tell me," she said.

Maria took a pot of chocolate, a cup and saucer and spoon, and a plate with two oatmeal biscuits up to Lady Maple's room an hour before noon. It was what she usually had at that time, her maid had explained.

Lady Maple was sitting up in bed, pillows piled at her back, a frilly cap on her head, and wire-rimmed spectacles halfway down her nose. She was reading a book, though she did set it aside when her door opened and peered at Maria over the top of her glasses.

"You missed a great deal of excitement at breakfast," Maria told her as she set down the tray on the table beside the bed and poured a cup of chocolate.

"I do not believe anything could excite me at breakfast," her great-aunt said.

"Brandon . . . *Justin* proposed marriage to Estelle this morning," Maria said, "and she accepted. They are going to marry here in October, and everyone is invited to come back for the wedding. All of Estelle's family will be invited too. It was announced at breakfast."

"And this is *news*?" Lady Maple asked, removing her spectacles and taking the cup and saucer after Maria had stirred the chocolate. Apparently she always drank one cup before eating a biscuit.

Maria smiled at her. "If you had told me two weeks ago that I would be happy about it," she said, "I would have called you mad."

"And it would have been a great impertinence," Lady Maple said. "One ought always to speak to one's elders with courtesy, you know—or some such nonsense."

"I am really dreadfully sorry for what I said to you that one morning," Maria said.

"The fault was mine, child," her great-aunt said. "I ought not to have opened my mouth on that topic even though I did not realize you were within earshot. A girl should be left alone with her memories of her mother."

"Not when they are false memories," Maria said. "Not when they cause her to treat living people unjustly. Mama's jewels were never stolen. They were in the safe in Papa's room all the time. Papa sent Justin away because there was something between Justin and Mama. I am no longer so naïve that I cannot work that out for myself. And much as I loved Mama—much as I *love* her and always will—I cannot believe that the fault was with Justin. He adored Papa and he adored me. He would not— Well, *he* would not. I am not going to stand in judgment upon Mama, though. The only thing for which I really blame her is the lie she told me. She might have just remained silent on the subject, as Papa always did. She lied instead."

"Put the cup back on the tray," Lady Maple said. "My hands are not quite steady this morning. You are a good girl, Maria, and always have been, I suspect. Now you have your brother back and will soon have a sister who is already your friend. You have a larger family to love you too. Even the Sharpes have taken you to their bosom. I am glad. And perhaps at last I will forgive myself."

"Oh, Great-aunt Bertha," Maria said. "It was not your fault, what happened."

"There is no point in dwelling upon it anyway," Lady

Maple said. "Ring the bell for my maid, please. It is time I got dressed."

"Great-aunt Bertha." Maria did not move for the moment, and Lady Maple looked up at her. "Justin and Estelle will be newly wed and wishing to be alone together at least some of the time each day. I have had several invitations, all of which would involve some traveling alone—apart from all the servants Justin would undoubtedly send with me. I was wondering . . ."

"Well, out with it, girl," her great-aunt said. "Or I will be missing luncheon in addition to breakfast."

"I was wondering," Maria said, "if you might wish to come and live here. Oh, not necessarily for always. I know you have your home in London and your friends and your social life there. I do not suppose it would be terribly exciting for you to spend your days with a . . . a girl. But . . . Justin has said I may ask, and Estelle thinks it is a good idea. I asked her before I came up here. So . . . I thought I would ask."

Lady Maple blinked a few times, remembered that her book was still open across her lap, and busied herself putting a folded handkerchief between the pages to mark her spot before closing it.

"Well," she said at last. "I suppose I could come back here for the wedding and then stay for a while. And you will certainly need company if those relatives of yours in Cornwall persuade you to go there or if the family in Yorkshire wants you to go there for a while. You will need a chaperon when you go to London next spring, and you cannot expect that Lady Estelle will always be either able or willing to accompany you. It would not be fair either to her or to Brandon. *Will* you ring my bell, girl, or must I do it myself?"

"I will do it," Maria said, smiling at her. It had not really occurred to her until Justin spoke to her just after breakfast that perhaps Great-aunt Bertha was lonely and had been for a long time. It was bad of her not to have noticed. She really must cultivate a greater sensitivity to other people. Like her brother had.

Twenty-four

They arrived at Redcliffe Court in the middle of a wet afternoon. They had traveled in a carriage together, the three of them, though two other carriages came behind them—Justin's, in which the two valets and Estelle's maid were riding at their leisure, and Bertrand and Estelle's baggage coach, which was empty apart from their bags.

The two men got along well together, Estelle was pleased to discover. They had both studied the classics at Oxford. Both had been on a rowing team there. Both had an interest in politics and religion and philosophy. Both were also sensitive to the fact that they were not alone together. Their conversation always included Estelle, except occasionally when she had been settled for a nap in her corner of the seat facing the horses, though she had not always been asleep. And it was not as though they felt obliged to discuss the newest fashions in bonnets or the weather or other mere frivolities when she was not asleep. She too was interested in the topics they favored, with the possible exception of the ancient classics. She had views and opinions of her own to express.

Justin was planning to spend a few days at Redcliffe— *unless your father tosses me out on my ear after taking one look at me,* he had told Estelle. Then he was going to go to Gloucestershire to attend Wesley Mort's wedding to Hilda, and to persuade them to move to Everleigh if they were wavering. He wanted it too much himself to be confident of success, Estelle suspected. Ricky had known of the possibility before they left Everleigh. Apparently the blacksmith had inadvertently talked about it in his hearing. By the time he came to say goodbye to everyone, Ricky had been moving rather as though he had springs beneath the soles of his boots and was so excited about coming back and living in that house up in the village, where he would have a room all of his own that was not even up in the attic, that his words fell all over one another and were barely coherent.

Justin was going back home after Wesley's wedding in order to prepare for his own. Though he predicted that he would have little say in the matter. After drawing up endless lists the day before their departure and consulting both Mr. and Mrs. Phelps and the head gardener and even the vicar in a brief visit to the vicarage, Lady Crowther had announced during the evening that she was staying.

"I cannot possibly organize everything from Cornwall, Justin," she had declared, as though he had asked her to do just that. "And we cannot expect the Marchioness of Dorchester, Lady Estelle's stepmother, to come here in person to organize the wedding. Maria has no experience in planning anything on such a grand scale, besides which she is going to spend a few weeks with Rosie, which is an excellent idea as the past few years have been very gloomy and stressful for her. I know Everleigh. I even know many of the people here. I am staying. So is Felicity. Everyone else will go home, as planned, and return for the wedding."

And when Lady Crowther, Justin's aunt Augusta, decided something, Estelle had realized, no one argued. It must have felt strange to Justin when he left Everleigh with Estelle and Bertrand to be waved off by two of his guests. He had even apologized to his aunts for abandoning them.

"But of course you must go to Redcliffe, Justin," Lady Felicity Ormsbury had assured him. "It is only right that you apply formally for Lady Estelle's hand to the Marquess of Dorchester. Besides, we do not need you here. There is nothing for you to do."

They had laughed about it in the carriage, the three of them.

"Relatives," Justin had said, shaking his head as the carriage rumbled over the Palladian bridge before tackling the climb out of the valley.

"Are they not wonderful?" Estelle had said. "I am so glad you did not fight your aunts on the issue, Justin, and order them to leave your house. They will enjoy themselves enormously in the coming weeks. And they will organize a really magnificent wedding, with a great deal of help from your servants and your secretary. You will surely find that there really is nothing for you to do."

The two men had exchanged sober glances.

"Except put in an appearance at church at the right time on the right day to marry my sister," Bertrand had said.

"I think I can manage that," Justin had said. "Provided someone reminds me the day before."

"I will do that," Bertrand had said. "Provided *Estelle* reminds *me.*"

"I think I can manage that," she had said.

They arrived at Redcliffe on a rainy afternoon. Unexpectedly, of course. They had sent no advance notice that they were on their way. But they must have been spotted from the drawing room windows. The marchioness was hurrying down the stairs even as they came dashing through the front doors out of the rain. She looked her usual elegant, lovely self, her face lit up with a smile of welcome.

"Well, this is a wonderful surprise," she said, catching first Estelle and then Bertrand up in her arms and smiling politely at Justin beyond them. "Marcel is with Oliver in his office. He will be here in a moment. He is going to be *so* happy to see you."

Oliver Morrow was the steward at Redcliffe—Estelle and Bertrand's cousin, Aunt Jane and Uncle Charles's son.

"The Earl of Brandon has come with us," Estelle said. "The Marchioness of Dorchester, our stepmother, Justin."

"But of course," she said, extending a hand toward him. "Estelle and Bertrand have been staying at Everleigh Park with Lady Maria Wiley, your sister, have they not?"

"They have indeed, ma'am," he said, shaking her hand. "To my great pleasure."

"Justin and I are betrothed," Estelle told her.

"Oh?" Her stepmother looked from one to the other of them. "Oh, goodness."

But the marquess was striding into the hall, looking dearly familiar to Estelle—tall and solidly built, still wondrously handsome though he was close to fifty and silver hair had almost overtaken the dark at his temples.

"What is this?" he asked as he came toward them, smiling. "No warning? You are going to be giving our cook an apoplexy."

"Papa." Estelle did what she had always longed to do as a child and young girl. She dashed into his arms, which closed tightly about her and made her feel instantly safe. "We have come home. Oh, Papa." She had had no idea she was going to be so emotional.

"What is it?" he said, his voice suddenly full of concern. "You are not crying, are you, Estelle? Has something happened? Bertrand? Why has the mere sight of me reduced your sister to tears? Ah. Brandon. You have come here with my twins, have you?"

"I have, sir," Justin said. "And I think I may be a bit responsible for Estelle's tears. I have come to ask if I may take her off your hands. For all time, I mean. I hope to marry her. I am *going* to marry her. But I would rather do it with your blessing, if it is something you are willing to give."

"I am not *weeping*," Estelle protested, horribly embarrassed. She loosened her hold on her father and swiped at her eyes with two fingers. "I am just happy to see you and Mother again and to be back home. Temporarily. I am indeed going to marry Justin, but I would rather it be with your blessing than not, Papa. Bertrand approves."

"Well, that is a high recommendation indeed," her father said, sounding perfectly serious. "But here are Viola and I, coping with the double surprise of your descending upon us without warning and your announcement that you are betrothed to Brandon, with whom I have the slimmest of acquaintances and Viola none at all. You must all make allowances for our advancing age. *Shall* we sit down in the drawing room to discuss these matters and perhaps sip on a glass of wine while we do so? Possibly champagne—if, that is, I discover that my blessing is available to be given. And see how you have all sent my manners packing? Welcome to Redcliffe, Brandon."

He strode toward Justin and shook his hand.

* * *

The following weeks were busy ones for both Estelle and
her stepmother, even though they did not have a full wedding to plan. It seemed to Estelle that they spent more than
half their days in the morning room, one of them at the
escritoire, which had been placed beside the window to
catch the morning light, the other at the table, which was
usually used to hold needlework supplies.

There were invitations to write and send out to all the
people on the list Estelle had compiled on the last day at
Everleigh. It was a lengthy list, even though the decision
had been made on both sides to confine the guests to family
members. They had been fortunate with Justin's family, of
course—all of them had been at Everleigh to be invited in
person, except for Sarah and Thomas Wickford.

Estelle divided the list of her own family members with
her stepmother and they set to work. Then, of course, over
the coming weeks there were the replies to read and com-
pile into two lists, of those who could and would come to
the wedding, and those few who could not for various reasons. The former list had to be sent on to Lady Crowther at
Everleigh so that she could plan accordingly.

Estelle's stepsiblings—Camille, Harry, and Abigail—
would come, though Camille's family was too large to
travel en masse. They had done it in the spring for Harry's
birthday and surprise wedding, but it had been a heroic
undertaking. This time Joel would remain at home with
most of the children while Camille came with Winifred,
her eldest daughter, and with Andrew, her deaf son, and
Robbie, the son who gave them the most trouble, though he
was devoted to Andrew.

Anna, Duchess of Netherby, would be unable to travel,

as by October she would be getting close to her confinement. But the duke would attend with Josephine, his eldest daughter, and Jonah, his son. Mrs. Kingsley, the marchioness's mother, would come from Bath with Camille. The Reverend Michael Kingsley, Viola's brother, and his wife would come all the way from Dorsetshire. The Earl of Riverdale, head of the Westcott family, would come with his countess, though Elizabeth, the earl's sister, Lady Hodges, and her husband sent their regrets as they were about to embark for Ireland, where Lord Hodges had relatives. The Dowager Countess of Riverdale, once Viola's mother-in-law, and her sister also declined with regrets, as the countess's physician—*"that old tyrant"*—had ordered her to travel less if she hoped to live into her eighties. Her daughters would attend, however—Matilda with Viscount Dirkson, her husband; Louise, Dowager Duchess of Netherby; and Mildred with Lord Molenor, her husband. Jessica, Countess of Lyndale, the dowager duchess's daughter, was in the early stages of a second pregnancy and was suffering wretchedly and annoyingly just as she had the first time. The mere thought of a carriage ride was enough to prostrate her.

Sometimes Estelle felt she was inviting half of England to her wedding. She even briefly regretted not suggesting to Justin that after all they do what Anna and Avery had once famously done and go off somewhere to marry privately without a word to anyone until afterward. For all she really wanted was to be married to Justin and living with him at Everleigh.

Though no, she always realized just moments after entertaining these treacherous thoughts, that was not *all* she wanted. She wanted to be married to Justin and living at Everleigh with him, with strong, active connections with every single member of their families, including the extended branches—the Westcotts, the Yorkshire group, and the Morts. She wanted her marriage to be a family affair—and her wedding too.

So she returned to all the letter writing.

Aunt Jane and Uncle Charles and Ellen would come, of course. So would Uncle André, Estelle's father's brother, and Aunt Annemarie, his sister, with Uncle William and their children. Cousin Isabelle and her daughter, Margaret, would be there with their husbands.

Letters came from Everleigh with great frequency. The Ormsbury ladies were as relentless in their planning as the Westcott ladies' committee had ever been in Estelle's experience. They were planning everything down to the finest detail and were meticulous about keeping the Marchioness of Dorchester informed. All their letters were addressed to her. Estelle, it seemed, was as unimportant to the process as Justin was. There was apparently nothing for either of them to do—except play the parts of bride and groom when the time came.

A few years ago, Estelle's stepmother had discovered a young dressmaker whose work was exquisite, in her expert opinion. She was also a talented designer and did not rely upon fashion plates, as other dressmakers did. She lived a mere three miles from Redcliffe and was beginning to thrive as word spread that she had the exclusive dressing of the Marchioness of Dorchester, who was known far and wide for her taste and elegance.

The dressmaker was brought to Everleigh and given accommodation there for three weeks while she and her two assistants designed and produced Estelle's wedding gown and a selection of bridal clothes, as well as an outfit for the marchioness herself and one for Oliver's wife. Both Estelle and her stepmother spent hours looking over designs, making suggestions, rejecting, approving, and being measured and fitted.

Bertrand and his father meanwhile did what men were inclined to do when there was a wedding looming. They went out together for hours on end about estate business with Oliver. They went fishing. They spent time, Estelle suspected, at the village tavern, though Bertrand did not drink alcohol.

Estelle's father had given his blessing to Justin, though he had acknowledged that it was not necessary. Estelle was of age. More important, she knew her own mind and had always been extremely discriminating. If she believed she would be happy with Justin Wiley, Earl of Brandon, then that was recommendation enough for her father. Nevertheless, he did take Justin away to his own private domain that first evening and questioned him over everything in his past and present that might disqualify him as a husband for his daughter. And he took Estelle to the same place the following morning and spent a whole hour with her there making sure that she had not simply had her head turned by a practiced charmer and woman chaser—*though I have never heard of his being either of those dastardly things, Estelle.*

He gave his blessing formally at dinner that evening, when he did indeed propose a toast with champagne—he had drunk a glass of wine in the drawing room the first day while everyone else had drunk tea.

Justin had left a couple of days later to go to his friend's wedding. Estelle would not see him again until their own wedding in October. Six long weeks.

"But I will write," he had assured her as he hugged her to him before climbing into his carriage. "Every day."

She had smiled a bit ruefully as she waved him on his

way a few minutes later. *Every day,* she thought. *Perhaps once a week if I am fortunate,* she had told herself.

He wrote every day. Mostly just a single sentence or two, sandwiched between the rather flowery opening, "My beloved Estelle," and the closing, "Yours forever and perhaps beyond that, Justin." She came to live for the arrival of the daily post and that single sentence or two.

"Wes as a happy newlywed is a fearsome sight, but I am envious! Not to mention impatient."

"I love you."

"Ricky loves 'that nice lady, Juss,' and looks forward to seeing you again. So do I!"

"Captain loves you too—he was delighted to see me back but searched the carriage in vain for you and then looked mournful as only he can."

"The aunts are driving me insane. I have come to the library to dream of you."

"Writer's cramp? Stop writing this minute—though not to me."

"The grotto felt lonely without you this afternoon. I want my female resident hermit back."

"I had a letter from Hilda today to say they really are all coming next week. I wish you were coming next week too."

"What was I saying yesterday? I wish you were coming today."

"I do not suppose I could interest you in eloping?"

"I love you."

"I watched the sunrise from the Palladian bridge this morning. Come home!"

"I miss you more each day. Have I also mentioned that I love you?"

"I love you."

"Bill Slater moved out of his cottage yesterday and a small army is in there today, preparing the house for Wes and Hilda and Ricky. The countess's room next to mine has been prepared, but where is the countess?"

"What did I think about, what did I dream about, before I met you?"

"One week left. Will it be as long as the last weeks have been?"

"I am wasting away, a mere shadow of my former self. Come soon."

"I love you and long for you."

"What do you mean—only a week? Have you no heart?"

"Of course you have no heart. I have it here with me for safekeeping." There was a drawing on that particular page of a heart colored with red ink cupped in two large wedge-fingered hands.

"I am counting hours now rather than days."

Estelle kept all the letters, bound together with a silk ribbon. She read them all each night when she went to bed and smiled and even laughed over them. She shed a few tears too. For no, it was not *just* a week when indeed seven days remained before her return to Everleigh for her wedding. It was an endless eternity.

Justin's aunts had faced a number of problems, such as how to fill the church and the house with flowers for the wedding when it was October and most flowers had either gone to ground for the year or were looking distinctly sad. But the most serious problem, unless *someone did something about it*, concerned the fact that the bride and groom might be sleeping beneath the same roof, albeit a very large roof, on the night before their wedding. How were they to be kept from seeing each other on their wedding day before they met at the altar inside the church? The slightest blunder and they would be doomed to all sorts of bad luck for all their married life. It was not to be contemplated.

They had found a solution in their friend Jemima, Lady Hodgkins, who had gone into transports of delight when she had been asked if she could possibly offer the bride a bedchamber in her house for the wedding eve. Not only could she accommodate the bride, she had declared, but the bride's mother—*What? Stepmother? Stepmother, then*— and father simply must stay with her too. What else were she and Hugh to do with their twelve spare bedchambers? And Lady Estelle's dear, handsome twin too if he wished. Indeed, they must all come during the afternoon of the wedding eve, in time for tea. And they must dine and spend the evening as well as the night. And they would be fed breakfast too, of course, though brides never had hearty appetites on their wedding day. A soft-boiled egg might be just the thing to tempt Lady Estelle. Lady Hodgkins simply could not be happier about anything.

Another problem had been solved.

So had all the others as they arose. Justin had spent almost six weeks feeling utterly helpless as his aunts took over his home and his servants—*including* his secretary— and his life. There was something undeniably heartwarming about it too, however. They were his *family*. They *cared*. They had given up weeks of their own lives for his sake and Estelle's. They sang her praises almost every day, largely, Justin suspected, because she had turned over her end of the wedding planning to her stepmother, whom the aunts deemed to be a sensible woman. They had both met her a time or two in the past when she was still the Countess of Riverdale and universally respected—*though River-dale was a scoundrel of the first order, Justin, as witness the fact that his lengthy marriage to the poor lady before his death was bigamous from the first moment.* The marchioness sent the information the aunts needed and answered promptly any questions they had without any fuss or bluster.

Justin spent some of his time alone with his dog, tramping about the park and the farm. He spent time in Wes and Hilda's cottage after they had moved in and at the smithy after Wes had started work there, watching his friend learning his new trade, or rather reviving skills he had acquired as a boy and never forgotten. He took Ricky to the sheep pens a few times and left him to the care of the head shepherd, who assured Justin that the young man had a future there, since he obviously loved the animals and had endless patience with their frequent stupidity.

"And if you ever have a lost sheep," Justin had said, grinning, though he was not quite sure the shepherd understood the biblical reference, "Ricky is your man."

But finally the waiting was almost over and the guests began to arrive. Family only. But it was a very large family. Or group of families, to be more accurate. It was amazing to know that he or Estelle—soon to be he *and* Estelle—had a close connection to all of these people. Their anchor to this life. The network of family connections that would sustain them and enrich their lives and be passed on to their children. Who, please God, would begin to put in an appearance within the next year or so.

Maria was first to come, with Aunt Betty and Uncle Rowan and the cousins. It was lovely to see his sister glowing with youth and happiness, Justin thought as he met her down on the terrace and she dashed into his arms.

"Aunt Betty has come to help with the wedding preparations," she said. "I have too, though I doubt there is anything left to do except take credit for it all as your sister. Aunt Augusta and Aunt Felicity are *formidable*, are they not? When will Estelle be here?"

Not soon enough for him.

But over the coming few days he was too busy to be able to indulge in too much pining. A surprising—surprising to him, anyway—number of the Westcott family came to Everleigh, as well as Estelle's blood relatives on both her father's and her mother's sides. Justin was particularly interested in meeting the woman he thought of as the formidable aunt—Jane Morrow, who had raised Estelle and Watley. She came with her husband and daughter.

"I owe you a deep debt of gratitude, ma'am," Justin told her when he met her, taking her offered hand in both his own. "I understand you raised Estelle to be the woman I love. Thank you, and welcome to Everleigh."

She looked at him with pursed lips and suspicion in her eyes, nodded briskly, and answered him. "She is someone I love too, Lord Brandon," she said. "I will expect you to make her happy."

Avery Archer, Duke of Netherby, elegant and apparently indolent as always, shook his hand after presenting his stepmother and his eldest daughter and his son. "My guess is, Brandon," he said, "that you are not going to be particularly popular with a certain element of the male population of London next spring when it is discovered that you have made off with Estelle Lamarr behind their backs. Congratulations. Anna sends her best wishes."

"She is well?" Justin asked.

"She is *cross*," Netherby said. "She believes herself to be large and ungainly and useless. And other such nonsense while she fills my heart with terror for her safety."

And finally, two days before the wedding, Estelle arrived in a carriage with her brother; her cousin Oliver Morrow, Dorchester's steward; and Oliver's wife. The marquess and marchioness came in a carriage behind them.

"It feels like years," Justin said, turning to Estelle after he had greeted everyone else and they had disappeared under the portico and into the house. "It feels like eons. I am not going to let that happen ever again. I am never going to let you go anywhere without me for such a long time."

"The autocrat already, Justin?" she asked him. But her eyes were dancing with merriment, and her lips were curved into a smile, and though the terrace was swarming with servants unloading all the baggage, he caught her up in his arms.

"Well, you *are* going to promise the day after tomorrow to obey me, are you not?" he said.

"I will *think* about it," she told him. "Oh, Justin, you are so very *large*. I have missed you."

He drew back from her, leaving his arms still about her. He spoke very softly. "Are you with child?" he asked her. It was a possibility that had plagued him since that night at the summerhouse.

"No," she said. "You are going to have to try again, I am afraid."

Her cheeks turned pink. He laughed.

"Oh, I will," he assured her. "Again and again and again."

Twenty-five

And suddenly it was his wedding day.

"Brown," Aunt Felicity had told him, though he had not asked for any help or advice with what he would wear to his wedding. "Brown if you possibly can, Justin. It is all I am going to say."

It was enough.

He was wearing a brown coat with fawn pantaloons and black Hessian boots and white linen. There was lace at his cuffs, and his neckcloth was tied into an elaborate creation that delighted his valet, though the man had ruined eight starched neckcloths before he got the folds just right with the ninth. If he looked directly down at his feet, Justin thought, he was sure he would be able to see his reflection in the high gloss of his boots. He did not look directly down. In the folds of his neckcloth he was wearing a diamond pin he had not worn for thirteen years. His father had given it to him for his twenty-first birthday.

And now he was seated at the front of the village church,

which, according to the aunts, was going to be just large enough to seat all the guests. He was sitting in the front pew with Wes beside him and Ricky beside Wes. Wes had *not* been delighted when Justin had asked him to be his best man. *"What?"* he had exclaimed. "With all those nobs looking on as I drop the ring, Juss? Forget it! Absolutely no way on this earth—or on the moon either. Do you want me to knock your teeth down your throat?"

Ricky had been Wes's best man a few weeks ago, but Justin had sat beside him in order to let him know when it was time to step forward with the ring.

"Ricky can sit by you to tell you when to hand me the ring," Justin had said. "He has experience. And if you drop it, Wes, and it rolls out of sight, he will be there to find it for you. I have considered asking a cousin. I have a number of them. But I want you. You are not going to disappoint me on my wedding day, are you?"

"Blast you to hell and back, Juss," Wes had said before apologizing because he had uttered a blasphemy in Hilda's hearing. "Don't put it that way."

"I just did," Justin had said, grinning at him.

"It really doesn't matter that he is an earl and rich as a king, Wes," Hilda had said. "It matters that he's your *friend*."

"Aren't wives supposed to be quiet and mind their own business?" Wes had asked.

"Who put that daft idea in your head?" his fond wife had asked. "Besides, you *are* my business."

So here Wes was, wearing his wedding suit, which really made him look quite handsome, though he looked anything but comfortable in it and had sworn on his wedding day that he would never wear it again. He was scowling. Beyond him was Ricky in his best man's suit, beaming happily and finding it difficult not to keep looking over his shoulder at the gathering guests.

No one was talking out loud, for they were in church. But there was a hum of subdued conversation anyway, noticeable only when it stopped and silence fell and then the organ began to play as the vicar arrived at the front of the church and signaled to Justin and the rest of the congregation that it was time to stand.

His bride was arriving.

His wedding was about to begin.

At last.

Justin stood and turned to see Watley escort the Marchioness of Dorchester to the front pew across from his own. And then his eyes focused upon the other end of the nave, where Estelle was coming toward him on her father's arm.

Lady Hodgkins, forever cheerful, was a talker. She had scarcely stopped since the afternoon before, when Estelle had arrived at her house with her father and stepmother and Bertrand. The lady's husband and children, though they appeared to be an amiable lot, could scarcely get a word in edgewise. Nor could anyone else. They all recognized the lady's good nature, however, and the lavish display of her hospitality. They relaxed into their roles of guests and listeners.

But finally she relinquished her house to the four of them as she left for the church with her husband on the morning of the wedding, loud in her satisfaction at being the only invited guest who was not a member of either family. Except for the Morts, of course, but they scarcely counted in her estimation.

"Oh, Estelle," the marchioness said as she watched Olga put the finishing touches to her hair. "You look *gorgeous*."

Estelle, all modesty aside, could only agree with her. Her gown, clinging close to her body from a high waist, was cream lace over the same color silk, deceptively simple in design, expert in execution. It had a scooped neck, though it was not too low, with long, close-fitting sleeves of lace without the silk underlay. There was a matching spencer with a stiff stand-up collar to be worn over the dress if the autumn weather should happen to be chilly. Estelle would indeed wear it, for it was a chilly day, though bright and sunny. She would remove it later for the wedding breakfast.

She and the dressmaker and her stepmother had decided against a bonnet. Instead, her hair was dressed high on her head and intertwined with multicolored autumn leaves, which had been waxed to preserve them. One long curled ringlet was pinned diagonally across the back of her head and hung down over her shoulder. That too was woven with leaves. Her kid gloves and her shoes were tan colored.

She looked, Estelle thought, like an autumn bride. She felt like a bride whose stomach was filled with fluttering butterflies.

This was her *wedding day*.

Bertrand was in her dressing room then, and Olga left. Their stepmother went into the bedchamber.

"Stell." He took both her hands in his and held them very tightly as he took a half step back to look her over from head to feet. "What is there to say? You look lovely."

"Will you be lonely without me, Bert?" she asked, and their eyes connected. "Will you live at Redcliffe?" Strangely, they had not talked about it during the past weeks.

"I'll go there often," he said. "I'll come to Everleigh often. And of course I will miss you, Stell. I will live at Elm Court. It is home. It will always be home for as long as Papa lives—and I hope that will be until he is at least ninety. I will not be lonely. I have my books and my life. And when I *get* lonely, as maybe I will in a few years' time, then I will take a bride of my own. Life moves on, and we must move with it. He is perfect, Stell?"

"Of course he is not," she said, "any more than I am. But he is perfect for *me*, Bert. And I think I am perfect for him."

He smiled at her, squeezed her hands more tightly, and kissed her forehead, leaning carefully forward so that he would not disturb her hair or her clothing. Estelle swallowed what felt like a lump in her throat and smiled back. She could hear her father talking with her stepmother in the bedchamber. Bertrand stood back so that she could precede him into the room.

"Well, just look at you," her father said. "Good God, is this really *my daughter*? Dash it all, Estelle, come here."

Estelle laughed as she set her hands on either side of his waist. "Mind my hair," she warned him. "It took Olga a whole hour."

It was time for them to leave then for the short drive to the church. Carriages were drawn up all about it, and a small crowd of villagers was gathering about the gate. And Justin had been *so* right about the time of year, Estelle thought. The valley was indeed breathtakingly lovely with all the autumn foliage. The village was too. It was surely the very best time of the year to marry, with Christmas approaching and the coziness of the winter months and the promise of spring not too far off.

After a final hug inside the church doors, Bertrand and their stepmother went together to take their places in the front pew. The vicar waited at the front of the church, and the organ began to play.

"Come," her father said, smiling at her and offering his arm. "Your mother would be so very proud of you today, Estelle. She loved you both very dearly."

"Oh," she said. "Thank you, Papa. How blessed I am. For Mother loves me dearly too."

She set her arm within his, solid and dependable, and walked toward her bridegroom, who had risen with the rest of the congregation and stepped a little into the nave so that he could watch her come.

And ah, she loved him. Her throat was still a bit tight from Bertrand's hug and her father's words about her mother. But her future, the rest of her life, was awaiting her in the large form of Justin Wiley, Earl of Brandon, and it was going to be good. It was going to include everyone from her past, everyone from her family and his. But it was all going to center about *him*.

He did not take his eyes from her while she walked to meet him or while her papa gave her into his keeping. Or even when the vicar began to speak.

"Dearly beloved," he said.

And they were married.

Husband and wife.

Earl and Countess of Brandon.

The nuptial service was at an end, the register had been signed, and they were making their way from the church, smiling from side to side at all their relatives. For all of them were now indeed *their* relatives. Not his and hers any longer, but *theirs*.

And some of those relatives, mostly the younger ones,

were outside in the churchyard awaiting them, armed to the teeth, of course, with yellow and wine and russet flower petals they had got from somewhere. They were lined up, waiting to pelt them as they made a dash for their carriage.

"I love this part of a wedding," Estelle said, grasping Justin's hand and laughing. "Though I have never before been at the receiving end."

"Enjoy it, then," he said, laughing with her.

"It is a shame to run," she said. "But they will be disappointed if we do not."

"Here we go, then," he said, and they dashed along the path while autumn rained down upon their heads. *Not* autumn rain, but autumn colors, already vibrant about her person and on the trees all about them. The children were shrieking with laughter as they hurled their loads. Everyone else grinned and laughed. Villagers applauded and smiled.

And he belonged again, Justin thought. He had been fully accepted back at last. Perhaps because he had *wanted* to be back.

He handed his bride into the carriage and followed her in.

"Protect your ears," he said.

She tipped back her head and closed her eyes briefly as the church bells pealed to announce their marriage. The congregation—their family—was beginning to spill out of the church.

"Oh," she said, turning shining eyes in his direction. "This is the happiest day of my life, Justin. I know that is not very original, but—"

He did not hear the rest. For the carriage was in motion and so were all the pots and pans and Lord knew what else tied beneath it. It created a ferociously deafening din.

He set an arm about her shoulders and turned her toward him.

"Why waste time trying to talk?" he said, though neither of them heard his words. He kissed her.

Unknown to either of them, a cheer went up from those gathered outside the church gates—and those in the church-yard too.

The entry hall at Everleigh was decorated in autumn colors and would have quite taken her breath away if there had been any more to take, Estelle said, laughing, when they entered it—to find all the household servants lined up in two rows to greet them with applause when they stepped over the threshold.

The state dining room in the north wing was similarly decorated, as was the nearer of the smaller reception rooms on one side of it and the ladies' withdrawing room on the other. Estelle and Justin moved from room to room trying to greet everyone personally before everyone was seated for the wedding breakfast.

Estelle hugged her stepsiblings—Camille, Abigail with Gil, and Harry with Lydia, who interestingly appeared to have lost some of the slimness of her waist since Estelle last saw her at her own wedding in the spring. She shook hands with Thomas Wickford from Yorkshire, and hugged his wife, Sarah, the youngest of Maria's aunts. She hugged all of the Westcott sisters, her stepmother's former sisters-in-law—Aunt Matilda, Aunt Louise, and Aunt Mildred. She laughed and chattered with various cousins, and kept an arm about Andrew's shoulders as he hauled out of a bulging pocket his latest stone carving to show her; it was inspired, she believed, by the carvings on the Palladian bridge. His sister Winifred explained that Ricky Mort had found the stone for him. Ricky had sat with the boy while he carved, and the two of them had somehow been able to communicate even though Andrew could neither hear nor talk.

Estelle hugged and thanked the Ormsbury aunts when she saw the state dining room, which was gorgeous in the splendor of its decorations and table settings.

"How would we have managed without you?" she asked them.

"Very easily, Estelle," Lord Crowther told her. "All you really need for a wedding is a clergyman and a license and a willing bride and groom."

"If I did not know he was merely trying to provoke me," Lady Crowther said, tossing a glance at the ceiling, "I would give that idea the answer it deserves. Thank you, Estelle. Felicity and I worked hard. And we enjoyed every moment. I can see a dozen other ladies in this very room who would have been only too happy to take our place if we had been unavailable. *At least* a dozen."

The meal was sumptuous. It was followed by speeches and toasts and the cutting of the bottom layer of the four-tier cake. Sidney Sharpe gave the speech the best man would normally have given. Wesley Mort had apparently agreed—very reluctantly—to be Justin's best man, but only on the condition that he would not also be expected to attend the wedding breakfast. He would, however, be at the ball this evening. His wife would see to that. So would Ricky.

"We have a few hours," Justin said when the breakfast was over. He had Estelle's hand clasped in his. "How would you like to use them?"

"I am quite weary," she said, surprised by the truth of her words. "The summerhouse? The lake? The grotto? The library?"

"We made the bed at the summerhouse work for us once upon a time," he said. "But for the next time, Estelle, I want something altogether more spacious. I think this afternoon should be the next time. And I have not yet shown you the countess's bedchamber, have I?"

"It might be considered scandalous if you had," she said.

"Come and see it now," he said.

"We will not be missed?" she asked him.

His eyes laughed at her. "I would expect that *everyone* will miss us," he said. "But everyone will know where we are, so no one will come looking."

"I think," she said, "I am blushing."

His eyes roamed her face. "You are," he said. "Blushes become you."

"Ah, Justin." She sighed. "Take me to see the countess's room, then. *My* room."

They spent three hours there before Justin rang for her maid and his own valet. And for those hours Estelle seemed to forget her weariness except during a few brief intervals while they both dozed. They made vigorous, joyful love on either side of those intervals. And talked love words and nonsense and smiled and laughed.

"It is the laughter and the joy that I remember from my childhood here," he told her. "My parents were forever talking silliness to each other and tickling me and pretending to eat me up and hugging me while they told me what a little pest I was. That was when Everleigh felt like home."

"It will feel like that again," she promised him.

"Oh," he said, "it already does, Estelle. Will you think me *very* greedy if I have you one more time before we get ready for the ball?"

"Yes," she said. "But I am greedy too, you see."

"Mmm," he said, covering her mouth with his. Again.

*   *   *

The wedding and the breakfast had been for family. The ball was for the community too. Justin had signed all the invitations that had been put before him after his return from Wes's wedding, and they had been sent out to families at the village and in the countryside for miles around. All, almost without exception, had sent back acceptances and came promptly at the appointed hour. Justin stood with his bride just inside the doors of the grand reception hall, the dome soaring above them, tasteful wine and gold decorations all about them, wound about the great stone pillars and in festoons over the balustrade of the gallery. The orchestra platform was surrounded by pots of autumn-hued chrysanthemums. They were greeting their guests.

Estelle was at her most elegant and beautiful in a high-waisted, simply styled gown of dull gold, her dark hair almost severe in a smooth chignon that shone in the light of myriad candles. She was at her most charming too, and she had a word and a smile for everyone. Even setting aside the fact that he loved her, Justin could see that she was going to be the perfect countess. But of course that was a nonsense thought, for he *did* love her. More than he had ever thought it possible to love. And, wonder of wonders, she seemed to love him just as much, callused hands and broken nose and overblown muscles notwithstanding.

Maria, who came into the room in the midst of a cluster of cousins, most of them not even her blood relations, hugged them both and clung to Justin for a few moments.

"Thank you, Justin," she said. "Thank you for bringing me home."

That was all, and she was off to be a part of her group

and to join a few other young people. But it almost brought Justin to his knees.

"Did you hear that?" he asked Estelle.

"I did," she said. "Maria has been *sparkling* today."

Lady Maple, Justin could see, was sitting in a group with Mrs. Kingsley and a couple of older ladies from the neighborhood. Leonard Dickson and Irwin Chandler were deep in conversation with the Duke of Netherby. Maria was gathering young Winifred Cunningham into her group. The Earl and Countess of Riverdale were talking with Patricia Chandler and Sarah Wickford, her sister. Estelle's aunt Jane appeared to be holding her own with Lady Hodgkins. A couple of young girls from the village were flirting with Viscount Watley, who was humoring them good-naturedly without in any way flirting back. Wes seemed to be about as uncomfortable as it was possible for a man to be while Estelle's father and stepmother chatted amiably with Hilda and him. Ricky was smiling brightly as he chattered away to the Westcott sisters, all three of whom were listening with what looked like genuine interest.

"Your friend Hilda Mort is a surprise to me," Estelle said. "For some reason I expected a woman who was large and managing. Instead she is petite and pretty—and those two very large men clearly adore her."

"The power of womanhood," he said, grinning at her.

And then the dancing began with a country set that everyone knew and in which most participated. Justin led it off with Estelle.

"So," he said. "Were you right? Does this make a good ballroom?"

"Absolutely the best," she said. "Justin, I am so glad our wedding has been here. It seems so right that we are celebrating this evening in this round room, surrounded by our family and our neighbors."

"And it is always easier to waltz in a circular room," he said.

She raised her eyebrows.

"No corner to negotiate," he explained.

The waltz was next. Justin had been determined that Estelle would be his partner, of course, but he had not given any instructions that they dance it alone. It happened anyway, and Justin suspected his aunts had indeed considered every fine detail of this wedding. When the dance was announced and he led Estelle onto the floor, no one else joined them there. Everyone stood around the perimeter. Some had even gone up to the gallery. And there was a murmur and a smattering of applause.

He smiled at Estelle, and she smiled back.

"I hope," she said, "you know the steps."

"What steps?" he asked, setting his right arm about her waist while she set one hand on his shoulder and he took her other hand in his. "Help!"

She laughed. "Well, you know," she said, "I have never seen you at a ball in London."

The music began and he led his bride into the waltz, twirling her slowly while they caught the rhythm and arranged their feet so that they did not step upon each other's. Then he twirled her more boldly as he smiled into her eyes and she smiled back.

"I love you," he said.

"I am glad," she said. "For I love you too."

Some of the spectators were clapping to the rhythm. A few wags called out encouragement. Someone whistled.

After a few minutes the Marquess of Dorchester stepped onto the floor with the marchioness, and Watley with Maria, and Harry Westcott with his wife, and Sid Sharpe with Angela Ormsbury, and Nigel Dickson with Winifred Cunningham. And gradually the floor filled with dancers, and their guests celebrated a wedding.

He had felt so terribly alone, Justin remembered. Then he had gone to fetch Maria. And invited his relatives and hers to come here in a desperate, potentially disastrous attempt to make her feel at home. And then he had come across a woman alone on a riverbank, her dress up about her knees, her feet dangling in the water, her hair loose and untidy down her back.

And here he was, a mere few months later. At home. No longer alone. Dancing in a room full of people with whom he belonged and always would. Waltzing with that woman from the riverbank.

His wife. His countess.

"Happy?" he asked.

She nodded. "Happy," she said.

His love.

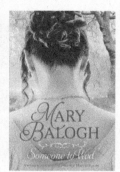
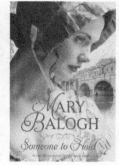
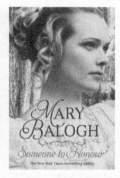

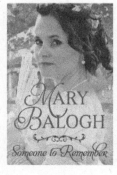
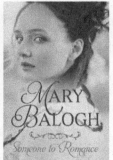

Do you love historical fiction?

Want the chance to hear news about your favourite authors (and the chance to win free books)?

Suzanne Allain
Mary Balogh
Lenora Bell
Charlotte Betts
Manda Collins
Joanna Courtney
Grace Burrowes
Evie Dunmore
Lynne Francis
Pamela Hart
Elizabeth Hoyt
Eloisa James
Lisa Kleypas
Jayne Ann Krentz
Sarah MacLean
Terri Nixon
Julia Quinn

Then visit the Piatkus website
www.yourswithlove.co.uk

And follow us on Facebook and Instagram
www.facebook.com/yourswithlovex | @yourswithlovex

PIATKUS